SLEEP DEBT

THE DEBT COLLECTION

BOOK 5

ANDREW GIVLER

SLEEP DEBT
Book Five of The Debt Collection

Editor: Laura Jorstad
Cover Illustration: Chris McGrath
Cover Design and Interior Layout: STK•Kreations

Hardcover ISBN: 978-1-958204-18-4
Trade paperback ISBN: 978-1-958204-17-7
eBook ISBN: 978-1-958204-16-0
Worldwide Rights

THE DEBT COLLECTION SERIES:

Soul Fraud

Piper's Price (Novella)

Dandelion Audit

Star Summit

Death Tax

Sleep Debt

Present Day

IRONBOUND:

Ironbound

Cold Wind (May 2026)

STAY UP TO DATE

Scan the code or find me on these social media platforms to stay up to date on my upcoming projects and book releases!

Sign Up for my Newsletter by visiting andrewgivler.com

Book YouTube Channel: @GivReads

Instagram: @sigils

Twitter: @Sigils

Facebook: @andrewgivler

To the 2 to Ramble boys, Austin and Richard,
who dared to ask me, "what have Robin and Ash been up to?"
and gave me the idea for half of this book.

SLEEP DEBT

CHAPTER **ONE**

I'VE BEEN IN the bad business for a while now. I know that's not a specific industry, but it's the only way I can think of to describe my life. Ever since a demon stole my soul, it's just been one nightmare after another. I have a lot of enemies and an unfortunately easy-to-find address.

It turns out that the supernatural world sucks. I don't recommend getting involved in its intricacies. For every wonder, there are a dozen terrifying things that go bump in the night and are very hungry. I've got a laundry list of things that I wouldn't want to have knock on my front door. Vampires, ghouls, demons, you name it—none of them are welcome to wipe their feet on the doormat.

But at the very top of the list is the Internal Revenue Service of the United States of America.

Unfortunately for me, I never get what I want, or get to do things the easy way. So I wasn't as surprised as I should have been when I answered a knock on my front door to find two genuine suit-and-tie-wearing Feds waiting for me on the other side.

When you're facing off against something that isn't human, there are tells to identifying what kind of thing you are squaring up with. Nephilim have more or less pointy ears, depending on how much demonic blood they have pumping in their veins. Demons have black eyes, and angels have white. Roman gods' irises are purple, for some reason. Not sure who handed out the color coordination rules when teams were being picked, but that's how it shook out.

Similarly, Feds are easy to spot for anyone who is paying attention. The ties are always too wide, the suits too boxy. There's always a noticeable bulge on the hip or shoulder, hinting at where their service pistol is holstered. Occasionally you'll see one go rogue and wear it on the back of their belt. Those are the sneaky ones. Watch out for them.

But more than anything else, it's the sunglasses that are the giveaway. Feds love their aviators. I mean, who doesn't? They're an excellent fashion accessory, but come on, variety is the spice of life.

"Officers," I said before either of them had a chance to identify themselves. "What can I do for you?" Despite my chipper tone, a sense of dread washed over me as I studied them. My last run-in with the Feds hadn't gone so well. Thanks to an overzealous FBI agent, I'd spent most of the next six months hiding in an underground mad scientist's lab because I'd sort of been wanted for terrorism.

Now, just to be clear, I didn't commit any acts of terror. In fact, I stopped one in progress by helping to kill a giant dragon that was trying to burn down half of Downtown Los Angeles. But the Feds like to cast wide nets, and when they don't understand something, they don't always wait to ask questions.

They're also not as clued in to the world beyond the mortal one as they think they are. Agent Richter, who'd been in charge of the case against me, had only known enough to be dangerous to himself—and sometimes me.

"Mr. Carver, this is Agent Peters," the Asian woman standing on the front step said, nodding at her ginger partner who was still wearing his aviators. She had at least been polite enough to remove hers. "I'm Agent Wong. We'd like a moment of your time. Can we come in?"

"Can I see some ID?" I asked, trying to stave off panic as I mentally processed what illegal items might be lying around the house. I knew there was a fully automatic assault rifle in pieces on the dining room table. Alex had promised he'd finish cleaning it today, but that meant he'd get to it around 11:45 p.m. The living room had at least half a dozen knives and maybe a grenade? I couldn't remember if I had taken that up to my room or not.

Probably best if I didn't let them in.

Agent Wong reached into her jacket pocket and flipped it open so I could see the bright shiny badge. My fear shifted to shock as I read it.

"The IRS? What do you guys have to do with—" My mouth snapped shut as my brain frantically caught up with the question that had snuck out of my mouth. Warning alarms were flashing in the control bridge of my psyche, but it was far too late.

I knew from firsthand experience that not everyone in law enforcement knew about the monsters and scary things beyond our mortal lives. So, while Agent Richter was sort of a fop, he at least knew something about something. Many of the other departments hadn't even gotten that far.

"We're familiar with your file," Agent Peters responded coldly, still not taking off his glasses. "This is unrelated into the investigation of the Downtown Inferno."

Inferno. That was certainly the word for what the dragonfire had done to several city blocks. I gave him a tight smile, forcing myself to not watch my own reflection in his glasses. It was just so distracting! I'm no model, but I've been working out a little, and I couldn't help but admire the results.

"Mr. Carver, we're here to serve you a lien." My eyes narrowed as I tried to figure out what that meant. I have a college degree, but it is (1) in English and (2) fake.

"Ah," I said, trying to hide my ignorance. "A lean, of course." Realizing that I was slouching, I forced myself to stand up straighter. Just in case.

"A lien is a legal claim to your assets as a guarantee to secure your outstanding debts to the US government," Agent Wong explained, somehow seeing through my attempt at bluffing. I didn't like her. She seemed smart. That's not how I prefer my federal agents.

"I owe a debt to the US government?" My voice went up an octave or two. "What kind of debt?"

"Your taxes, Mr. Carter," Agent Peters supplied unhelpfully. I didn't like him either, but that was mostly because he seemed rude, not because he was smart.

"Our records indicate that you are the sole owner of an LLC registered here in Los Angeles, California, that is in its second year of business but has not filed any state or federal taxes in that period." Wong popped open her briefcase, apparently accepting that I had no intention of inviting her and her partner in.

She pulled out a manila folder and handed it to me, ignoring the stunned look on my face. I accepted it robotically, flipping it open to paw through a dozen pages of government money babble that didn't even seem like it was written in English.

The only thing that stood out to me was the line that read:

MATTHEW CARVER INVESTMENT AGENCY WORLDWIDE ETC LLC.

"Well, that's certainly my name on the company," I admitted. "Are they allowed to do that?"

"Are who allowed to do what?" Peters asked.

"Name a company after me."

"Are you saying that you have no knowledge of this company named after you that is also registered in your name?" Wong pulled a pen out of her suitcase, as if preparing to take some notes. "I just want to make sure I have that right, for the record."

"Uhm, no." I scanned the page again, looking for anything that made sense. There was an address listed that didn't seem too far away based on the zip code. "I am not saying that or anything." I arched an eyebrow at them to see if that triggered a reaction. The two IRS agents stared at me stone-faced.

"So how does this work. Am I under arrest?"

"No, Mr. Carver, the lien is set to garnish your wages until you pay off your debts and get your taxes up to date." Wong's voice had a long-suffering quality to it.

"Okay, great. What's the total? Do you guys take credit cards?"

"Last page," Peters answered. A man of few words, that ginger.

"Ah." I gave him a polite smile before thumbing my way to the back of the folder. I didn't have a job per se. The last time I made any money was on my birthday, when the CFO of Hell handed me five million dollars in a duffel bag. I highly doubted that Zagan had reported that transaction to the IRS. Wasn't that the whole point of getting paid in cash? My train of thought abruptly derailed as I read the number that the government claimed I owed.

"Seven million, four hundred thirty-nine thousand, eight hundred and twelve what now?" My eyes shot up from the page to stare at the two Feds with unabashed shock. "Dollars?"

"That number is based off reported earnings from your company as well as short- and long-term capital gains..." Wong trailed off as I held up a hand begging her to stop. I couldn't handle hearing a single more math word.

"There must be some mistake," I told her, snapping the folder shut and shaking my head. "There are probably two very handsome men named Matthew Carver. Happens all the time. But I do not now have, nor have I ever had, seven million dollars."

"Your Social Security number is a match."

"Then someone has stolen my identity!" I felt a flush creeping up my neck as I struggled to contain the panic building inside me. I have been hacked, defrauded—of money, this time, instead of just my soul. This seemed lazy and repetitive. Surely someone could invent new disasters for me to suffer. But who could have done this? Was this the last move of dead Lazarus? Some sort of trump card, a doomsday plan enacted in revenge for killing him?

"If you are able to audit your finances and show that the number is incorrect, the lien will be adjusted accordingly," Wong promised me, her face schooled into a professionally smooth rock. "I would encourage you read to through the file. It is quite thorough."

"What happens if I don't pay off this lien?"

"You go to jail. I highly recommend you make your payments." Wong's face was expressionless, a classic Fed.

"I gotta call some people," I muttered, realizing that I should stop talking. I have learned firsthand that law enforcement is not always my friend. The last thing I needed to do was say something stupid that would give them leverage over me. "Am I free to go?"

"This is your house," Peters answered with disgust.

"So it is!" I snapped, embarrassed by my panic. "Good day, Agents. My people will be in touch and et cetera." I turned on my heel and stormed back into my house, closing the door and locking the dead bolt in their faces.

"What do you think he was on?" I heard Peters ask Wong dimly as they started to turn away. "He looked like he hadn't slept in a week." I gritted my teeth to keep myself from snapping a response at the retreating agents. He had no idea how right he was.

"Did you order something?" my best friend Alex called from the living room as I paced through the entry hall. "Thought I heard talking out front." I entered our living room to see him lounging on a giant, white, L-shaped couch, participating in his favorite pastime, watching cartoons.

He was a tall, lean man with his blond hair perfectly, artfully mussed so it just barely hid the rounded tips of his ears marking him as a lesser Nephilim.

"That was the International Revenue Service."

"The who?"

"You know, the IRS?

"I think you mean *Internal* Revenue Service."

"I mean *Idiot* Revenue Service." I collapsed into one of the matching plush white chairs and rubbed my face with my hands. "Shoot me."

"What did they want? Forget to pay your taxes?" Alex's mouth was full of chips as he asked what he thought was a funny question.

"Yeah, apparently I have a company? Did you know I have a company?"

"*You?* Why would they let *you* have a company?"

"Well, apparently I'm really good at it, because it owes over seven million dollars in taxes." My face was still buried in my hands, so I was surprised as the sound of the TV abruptly turning off. That meant Alex was taking this seriously—which, frankly, was a bad sign. I pulled my hands off my face long enough to toss my stunned friend the manila folder Wong gave me.

"Dark Abyss, you're not kidding," Alex breathed as he flipped through it. "Who named this thing? It seems melodramatic and egotistical—even for you."

"I can't even spell *et cetera,*" I groaned in complaint.

"What are you going to do? Do you even have that much?"

"No! I don't have *seven million dollars.* That's more money than I made last year, which doesn't even make any sense. I'm not really sure how the math is supposed to math, but I don't think they mathed it right."

"There's an address here," Alex pointed out, already wearing his investigative reporter hat.

"I saw. Doesn't seem that far."

"Well…"

"Let me put on shoes." I sighed, leveraging myself out of the couch. "Might as well go see what's been making me all this money."

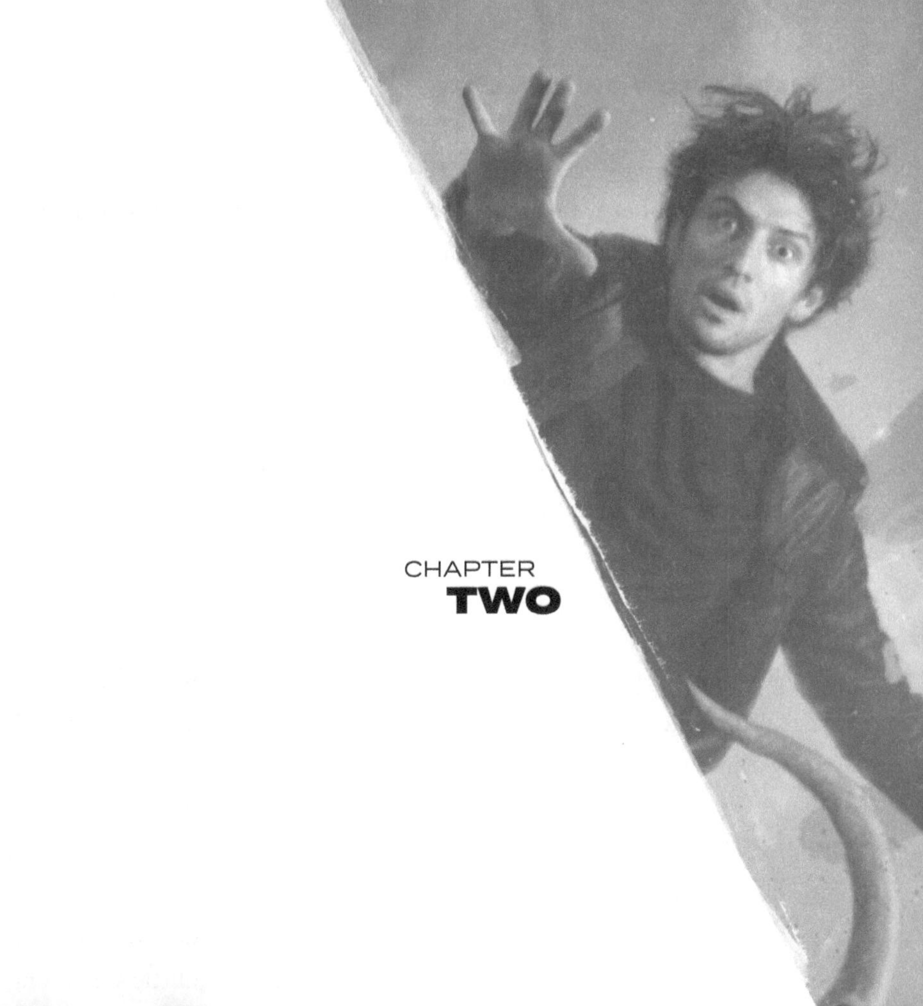

CHAPTER TWO

MY COMPANY APPARENTLY operated out of a multi-floored professional building on the edge of the Northridge area. It was a plain, glass-enclosed building that stood about fifteen stories tall. There are a million other buildings that look the same spread across LA.

The first rule of any operation is to get a lay of the land, so we prowled around the public area, looking for a clue about what we might be getting ourselves into, but there was nothing to see. No one staffed the little security desk in the drab lobby, and no matter how long we watched, no one seemed to enter or exit the building. There were cars in the lot, but whoever was working there wasn't coming out.

The longer we watched, the more my sense of unease began to grow. Something about this felt *wrong*. I mean, all of it did. I didn't think I started this company. Well, I was 99 percent sure I hadn't done it by accident. Which meant that someone had done it without my consent, maybe to get me in trouble with the IRS.

The list of my enemies who are clever enough and rich enough to do something like this was unfortunately long. Zagan, Samael, and Lazarus were all at the top, but that was by no means exhaustive. The longer we waited, the more certain I grew that this was a trap.

"We can't exactly peer in a window," Alex grumbled when boredom had overcome our better instincts. According to the address that the government gave me, my self-named company was in Suite 1301. Yet another reason I was skeptical—American buildings aren't made with a thirteenth floor. It's unlucky.

But sure enough, the directory in the lobby showed MCIAW ETC LLC as being in that suite. The elevator even had a button for the thirteenth floor. Alex and I exchanged nervous glances as the lift's doors closed.

Unconsciously my hand dipped beneath my jacket, loosening the clasp on the holster that hugged my ribs. I felt a little silly doing so—I carry far more dangerous things with me than guns. Mentally, I checked the corner of my mind where two conflicting powers waited. The warm, cheerful ball of fire, Willow the Faerie spirit, leapt to my query enthusiastically, eager to be used.

Beyond it lurked the cold, absolute power of Death. My access to the dark power was greatly reduced from when I was the heir of the Grim Reaper, but it was still enough to make me dangerous to any Immortal who dared to cross my path.

In my free hand, I carried the manila folder explaining my debts, just in case there was someone to talk to instead of a bunch of thugs ready to kill me. No matter what was waiting for us on the thirteenth floor, I had a bunch of weapons ready for any situation.

Across the elevator, Alex copied my movement, his normally cheerful face set in a grim expression. I shrugged my shoulders, straightening my spine as the floors dinged by.

Ding 9.

Ding 10.

Scenes like this, right before a fight, made me miss Orion, our mentor. These aren't the only moments that I do. First and foremost, the Nephilim-formerly-known-as-the-Hunter was my friend. He put his life on the line for me, and I will never not owe him for that. But he was also one of the most dangerous beings ever to live. I've met the Grim Reaper, and even *he's* a fan of the Hunter.

Ding 11.

Everything I know about violence, I learned from him. Going into a dangerous situation without him felt wrong. It also felt stupid, like leaving your best bullets at home. Shaking my head to pull me out of my gloomy reverie, I shot a glance at my friend. He knew what I was thinking without me even saying.

"I miss him too." Alex snorted. "Can you imagine what he would say if he knew we were riding the elevator to a possible ambush?"

"What's wrong with the stairs?" I tried to make my voice as deep as possible to mimic the elder Nephilim's bass tone.

"You should have rappelled down from the roof." Alex copied my attempt, smiling fondly.

"Now that you mention it, we probably should have."

Ding 12.

"Too late now."

Ding 13.

The two of us stepped out of the elevator at the same time, hands hovering just over the grips of our pistols. Generally speaking, it's a bad idea to run around the mortal world with your guns drawn. And this is California, not Texas—there are *rules.*

But I wanted as little time as possible to pass between seeing an enemy and drawing my gun. By conditioned training, I broke to the left as Alex went right, stepping into the empty hallway to assess the scene.

A flicker of movement in the shadows startled me, and I reached for my gun. For a moment, I saw a pair of bright-red eyes on a creature with sharp claws leaping out of the darkness. But before I could finish pulling my weapon, I blinked, and the creature was gone. It was just an empty corner.

I took a deep breath, holding it for a moment before I let it out in a long, shaky sigh. *Get it together, Carver,* I hissed at myself. This was not the first time I'd been plagued by hallucinations, but now was not a good time for me to be imagining monsters hunting me. There were enough real ones lurking around without me adding to their number.

Like the rest of the building, the floor was empty. There were a handful of suites with closed doors, but I ignored all of them. At the far end of the hall was door 1301, our target. A helpful plastic placard on the wall read: MCIAW ETC LLC.

Just in case that left any confusion, there was a large caricature artist's rendition of my face painted right on the door like a logo. Alex and I both drew up short, tilting our heads in sync to study it in stunned silence.

"I don't think my nose is that big."

"Well, they did get your ears right."

"I think you're confusing me with Dumbo."

"No, you just have big ears. You do have a big nose, but it's not *quite* an elephant's trunk."

"Enough of this," I growled, stepping forward to grab the door handle with the same hand that carried the Feds' manila folder. Now I was mad. Before it had all been surreal, some sort of fancy math mistake. But now it felt personal. It was one thing when they set me up to somehow owe the government seven million dollars. It was another thing entirely to mock me while they did it.

Quick as lightning, the jokes were gone. Alex slid behind me, gripping his pistol, ready to draw and follow me in.

"On three?" he asked.

"Three." I twisted the handle and shoved it open, bursting into the office with the fury of a hurricane.

"Oh!" The woman sitting behind the receptionist's desk looked up from her computer screen, watching us enter with mild curiosity. My eyes snapped away from her, scanning the rest of the room for any lurking threats.

The little sitting area was much like the rest of the building. The carpet was nicer; maybe it had been replaced recently. The walls were painted a bright white, and a giant black-and-white painting of a dandelion head hung on the wall. The couches were worked with golden trim. It felt at once incredibly fancy and hauntingly familiar.

I sensed no immediate danger. There was a hallway leading farther back into the office that could be concealing any number of horrors, but the room we were in was empty and calm. Convinced of our safety for the moment, I turned back to the woman, who had risen from her seat.

"Sir! I am so sorry. I did not know you were coming in today." A pretty, college-aged brunette, she was dressed in a black pencil skirt with a white blouse. A look of concern crossed her face as she spoke. "Are you feeling all right?"

"You know who I am?" I ignored her question. There was no way for me to describe how I felt without sounding like a lunatic.

"Well, of course." She gestured at the drawing on the door behind us as if that was somehow relevant. I could hear Alex choking down a laugh.

"If you give me a moment, I'll let the COO know you're here." My eyes narrowed as I tried to understand what was happening. This had to be the worst trap I'd ever been caught in. In fact, it really didn't even seem like a trap at all. It looked like the office of a legitimate business. Maybe even evil companies bent on destroying my life needed receptionists.

"Yes," I said after thinking for far too long. "Please do."

"One moment." She picked up the phone on her desk and pressed a button, then held the receiver to her ear as someone picked up on the other side.

"Sir, the president is here for you." Alex and I exchanged surprised glances.

President, he mouthed as if he had never heard the word before. I resisted the urge to roll my eyes.

"He'll be right out," she announced, hanging up. "In the meantime, can I get you anything? Coffee? Water? Tea?"

"I'll take a water," Alex answered without hesitation. I shot him a glare, but he only shrugged. We might as well get something out of my giant, debt-creating machine.

"I'll take one too, thank you," I replied. But any thoughts of hydration fled my brain as the door down the hall opened, and a dozen puzzle pieces clicked into place. Something had been bothering me about this whole deal, and now I finally knew what it was.

It was the damned Fae.

Robin Goodfellow, counselor to the Dandelion Throne and my personal lawyer, walked out into the room with a delighted smile on his face. His blond hair was slicked back like Norman Bates, and his usually golden eyes were a human blue. But there was no hiding his pointed ears or impish smile.

"You have got to be kidding me," Alex scoffed. I said nothing, because I knew he was not. No, no, the mystery was already solved. All that was left to find out was just how bad the damage was going to be.

"Matthew! What a delight to see you!" Robin trilled, holding out his arms like a long-lost father greeting his wayward son. I glared at him, but he ignored my dark look with his usual unflappable humor.

"Nice of you to finally come into the office. Leila has been wondering when she would finally get to meet our founder. Here he is." He paused as if truly seeing me for the first time. "Although he usually looks a little less like the dogs have been chewing on him. You need a nap."

"Everything you said he would be, sir," Leila responded brightly, handing Alex and me a pair of chilled water bottles. I give her a small smile, refusing to let myself be distracted. Cold rage flared in me as I glared at the Faerie.

"What have you done?"

"Oh, you're gonna love it," he assured me, which only made me angrier. "Come, come." He waved before leading us down the hallway deeper into the office. What I found there brought me to such an abrupt stop that Alex ran into my back with a grunt of complaint.

An open-air cubicle farm ran the length of the building. More than twenty men and women in suits sat at their computers, working away. The space buzzed with the efficient energy of a serious office.

"Dark Abyss," Alex swore when he got a look for himself.

"Robin," I asked through gritted teeth, "who is paying all of these… expensive-looking people?"

"Oh, well, you, of course."

"Of course."

Robin led us through the bullpen, waving brightly at the workers as he went. A number of them reacted to me in surprise, clearly recognizing me from the logo. I felt my left hand curl into a fist as I tried to contain my growing irritation. Would it be insurance fraud if I used Willow to burn the whole place down?

On the other side of the open-concept working area, Robin led us through another hallway past a bunch of executive-style offices with nameplates on the doors. I glared at the one that read ROBIN GOODFELLOW—COO as we passed it.

"You have really done it this time," I snapped at my lawyer, who looked at me with vague surprise. Still moving forward. "I feel like an idiot even asking this, but do you know how much trouble I am in?"

"Here we are," he said, turning the handle on the door next to his. "I think you need to speak to the CEO." I had just enough time to see that the nameplate read MATTHEW CARVER—PRESIDENT/FOUNDER as we entered. My complaints died on my lips as I got a glance of my office.

It was spacious—impressively so. A large mahogany desk that reminded me far too much of Kane's sat along the back wall. A row of bookshelves filled with tomes I'd never read ran along the left side, while the right had a large leather couch and a pair of chairs.

It was a pretty nice office. I wouldn't mind working here if I, you know, had a job or marketable skills. But that wasn't what shut me up. It was the CEO who was waiting for me, her lips compressed in a tight smile.

The dusky-skinned woman's green eyes sparkled with mischief at the irritation on my face. Her red hair was bound up in a tight, professional bun that fit the rest of her business attire. The only clue that she was not human was her pointed ears, which looked like a Hollywood vision of an elf's.

Her name was Ash, and she was the Lady of Autumn in the Dandelion Court. She was kinda my girlfriend...and betrothed. It's a long story. The girlfriend part sort of came after the betrothing. The Fae have a funny way of doing things.

She was also the daughter of the Devil himself.

I know.

In my defense, I didn't find that out until it was too late, and so far it had actually mattered a lot less than I would have expected. She was *very* different from her absentee father.

"Not you too," I groaned.

"Hello, darling," she replied, her smile growing. "You've ruined your surprise."

"*I* didn't ruin it. The federal government did."

Her expression grew clouded as she glanced between Robin and me. "What is he talking about?"

"Oh, who knows?" Robin sighed airily. "You have no idea how exhausting it is being his lawyer. There's always *something*. I tend to tune him out most of the time."

"You should try living with him," Alex offered from behind me.

"You should try *dating* him." Ash's eyes flashed with amusement. "That is what it's called, right?"

"Very good," I snapped, feeling my irritation rise. Before becoming my betrothed, Ash had never left the Faerie Lands, a world far away from here. Since coming to the mortal realm, she's had to muddle along with the three of us as her pop-culture tutors, for better or worse. "But all of your banter isn't going to help me find *seven million dollars* so I can stand up straight."

The two Faes' expressions cooled as they studied me with a new focus.

"He's talking about a lien," Alex offered helpfully.

"Yes, that."

"The IRS placed a lien on you?" Ash's voice was cool and imperious, like the princess she was.

"Yup! Apparently, I haven't been paying my taxes on the company I started?" The two of them exchanged a long, knowing glance that did not make me feel any better. Robin held out a hand, face impassive, and I offered him the manila folder the Feds had given me.

The Faerie flipped through the documents, eyes blurring as he read at an inhuman speed. Ash peered over his shoulder, eyebrows forming a red V. An identical scowl began to grow on both their faces as they progressed deeper into the documents.

"This says we haven't paid any taxes," Robin said, his voice dangerously mild. "Which is interesting, since our books say we have."

"Douglas?" Ash asked Robin, ignoring my complaints for a moment.

"Douglas." Robin's face was a scowl as he played with his long fingers. "I knew he was too good."

"Sorry, who is Douglas?" I felt like I was feverish. This was some sort of play where everyone knew their lines but me. At any moment a laugh track would kick in.

"He's our CFO. Wildly competent." I shuddered at the thought of having someone with the same title as Zagan working in my office. I guess that wasn't really logical, but the fallen angel had left something of an impression on me.

"What about this feels wildly competent?" I asked, letting a little more heat creep into my voice.

"The part where he's probably been embezzling millions of dollars from the company instead of paying the taxes we owe." He flipped the manila folder onto my desk with a sneer, finally as irritated as I was.

"Oh." I felt a little better knowing this situation made sense to the two Fae. Although I wasn't thrilled that it did sound like I was millions of dollars in debt. I was sort of hoping that part was wrong.

"We knew he was a corporate spy. But didn't think they'd start with sabotage this early," Robin grunted.

"You *knew* he was a corporate spy?" I snapped. "And you left him in charge of the *finances*?"

"Better the devil you know and all that," Robin muttered, waving his hand in a dismissive gesture.

"Not in my experience!"

"That's crazy," Alex breathed, awe filling his voice. "You're now a victim of two different types of fraud."

"Yes, thank you, Alex," I managed through gritted teeth. "Out of curiosity, what exactly is it that my company does that it has corporate spies infiltrating it?" My head hurt. Ever since Dan the Demon stole my soul, I've been playing catch-up on a lifetime of knowledge about the supernatural world that exists in the shadows of ours.

But this was supposed to be *my* side of the fence. Somehow I was behind yet again, outpaced by these Immortals who were flourishing in the mortal space. It wasn't fair.

"We're an angel investment firm that specializes in emerging tech, medicine, and thaumaturgical research," Ash answered as if those words meant anything.

"Thauma what now?"

"It's the modern intersection of science and magic," Robin explained with a halfhearted shrug. "The Lazarus Group was heavily involved in that space."

The Lazarus Group. An involuntary shudder ran down my spine as I remembered what I'd gone through at the hands of the twisted billionaire's technomancers. They had used technology and occult power together to kill me for a short time and send my soul to the Veil.

It was not a particularly pleasant experience. I haven't been able to sleep since I got back. I lost something of myself in there, and I am not sure I will ever get it back. All that is to say, I'd had more than enough experience with the kind of research they were talking about.

"Where did you even get the money to start an investment—" I interrupted my own question as the understanding clicked. "The demon money," I groaned. Part of my ten-year fraudulent contract with Hell for my soul was a yearly payment of five million dollars. Zagan had personally delivered the first installment to me on my birthday, the same day that Ash came to the mortal world. Operating as her agent, Robin negotiated a stipend of a million dollars for my betrothed's needs. I had assumed that was for necessities like housing and clothing. Silly me.

"Why?" I had a thousand questions, but that seemed like a good place to start. It encompassed the overwhelming sense that I was drowning.

"Why did I start a company in your name?" Ash's voice was cool and calm. The Lady of Autumn was a spirited woman. She was most dangerous when her voice was steady. But I was too frustrated to care.

"Yes, that is a great place to start." Robin and Alex visibly took a step back, giving my dear beloved and me some extra space.

"Because you are the only one of us with a Social Security number. We do not exist. Only you do. But that is secondary to the more important reason."

"Which is?"

"I am the Lady of Autumn. We are betrothed. Your life will become my life, and my life will become yours. We will share rivals, more than we already do. What else did you expect me to do than build our House to withstand the storm that is coming?"

I had to admit, she had a point. The two of us have a lot of enemies, and there was a ticking clock until her father could claim my soul and cart me off to the big fiery downstairs forever. I've seen the circle he's preparing for me. It wasn't nice to visit—I have no desire to stay there long-term.

"Well," I said, feeling cantankerous despite beginning to understand. "Not to be too ungrateful, but being seven million dollars in debt to the US government does not particularly make me feel like I am in a stronger position than I was before I had a company." To my surprise, Ash didn't look angry or ashamed by my comment.

"That," my betrothed said with a sudden twinkle in her eye, "is because you do not know what you have bought."

CHAPTER
THREE

"THE MCIAW ETC LLC portfolio has become quite robust over the last year," Robin explained to Alex and me. He stood in the center of the room while the two of us sat on the couch with Ash. It was quite comfortable and luxurious. I wondered if we could sell it to help pay off my debts.

"That is just an awful name," Alex pointed out.

"Yeah, even Lazarus Group sounds cooler," I agreed. "Why did you have to make it lame?"

"Interesting companies get audited," Robin replied with a shrug.

"Well, I'm getting audited, *and* I have a lame company name, so it doesn't seem like that plan worked."

"As the Lady of Autumn said, we have focused our investments in three primary verticals," he continued, ignoring me as he always did when I was right. "Technology, medicine, and thaumaturgy. Our ideal partners work in some combination of those. We've invested in companies that are creating hybrid products using things like alchemy, quantum computing, or weapons manufacturing. In all cases, we're looking to locate unicorns."

"...unicorns?" I repeated the word slowly, almost certain I hadn't heard it correctly. "Surely you don't mean—"

"In investing terms, a unicorn is a start-up company that goes from a negligible net worth to over a billion dollars after you invest in it, creating a return with many zeros in it," Robin explained smoothly. "But honestly, we'd consider either kind a win." That didn't make me feel any better.

"Okay, but we're still broke, right?" I held up my hands to stop the lecture. "This all sounds great. I can't wait to learn more, but I owe the US government more than seven million dollars, and my next demon payment is only going to be five million."

"We own assets that have value," Ash replied, cocking her head to the side. "It wouldn't be impossible for us to bring in outside investment to cover our capital expenses while allowing us to retain most of our ownership."

"We'd have to be careful about who we let into the fold," Robin mused, rubbing at his chin. "It would be a shame to invite the wolves in just to put out a fire."

"But doable?" I looked between the two of them, not entirely sure I was following. It sounded like they were talking about selling a part of the ownership of the company to someone else in exchange for the money we needed to pay our bills.

"Doable," Ash agreed.

"I'm sure we can come up with a payment plan they will accept. The IRS is truly the most reasonable branch of the Feds."

I blinked at Robin in surprise. "I'm not sure anyone has ever said that in the history of the United States."

"That's because most people can't read."

"My birthday was three months ago. Shouldn't I be getting another deposit of five million dollars from el Banco del Diablo?"

"Oh, that already came through," Robin replied, as if surprised I was asking.

"What?"

"As your lawyer of record, they made the delivery to me while you were still…dead. I think Zagan did it then to be petty." That did sound like the fallen angel. He had probably been crossing every *t* and dotting every *i* in case I had died for real while I was down in the Veil.

"So where is it?"

"Since the relationship between you and the Lady of Autumn had not changed, I distributed the funds in the same allocation we used previously."

"So a million to Ash, a million to you for retainer, and my three million is…"

"Invested in the company's operating fund."

I sighed, rubbing my face with my hands. This is what I got for letting my Faerie lawyer run on too long of a leash. Things had been quiet for a few months, and I should have known better. The Fae are like puppies and toddlers: If you can't hear them, they're getting into trouble.

"We will discuss this further," I promised him in what I hoped was a threatening tone. "But that guy who stole our money…Douglas, was it? Why don't we just make him give it back?"

"Oh, that money is almost certainly long gone," Robin replied with a sad shrug. "I'm sure it hopped through the Cayman Islands before it found its way into some Swiss bank account where no one can touch it."

"You know way too much about our banking system for someone who isn't from here."

"Please, you think a mortal came up with it?" He snorted in disgust. I decided not to pursue that line of questioning. I can only handle having my world reframed so much at one time.

"Well, how about we stop him from taking any more money? Do we know who he is working for?" I was so far out of my depth. This was *technically* my company, but that mattered little. I just wanted to stay out of prison.

"At first I assumed that it was the Journeymen or one of those other supernatural investment groups," Ash murmured, drumming her fingers on her thigh as she thought. "But this theft makes me think otherwise."

"Why?"

"It's largely useless." She shrugged. "More annoying than damaging. If he was really working for a competitor, they would stand to make a lot more money by having him steal insider information."

"You're saying stealing seven million dollars is useless?" I couldn't keep the incredulity out of my voice.

"It's a rounding error at the level most of these companies operate on. Even if they stole the money for themselves, which they likely didn't, that would be too traceable. It wouldn't make a dent in their fortunes."

"It feels almost personal when you put it like that," Alex suggested.

"I agree." Robin nodded, his face troubled. "Although unfortunately that doesn't narrow down the list of suspects." He glanced at me with a dour expression. "You're not a well-liked man."

"Don't I know it," I muttered darkly. "So Douglas is working for someone who hates me on a fundamental level, sabotaging the company for spite instead of for material gain, because seven million dollars isn't enough money for the heist to be worth the risk?"

"That's essentially it," Ash agreed.

"Must be nice," I grumbled. "Okay, so how do we find out who he's working for?"

"We could always ask him," Alex offered, a tight, unpleasant smile blossoming on his face. I frowned to see the expression, but I didn't disagree. Ever since Orion got locked up by Polaris, my best friend has been on edge, trying to fill shoes that cannot be filled. I was worried about him, but that was a problem for a different day.

"We could," Robin agreed, tapping his chin thoughtfully. The lanky Fae was no stranger to violence. But he was far more like a stiletto than Alex or I tended to be. "Once he knows that we know, however, there will be no opportunity to put the cat back in the bag."

I didn't think that was exactly how the expression went, but I decided to let him have it. "What do you propose?"

"Let me dive into the books, see what I can find. If we're right and he's just here to smash things up, it should be easy to find traces of his work. Maybe there's a pattern that will give us some clues about who he's working with."

"How long will that take?"

"A day or two?" He shrugged. "I work quickly, and it will be my second highest priority."

"Why second?" I asked, eyes narrowing in suspicion.

"We're leading a round that is about to close with an arms manufacturer called Nothung."

"Nothing?" The name gave me so much pause it made me forget I had no idea what "leading a round" even meant. It sounded like something middle schoolers did during recess.

"Nothung. You have to pronounce the *u*."

I shook my head, not willing to argue with the Faerie anymore. "Well, not to be too rude, but it is my company…"

"Actually, you're not a part of the day-to-day operations, just chairman of the board," Ash explained, as if that meant anything to me.

"But I own the thing."

"And part of the operating agreement was that you would recuse yourself from managerial duties in exchange for a discount on our 'unique expertise,'" Robin was quick to answer.

"An operating agreement, huh? That sure sounds like something I need to sign for it to be effective. But I don't remember doing that." The two Fae had the good grace to look embarrassed. For a moment an unreasonable amount of rage bubbled in my chest.

Dan the demon had forged his infernal contract with my name against my wishes, and now my lawyer and betrothed had done the same. It's a miracle I don't have *more* trust issues.

"We will be amending that agreement," I managed through gritted teeth. Robin opened his mouth to object, but I gave him no time.

"Seven million dollars," I growled.

"That was always the plan," Ash admitted from beside me. "This was meant to be a wed—a surprise." A moment of tense silence hung around her slip, but I chose to ignore it. Now was certainly not the time for that terrifying conversation. I would almost rather go back to Hell and face her father. Which, now that I thought about it, maybe I was supposed to before—Nope. Not the time.

"Okay," I said, flexing my newfound business muscles. "I want that modified agreement in my hands ASAP. I don't know about this Nothung, but do we even have the money to invest?"

"The funds are already in escrow," Robin told me, as if that meant anything. I was pretty sure that was the country next to Norway, but I was too afraid to ask.

"Fine," I snapped, embarrassed once again by my own lack of knowledge. I should really read more books. Maybe after I get my soul back. "Finish this round thing, but every other resource you have goes into figuring out who this Douglas character is working for and where the money went. Capisce?"

"You don't have to yell," Robin grumbled, crossing his arms like a wounded teen. I resisted the urge to roll my eyes. "But yes, that should be a simple matter for someone of my talents." He smiled widely, showing far too many teeth.

"What about me, am I fired?" Ash asked, turning to look at me with a slight smirk. Somehow she knew I wasn't as angry as I should be. Maybe she took it as a compliment that I wasn't able to get upset with her. The truth was that I could barely even feel this. I was simply too tired to do anything but plod forward. One more problem to solve while the game clock on my life ran down.

"Probation," I told her, returning her smile with a weak one of my own. "We have accountants we can trust, I assume?"

"A few. You have to be careful with accountants. They're all a little sneaky."

"Well, see if you can get some of them to be sneaky for me, and find a way where I don't have to pay the government seven million dollars."

"Can do." She smiled for real this time. "Technically the lien is against anything you own, which means the company as a whole."

"So you're saying it's your problem too."

"It's our problem too."

"Hey," Alex said, breaking into the conversation after being mercifully silent for a few moments. I'm not sure I could have handled all three of them going full blast at the same. "Why am I the only one who doesn't work here? Can I have a job?"

"We do need a new janitor," Robin mused.

CHAPTER FOUR

LOOK ON THE bright side," Alex said as his faithful white minivan pulled out of the MCIAW ETC LLC's parking lot. "At least she got you a present. No one's ever gotten me a company before."

"Want mine? I'll sell it to you," I asked from where I slouched in the front passenger seat, feeling exhausted and overwhelmed. The exhaustion wasn't new; it had been following me since I came back from the Veil. The scientists who'd sent me to the Underworlds emphatically insisted that I was never "technically" dead, but my experience is that death is more like a set of guidelines than hard-and-fast rules.

Since my trip to the other side, things hadn't been the same. I may not have died, but I wasn't sure I was properly alive either.

A massive stack of papers sat in my lap, dossiers on all the different companies MCIAW was invested in. I didn't know why I had to carry them. When I'd asked Robin to email them to me, he'd gasped like I had asked him to kill his own mother.

"*Think of the operational security!*" he'd said. I didn't even bother to remind him that someone had already stolen millions of dollars from us. At a certain point I was just starting to sound bitter.

"On the plus side, I think the debtor prison isn't that bad compared to the ones where they send all the violent criminals," Alex offered, merging into traffic.

"Perfect. It will be easier for you to bust me out."

"True," he said without hesitating. I snorted in appreciation. He was a good friend to have. "I would, you know."

"I know."

A heavy silence descended upon us, a shared unspoken thought. Our mentor and former boss, Orion, of the constellation fame, currently languished in Tartarus, a prison for Nephilim. He had been sentenced to five hundred years for killing Doyle, the mad dragon that had rampaged through LA.

The penance itself was a slap on the wrist. Orion was immortal, and he would emerge from his stint behind bars no worse for wear. But the passage of time would still be damaging for him. He was ostensibly the big alpha of Los Angeles, which wasn't a formal position; he wasn't a king or official. He was just dangerous.

This meant that a lot of scary things steered clear of the area. Especially ones that preyed on humans and Nephilim. When the Hunter was on the prowl, the risk wasn't worth the price of admission. But with him gone, I could only assume things would begin to change. It wouldn't take long for his territory to be overrun.

On a personal note, I would never see him again. By the time he returned to the world, my bones would have turned to dust, even if I did manage to get my soul back from Hell. Even Alex, who was already over two centuries old, might run out of days by then. He carried a lot less demon DNA in his blood than the Hunter. There was a chance he was merely long-lived rather than truly immortal. He'd find out at some point.

If we could save him, we would. But Tartarus was no ordinary prison. It was built to hold the most powerful of supernatural creatures. Alex and I didn't even know where it was. So yeah, I knew Alex would bust me out of a simple mortal cell if the IRS carried me away, but both of us carried the guilt of not being able to help our mentor in the same way.

My phone rang, rupturing the heavy silence between us. Not with an actual ringtone—I'm not a loser—but its vibration was loud enough that my sharp-eared friend could hear it easily.

"What do you bet it's good news?" he asked as I fished my phone out of my pocket. "Today's been going so well."

"Don't tempt Fate," I scolded, glancing down at the screen, surprised to see that it was Father Pike. "I've already upset her enough."

I put the receiver to my ear. "Hello, sir," I said brightly. "What can your favorite sinner do for you?" Father Gerald Pike was my priest. Sort of. I was nominally—*nominally*—Catholic. My grandmother was devout, but just like trickle-down economics, the phenomenon seemed to dry up as it worked its way down to my mother and then to me. It was more like a hometown sports affiliation at this point. Maybe that was because my Faerie father's name was Damien, after all—far too close to *demon*.

When I first discovered that my soul had been stolen, I made a pilgrimage to the other team's base to see if there was any help to be had. The reception was...underwhelming. The best thing that I can say about it was that at least I didn't burst into flame as soon as I stepped on the grounds. But it turned out coming in off the street and telling a man of the cloth that the Devil owned your soul wasn't a great opening. Faith comes in many different levels, I guess.

Fortunately for me, Father Pike overheard me telling my story to the first priest and caught me before I left. Unlike his counterpart, he believed me and even offered to help. He hasn't been able to find a solid solution to my overlying problem, but he has been unwaveringly in my corner. He's good people.

"All men are sinners, Matthew," Gerald chided me gently, "and I have love for them all."

"Why do I feel like there's a 'but' coming?"

"There's a 'but' coming. How did you know?"

"It's been that kind of day. What's wrong."

"Can you come by Saint Sebastian's? I need your help."

"Yeah, we're headed toward that part of town now," I replied, glancing at the highway's traffic as Alex merged us onto the 405 heading north. "Maybe twenty minutes?"

"That's fine. I will be here."

"Father, what kind of help is this?" I asked, already knowing I wasn't going to like the answer. "Is it the lifting-heavy-boxes kind or the fighting-monsters kind?"

"It's to save someone's soul."

"Oh boy."

It took closer to thirty minutes for us to make it to the church, but this is LA. Everyone knows that travel estimates are about as reliable as weather forecasts. Traffic jams creep up out of nowhere like a blustery wind or vanish in a heartbeat.

St. Sebastian's was a rotund little chapel in Northridge that didn't look like the castles Catholic churches often seem inspired by. It had seen better days; the mortar on it was cracked, and the announcement board was always missing letters.

But there were always a few cars in the lot, and it seemed full of good, hardworking people looking for answers, which I took as a testament to the quality of some of the shepherds who worked there.

"Why do we always end up here?" Alex complained as he parked. He'd never liked coming here. Given his heritage, I can't exactly blame him for feeling uncomfortable on the premises.

"He helped us identify Ascalon," I reminded him. Orion had gotten his hands on Saint George's dragon-killing lance, and the good Father had been able to confirm for us that it was the relic we'd hoped it was. "We owe him a conversation at least." Alex grunted in reluctant agreement, following me out of the van.

I opened the big wooden door set with a bit of stained glass to enter the narthex, which as far as I could tell was just a fancy word for "northern entrance." Neither of us spoke as we slunk through the hall and down the side toward Father Pike's office. His counterpart, Father Bryant, was the man who'd originally tried to throw me out, and I was in no mood to put up with his scathing commentary.

"Come in," Gerald called when I knocked on his door. I obeyed and stepped into his whirlwind of knowledge. Books filled every possible surface, facing every direction. More were stacked in piles on the floor. A pair of plush overstuffed chairs sat in front of his paper-covered desk. The priest looked up at the two of us with a small smile of welcome.

Father Pike was a tall man in his late forties. He'd immigrated to America from Uganda because he felt that we needed him here more than his homeland did. Laugh lines were etched into his cheeks, and he peered at us over a pair of silver, wire-frame glasses that glinted with the light of the fluorescent bulbs in the ceiling.

"Matthew, Alex, thank you for coming," he said, gesturing for us to sit. His accent was unique. It was easy to hear the British influence on it. He also drank tea instead of coffee, which seems like a bigger sign of colonial trauma.

"Are you feeling well?" His brows narrowed in concern as he took in my appearance. "You look a little under the weather."

"What's going on, Father?" I asked with a sigh, letting his question go unanswered. I slid into one of the seats while Alex sat next to me.

"Someone who has been coming to me for counseling has vanished without a trace. I am worried about her—and I am hoping I can prevail upon the two of you to help me find her."

"I mean, we could try," I said slowly, exchanging looks with a skeptical Alex, "but we're not exactly private detectives. I'm not sure what we could do that the police couldn't."

Gerald smiled softly as if unsurprised by our hesitation. "This particular woman, Maria Gonzales, came to me because she thought she was being tormented by demons. Over the last six months I've been helping her wrestle with faith and the things that plague her."

"Meaning no disrespect, Father," Alex replied, his face set in a firm line, "but just because someone thinks they are being persecuted by the supernatural doesn't always mean they are. Plus, we're not exactly missionaries."

"It's true. One of the hardest parts about this job is figuring out how to help those in need. Many people are victims. Others are their own demons. But every once in a while, there is someone whose story defies explanation. And sometimes the danger isn't only spiritual." His gaze landed heavily on me, and I resisted the urge to wince. Gerald had believed me right away, making him one of a very small number of mortals.

"Why do you think Maria's case is like mine?" I asked, trying to be open-minded. Privately I felt similar to Alex. I had a lot on my plate. I didn't have time to go looking for a missing woman. I needed to find the missing parts of myself first.

"When she first came looking for help, she told me the Devil was trying to buy her soul," Gerald said grimly. My mouth twisted into a grimace. That sounded a little too familiar. "Believe it or not, that part is not that uncommon," he continued, seeing the expression on my face. "It was the way her story evolved that left me concerned."

"What do you mean?" Despite his earlier resistance, Alex's expression was sharp and focused.

"She told me there was a particular demon set to torment her—again, I have been told that before, but there was something unusual about her story. She spoke of the demon as if he were a smarmy salesman. His name was Greg, and he was short and red as a fire engine." I swallowed, beginning to understand why Gerald thought we might be able to help with this case.

"I have only ever heard of a demon having a simple, modern name once before," he told us softly, dark eyes flicking between the two of us, waiting for us to reach the same conclusion he had.

"Dan," I said it for him. The Father inclined his head at me, too gracious to say *I would not waste your time, young man.*

"So I was already suspicious. Then, Maria told me a *new* demon had come to pressure her. It was an overseer, a being that this Greg reported to. His name was Zagan." I went still, too stunned to speak.

"Dark Abyss," Alex swore under his breath, his tone a mixture of awe and anger.

"Now, Zagan is a name that is known to me. There are records from the fathers of the faith who list him among the fallen angels cast out of Heaven with Lucifer. But similarly, I have only ever heard his name spoken by someone looking for help one other time." I hung my head, feeling tremendous sympathy for this woman trapped in the same machinations that had caught me. I knew firsthand how miserable it was to be ground by their gears.

"Greg and Zagan made tremendous promises to Maria, and the poor girl is plagued by many problems. Her faith was strong, but her body is weak. She told me she would never accept their twisted gifts, but denying them was growing harder with each day she suffered. Two weeks ago, she did not show up for her appointment. I have not seen her since. I went to visit her, but she did not answer."

"Do you think she signed it?" Alex asked the question hanging over all of us.

"I do not believe she would, but anything is possible. Lucifer and his creatures are skilled in their fell arts," Gerald replied with a hint of disgust. "I worry something else has befallen her." He did not have to look at me to imply exactly what we all were thinking.

What if I was not the only soul that Hell had forged a signature for?

Alex and I exchanged long glances. His expression matched my own, a grim resignation to the monumental task before us.

"What would Orion do?" he asked softly. Father Gerald's face twitched with the ghost of a smile. He had a particular shared affinity with the Hunter. Orion wasn't a devout man, but he had a passion for the lost. I knew that better than most.

If he'd heard this story, he would already be out the door, with his hand on the hilt of his Immortal-killing blade. He would abide no poaching of the innocent in his territory. I saw no reason that we, his squires, should suffer it in his absence. We might not be able to rescue him from Tartarus, but we could carry on his work while he was gone.

There was also a small chance that this could benefit me. If Zagan and his demons had really forged her signature too, then there was a chance Maria and I could help each other. Maybe we could start a class-action lawsuit or something. Alex gave me a minute nod, telling me he was with me.

"Give us what you got," I told Father Gerald. "We'll find Maria."

CHAPTER
FIVE

"OKAY, WHAT DO we have?" Alex asked from the driver's seat as we pulled out of St. Sebastian's parking lot. The sun was beginning its late-afternoon descent, and rush-hour traffic had already begun to pick up, meaning we would be moving at a sedate pace toward home.

"Maria Gonzalez, age forty-eight," I said, flicking through the thin folder Father Gerald had given us. It didn't have his more personal records of counseling, just some high-level notes along with an address. A small Polaroid photo showed a woman in her forties smiling where she sat next to Father Gerald in his office.

"Looks like she has some chronic pain and an addiction problem," I murmured, scanning his notes. "To the best of his knowledge, she lives nearby." I checked her address against my phone's map. "Five-minute drive."

"Wanna swing by?"

"No point in waiting."

Alex got off the 405 two exits later, taking us through a run-down neighborhood. Northridge is not one of the nice parts of LA that you hear about in songs and movies. It's most famous for being devasted by that big earthquake in 1994 that killed more than fifty people.

It's home to a lot of immigrants and working-class folks. Money is tight, and people work hard to survive. I knew this because it was where I grew up, although now that I knew my father was a Faerie Lord, I suspect some of that might have been him trying to hide. Whatever the reason, I spent a lot of time in hand-me-downs as a boy.

"It's on this block," I told him as we turned down a residential street full of small houses with peeling paint on claustrophobically tiny lots. Alex parked in an empty spot, and we got out of the van, preparing to walk down the street.

"Bring your lockpick kit, just in case," I told him. If something had happened to Maria, we'd need to get inside to find clues to hunt her down.

"Way ahead of you." Alex patted his back pocket where he had tucked away his tools. Together we made our way down the street, trying to look like two normal members of society who belonged here.

"One-one-four-seven, four-nine, five-one," I counted as we approached Maria's last known address. My instincts, honed by two years of living dangerously, were going wild. The squat white house was dark, showing no signs of life. An older sedan was parked in the driveway, dust on its windshield. Nothing had moved here for a while. Alex and I exchanged a knowing glance, telling each other that we both felt a sudden sense of foreboding.

"Well, guess we know what kind of adventure this is going to be,"

Alex said, staring at the closed door. Bad—he meant it was going to be a bad one.

"Might as well get it over with," I agreed. I held out my left fist without looking, and he rapped his knuckles against mine, our sacred ritual before we made stupid decisions. We do it pretty often.

I walked up the path to the wooden porch. My footsteps were too loud, like I was disturbing a silent place. I pressed the doorbell but didn't hear a sound through the thin door.

After a moment of hesitation, I tapped my fingers against the door itself. "Hello, Maria?" I called, leaning forward to catch any sound of movement on the other side. "We're friends of Father Gerald; he asked us to drop by. He thought we might be able to help you with some of your…problems."

Silence.

I knocked again, firmer now. "My name is Matthew Carver, and I'm with Alex Johnson. We just want to help."

This silence was louder this time.

Alex and I traded uncomfortable looks. There was a heavy weight to the property that felt familiar—the kind of ponderous silence that can be found in graveyards. Kane, the Grim Reaper, wore it like a cloak. A piece of that quiet lurked in the back of my mind, a party favor from my time as an employee of Death Corp.

Alex sighed, understanding what I wanted to do next. He dug his tool kit out of his back pocket. Before I met him, Alex had done many things, but his most recent job was as an investigative reporter, one who sometimes went above and beyond for a story. Originally that was why he'd offered to help me—for a chance to break my story.

After he was recruited into the Hunt, his priorities had changed, but the skills he'd acquired in his previous life still came in handy from time to time. I glanced over my shoulder, scanning the street as he crouched to dig at the lock.

No one was out for a walk; dusk was just beginning to twinkle into existence. A car drove by but didn't seem to notice the two men messing with someone's front door. There's a lot of power to not looking like you're doing anything wrong. We wore no masks, made no effort to hide what we were up to. After all, who would break into a home out in the open where everyone could see?

Only idiots.

"Got it," Alex said, his voice accompanied by a heavy *click* as the dead bolt retracted. He placed his hand on the knob and twisted before hesitating, looking at me one last time to see if we were really doing this.

I reached over his shoulder and gave the door a light shove. The two of us watched as it slowly swung open, its unoiled hinges creaking like the dead. For a moment the two of us stood at the threshold, listening. The silence was heavier now, as if responding to our disturbance.

You already know what you're going to find, my mind whispered to me, in sync with the cold power that coiled in my head like a sleeping serpent. I ignored my instincts, calling out in a loud voice, "Hello? Maria, are you home?" My voice almost seemed to echo in the darkness. There were no lights on, no fans running. The windows were all covered in cardboard and newspapers.

"Oh, she's here," Alex said softly from beside me, sniffing loudly. I copied him, leaning forward slightly, since my senses aren't as enhanced as his Nephilim ones are. But he was right: A foul odor floated on the still air. Death had made itself at home here.

Fishing a flashlight out of my jacket pocket, I clicked it on before I took a step into the home, wincing as a floorboard creaked under my weight. It felt rude, like I was intruding in a place where I wasn't meant to be. Well, I *was* intruding, in the legal sense of the world. But this was a different kind. It felt like we were breaking into a mausoleum, not a home.

Alex followed in my wake, pulling the door shut behind me. His light turned on, sending a second beam cutting through the darkness.

"Let's go see what we came here to find," I whispered.

It was easy to know where to go; I just followed my nose. Slowly we made our way through the small living room and into the kitchen.

Maria was waiting for us on the table. My stomach roiled in disgust at the sight of her. She had been here for a while, and Mother Nature had been about her work. But it was not the state of decay that made me sick. It was the clear signs of what had been done to her.

She lay on her stomach, hands outstretched as if straining for help that was just out of reach. A black knife made of a material I couldn't immediately identify stuck out of her back. The part of its blade that I could see was covered in jagged edges and teeth. It was a cruel weapon, made to devour.

"Dark Abyss," Alex swore when he stepped in beside me to study the scene. "That's an athame."

"Sounds bad."

"Traditionally used in dark rituals."

"Gee, thanks for the clue," I replied dryly. As I surveyed the horrors before us, I was suddenly glad I hadn't been sleeping. Now I couldn't dream of this.

In silence we both panned our lights across poor Maria, searching for more clues.

Our beams froze on the writing at the same time. I could feel myself turn pale as I tilted my head to read the upside-down words. She had written them in her own blood, one last defiant act before the Reapers came to collect her soul.

I DIDN'T SIGN IT

I DIDN'T SIGN IT

I DIDN'T SIGN

Neither of us spoke for a long time. A thousand emotions roiled through me as I stared at the words. The skeptic in me wanted to say they could mean a thousand things: Maybe a relative had faked a last will and testament, or a predatory loan shark had taken her house. But the longer I stared at her writing in blood, the more I knew that wasn't true.

Someone had done to her exactly what had been done to me, then taken it one step further. They killed her. But why? When Lilith had planned on murdering me, she had admitted that it would make Hell's case weaker. She had just been counting on the fact that I was dead to keep anyone from looking into it too much. But the implication was that this was not the smart way to go about committing soul fraud. So why had it happened?

"A copycat?" Alex guessed, reading the situation similarly.

"Either someone decided to steal Dan's playbook, or I was not the first." My gut told me it was someone following in his footsteps. So far everyone involved in my case had acted as if this was the first time they'd ever encountered a situation like this. Even Lilith was surprised. If someone was doing this regularly, surely *someone* else would have heard about it.

Guided by instinct, I moved my flashlight's beam up to the knife—er, athame—sticking out from her back. Instead of iron, it was made of an all-black material. It was familiar, but it took me a moment to register where I had seen it before. It ate the light that I shone on it eagerly, like fire devouring wood.

Slowly, I lifted my left hand and reached for the dark power that was lurking in the back of my brain. Willow's familiar presence brushed against my senses, offering to come to my aid, but gently I rebuffed that warm light. This was not a task for them.

The cold came to me without hesitation. Pure shadow coalesced in my palm, darker than the rest of the room. It was frigid, and a shudder of revulsion ran through my living body at its touch as it formed into a scythe taller than I am. This was something I suspected I was not supposed to have. A piece of Death, given to the Reapers who serve beyond the Veil. When I returned to the land of the living, it came with me. For a while, I'd thought Kane didn't know, that I'd stolen it like Prometheus took the fire from the gods.

But now, as I compared the pure darkness of my Reaper scythe with the athame that stuck out of Maria's back, a sinking certainty in my gut told me that wasn't the case. Death, the person, the Horseman of the Apocalypse, was tasked with one duty: the safe delivery of souls to their respective places of rest. He's the Postman.

While I served as his heir, I saw that there were problems with the mail. Things weren't always ending up where they were supposed to go. I had stopped Pluto, the Roman god of death who had been siphoning off his souls to a mysterious place, but the Grim Reaper had told me that he was only a piece of the greater puzzle.

Kane was old. As old as it gets, if he is to be believed. He didn't *forget* to take his power back from me. He let me leave with it because I was going to need it. I squinted as Alex's light shone on my face, highlighting the absolute dark of my scythe—a perfect match for the athame.

"Dark Abyss," he swore.

CHAPTER SIX

I TOOK THE ATHAME with me when we left even though it felt wrong to disturb the crime scene. We play fast and loose with the rules on the supernatural side, but this was a murder—a human murder. Still, I knew LAPD would have no idea what they were dealing with here. We were the only people who stood a chance of solving this case. Which meant I was going to need every piece of evidence I could get.

"Okay, we're looking at a pretty serious thing here," Alex said, breaking the silence on our ride home. It was fully night now, and the earlier traffic was long gone. I grunted in agreement, my thoughts still a whirl. This was not my first time seeing a dead body. Despite my protests to Gerald, this wasn't my first time working a murder case. The Hunt had handled more than one during my time with it.

But none of them had affected me personally. For the last two years, my whole life had revolved around Dan's act of soul fraud. After my most recent birthday, the time on the game clock was officially less than eight years; then Lucifer and his demons could come collect me.

While I was still nursing a ray of hope about completing my Impossible Task, I hadn't made much progress on it yet. I didn't even know where to *find* an apple of Iðunn. After that, I had to slay something called Leviathan, which didn't sound good. Every time I looked him up on the internet, I found a worse theory of what that might involve. Some people claimed he was a monster large enough to devour the world, perhaps another name for *Jörmungandr*, the serpent from the Norse Ragnarök prophecies. A few theologians claimed he was a metaphor for the Devil himself. That was the worst possible outcome in my book, which meant that it was probably true. It felt a little personal, and Atropos had been quite upset with me when she approved my Impossible Task. My current favorite theory was that Leviathan was actually the Loch Ness monster. Mostly because that seemed like the least violent version. Nessie hadn't eaten anyone as far as I knew. The hard part would just be finding her.

If I somehow managed to pull off the first two tasks, my last step was to break the Four Seals of the Apocalypse—which…don't even get me started. It sounded so far beyond impossible, I was tempted to sue for false advertising.

These Seals were pretty famous. Everyone knows their names: War, Pestilence, Famine, and Death. Right out of the Book of Revelation. Despite needing to collect all four, I'd only ever met one, Kane, and he didn't live in this world but in the Veil that hung between the living and the dying ones.

All that is to say, if there was some sort of class-action lawsuit I could join to get my soul back, I'd much rather do that. It sounded like I'd have a much higher chance of keeping all my limbs. So far, I had found relatively few parties sympathetic to my plight. Plenty of individuals had given me aid, but on the institutional level, there wasn't much progress being made. Part of that was because in some ways, my case was very small. One mortal against the trillions who will ever live is barely even a rounding error.

The other reason was because of the possible repercussions. Stealing a soul was pretty major violation of the treaties that exist among the supernatural powers. A single rogue operative filching one little soul wasn't worth starting a war over. It was maybe better for everyone but me if it was just forgotten about. But if there were more? If there was some sort of organized cabal behind it? Then it got a lot harder to ignore.

A few pieces of evidence suggested that something bigger was going on. Death had told me that Pluto was selling the souls from Hades to someone. The Dragon Dons offered to bribe Dawn with ten thousand of them, which they must have gotten from somewhere. Now Maria might have had hers taken.

I might not be fake-dead anymore, but I was still on the case that Kane gave me when he made me his heir. Just because I returned to this side of the Veil didn't mean I was free of Death's games.

"You realize what this might mean for you, right?" Alex pressed. It's not his fault for assuming I hadn't put all the pieces together. I'm often an idiot. "Why aren't you more excited?

"You mean beside the cruel ritual murder scene that we just left? The one I'm going to have tell Father Pike about?"

"Oh." Alex has been around violence for almost two hundred years now. At a certain point, I think it starts to wear you smooth. Orion would not even have blinked at what we found. He would have gotten angry, he would have sought vengeance, but he wouldn't have felt it.

I've only been living this way for two years, and already I can feel it doing the same to me. I have walked the halls of Hell itself, descended through its nine levels to the tenth that waits for me. What's one little death compared with the face of eternal torture?

"Sorry." I sighed, leaning back in my seat. "I do know. Honestly, I'm still trying to wrap my head around it."

"What's there to wrap? They're forging contracts and stealing souls. Just like they did to you."

"Maybe," I agreed reluctantly. "We don't actually know that yet."

"You were the one who just found a weapon exactly like your Reaper scythe at the *murder* scene," Alex retorted.

"Yes," I agreed. "But that doesn't mean we know for sure they took her soul. We don't even know exactly what that thing is." I gestured to the blanket that the murder weapon was wrapped in at my feet.

"What do you mean? It's Death."

I frowned, not as convinced. It sure felt like my power, but I had never seen it manifested separate from a Reaper before. Where had it been made or taken from that it existed on its own?

"It could be a corrupt Reaper," I agreed slowly. "But my gut tells me it's something else."

"With access to the same power you have? Who could that be?"

"I don't know. Something about it doesn't feel right. Dan was pretty incompetent, and this feels calculated."

"You have been running around telling anyone who would listen what he did."

"It just seems so…small."

Alex glanced me in surprise.

"In scope, not in evil," I continued, holding up a hand to interrupt him. "The volume of souls they would be able to move just isn't that impressive. I know every little bit counts, but how many souls are in Hell? Several hundred million? A few billion? How many people have lived in the history of the world? Is this worth the effort and risk for so few?"

"I see your rather horrifying point," Alex murmured after a moment. "How in the world do we figure that out?"

"I have no idea," I admitted, unbuckling my seat belt as we pulled into the driveway of our home. "I guess that's the job."

"So are you saying we should rule Hell out?"

"Oh no." I chuckled darkly. "We'll for sure check them first. I just wouldn't be surprised if the answer isn't that easy."

"Since when do we get to do things the easy way?" Alex said.

"Exactly."

—— × ——

For a guy who was on a five-million-dollar-a-year stipend from Hell, I really didn't spend my money like it. Granted, it was a lot less after Robin and Ash got their hands on it, but that was still more than I had any business having.

I hadn't bought a mansion or a car.

We rented a nice house, but it was in *Northridge.* The first thing anyone who lives here does when they get money is move. Our place was one of those modern square castles made of concrete and sharp edges. It looked like it could have been made from Lego bricks. But it was solid. I felt confident that it would withstand earthquakes, fires, and invasions, which were three main threats in my life.

I punched the code into the keyless entry and stepped in, leaving it open for Alex behind me. I had been willing to spend a *little* of Satan's money on furniture because I had at least grown up a little. Our dining room had a long table with matching chairs that we had never used. All our mail was piled on it, ignored. I figured if someone needed to get ahold of me badly enough, they would email me.

Down the hall was our open living room, with a white L-shaped couch and a set of matching chairs curled around a large television where Alex liked to watch his cartoons.

Whatever this square building's version of a circular staircase was worked its way up from the edge of the room, stopping at the bedrooms on the second and third floors.

"Well, we certainly put in a day's work," I remarked to Alex as I began to climb my way up the stairs. "I'm gonna crash. See if I can finally get some sleep."

"I think I'll finish my episode, then do the same," my friend replied with a tired smile. "Big day tomorrow."

"Aren't they always?"

My room is another area of the house that I really didn't spend much money on. I don't find myself in there that often. I bought a big bed—because anyone six feet or taller deserves to sleep on a king-sized mattress so their legs don't dangle off the edge. A smaller TV was mounted on the wall, but the only other stuff was my sparse wardrobe in the walk-in closet.

Sometimes I worried that I was so busy trying not to die in ten—er, seven-something—years that I was forgetting to live. But then I remember who gave me the money and how they invented the art of temptation. Maybe it was just there to distract me and take away my edge. Complacency kills in this business.

I shook my head and went about my evening ritual, showering and preparing for bed. I performed each step with care, as if doing it perfectly would help bring sleep to me. But deep down in my heart, I knew this was an exercise in futility.

Dying broke me.

I guess that wasn't surprising. It breaks everyone—that was sort of the point. But while I was a Reaper serving my time in the Veil, I was unable to sleep. I could *rest,* but it was a different thing. Wilbur, the guy who got stuck with my job as heir, told me that sleep was for the living.

I assumed that meant I would get it back when I returned to this side of the Veil, but so far, no luck. I hadn't slept once in the last five months. I'd meditated. I'd kind of rested. But I hadn't *slept.*

Like I said, I don't know how to explain what was happening to me without sounding like I'm insane. I knew it wasn't pure insomnia. A normal human being can't go five months with no sleep without breaking. My brain didn't seem as broken as it should be, which might be setting the bar low. Still, whatever was happening to me wasn't natural.

That's not to say that I was getting off scot-free. I was weary, bone-weary. The kind of tired that only parents of newborn triplets should be. I could feel the lack of sleep pulling on me like a hundred hands, weighing me down. I was slower than normal.

Sometimes I saw things. Like the red eyes in the hallway outside of the MCIAW offices earlier today. Little things went wrong in the corners of my vision, like nightmares haunting me in the waking world, desperate to get their claws into me. Maybe they missed me like a spurned lover.

All that is to say, it was with a skeptical sense of routine that I lay down in bed, turning on some movie that could play in the background as noise to distract me while I hovered in that place between waking and dreaming. Then, with the quiet laugh of man who knows he is going to fail before he begins, I closed my eyes and waited for the dark to claim me.

But it didn't come.

Something else did.

I blinked into consciousness, pulled from my almost trance-like state by a deep-purple light. It was blinding, and I squinted, holding up a hand to shadow my eyes. It was no use; the glow came from every direction.

With a jolt, I realized I was falling, tumbling through a vast abyss of dark purple. Reality around me seemed to twist and change, as if space itself was being warped. The world stretched thin, then expanded.

A thousand things flew past me: monsters with too many heads, scenes of everyday life. It felt like I had fallen into a television set and was tumbling past every channel playing at once.

Then with an abrupt jerk, I landed on an empty leather chair in the middle of nothing. Slowly, I lowered my hand, turning to take in the strange place I found myself in. At first glance it seemed like a limitless expanse, a white world that extended as far as I could see. It reminded me of the Nothing, only inverted. Instead of being achingly empty, it was full of limitless potential.

I made a full revolution, taking in the expanse of this blank canvas, trying to decide if this was real or not. It didn't feel real—it felt like a dream. But I had not dreamed in months. This would be a wild welcome back.

The world flickered, changing in the space between thoughts. Instead of a white void, a living room began to build around me. It was modern, made of sharp edges like my own home, and they seemed to slide together like puzzles pieces to form a building. A second, empty chair appeared in front of me. Every wall was painted in a different shade of gray, like a study of despair. A giant glass window showed the glowing tip of the sun about to rise. I glanced over my shoulder and saw a second window, which showed it setting.

The sound of wrinkling leather told me I was no longer alone.

Dread coiled in my guts as I turned back to face the seat, which was now filled with a god wearing a toga. My eyes narrowed as I traced the contours of his sharp jaw and short, dark hair. He was tall and powerfully built; golden armbands encircled both of his biceps. He smiled warmly at me, but that friendliness did not reach his eyes.

His solid-purple eyes.

"Oh boy," I said, without needing him to speak. I did not know his name, but I knew what team he was playing for. He had been nice enough to show up in uniform. He was a member of the Greco-Roman pantheon. I didn't know if it was Greek or Roman, but according to Midas, who I met in Hades, it didn't really matter. Most of them had just rebranded after their first failed venture when they launched their second start-up.

"I have been waiting quite some time for this," he told me, leaning back in his chair with a smug smile. His voice was soft and smooth, almost like a lullaby. I felt the exhaustion within me stir, like a cobra before a snake charmer.

"I don't suppose you're here to thank me?" I asked, arching an eyebrow. As part of my time as Death's heir, I had been responsible for the destruction of Hades, the Underworld of the Greeks and Romans. It wasn't totally my fault. Pluto had already knocked out all the support beams long before I got there. I just happened to be the lucky guy who landed the last blow that sent the tower toppling over.

"Thank you?" the god mused in his too-calm voice. "For what do you deserve thanks? The release of my mad cousin Aite from her fallen world? Perhaps it is for finding the lost key of my cousins Janus and Portunus?"

Crap.

"Never heard of them," I replied a little too quickly, resisting the urge to reach for my pocket to check for the key. I wasn't sure if I was really here or not, but it didn't matter. If there was a door here, my relic could open it.

"Ah, I know what it is, the destruction of my ancestral home!" He tilted his head to study me as I remained studiously silent. What was I supposed to say, *sorry*?

"No? Hm. What other services have you rendered unto me, mortal? Ah yes, I remember. Perhaps I am to thank you for the murder of my older brother Pluto." His voice gained a slight edge for the first time, losing a bit of its mesmerizing, tranquil quality.

Double crap.

"Technically, I didn't do that last one," I pointed out, holding my hand up like a student in front of a teacher. "That was Aite. I am an eyewitness. I will gladly testify if you're pressing charges."

"Do you know who I am?" The god ignored my protests like a tired father.

"I mean not specifically, but I know who you hang out with."

"My name is Somnus." His perfectly manicured brows narrowed in irritation as he noticed the confusion on my face. "The Greeks knew me as Hypno." I gave him a tiny shrug, and he let out a tiny sigh. "I am the god of sleep. This is my home, the House of Dreams."

"Ah." A dozen puzzle pieces clicked into place. I have heard sleep referred to as the little death. Every night when most of us close our eyes, we descend into the darkness much as we will when we finally die. It is only when we wake that we live again. It made sense that he would be the younger brother of the god of death. Somnus leaned back in his chair, pleased at the effect his revelation had on me.

"Look at you, worn and bedraggled. Your mind is so close to breaking. I wonder if you know that it is I who has closed the realm of dreams to you."

"I did get there, yes." I tilted my head, studying him, trying to understand what was going through the god's mind.

I'm still not entirely sure what qualifies someone as claiming deity status. There doesn't seem to be a specific rule set. The most important part seems to be that if someone has the gumption to claim godhood, they usually have the firepower to back it up. Well, that and a little bit of madness. But as I stared into his solid-purple eyes, I couldn't help but feel like he seemed a lot more sane than his relatives. Which next to Aite wasn't saying much, but it was something.

"You owe my family a debt," Somnus rumbled when the silence between us had stretched long enough. "Do you know what a *weregild* is?" The only thing I could think of was some sort of guild for werewolves, and I was fairly confident that wasn't it, so I merely shook my head.

"A lovely invention by our Nordic neighbors. It is a way of atonement in which a guilty party can compensate a family for taking the life of one of their relatives." A chill swept down my spine as I considered what the life of a god might be worth. I was already in too much debt, and I doubted Somnus accepted credit cards.

"And how much do you want for this *weregild*?" I asked, hating that this was the second time today I'd had to ask that kind of question. At least this one was kind of my fault.

"I fear the size of your debt is no small amount," Somnus said, steepling his fingers in front of his face to peer at me with the patience of an alligator. "Not only did you kill my older brother—" He held up a hand to stop my protest. "Aite was your weapon. She is more attack dog than goddess after so long in the clutches of the Nothing. A lack of sleep will do that to you." The grin on his face was wickedly cruel. It sent another shiver of fear down my spine. I suddenly had a lot more sympathy for the fly caught in a spider's web.

"Not only did you murder Pluto, but you caused the destruction of our ancestral home." I narrowed my eyes but did not speak. Technically that was true. I'd killed Midas suspecting that it would tear the whole Underworld down with him. In fact, I was happy to do so after I discovered what Pluto had been using it for.

"Yes, yes." I rolled my hand in impatience, urging him to get on with it. "You've exhausted your list of grievances. Just give me the total on the bill."

"A soul."

"What?" I was so caught off guard by his answer that I couldn't hold back my question. "What are you going to do with a soul?"

"Rebuild." Somnus shrugged as if that was obvious. "We still own a prime piece of real estate for an Underworld. All I need is a mortal soul to power our reconstruction, and we will rise from the ashes. You of all people should know that dead things don't always stay dead."

I rubbed my chin in thought, thinking through his plan.

As it has been explained to me, human souls are the energy that feed Reality. The universe was made for mortals; it belongs to us. All these Immortal interlopers are squatting on our property. They need our souls to keep the Nothing from devouring their little bunkers. When Somnus said "real estate", what he meant was *real* estate, as in it was real, it existed. I'd thought that the crushing, hungry dark had devoured the entirety of their Underworld, but there must still be some tiny shard left, holding on for dear life.

It suddenly put into perspective the princely sum that Dawn turned down from the Dragon Dons to betray Orion. The Faerie Lands existed in a sort of permanent low-power mode, in order to survive off the souls they did have for as long as possible. My assumption was that she rejected the deal because her people weren't particularly good at bringing in new souls, so it would not solve their bigger problem. But it seemed Somnus wasn't worried about that. As far as I knew, the Greco-Roman age was long gone, perhaps even further than the Fae era. Where did he think he'd be getting more souls from?

A ghostly image of Maria's rotting body hovered in the back of my mind, burning like a beacon. I swallowed in fear, trying to ignore her. But I knew I couldn't.

"What good will one soul do you?" I pressed, crossing my arms. He might hate me for killing his brother, but I didn't get the sense that I was in any physical danger from the god of dreams in this moment. He needed me alive. "You're missing a death god to bring new ones in to rebuild."

"That's true." His lips quirked in amusement. "But that is not a concern for you. Until you make good on your debt, you will continue to suffer under my punishment, unable to sleep, unable to dream. If I were you, I wouldn't tarry. Being too long without dreams is bad for your soul. Even your connection to Death can only shield you for so long."

"Holy crap." I laughed in disgusted amusement. "You're putting a lien on my dreams."

CHAPTER
SEVEN

I **WOKE FROM MY** encounter with Somnus—I hesitated to call it a nightmare, because that would make it a dream, and it was certainly not that—feeling dried out. It was like I was dehydrated but not on a physical level. I was withering on the inside. I had been deluding myself before that my lack of sleep wasn't affecting me. Whatever the god had taken from me, it was strangling me as sure as a boa constrictor.

I was carrying enough stress that if the Devil didn't get me, a heart attack would soon enough. But there was no point in lying in bed worrying about it. That wouldn't give me any rest. The only way I was going to survive was getting up and doing something about it.

"Somnus?" Alex asked in disbelief as he drove us to get coffee.

Okay, there is one other splurge I've allowed myself since getting el Diablo as a sugar daddy. I don't drink cheap coffee made at home. I know it costs like eighteen dollars a day, whatever. I prefer my morning mocha in milkshake form.

"You know, I had seen like exactly two gods in my entire life before I started hanging out with you," Alex complained, slurping on his sweet drink as we pulled out of the drive-thru. "And one of them was Bacchus, who was DJing a show that I went to, so it barely counts. But that's, what, three in the last six months?"

"Bacchus DJs? Of course he does. Also, technically you haven't seen any of them," I pointed out. My other two godly encounters had taken place across the Veil, where Alex had not been able to follow.

"Great, so I'm too much of a sidekick to even be a part of the encounter," he grumbled to no one, merging into the traffic of the 405. There was a note of authentic bitterness to his voice that made me wince.

"That's not what I meant," I protested. Alex didn't respond for a few moments, so we rode in uncomfortable silence, punctuated by the sound of his engine and the faint hum of the tires meeting the road.

This was the only sore spot in our friendship, and I had blundered into it blindly, not thinking about anything other than my joke. Alex was a two-hundred-year-old Nephilim. He was stronger and faster than the average mortal by a noticeable amount. But among his kind he was considered something of a runt. The original members of his race were born of the union between men and demons. They were terrifyingly powerful and monstrous.

That ratio diluted through the generations as more and more humanity found its way into the bloodline. Orion teetered somewhere around 30 percent demon if I understood correctly. Alex didn't even have a third of the juice that our master did.

His whole life had been spent being the weakling among the

strong. The last guy to get picked for the kickball team. Then he met me, and for a little while he was my guide to the supernatural world. But my unique circumstances have led me down roads that are closed to him. It's hard not to feel overshadowed by a mortal who accomplishes more in two years than you do in two hundred, no matter what the contributing factors are.

"I know," he admitted at last, taking a sip of his frozen coffee. The tension faded out of his shoulders as he relaxed. "Even if you did, I shouldn't let it bother me like it does."

"Yeah, bottle it up like the rest of us."

"Can you imagine Orion letting a little thing like a feeling slow him down?"

"Slow him down? No. Send him on a wild quest that leaves hundreds of villains dead and teaches two idiots how to survive in a world far too dangerous before being thrown into a supermax fantasy prison? Yes."

"That's a good point," Alex chuckled sardonically. "That's a good point."

"I know, that's why I made it."

"Before you get too smug, let's get to work, huh? Make sure we have the lay of the land."

"We've got three cases."

"Oh, is that all?"

"Quiet! I have the talking stick. Yes, three. Number one: Figure out how not to go to jail because I owe the IRS seven million dollars."

"Not really our area of expertise. Sounds like a lot of math."

"True, but Ash and Robin suspect sabotage, so we should figure out who's out to get me."

"Everyone." Alex waved his hand across the window, gesturing to the whole of LA lying before us.

"Number two: Solve Maria's murder. Find out if someone stole her soul, locate where they took it, and then stop them from stealing any more."

"Agreed." Alex's voice was harsh, an echo of mine. The Hunt may not have existed as a legal entity any longer, but that's like a judge ordering a motorcycle gang to disband. Permission wasn't really what made it what it was in the first place. The Hunter would not stand for an atrocity like this to happen in his territory. As his squires, we could not either.

"Number three: Get Somnus a soul so he can start rebuilding Hades before my mind cracks."

"That one is trickier."

"Much trickier," I agreed.

"Although there is a way that two of the problems might solve themselves," Alex said slowly. "But it would be morally *gray* at best."

"What do you mean?"

"Well, if someone has figured out how to steal souls for Hell, it theoretically wouldn't be hard to modify the process and change the delivery address." We were both quiet for a moment, measuring the size of that atrocity.

He was right. It could make my survival *much* easier. It wouldn't have to be an innocent person like poor Maria. We could find some monster, say a serial killer, and send him packing to a place that wasn't any worse than where he was going anyway.

But at the same time, there was a perversion of justice there that made me feel itchy. I had judged the Reapers for participating in a similar scheme while serving in the Veil. It would make me a hypocrite to do the same thing now when it was my future in the crosshairs.

This whole circus—the entire *point* about my crusade to get my soul back—was that my rights had been impinged on. Hell had taken my free will and thrown it into a dumpster. Because I'm a mortal, that's pretty much my only inalienable right as far as the universe is concerned. Sure, George and the rest of those dudes in white wigs tried to create a few more, but what they ended up with weren't laws of Reality, just a bunch of humans screaming at the dark.

When it all boiled down to the very basics, there was one simple rule. Mortals have the free will to decide how they will react to things and where they want to go. We use it for good and for evil, but each of us has it. Immortals do not. That's the trade-off between living forever and not having a soul.

"I won't condemn someone to the Greco-Roman Underworld who wasn't supposed to go there," I said at last, and some of the tension flowed out of Alex's shoulders as he nodded. I knew he would feel the same.

"All right, the straight and narrow it is. The question becomes—where do we start with this pile of nonsense?"

"The pet store."

"Are we getting a fish tank?"

"No. Although that is a good idea." I laughed, trying to hide the fear I felt. "We're going to do a summoning."

"Ah, so that's how it gets worse."

"Yup."

We made a few more stops after the pet store. A hobby shop for some paint and candles, then a grocer's for some cheap, ceramic plates. Fully supplied, Alex and I went to rent a storage shed at one of those places that's a sea of orange doors.

I paid for a month in cash under a fake name and told the manager we'd be out before then. In fact, I had no plans of using it ever again after today, but it never hurt to be prepared. Alex drove down the rows of long, low buildings until we found unit C17 halfway down the line.

I grabbed the bags as my friend unlocked it, whistling like I didn't have a care in the world for the CCTV cameras that I knew were trained on us. The door rattled as it rolled up, loud in this quiet place. Together we walked into the small, square unit before pulling the door down behind us.

The concrete space had no windows. A pair of fluorescent lights flickered down from above, bathing the otherwise empty room in gross yellow light.

"You know, I really hope we don't burn this place down," Alex remarked as we began organizing our supplies. Historically speaking, the locations that have played host to our summonings have not fared well. Lilith set the first one on fire, and Zagan smashed most of the second.

"Don't worry," I told him as I grabbed the can of black paint and a roller. "For once we're calling someone who likes us. Well—more than usual."

"No one likes us."

"Ain't that the truth," I grumbled, dipping my brush in the paint and beginning to inscribe a rough circle in the center of the room. It didn't have to perfectly round; as long as the two edges touched it would be good enough. I crouch-walked forward as I painted, making sure the radius was big enough to hold a human without feeling cramped.

"It feels like a lifetime ago that I taught you how to do this." Alex remarked, pulling out four of the plates from their packaging. "Now you're doing it without telling me who we're summoning."

"Well, there's a good reason for that," I grunted, standing up to survey my finished painting job. "If I did, you'd tell me it was bad idea." The black circle took up over two-thirds of the room, leaving plenty of space for us to maneuver around it without being rude.

When I finished, I reached into my mind for the warm, bright power of Willow. The Fae spirit came to my call willingly, like an excited puppy. Fire burst into being in a nimbus around my hands, casting a pleasant glow in the room.

Mindful of the fact that Willow has a limited supply of power here in the mortal realm, I channeled a little of my will into them, sending a line of fire down to the ring, drying the paint instantly. No point in taking risks on something getting smudged.

"How hard would I try to stop you?" Alex asked when I was done.

"Let's call it a seven out of ten." A tense silence hung between us as Alex glanced at the dark ring and back at me. I gave him a small smile and shrugged. This had to be done. He would understand once he saw.

"At least this time you can't blame me when it goes wrong," he said brightly. "Where do you want these?" Following my instructions, he placed three of the plates around the perimeter of the circle, and the fourth in the center.

Crossing the line for the last time, I pulled out the dark athame that was used to kill Maria and placed it on the dish in the center. It felt cold in my hands, even to someone who was used to the touch of Death.

On two of the surrounding plates, we set lit candles of black wax. Their scent was called Decadent Mahogony. A woody smell began to pervade the unit, though it was much less cloying than the apples and cinnamon we'd used to summon Lilith.

At last, I sat cross-legged before the final, empty plate and pulled out the dead mouse we'd bought at the pet store. It was meant for weirdos who keep pet snakes, but today it would work just fine as a different sort of treat.

Technically you don't need all these accoutrements to call on a supernatural being. It just makes the number easier to dial. It's a little like putting in the area code even when you don't have to.

Squaring my shoulders, I took one last look over the summoning ring, making sure I hadn't missed anything. Technically these things are pretty simple—a circle is one of the most basic shapes. A toddler can draw one. But most weren't used to contain supernatural creatures that could eat your face. It was worth taking a few extra moments of precaution before swimming with the sharks.

As I understand it, when someone creates a circle, they are essentially making their own world for a moment. Anything supernatural that is pulled into that world cannot exit it without breaking the circle or the will of its owner. That doesn't mean the circle created a magical force field that would protect me from anything. When I trapped the CFO of Hell, Zagan, he had merely pulled a Desert Eagle out of his pocket and threatened to shoot me. He couldn't leave the ring or smite me with his fallen angel powers, but the bullet would have worked just fine.

"Look good to you?" I glanced up at Alex, who was hovering nervously at my shoulder, studying the ring with a skeptical look.

"I mean, it's not designed for a demon," he answered slowly, brow furrowed in thought. "There's no pentagram, and red is a better color for them, as you know."

"No demons," I promised.

"It should work as long as you're trying to summon something sort of dead or dying..." His voice trailed off as he understood my intent. "Please tell me you're not doing what I think you're doing."

"I...cannot do that." I laughed. "That would be lying."

"I hate you so much."

"Good, let it fuel you. Now if you'll excuse me. I need to perform a ritual." Alex's lips compressed into a flat line, but he held out his hand in a *go-ahead* gesture.

"Thank you." I closed my eyes, inhaling once and holding it for a moment, forcing my dehydrated, sleep-drained mind to focus, to grow sharper. Slowly I formed the circle in my mind, willing it to exist, to become a part of this world. When I felt ready, I let out the breath, keeping my eyes closed, embracing the darkness.

"Attend to me, Grim Reaper." At the sound of my voice, the room went unnaturally still, as if the air itself had died.

"Heed my call, Pale Horseman." My skin crawled as even the light that shone through my eyelids seemed to dim.

"Come, invited guest, accept my offering. Be welcome in my house and treat with me, O Death." A hush settled over me as I waited. My eyes were still closed, bathing me in the darkness of the grave, but I knew the moment he arrived. The silence grew sharper, like a cold wind. I was tempted to sigh in relief, but summoning the correct being was only the first hurdle. I plastered a smile on my face, preparing to greet my old boss, Kane.

Instead, when I opened my eyes, I found a different man waiting for me. He was tall and gaunt with an embarrassed smile on his face. He wore a dark cloak and carried a pitch-black scythe in his left hand. With his right he gave me a small wave of greeting.

"Hello, Matt," Wilbur said abashedly in his southern drawl. "I didn't think I'd be seeing you so soon."

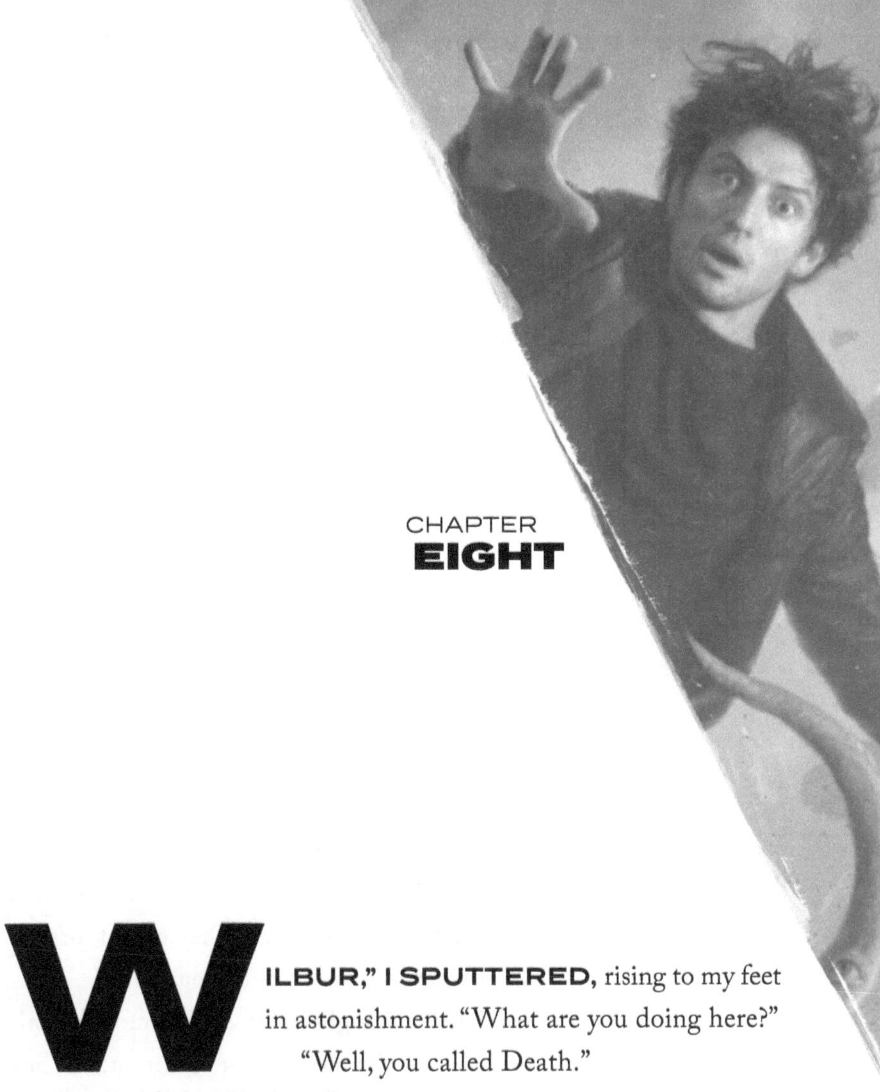

CHAPTER
EIGHT

WILBUR," I SPUTTERED, rising to my feet in astonishment. "What are you doing here?"

"Well, you called Death."

"I called Kane! You're—"

"His heir, remember? Sometimes he has me cover for him when he's busy." He held out his right hand to show me the giant death's-head signet ring that rested on his fourth finger. "I don't know if you realize this, but the Death Board is always meeting and—"

"Never meeting. I know." I frowned in thought as I wondered why Kane had ignored my call. Was he avoiding me? Atty was his right hand. Had she told him that his name was on my Impossible Task?

"You seem awfully unhappy to see me, even though this is sort of your fault. Are you feeling okay?" His brow crinkled as he took in the dark circles under my eyes.

"I'm fine," I snapped, irritated by the question.

"Hang on, did you get wrapped up in his schemes and have your life completely hijacked too?" Alex interjected from behind me. "Trust me, I am *familiar.*"

"Something like that," the dead country boy agreed, peering at my living friend with a curious glance. "Name's Wilbur. I'd shake your hand, but..." He gestured at the invisible barrier of the circle between us helplessly.

"I'm Alex."

"Oh, he told me stories about you."

"He did?" Alex looked at me in horror.

"I would never..."

"Wasn't he the one who got caught wearing the chicken suit—"

"No, that was another friend," I interrupted hurriedly, feeling a sense of horror having these two intersect. Wilbur was my closest companion while I was playing dead, but I never imagined a world in which he and Alex would meet. Any second now they would turn on me, I could feel it. "I called Death because I need your help."

Wilbur's face squinted up in thought as he considered what his boss would want him to do. I like the guy a decent amount, but he's not the sharpest scythe in the toolshed. "We don't really do help..." he said after a moment.

"This is different," I promised, gesturing at the plate holding the athame at his feet. "Do you recognize that?" Wilbur might not be Kane, but I knew from experience that he was tapped straight into the source of Death's power. He might be able to get a better sense of what it was made of than I could.

"That's a strange-looking knife." Genuine curiosity entered the heir's voice as he studied the athame. He crouched, banishing his scythe in the same motion so he could pick up the weapon. I held my breath, waiting for him to feel the same thing that I did.

"Well, I'll be," Wilbur half whispered in reverent disgust, twisting the evil-looking blade in his hands. "You know what this feels like." He glanced at me with a concerned expression.

"I do," I confirmed. It felt like the cold, dark power that I still carried with me even after my time as a Reaper in the Veil. It felt like True Death.

"Is it ours?" I pressed, wishing again that Kane had been willing to take my call. Wilbur had access to plenty of Death's power, but he was still new to his role. The Grim Reaper had been doing this for a long time. He'd have a far better idea of who might dare to cross him like this.

"It's not," Wilbur stated confidently, still turning the weapon in his hands.

"You're sure?" A dozen theories raced through mine as he confirmed what I was afraid of. While I was relieved one of my co-workers wasn't abusing Kane's powers behind his back, it meant that someone else was trying to imitate him, which might be worse. It takes a certain kind of madman to impersonate Death.

"My power is an extension of the big man's. I'd know if this was us." So it was option two then. A frown worked its way across my face as I tried to build a suspect list of who might be behind this.

"Just to be clear, you're saying that is counterfeit death?" Alex asked in surprise. "As in, someone has manufactured a new type of *mortis* that is separate from the foundational power of the universe?"

Slowly, Wilbur and I looked at each other. I could tell from the pained expression on his face that he was thinking the same thing I was. While I was a Reaper, I had convinced Wilbur to help me take down a cabal of crooked deliverymen who were funneling souls to other places. Standard mail fraud.

But what if there was a way to keep the souls from ever even reaching the DMV in the Veil? What if there was another courier service that was picking them up before they got into Death's system so it couldn't track where they were going? Death was supposed to be a monopoly. This might be the one time in the history of the world that having a competitor would be a bad thing.

"Wilbur, do you have a way to look up who died?" I asked, my voice suddenly a little hoarse with stress. My worst fear was coming true. I had still been holding on to hope that Maria had simply been murdered, which was horrible, but at least it would be over. She would be free to experience whatever waited for her on the other side. But after Wilbur's confirmation, I didn't think she'd even made it that far.

"Of course. It's all right here." He tapped the side of his head with a long finger. "Didn't you when you wore the ring?"

"I never got any instructions," I managed through gritted teeth, not letting my irritation distract me. "So you have that knowledge-something with you inside the circle?"

"Yes." Wilbur's eyebrows narrowed as he looked at me. "Why?"

"Do you have an entry for a Maria Gonzalez?"

"Uh, I can check." Wilbur's eyes rolled up into the back of his head, so that only the whites were visible. A shudder ran through me as I watched him interact with a power that held far too much knowledge.

"I am going to need a little more information to find a single person from the history of the human race," he said, his voice airy and distant.

"Yeah, that makes sense. Let's see, she was in her forties. She would have died in the last two weeks, here in Northridge."

"Cause of death?" Wilbur's voice was even more robotic, as if he was lost to the flow of information that was flooding through him. I couldn't imagine what it was like to carry that kind of knowledge.

Secretly I was more than a little glad I had never found that button on the dashboard.

"The weapon you're holding."

A long silence built between us as he scoured his records. With every passing moment, my dread only grew. Alex was right. Someone had found a way to steal souls from Kane. They had broken the Death Treaty, and when the Underworlds found out…there would be hell to pay.

"Nothing," Wilbur gasped, his eyes snapping back into place. "I don't see anything that fits your description. Not in the entire history of the world."

"Dark Abyss," Alex swore.

"Someone's messing with the mail." Indignation flooded through Wilbur's voice as we stared at each other through the invisible barrier of the circle.

Death as it exists in the modern world is sort of the postman of souls. Reapers collect everyone who dies, then deliver them to where they are supposed to go. It was Kane's directive, and therefore Wilbur's, to make sure things got to their destination.

"Well, this is bad," Wilbur said, looking down at the athame in his hands with a new level of intensity. "Uh, can I keep this? I think the big man is going to want to see it."

"Only if you take it to him ASAP—As Soon As Possible." I translated the acronym when I saw the look of confusion on his face. Wilbur had been the most recent recruit into the ranks of the Reapers until I arrived, but he had been dead for a while. Some of the modern parlances didn't quite land with him.

"We can't do much on our end without some guidance from Kane." I shrugged helplessly. "Tell him I want to stop this as much as he does." That was true. After seeing the Underworlds with my own eyes, I couldn't bear the thought of more innocent people being sent places they did not deserve. Especially not if they were like Maria, already downtrodden and crushed by society. Scavengers preying on the weak? Not in my city.

Orion's city.

Not in Orion's city.

"What if I could give you a way to track it?" Wilbur suggested, his eyes half closed in thought.

"You could do that?"

"Sure. It's pretending to be part of whatever we are. It's similar enough that I can give you a little more juice so that you can sense it too."

"Why does it feel like there's a 'but' coming?" I asked, narrowing my eyes. Wilbur gets embarrassed before he has to deliver bad news. He'd make a terrible poker player. His expression was drawn, telling me that I wasn't going to like what I heard.

"Well, I can't exactly reach you." He kicked at the edge of the paint, his foot bouncing off an invisible, impenetrable wall. "Not much I can do from inside this circle." My heart skipped a beat as I slowly tracked my gaze up from the spot he had bumped to his flat, expressionless eyes.

The ring was mostly a focus, a way for me to pull someone like him from another realm to ours and let us converse. It was a phone, a means of communication. But it was also a shield, like the ones they use in prisons to keep everyone safe. Wilbur was my friend. I trusted him. But that did not mean he wasn't *dangerous.* He was, after all, a piece of Death himself. Breaking the circle would be a little like choosing to swim with Shamu. Safe until it certainly wasn't.

"Wilbur," I said in a very slow, deliberate voice. "Am I on your list?"

"No." The lanky Reaper shook his head, a slow, ponderous motion. "I don't get lists anymore. Kane has me working on more important projects."

"Matt..." Alex groaned in a low voice behind me. I ignored him, not because he wasn't important, but because we both knew that I knew what he was going to say.

"If I let you out, you'll give me the ability to hunt for more pieces of this fake death?"

"I will."

"You won't try to claim Alex or me?"

"I will not."

I sighed in irritation, closing my eyes and letting everything fade for one long moment. My heart was racing; fear, an old friend by now, clung to me. This pause was performative, and we all knew I was going to do it. I was just trying to convince myself that it wasn't a *bad idea.*

It was.

"Do I get a vote?" Alex's voice cut through my mental gymnastics, and I opened my eyes to look at my friend. He stood behind me with his arms crossed and a hint of a scowl on his face.

"Sure. What do we do if it's a tie?"

"I vote yes."

"You do?" I was so startled by his choice that I turned to stare at him, my mouth dangling open a few inches.

"You know him, right?"

"Yes."

"You trust him?"

"I saved his life—er, well, his death, I guess," I replied, cocking my head to study Wilbur with an aggressive stare. The tall man inclined his head in agreement. "I figure that counts for a lot."

"They killed that woman and stole her soul." Heat entered Alex's voice as some of his anger flared to the surface. "And no one knows but us. No one is going to *do anything* about it but us." I was surprised by his intensity, but I shouldn't have been. He was the first one to step up to help me when my own soul was taken. He'd sat at the feet of the same mentor as I did for the last year and some change.

How could either of us be any different?

"Okay, Wilbur," I said, turning back to the Reaper. "I'm going to let you out. Don't make me regret this, okay?"

"I won't hurt you," he promised.

I reached into my jacket and pulled out my pocketknife, flipping it open with a satisfying *click.* Normally I use my scythe to cut through anything I need, but it wouldn't do any good here. The circle can only be broken by physical things from this world. Grumbling under my breath about stupid risks, I began to dig at the dry paint. It flaked easily thanks to Willow's earlier fire.

As I cut through the line, my sense of trepidation grew. This was not the stupidest thing I had ever done. But that was not setting the bar very high. If being an idiot was an art form, then I would be listed among the greats, the Michelangelo or Van Gogh of my craft. I once willingly walked into Hell itself. This was nothing.

But still, there's something to be said for inviting the wolves into your home. I knew that he was wild. Being dead does something to you. Wilbur was a man, but he was no longer *human.* Not in the same way he was before. He was Death, and Death's hunger could never be satisfied.

"Here goes nothing," I said to no one in particular, scratching out the last piece of black paint that was holding the ring together. Wilbur let out a little sigh of release as the circle broke, as if he had just been freed from a heavy pressure that was weighing him down. Feeling a little like Red Riding Hood, I rose to my feet and looked at the Reaper with an arched eyebrow.

"How do we do this?" I asked Wilbur as he stepped over the line.

"Just take my hand." The tall man smiled, leaning forward and extending his palm for a shake. I licked my lips as I reached for him, bracing myself for the chill that was coming. As I expected, a cold deeper than the darkest days of winter swept through me when we touched.

For a moment, I felt the familiar hunger that drove the heir. Then something else flowed into me, a dark knowledge, alert and hungry like a hawk. I could feel it watching, searching, ready to hunt at a moment's notice.

It was as if the Reaper power that I retained after I gave away my title as heir gained a new lever. A different muscle that I could use at a moment's notice. I understood it instinctively, the same way I knew how to move each of my fingers.

Then it was done, and Wilbur withdrew, studying me with a curious expression. "Do you want me to give it to him too?" He nodded toward Alex. "I think I could sign him up—" His sentence stopped abruptly as he vanished—here one second, gone the next.

Alex and I tensed, turning to stand back-to-back in the tiny storage unit, looking for any sign of a threat. But there was nothing. The room was empty other than the candles and the paint. Wilbur was just gone.

"Guess his batteries died or something."

"Somehow I hate this more than if he had just attacked us," Alex remarked after the silence stretched into awkwardness. I could feel him shifting behind me, trying to watch every direction at once.

"Yeah," I agreed, thoroughly spooked. Something had *yanked* him away, and the list of people who could do that was very short and very scary. "Let's get out of here."

CHAPTER NINE

LET'S MAKE A rule," Alex said when we were loaded up in his minivan and safely on the highway. It was early afternoon, and the rush-hour rush hadn't begun yet. Plenty of cars dotted the lanes, going ten miles an hour above the speed limit. "No more summoning, *ever.*"

"That's a pretty good rule," I grunted in agreement. "But what if it's a life-or-death situation?"

"When's the last time we weren't in a life-or-death situation?" My blond friend shot me a side-eye glance. "Go ahead, I'll wait."

"Well...technically Lilith wasn't."

"You were going to die in ten years. It counts."

"Okay, fine. *No* more summonings." There was a long pause of amused silence before we both started chuckling at the same time. Neither of us believed that promise. At least we could laugh about it.

"Do you think I inspired a copycat?" I asked into the bemused silence, voicing a fear that had been gnawing at my insides ever since Wilbur confirmed the athame did not have Reaper origins. My friend was silent, unsure how to respond to a question we both knew the answer to. Yes.

My phone rang, saving him from having to lie. I fished it out of my pocket and stared at the caller ID in surprise. It read: DAWN—QUEEN OF ALL FAE. "Huh, I guess Dawn's back in the mortal world," I remarked to Alex before answering it. The newly minted queen tended to spend a lot of her time in the Faerie Lands, lurking in Goldhall, the seat of her power. But that was another world; there was no cell reception there. If she was able to call me, that meant she had come to the mortal realm for some reason.

"Matt's phone, this is Matt speaking," I said as I answered.

"Your sister just tried to kill Mav. *Again.*" Dawn's tone was flat and unamused. "You need to talk to her." I couldn't help but chuckle in dry amusement.

"I'm not sure what you want me to do about that." Megan had taken to her newfound powers with a gusto. To no one's surprise, dear old daddy Damien had been more than happy to swoop in and take her under his wing to teach her everything he knew. Some things never changed.

"Matthew, this is serious. My sister is the *Lady of Winter.* I can't let this go unanswered."

I rolled my eyes, letting the queen vent. Mav was a traitor, bound and controlled by a golden collar. Dawn didn't care about her personally at all, but the icy Faerie was useful to her. The queen had promised my father she would execute her sister in four hundred years when her rule was more stable, but Megan shared my impatience. I had no interest in dying before seeing justice done.

"Mav did kill Megan," I pointed out. "Not to mention my mother and my *other* sister. This all seems like fair game to me."

"Well, obviously she didn't do that good a job since your sister is running around giving me headaches. Besides, an eye for an eye blinds the whole world, Matthew," Dawn replied with a vicious sigh as if she weren't the pettiest creature I'd ever met.

"Then we will fight in the shade."

"Whoever taught you to read did the world a great disservice," the queen sniffed into her phone. "Will you talk to her before I have to do something *drastic*?" For the first time there was a hint of some cold in her tone, which made me sit up in my seat.

"If you touch her, I will—" I began, surprised at how much anger burned in my voice.

"Matthew, that is exactly what *I am trying to avoid.*" Dawn sounded exasperated, like I wasn't listening to something very obvious. I forced myself to take a deep, calming breath and think.

Dawn was a Faerie, which meant that she did not have a soul—did not have free will in the way that I did. Her power came with rules and regulations. As Queen of All Fae, she was responsible for her people in a foundational, primal way. If Megan killed Mav without her blessing, Dawn wouldn't just be angry; she would *have* to do something about it. It was coded into her DNA.

That was why she was calling me. It wasn't just that she was a control freak who wanted to have her cake and eat it too. She was trying to prevent things from getting to the point of no return. It was a kindness, just wrapped up in a selfish-sounding burrito. The Dawn special.

"Okay," was all I said when I finally understood the conversation we were having. "I'll talk to her. But maybe put the Winter Lady on ice for a bit?"

"She is somewhere safe. But I will need her soon." I resisted the urge to shudder at the darkness in her tone. Mav was Dawn's deadliest servant. The path of ice was dangerous, and the Lady of Winter was a cold-blooded killer. If the queen was anticipating using her sister's skills, that could only mean trouble.

"I'm on it," I promised.

"Good. How are you?"

I blinked in surprise at the casual question. Dawn and I are not friends. She is my queen; technically I am a member of her court, betrothed to her sister. But we don't *hang out.* She certainly doesn't just call to chat.

"Not great," I admitted. "Dealing with a couple of issues over here."

"Need help with any of them?" For once her sarcasm was completely absent. I was so stunned, I almost dropped my phone.

"Uh, I'm not sure—there's a counterfeit death—are you okay?" Something about this entire conversation was setting off all my Dawn alarms, but I had no idea what they could mean.

"Who, me? Never better, darling. If you need *anything,* just give me a call. I'll be in the mortal world for a while."

"You got it," I agreed slowly, unable to keep my confusion out of my voice. Alex looked at me from the driver's seat, curiosity burning on his face.

"All right, my mimosa is here, *ta*!" She hung up before I could reply. I stared blankly at my phone for a moment before slowly returning it to my pocket, trying to dissect her strange behavior. Dawn is not vapid, but she can wear a party-girl persona like a set of armor.

The game was afoot. I just didn't know which one it was.

"What did she want?" Alex asked as I shook myself.

"Oh, you know. The usual."

"Megan tried to kill Mav again?"

"Yup."

"Classic Megan. You really gotta appreciate how consistent she is. You could learn a thing or two from her."

I ignored him. "Then Dawn asked how I was doing."

"What?" Alex's shock was a mirror of my own.

"I know."

"She's a strange one," he mused. "Cute, though."

"Alex. No." I mimed squirting him with a spray bottle like a disobedient cat. "Absolutely not."

"Think about it, we could be *brothers-in-law.*" I groaned. I may not be able to sleep, but my nightmares were certainly following me to the waking world.

Alex and I both agreed that the counterfeit death situation was too pressing to wait. I hadn't called Father Gerald yet, and when I did, I wanted to have some sort of good news, instead of just being a dark messenger.

Maria was dead, but if her murder was avenged—sorry, *brought to justice* was probably more in line with the parlance the good Father would appreciate—then I could at least tell him we helped. I was getting very tired of being the bearer of bad news. Just once I wanted to be a good omen rather than a fell one. But until that day, I could at least do something about the evil I found myself in the middle of.

So in the passenger seat of a beat-up white minivan, I closed my eyes and welcomed the new dark power that I carried, unleashing it to serve its task. It turned out that the bloodhound ability Wilbur gave me was *terrifying.* I already knew Death pervades everything around us. The mortal realm is one where there is only one king, and that is atrophy.

All things end. Every light goes out. The bill always comes due.

But I had not considered just how deep that infection went. My awareness swept out across Los Angeles with a sense of *knowing.* It felt like an echo of Fate, a knowledge of all things dead and dying.

A patch of grass, dehydrated from LA's incessant drought, would succumb to the heat soon.

Underground, a colony of ants starved without their queen.

Three different rats were succumbing to poison from an exterminator's trap.

An old man named Murv was dying three blocks over.

I felt all their pain, their terror. I felt the certainty of an alligator circling its unsuspecting prey on the surface of the water. All of this bright, burning existence is a futile shout in an empty room that only gets emptier.

My mind threatened to break under the burden of this. It was too much. Man was not made to know things like this. We are creatures of mystery and feeling. We rage against the dying light because we are fools. We do not know that the darkness always wins.

But now, enshrouded in this horrible certainty, I felt my mind crack as my illusions were torn asunder. No wonder they usually only give this power to someone who has already died.

"Gah!" I opened my eyes, thrusting away the coldness, scrabbling for life. I felt like I had been unconscious and heading toward the light at the end of a long tunnel.

"Are you okay?" Alex asked worriedly from the driver's seat. "What did you find?"

"It's too much," I gasped, pushing myself back into the seat to feel its comforting embrace. I was on the brink of a panic attack, although there was a definite, concrete reason for this one. Adrenaline surged through my veins, making me feel more alive.

"Holy crap, Wilbur, I think you gave me too much juice," I complained. The heir was long gone, but just in case, I wanted to lodge a formal complaint.

"It won't work?"

"I didn't say that," I said with a long exhale. I wanted to say that. It would be so easy to just quit. But that wasn't what Maria deserved, or me, for that matter. No one else was going to do this hard thing. "It's just going to take me a little to get used to drinking from the firehose."

"You're sure you can handle it?" Alex gave me a long, measured look. To an untrained observer, it might look like he was worried about me, but I knew he was just assessing whether this was the right time for another joke.

"I am."

"Well, get to guzzling, then, bucko."

I shook my head, leaning back into the chair and steeling myself to plunge back into those frigid waters. We're just children, playing with the fundamental *things* of the universe.

Once again, I reached for the darkness that lurked within me, and it leapt into my arms, delighted to see me. I gritted my teeth against the deluge of information and terrible knowledge.

This time I was more prepared and forced my vision upward, away from the street. It was an out-of-body experience. I didn't seem to have a physical form, and yet I could move through this sea of information like it was the street. Also—I could fly. That was cool.

I soared upward, letting myself scan the city. There was no wind, only the empty cold of the grave. Los Angeles was laid out in its familiar sprawl. From above, my massive city is beautiful at night. People always complain about how the overwhelming light means we can't see the stars, but even before I started meeting them personally, I thought there was something beautiful in that. If darkness is the natural state of the world without humanity, then light pollution is incorrectly named.

We are not "polluting" the dark. We are defying it. The empty sky is a sign of the human race throwing back the endless night. Our ancestors cowered in their caves and huts, hiding from predators and terrors. Now we walk in it, unafraid.

In the depths of the Grim Reaper's power, the city looked similar, but it was inverted. Instead of bursts of light, the entire city was etched in lines of darkness, where Death visited. Hospitals burned darker, a nexus place for the end.

I didn't have lips, but I still felt my mind trying to compress them as I stared down in horror at the dark tapestry. So much death happens in the wings of our lives. More than a hundred people die every minute. A century of priceless human souls going out. But despite that, we are so rarely affected by those tragedies. We suffer that loss comparatively few times before it is our turn to be lost.

As I hovered, I felt my understanding of the city reshape and mesh with this death map. Hollywood Avenue was just to my west. The 405 ran below me, going north and south. This was still my home, just in a different light.

Slowly, I moved my awareness farther, looking for something *wrong*. As silly as it might sound to say, THE END is not unnatural; it's a part of the story. Yet the athame that was used to take Maria's life was different. It was an ending, but a stolen one. Its darkness was different, its hunger tainted.

My senses swept across West LA and toward the center of the city mass. I felt a hundred looming tragedies, but nothing that was out of place. I flew farther, passing above Hollywood and Studio City. My empty eyes ranged over East LA, and I began to despair. Whatever I was looking for was nowhere to be found.

But I refused to give up, turning my attention south. A tremor of surprise ran through me as I looked past El Segundo to Long Beach, where the Port of Los Angeles sits on the shore. As in the rest of the city, the darkness was thick there, but there was something *wrong* with it. I allowed myself to descend from my heights, drawing closer to the individual stories that threatened to overwhelm me.

There, nestled in the shadows, was a stranger shadow. It was the wrong shade; it leaned in the opposite direction, as if it was affected by a different source of light. It tried to look like a panther, but in reality it was a leopard with no spots.

"Got you!" I gasped, ripping myself free of the darkness and returning to my own body.

"Ack!" Alex screamed, looking at me in horror. "Don't do that."

"Sorry," I panted, rubbing my hands up and down my arms, trying to get some warmth back into my body. "I was just excited. I know where to look."

"I mean, don't use that power," Alex snapped. He gave me a long look, his pupils wide with terror. "I thought it killed you."

"What? Why?"

"You stopped breathing and went cold."

"It's been like five minutes."

"It's been twenty!" He gestured at the dashboard readout with a furious finger. Alex's clock hadn't been adjusted for Daylight Saving and was off by seven and a half minutes. I felt my face grow paler as I did the math to realize how long I was lost in Death's power.

"Two rules: No summonings, and no whatever that is!"

CHAPTER TEN

I CAN'T BELIEVE WE'RE going to *Long Beach*," Alex complained for the fifth time since he'd turned the car around. I ignored him and turned up the van's heater a few more notches, still struggling to get warm after going so deep into Death's embrace. It was a testament to how worried about me he had been that he didn't complain about the temperature.

"Nothing good ever happens in Long Beach, mark my words," he continued.

"They are marked," I promised, only half listening. For the first time in my life, I was grateful to be caught in rush-hour traffic. It was giving me time to adjust to being inside my body again. Feeling the entire scope of death in Los Angeles had been beyond overwhelming. I was terrified at how far it spread. At least I knew I wouldn't be plagued by nightmares tonight over what I had seen.

It was all so bleak.

What was the point of life, of everything we were doing? Even if I got my soul back, one day the Grim Reaper would come for me too. Unless I became an immortal.

The stray thought wormed its way through my mind lazily, like a hawk floating on the breeze. It did not seem to have any effort or motion behind it. It just existed. But its presence sent a cold spike of fear running down my spine, further cementing myself back in my flesh.

That actually was an option.

According to Dawn, I was eligible for Fae citizenship. Thanks to Damien's DNA, I was roughly half Faerie, which meant I was allowed to choose it. I might have born a mortal, but there was a way for me to give it up.

All I had to do was say "I wish to I was a Faerie" three times and my pesky soul would be gone. That didn't mean all my problems would instantly go away. There would be some *repercussions.* Hell would have a chance to claim me, flesh, bones, and all, unless I could provide them with a suitable replacement soul of equal or superior value.

Odds of that weren't great, considering that el Diablo was in the process of building me my own personal circle of Hell for killing his girlfriend. I don't want to sound arrogant, but I'd be willing to bet a lot that his appraisal of my soul was quite high. But if I could solve that little snag, I would be well and truly immortal. I would be free of sickness and time. I'd already said it once. Just two more times and I could be free of Kane's clutches.

It had never seemed as appealing as it did now.

"Okay, Mr. Death GPS, where to now?" Alex asked when we took the Long Beach exit. The sun was already behind the horizon, but in the distance all the heavy cranes of the Port of Los Angeles glowed with their floodlights, continuing their work.

"Let me check, I've lost track of where we are."

"I really don't like the idea of you using that power more," Alex reminded me, his voice strained.

"I'll use less gas this time," I promised, hoping that would make a difference. "But we don't really have a choice." My friend let out a dissatisfied grunt. He knew I was right, but that didn't mean it was a good idea. I didn't think it was either.

Reluctantly, I slipped into a lighter version of the cold trance, like dipping my toe in the frigid water, using it to guide my friend deeper into Long Beach. The city is a weird blend of industrial and residential. All the cruise ships sail out of here, and it's where many of the goods from across the Pacific arrive. But it's also a city. A lot of people live here. They even have a large aquarium.

The path toward the counterfeit death strayed away from the residential side and deeper into the sea of warehouses. I flicked in and out of the dark map, guiding Alex as we grew closer.

"That's it," I announced breathlessly, feeling the chill once more. I nodded at a long, squat building up ahead on the right. We were only a few blocks from the port, and I could smell a hint of salt making its way in through the filters of the air-conditioning.

"Copy," he said calmly, driving past it at the same speed, not even glancing in its direction. I scanned it, but with a bored expression on my face. To anyone who might be watching, we didn't seem the slightest bit interested in that particular warehouse compared to any of the others that lined the street.

To be fair, it looked no different from any of the other buildings in the area. Its lights were off, and its loading bay was empty. There didn't even seem to be anyone standing guard, although I *highly* doubted that. You don't go into business trying to cheat Death and then have lax security.

Alex continued down the block and turned off at the next intersection, hiding us behind another building before parking on the street.

"Ready?" he asked, giving me a broad smile that did not reach his eyes.

"Never better," I promised, my tone just as empty as I opened my door and making my way to the back. Alex popped the rear door, and together we rooted through the arsenal of weapons we carried with us wherever we went.

"You thinking subtle tonight?" he asked, hand hovering over one of the bags with much bigger guns. I glanced at the dark row of warehouses, feeling a grim apprehension building in my bones. I already knew this wasn't going to go well.

"Nah," I said. "Let's go in hot."

"Firepower it is," Alex replied cheerfully, digging out a pair of assault rifles from one of the duffels and passing one to me. I tossed its tactical strap over my shoulder, grabbing a heavy belt full of magazines loaded with cold-iron bullets and sliding it around my waist. Some supernatural beings took more killing than others. These bullets were specially made to tear up anything that wasn't too Immortal to die of physical causes.

"What about..." Alex's question deliberately trailed off as he stared at a long, thin case that lay toward the back of the cargo area. He didn't need to finish it; we both knew what he was thinking.

I hesitated for a long moment, unsure of the answer. Before he was taken, Orion had given me custody of his sword. His Immortal-killing weapon was on loan from Azrael, the Angel of Death. I'm not sure anything in this *universe* can survive its judgment.

But the sword was a little...picky. It didn't particularly like me. Given the quality of its previous bearers, I didn't really blame it for not being thrilled by my performance. No matter how highly Lucifer valued my soul, I didn't compare to Orion or Azrael. The first time I ever drew it, I used it to kill Lilith, and it had repaid my foolish act by branding my right palm with its hilt. I still have the scar.

Since Orion had given it to me, it had *tolerated* me using it, but I got the sense that I shouldn't push it. The Hunter had the blessing of its angelic owner; I did not. I've met the guy, but we weren't the same kind of close.

I'd been avoiding using it by relying on my Reaper powers. The black scythe packed enough punch to threaten most Immortals. Even the sight of it was enough to make most of them hesitate. There was always a chance I didn't have enough Authority to bring one of them down, but most of them didn't want to risk it.

Now that Wilbur had fiddled under the hood of my connection with Death, the thought of touching it again so soon made me feel a little sick to my stomach. I was pretty sure I could summon the scythe without going into the trance, but I was tired of being cold. The sword might not like me, but at least it was warm.

"You know what? Maybe I will," I said after a few moments, reaching down to pull the black box toward me. I opened its top and slid the angelic weapon free, still feeling the same sense of awe I did every time I saw it.

The sword was not particularly ornate. It was about two and a half feet of steel with a narrow cross guard like an old Roman sword. Only the large ruby set in its hilt was opulent. It seemed to glow with its own light, like an angry eye watching the world around it.

Reverently, I pulled the scabbarded blade free of its box and slipped its belt across my other shoulder, letting it run diagonally across my back so I could draw it with my right hand. I felt like a child dressing up to be his favorite hero for Halloween. But no amount of spandex could fool anyone into thinking I was The Hunter. I was just going to have to be enough.

"It's good to see it again," Alex admitted softly. His face showed the same aching loss I felt in my bones. It would be better if the big man were here himself.

"Come on, brother," I said, clapping him on the shoulder and turning away from the van. "He's not here, but we carry on his legacy. Let's go and see who dares to poach in the Hunter's domain."

Together we walked down the dim sidewalk, avoiding the sparse streetlights whenever we could. This area did not seem to get a lot of night traffic. I was grateful for the darkness. It made it a lot easier for us to get close to the warehouse without drawing attention.

This close to the counterfeit death, I could feel it even when I wasn't in the trance. Its *wrongness* assaulted my senses like the smell of rotting fish. It made me feel slightly nauseous.

Alex stopped at the darkest part of the fence, pulling out a pair of wire cutters to tackle the chain links. I stood watch over him, not quite holding my rifle.

Pop.

Pop.

Pop.

The clippers cut through the fence with ease, and my friend pushed the hole open, crawling onto the warehouse property with quick, fluid movements. When he was on the other side, I ducked into the gap and followed him.

For a moment, the two of us lurked in the darkness, waiting to see if anyone noticed our little invasion. No spotlights kicked on, but that didn't mean anything. There were plenty of things that could see perfectly well in the dark.

No dogs or alarms wailed, but that also wasn't conclusive. I tried to be patient, trusting Alex's superior senses to decide when it was safe to advance. His Nephilim blood made him a much better scout than I am.

"I think we're good," he murmured after thirty tense seconds had passed. "Let's get out of the open." I nodded, and he rose to a tactical crouch, unslinging his rifle to carry it in his hands. Now that we were off the street, there was no point in pretending we weren't up to no good.

I copied him, grabbing my own weapon as we shuffled across the edge of the lot. Gravel shifted under our feet as we moved past their dumpsters. I sniffed lightly before making a face. They stank of rotting food and chemicals, another sign that this place was actively in use, so I shifted my grip on my weapon and kept my eyes open.

"You take me to the best places," Alex complained as we both tried to breathe through our mouths. For once I was not jealous of his superior senses. My regular human ones were more than overwhelmed by the stench.

There were no outside lights on the large rectangular warehouse, so it was simple for us to sneak across the empty parking lot. Alex went first while I covered him, before following in his footsteps. Together we leaned against the back side of the building, away from the street, working our way east, looking for any signs of life.

"Camera," I whispered, pointing at a small plastic bulb hanging off the bottom of the roof.

"I see it," Alex agreed, tilting his head to study its angle. "I think we're under it, but if there's one..." He didn't have to finish his sentence. There was a chance we'd already been spotted by another.

"Let's move faster."

We pushed farther along the back side of the warehouse, wasting no time. There was an ominous weight to the silence of this place. I *knew* the counterfeit death was here. I had felt it, practically touched it. But the longer we went without spotting any living guards, the more the back of my neck started to itch.

"*Hsst,* there." Alex gestured at a rusty, old fire-escape ladder above us. "If I boost you, do you think you could reach that?"

I tilted my head, judging the distance. "Yeah."

He handed me his rifle before crouching with his back against the side of the building, interlacing his fingers in front of him. I slung both of our rifles over my shoulder, taking a step away from the wall to give Alex room to get in position.

"One. Two. Three!" he whispered. I took a powerful step forward, getting a little momentum before I placed my left boot into his waiting hands. With a soft grunt, Alex strained, putting all his strength under me and throwing me upward.

I shot up into the air and easily grabbed the bottom rung of the ladder. It rattled in protest, and I winced at the sound. The goal wasn't just getting up here but doing it without making enough noise to wake the dead.

Slowly, I worked my feet against the building, pulling myself to the next rung and up the rest of the ladder. Sweat ran down my back from the weight of the two rifles, sword, and beltful of ammunition I carried. My arms were shaking by the time I made it to the top, but I managed it in relative silence. I dropped into a crouch on the roof, sliding Alex's rifle off my shoulder and placing it next to me. My eyes scanned the darkness as I seized my own gun, ready to face any threats.

"Clear," I called in a loud whisper when I found none.

The ladder rattled again as it protested someone climbing it. This time it was Alex, using his slightly superior athleticism to leap up to the bottom rung without any help. I stayed at the top, rifle at the ready, while he climbed, but no guards appeared.

This was starting to get spooky. Usually in one of these infiltration operations, someone would've shot at us by now. Either Alex and I were getting sneakier, or this place was empty. Or, the pessimist in me suspected, the truth was actually a secret, worse third thing.

"Come on," I whispered to Alex when he joined me on the roof.

"Let's take a look in through the skylights." A series of triangular panes ran in front of us, inviting us to inspect their secrets.

"Sure is nice of them to have some," the Nephilim murmured, following in my wake with his own rifle at the ready. "Way harder to spy on people who don't have windows."

Together we crouch-walked across the roof to the glass, careful to stay low in case someone looked up. It would be hard to see us in the dark, but there was no sense in being careless.

"Well, that's just cheating," Alex chuckled as we drew near. "They're not allowed to *do that*. How are we supposed to spy on them?"

I snorted, glaring at the black-painted windows. Someone had made sure no light was able to get in through them. "So much for that," I grumbled, looking around for a new plan. We had made it to the roof, but what was the point if there was nothing to see? My eyes fell on a rusted metal door at the far end of the building. A burned-out EXIT sign hung above it. "If they don't want to let us take a peek from the outside, I guess we'll have to go in and see for ourselves."

"Great." Alex's voice carried the same amount of enthusiasm that I felt. This was almost certainly a bad idea, but we both knew we were going to do it. It was what we'd been taught.

Together we padded over to the door, keeping our profiles low to stay underneath the wall that ran around the edge of the flat roof. I doubted there was anyone watching from another building, but it would suck to get the cops called on us for trespassing.

I kept watch while Alex dug out his lockpicking tools, slowly working the dead bolt until it slid back with a loud *click*. Both of us winced. So much for stealth.

"I'm sure these hinges are properly oiled too," Alex hissed in irritation before pushing on the door. As expected, it groaned a little, which was more than enough to be a problem. Supernatural creatures have really good hearing.

Shaking his head in disgust, Alex led me inside, rifle raised. I pulled the door shut behind us, moving it as slowly as I could. As much as I hated to make any more noise, I didn't dare leave it open. The last thing we needed was it banging around in the marine breeze.

Slowly, we worked our way down the staircase. I let Alex keep point, trusting his superior vision to guide us down safely. The roof access exited from a narrow stairwell to an open walkway on the second floor of the dark building. There were no machines this high, just a series of metal catwalks that ran the length of the warehouse. Below us I could make out towering metal shelves that held wooden crates. It looked suspiciously like a normal warehouse.

My friend shifted his rifle to gesture toward the north end, where several lights were on. Somewhere in the murk a forklift backed up, sending out warning beeps to anyone who might be in its path.

Someone was here, working under the cover of night.

I could feel my heartbeat begin to race as we started to work our way above the floor, moving slowly. We were shrouded in the dark, but not invisible. If someone heard us and looked up, it would not be hard for them to spot us.

Inch by painstaking inch we moved along the catwalk. I could make out the sounds of people coordinating their efforts. A man's voice echoed as he shouted directions over the beeping of the forklift.

"Dark Abyss," sharp-eyed Alex swore from the front, drawing up short. I dropped into a crouch behind him, squinting to try to make out what he saw. This close, I could see the outlines of figures moving about a complex setup.

A series of computers and server banks were on the far side of the room. I frowned, troubled by the sight of technology in a place that was making counterfeit death.

It felt a little too familiar.

Then a woman walked away from the server bank, turning to face our direction. For a moment she was perfectly framed in the light, and I felt my stomach do a flip of cold fear. I knew her and her mousy expression. Her name was Beatrice, and she was a technomancer. I hadn't seen her since she'd brought me back from the dead for Lazarus.

CHAPTER
ELEVEN

LAZARUS. EVEN DEAD and gone, the man who had been obsessed with defeating Death was still causing me headaches. The billionaire had run a secret-society-gone-corporate that had its fingers in *everything*.

Since Kane ordered me to kill the old man running it, Alex and I hadn't heard a peep from them. In fact, as far as we could tell, the organization had imploded without him there to hold it together. We even went by some of their safe houses, only to find them emptied and abandoned. That seemed like a reasonable response to having drawn the ire of the Grim Reaper himself. If I had been employed there, I would have backed away slowly and found a new line of work. But clearly some of his former associates hadn't left the industry behind.

Guess they didn't get the memo.

A sudden chill swept through me as I considered the fact that Beatrice had been responsible for sending me through the Veil and bringing me back. She and Lazarus had wanted me to steal the Crown of Immortality, but I had failed. That didn't mean her scientists didn't get anything of value from tracking my trip between the worlds of the living and of the dead. Like maybe a way to synthesize the power of Death himself. Now that their boss was gone, they had taken their talents in a different direction.

Dark Abyss, indeed.

Kane was going to kill me. Well…more than he already was going to. He technically already kills everyone—and doesn't. It's complicated. But I'm talking about murder. He would skip the whole "death" thing and just personally end me. Then probably unmake me.

"Welp, that's bad," I whispered to Alex.

"Beyond." His words were tight and clipped, an echo of my fear.

"Want to get closer to check it out?"

"Nope." But despite his words, he resumed his slow creep forward, trying to get us a better angle toward the abominable work being done below. As we got a clearer view around all the shelves, my fear only grew.

The far side of the warehouse had been cleared to make a large workspace. The computers sat next to a familiar-looking circle etched into the floor in metal. The main difference between this circle and the one I had been killed in was that the inner ring was scooped out and lined with metal. Further beyond it, some sort of kiln blazed red-hot with a fire far too bright.

Someone yelled something I couldn't quite make out, and as we watched, a worker dressed in a hazmat suit used the forklift to hoist a large bullet-shaped container from the top of the flames. The shadows danced as he maneuvered the glowing container to hover over the center of the circle. The voice shouted again, and the fork tilted, pouring out a slew of liquid metal from the bullet into the basin in the ground.

Beatrice and two more of her technomancers appeared, stepping forward to stand on triangular points around the circle. As one they began to chant, still wearing their white lab coats and safety goggles. The metal of the outer edge of the ring burst into darkness, a blazing beacon of shadow that devoured the light around it.

Even at our distance, I could feel the temperature of the room plummet as they invoked a touch of something that was *not from here.* I have said that circles are a way to merge two worlds, but whatever hunger they sought to contain was pushing at the walls like a tiger in a paper bag—like Lilith in a ring of red paint.

It reminded me of the Nothing.

Before our eyes, the liquid metal began to cool, shifting from a volcanic red to gray, then turning darker as it was fed by the shadow that lived in the circle with it.

"Now!" Beatrice shouted in an urgent voice. "Hurry, before we must close it!"

A man with long blond hair emerged from the edge of our vision, dragging behind him another person who struggled against his grip. I watched in stunned silence, unable to comprehend what I was witnessing before it was over. With a wrench, the man threw his prisoner forward into the center of the ring without crossing it himself.

A black knife flashed.

Blood fell.

The sacrifice landed on the partially cooled metal, and it drank hungrily, consuming his life like it was starving. As it fed, the center began to turn from dark gray to black, twisted by the ritual. This was how they made their counterfeit death. Matter and anti-matter, Everything and Nothing fused together, bound in blood.

I felt sick, trying to hold back my gorge and rage in equal measure. This evil was an order of magnitude beyond anything I could comprehend. The greatest monsters of the human race had only killed the bodies of those they oppressed. But these creatures were trying to take *eternity* from souls.

"It's not enough!" Beatrice shouted, urgency rising in her voice. "Hurry, we're losing containment." The long-haired executioner in the ring spun, and my rage went white-hot. I knew him too. It was Bellerophon, one of the Nephilim who worked with Polaris to conspire against Orion, who wanted to be him. It was he who helped drag our master away to the prison of Tartarus. I'm not sure who moved first, Alex or me, but both of our rifles snapped to our shoulders and together we unleashed a barrage of bullets at our hated enemy.

Bellerophon twitched as our first shots hit him. But he was far from human, and I wasn't going to hold my breath that they were enough to take him down. He dove to the side, breaking our line of sight on him. I snapped my sights toward the technomancers, who were much slower. According to their DNA, they were *Homo sapiens*, even if their souls were long gone.

I traced a line of fire through one man with his back to me, staining his pristine white coat red. Alex gunned down the third, which allowed Beatrice to escape. I was glad she was still alive; I intended to have some words with her before I sent her to meet my most recent co-workers.

Long, painful words.

"We gotta move!" Alex shouted, echoing Orion's relentless teachings. The enemy knew exactly where we were. In about ten seconds we were going to be shot out of the sky like a flock of turkeys.

"Let's go!" I leapt over the railing of our catwalk to land on top of the metal storage racks below. The drop to the main floor was too far for even Alex to land without shattering his ankles.

I was still up above my enemies, but my new vantage point had a lot more cover. Large wooden crates dotted the top, tall enough for us to duck behind. Alex and I exchanged brief glances before giving each other a farewell nod and running in different directions. We had no idea how many enemies lurked in the dark, and at least one was a dangerous Nephilim. Crossfire sounded like exactly what we needed to get us through this.

I ran south, pausing at a corner to jump east, letting me flank the open area where the ring was set up. To my horror, I saw Bellerophon was still trying to finish the ritual, dragging a bound woman toward the circle.

The metal in the center was black, but not as soul crushingly so as my scythe. I hesitated, trying to get a clear shot on the Nephilim, but I couldn't get an angle that didn't risk hitting his soon-to-be victim too.

So I did what any insane person would do and shot the ring instead. My best hope was that whatever they were cooking up was still raw and there would be no negative outcome if I broke the whole operation. Bellerophon flinched at the burst of gunfire from my rifle, looking over his shoulder at me. I saw his eyes go wide as he recognized me with his superhuman vision.

I ignored the heat of his stare, crouching to balance my rifle on the edge of one of the large crates. I leaned back in on my weapon, focusing my sights on the thick metal band that formed the outside of the circle. Sparks leapt from the concrete as my shots tore at the ground.

Go slowly, I heard Orion's voice scolding in my ear. *The first rule is, Do not miss.* A smile twitched at the corner of my mouth. Easy for him to say. But my teacher's wisdom was still as true as it had been before they locked him away.

Bellerophon was moving faster, trying to complete the ritual before I destroyed it. I couldn't let that happen.

I exhaled slowly, letting the air slip out of me. My hands and eyes worked together to find the target, the steel band no wider than my wrist. With the lightest touch I squeezed the trigger, praying I was not too late.

My shot hit perfectly, shredding through the outside of the ring, tearing it. Sparks flew.

Absolute darkness fell.

Whatever malevolent, shadowy hunger had been trapped inside the circle exploded outward, filling the warehouse instantly. My breath fogged out of my mouth as I gasped. Sound warped as a vast infinity enveloped us like a python to swallow us whole.

The warmth of my soul began tugging at its leash, trying to pull free, affected by a gravity that my flesh and bones did not feel. Dread mounted in me as I realized exactly what I'd done.

I'd brought the Nothing to Los Angeles.

Slowly, I rose from my crouch, scanning the abyss before me. Still standing on the metal shelving, I clicked the tactical light attached to the front of my weapon on, shining it into the hungry dark before me, but it did nothing; I might as well have been shouting into a hurricane. Reluctantly, I slung the now useless weapon's strap back over my shoulder, letting it dangle behind me.

I had something else with me that I suspected would do much better in the dark.

Hesitantly, I reached up with my right hand to place a hand on the hilt of Orion's—Azrael's—sword. The weapon was warm to my touch. Not in a threatening way, but a welcoming one. It seemed eager to greet me.

Despite the sword's apparent approval, better instincts kicked in, and I let go of it without drawing it from its scabbard. Now was not the moment to glow like a lighthouse. First, I had to get down.

Moving to the edge of the platform I was standing on, I dropped to a sitting position, sliding off until I caught myself with my hands and swung onto the next shelf down. I repeated the process once more before I was close enough to the ground to land on the scuffed concrete floor.

I crept forward, relieved when more of the room popped into view. Shadow hung over everything like a fog, but I could confirm that I was still in the warehouse. For a moment I feared that I had been trapped in my own little bite-sized chunk of Reality.

I cut to the right, heading closer to the ring. Bellerophon and his intended sacrifice were in this direction last time I saw them, and I had a score to settle with the scarred Nephilim.

Dismay filled me as I peeked around the corner, spying a dark form lying a few paces away from the ruined metal sheet. It seemed that once the second victim was no longer of use to him, Bellerophon had disposed of her anyway. One more thing to put on his tab when I checked him out of his life.

There was no sign of the Nephilim, so I moved forward to check on the victim.

A quick glance at the prone woman told me everything I needed to know. Even in the darkness I could see the ruin of her throat and the red blood that leaked from it. In the distance, I heard the sound of muted thunder. Alex must be engaged in a firefight, the noise warped by the touch of the Nothing. Snarling in fury, I rose, ready to race to my friend's aid.

A flicker of movement across the ring warned me that I was not alone. Bellerophon, one of the greatest slayers in the history of humankind, stepped out of the murk. A vicious scar ran down his face and over the bridge of his nose, where a chimera attack cut him up long ago. It could also have been a remnant from when he stole Pegasus, but it looked more like a gift from a talon than a hoof to me.

What? I looked him up since our last meeting.

"You *fool,*" he snarled, "you have no idea what you've done." For a moment all I could see was the memory of him holding down a beaten and bloody Orion before the Hunter was taken away. The fire of my anger was almost enough to banish the shadows on its own.

"Hasn't stopped me yet." I shrugged. "But I'm glad you're here. I've got something I've been meaning to give you." I held his gaze as I reached up and drew Azrael's—Orion's—blade free of its scabbard.

Light bloomed in the darkness, pushing back the murk of the Nothing like it caused it physical pain. In a couple of heartbeats, the entire workspace around the ring was as bright as day. Only the center of the circle—where the fell metal had been forged—remained thick with darkness.

Bellerophon recoiled a step in surprise, squinting his solid-black eyes as they adjusted to the light. I don't know how it worked exactly, since he didn't seem to have any physical irises, but it was otherwise essentially the same reaction a normal human would have.

When he recovered, he stared at the sword greedily, his hunger plain on his face. He was once on the short list for the Constellation of the Hunter but lost out to Orion. This would not be the first time he'd tried to take this sword, but it would be the best opportunity he'd ever had. I was not the swordsman that my mentor is.

"I will kill you." His voice was cold and hard.

"Promises, promises," I sneered.

Bellerophon reached behind his back and drew out a long blade, straight on edge with an angled tip, like a katana that wasn't bent. I didn't recognize its form. Some sort of saber perhaps. It didn't really matter; it was sharp and could cut me.

More important, it was black as night—made of the same dark material as the athame that killed Maria. The very counterfeit death they were trying to create here.

A little more of my confidence dripped out of me as I studied that foul steel. I had some protections thanks to my infernal contract. If I died right now, I'd probably end up back in Kane's office for like a thousand years. I wouldn't get my soul back, but I wouldn't wake up in Perdition. But if *that* thing killed me, I wasn't sure what would happen. I had no desire to find out, either.

Bellerophon took an angry step toward me, face curling into a snarl.

From the darkness, a clicking sound echoed.

A terrible feeling ran down my spine, like the thousand legs of a centipede. I'd heard something like that before. The Nephilim froze, like prey caught out in the open while a predator hunts. Slowly, I turned my head to the right, scanning for the source of the nightmare sound. There was nothing in my bright bubble, but I could *feel* its presence, a darkness awakening.

In a sudden burst of speed, Bellerophon threw himself backward, narrowly dodging being spitted by a pair of sharp, thin legs bursting from the floor. The bony appendages ended in sharp points, like spears. They were the color of rotting flesh, desiccated and faded. Dread bloomed within me as I recognized that pallid skin. I had seen it before on the monsters that lurked beyond the Veil.

Legion was here.

Two more legs exploded from the hole in the ring, slamming down like an ice climber's picks reaching for purchase. The haunting clicking echoed again, scratching against my mind like sandpaper. I could feel the madness within it.

Then with a burst of force, a nightmare pulled itself out of the darkness and into the light.

CHAPTER **TWELVE**

THE TWISTED SOUL-EATER was large. Far taller than any aspect of Legion I'd fought before. Except for one. At least it wasn't as massive as the Dreadknight, for which I was grateful. I had no desire to face one of those ever again.

It had the torso of a man, covered in massive tumors, which rested on top of the scuttling shell of something that loosely resembled a crab—if the crustacean had spent a thousand years inside a nuclear reactor. It had too many legs, half a dozen of which were as long and cruel as spears.

Its face flickered with every heartbeat, switching between the souls that it had consumed. A thousand faces rotated before me, their expressions locked in endless agony. That old anger began to grow within me at the sight of the destroyer and its great crime. I might be alive again, but I was still a Reaper.

Legion was a creature of the Nothing, something that had been cast into the Outer Darkness and become warped by what it lived off. There were a thousand faces to the collective, but they all served horrible things that were better left unspoken and unseen.

Trust me on that one.

Legion's ever-changing head turned slowly, taking in its new surroundings. I knew from past experience that the creature was able to visit this side of the Veil, but Kane himself had told me this was rare. Normally it sacrificed some of its power to do so. I was guessing that the portal the technomancers opened circumvented some of those limitations.

The thing turned to face me and let out a hiss of anger at the sight. Hatred flickered through its ever-changing faces, and it scuttled toward me, turning its back to Bellerophon.

Surprised, I flinched in the face of its rage. Did it remember me? I had killed more than a few of its other selves. Did they share their memories in some sort of hive mind? But as I moved, it reacted with a fury in the direction of the burning sword in my hand.

Oh.

It didn't care about me. It hated the light that emanated from my borrowed blade. Well, if I'm being more correct, it probably hated the Light—with a capital *L*—considering who this belonged to originally.

"Oh, I'm actually not with them," I told Legion with a small smile, taking another step back. "This is on loan." The monstrosity scuttled forward, the sharp ends of its legs clicking against the cement.

"Uh, a little help?" I called to the Nephilim. The scarred man ignored me, his eyes locked on Legion with complete, rapt attention. As I watched, he took a slow step backward, testing to see if the thing would react to his movement.

"That guy has a weird sword too!" I shouted at it, pointing at the retreating Bellerophon. Legion ignored my comments, keeping its murderous intent on the Light I carried with me. I let out a long sigh, forcing myself to stop retreating. The first rule of facing down a predator was not to be prey.

Besides, what was I really worried about? I'd killed a Dreadknight, a horror that carried over a hundred thousand stolen souls. Whatever this particular edition was called, I had no need to fear. What is a puppy when you have slain a wolf? Then a second pair of legs shot out of the dark behind it, and I really started to doubt the power of positive thinking.

"We gotta seal the hole!" I pleaded with Bellerophon, but he kept walking backward, his eyes locked on the creatures that emerged. This cowardice was exactly why he'd never made it on any of the *Top Five Slayers of All Time* lists I read on the internet. Perseus would have helped me.

Encouraged by more of itself arriving, the original crabby Legionnaire lunged forward, two of its skewers extended to spear me. I moved without thinking, ducking under the left one while slicing with the fiery blade toward the right.

I felt the shudder of impact as my weapon bit into its chitinous armor. Legion let out a scream, its thousand voices echoing over one another in horrid symphony. I dashed to the side, forcing it to twist as I surveyed the damage my weapon had dealt.

A vicious black line was burned into the thing's leg, leaving cracked and charred armor in its wake. A smile grew on my face as the monster pulled back, cradling its now-wounded appendage and studying me.

Behind it, the second one began to pull itself through the rift. I shuddered to think how many of them might be waiting on the other side, scrabbling like starving fish to fight their way into Reality. This was an invasion of the outside coming in. It was like leaving the porch door open with the lights on in the middle of a buggy summer night. No matter who I worked for, I couldn't let this continue.

Knowing I was running out of time, I pushed forward, shouting as I swung my sword. Legion scuttled backward, retreating from my fiery blade. There was no sign of Bellerophon; the cowardly Nephilim had taken advantage of my distraction to get out of Dodge. I wasted a little breath cursing the blond killer for leaving me to deal with his mess alone.

Now would be a great time for Alex to show up and save my bacon. I could still hear dim sounds of gunfire in the distance that told me my friend was busy dealing with his own problems. No one was coming to save Matthew Carver, so I was going to have to do it myself.

"You here for some free souls?" I shouted at the burned crab, still pushing my advantage. "Come and take mine, demon. You'd be doing me a favor!" The creature cocked its head, confused. Other aspects of Legion had spoken English, but this one didn't seem to have the language part down.

I threw myself forward, trying to force it into blocking my attacks. It seemed understandably hesitant to do so. Every time it touched the sword, it was wounded. That meant the only way it could avoid harm was by retreating. I pushed it back past the center of the ruined circle, giving me access to the next creature coming through.

With a grunt, I twisted away from the original Legion and swung my sword through one of the braced legs of the monster still outside our world. It exploded as the blade cut through it with ease.

Something on the other side let out a hideous scream, and its other legs convulsed as one. I dove into a roll as one of the limbs flailed over my head with impotent fury. Then they vanished with a *whoosh* as the creature was yanked back into the Dark. Terror bloomed in me at the motion. That was not the quick movement of an insect retreating; something had *pulled* the thing out of the way on the other side.

One problem at a time.

Alone and cornered, the original Legion could run no more. With an angry hiss, it exploded forward, twisting to send one of its longer legs sweeping at me from the left. I grunted in surprise, leaping over the low appendage, just in time to see a second one shoot forward, trying to impale me while my feet were in the air.

I swung the sword, only just managing to catch it in a panicked parry that would have had Orion screaming in rage if he could've seen it. But he wasn't here, only his teaching was. The rest I was going to have to do myself.

I landed awkwardly, staggering to the side as I bled off the momentum of Legion's strike. I should have known better than to fall for that trap. Emboldened by its success against me, the monster pressed forward, legs flashing as it tried to capitalize on its advantage. I retreated under the barrage of its attacks, desperately trying to get back into a rhythm. A year ago, I would have died.

But I was a student of the Hunter. The monster knew no tricks that my teacher hadn't already used on me. I weathered the thing's attacks, until bit by bit I was able to create some space to reset. For a moment, I considered trying to summon my scythe in my free hand to give me a second weapon against Legion's surplus of limbs, but I rejected it. The weapon was too large and unwieldy for me to try to use them both at the same time.

Now that I had control again, it was my turn to press the attack. I danced forward, feinting high before ducking low and lunging, trying to reach the center mass of the crab part of the monster.

BANG.

The entire world seemed to shake beneath my feet. Legion and I both staggered apart, equally surprised by the disruption.

What a terrible time for an earthquake. That's what I got for being in a duel near the San Andreas fault. It was bound to happen sooner or later.

BANG.

Everything shuddered again. My head turned in slow terror to face the hole as realization bloomed in my guts. This wasn't an earthquake; it was something hammering at the hole between Reality and Nothing.

Oh no.

I have walked the Rainbow Bridge between Underworlds. I have fled from the unexplainable horrors of the Elder beings that lurk beyond. I know the things that hide in the Dark. If one of them was trying to get through…well, it was beyond bad. There is not a word in the English language to express how calamitous that could be.

I didn't know what THE END was supposed to look like; Kane never told me. I didn't think he knew himself. But an Elder breaking into Reality could certainly be a candidate for it.

To my surprise, Legion let out a squawk of terror, looking over my shoulder at the hole. It took several paces back, almost as terrified as I was of what was trying to follow it. I took advantage of the situation, ducking forward to get past its long legs and close with its body.

By the time it noticed I was there, it was too late.

Orion's blazing blade sang as it bit into the human portion of its chest, angled upward to carve toward its heart. The many-faced thing threw back its head and screamed in agony as its flesh burned. The air stank of rotten meat, and the Light around me grew painfully bright, forcing me to close my eyes.

Then the creature collapsed, its legs giving out all at once, as if its life had been plucked from its body. The carapace of its crab body slammed into the ground with a *crunch.* The Light faded back to its normal brightness, and when I opened my eyes, its face had gone still.

Where did the souls go? When I killed the Dreadknight with my scythe, I had taken them into myself, acting as a temporary vessel until I could carry them back to the Veil. I could only hope that Azrael's sword had a feature that worked similarly.

BANG.

The world shuddered. Crates rained down from the metal shelves around me. I staggered, turning to face the ruined ring and its portal to the abyss. No time to worry about lost souls; I had to save Reality first.

Something moved on the surface of the darkness, like the giant appendage of a tormented octopus. It was a purple-black, studded with tumors and lumps—and eyes. My mind shuddered as I stared into one of them.

Surrender. Warp. Twist. Bend. Corrupt. A thousand voices whispered into me as the malevolent creature strained to fit its mass through the gap. The only reason everything wasn't already ruined was that it was bottlenecked, like a blue whale trying to fit through the opening of a milk jug.

BANG. The floor rumbled ominously, the concrete around the border of the hole into the Nothing beginning to crack as it endured a level of physical punishment it was never designed for. Given enough time, the Elder or whatever mad creature was trying to burrow its way in just might succeed.

There was no sign of Beatrice or any of the other former Lazarus employees aside from an occasional burst of gunfire in the darkness beyond. Which meant I was the only person who could do anything about this. I was worried about Alex's well-being, but unfortunately, my gut told me that stopping this thing from coming here was the most important thing I could do.

Like maybe ever.

I was also the one who'd broken the circle and created this rift. In my defense, I wasn't the one who had been trying to use the Nothing to make a counterfeit death. It didn't seem reasonable to give me *all* the blame. But there was enough that I had to do something about it.

The twisted tentacle probed at the hole again, trying to force itself through the straining concrete. Looking at it made my stomach do flips—equal parts disgust and terror. Slowly my gaze was pulled to the burning sword I held in my right hand. It still felt welcoming, but now its mood seemed to shift as if it was trying to tell me something.

It felt heavier in the front, like it was being pulled by a different center of gravity. I got the sense that if I let go of it, it wouldn't fall to the ground but shoot toward the Elder like a thrown spear. I felt a heavy yoke of responsibility settle on my shoulders as I tracked the trajectory from the weapon to the *thing*.

I knew exactly what it was telling me to do. It wanted to march right into the middle of that ruined circle and stab the tentacle right in the nearest suction cup. Fear—true Fear, not one of the lesser forms of Panic—clawed from my insides like a rodent trying to escape a prison.

If this Elder was anything like the one that chased me through the Nothing...Ubizekal, Kane had named it. Ubizekal had been the size of a city skyscraper. Running up to cut it felt a little like trying to duel King Kong with a butter knife. My magic sword was very magical, but it was also small enough that this thing could use it as a toothpick. It's hard to stab anything to death when the proportions are that far off.

Despite my Fear, the blade's pull increased, growing more demanding, like a dog on a leash that has seen a cat. This hatred felt primeval, basic. It had existed since there was only Nothing and before there was Everything.

I let out a sigh, trying to calm myself. I needed my hands to stop shaking. Reluctantly, I took my first step, crossing over the broken border of the circle toward the rift. *This is what Orion would do,* I told myself as if I was somehow worthy of his mantle. I tried my hardest to live up to his example, but just because we both played basketball didn't mean I could dunk like him.

Two more steps and I was at the edge of the rift, just out of reach of the moving tentacle.

BANG. It slammed against the hole once more, causing me to stagger to the side as it tried to wedge itself through a space far too small to contain its horrors. There was a crash behind me as one of the metal shelves fell like a great tree in a forest. The cracks grew, and my heart skipped a beat to see it making progress. It was now or never.

With a shout that was purely to give myself confidence, I drew the burning blade back, holding it in line with my ear as I prepared to leap forward.

"*ENOUGH!*" A voice boomed from everywhere at once. Its power echoed inside my skull, rattling around the free space where my brain was supposed to be. That's probably the scientific explanation for why I am such an idiot.

A blinding white light burst into being above the rift, growing from a sphere into a column of fire. It cast out the darkness like a pair of thick curtains being thrown open on a sunny day. I froze, my movement totally arrested by the command of the voice. The thing let out a shriek of fury that tore at my sanity with sharp edges.

"BEGONE, FOUL CREATURE. RETURN TO THE NOTHING FROM WHENCE YOU CAME."

Authority like I have never felt surged through the room, focused not on me but on the devourer trying to worm its way into the world. Even as the heir of Death I had never wielded a fraction of this power.

The heat that poured off the column of flame was absolute, warm and full of life, but just as consuming Doyle's dragonfire. I raised both my arms in a desperate attempt to shield myself from its strength. The Elder roared in protest again, and for a moment the darkness returned, although it seemed weaker than before.

"*NO,*" the voice said with the finality of a headsman's ax. The white fire pulsed once more; its heat swept around me, but I was not consumed. With a *pop,* like a joint coming back into place, the twisted presence vanished, condemned back to the Nothing.

The light faded. I blinked as its afterimage burned my corneas, leaving a glowing bar in its wake. Sound crashed into me as the world returned to normal. Gunfire ripped through the far side of the warehouse. It was overwhelming now that the volume had been cranked back up. As my vision cleared, I spied a figure standing where the rift had been.

She was tall and lean, with dusky skin that reminded me of Ash. Her chin and ears were sharp angles, proudly declaring her heritage to anyone who knew what to look for. Long black hair was bound in a tight ponytail, leaving her ready for a fight.

Her eyes blazed with a familiar white light, and they focused on me with an intent stare. Even if I didn't already know what she was, the fiery sword in her right hand that was a mirror of my own would be all I needed to see.

It seemed that the City of Angels had at least one in residence tonight.

"Angel!" a voice screamed in terror in the newfound silence. "The Host is here!" I heard weapons clattering to the ground and feet pounding on the cement as the remaining defenders scattered. My rescuer leapt into action, chasing after the fleeing criminals. I followed in her wake, still reeling.

We wrapped around several storage racks, following the guards as they ran deeper into the dark. My legs pumped as I pushed myself to my physical limits, trying to keep up with the supernaturals. But I was still the slowest kid on the kickball team.

Still, I kept close enough to see the criminals escape. A group of them clustered around Beatrice. I spotted Bellerophon's cruel face among them, watching our approach with a sneer.

The wizard-scientist made a gesture and threw something. There was a flicker of darkness against the shadows, and a door carved itself out of the air. There was no light on the other side of that waiting portal, just a deeper, more profound blackness.

For a moment, I feared they had opened some sort of path directly to the Nothing, but the hungry dark did not return. Instead, the villains fled through the opening, moving quickly to stay ahead of the pursuing angel. Bellerophon was the last one through, pausing on the other side to glare at me, his eyes promising revenge.

Then the frame of shadows imploded, and the door was gone, leaving me alone with a seriously pissed-off angel. The woman didn't move for some time, just stood facing away from me, glaring into the darkness as if she could hunt her enemies with force of will alone.

Maybe she could, I didn't know. I certainly wasn't versed in the capabilities of the Heavenly Host. That's where Alex found me, watching the motionless angel. I gave him a relieved smile as he joined me. We exchanged fist bumps as we studied the creature that was ignoring us.

"That what I think it is?" he asked, staring at her with something like awe.

"If it's what I think it is."

Suddenly she moved, spinning to take me in. For a moment we stood like two gunslingers measuring each other. She didn't seem to know what to make of me. I knew exactly what I thought of her.

I was terrified.

I have met exactly three other angels. The two who had come to inspect my shipment of souls that were delivered to Hell had failed to impress. Azrael was another beast entirely.

"Um, hello," I ventured after I could bear the tension no longer. "I'm sure you are wondering how—"

"You just blew my cover," she growled, irritation rolling off her in waves. "Do you know how long it took me to infiltrate this group? Now they're gone, fled to the wind."

"Oh, uh, sorry about that," I said, wincing. Mentally, I sifted through what I knew of how everything worked, trying to understand why she was here. Theoretically, any of the Underworlds—especially one of the bigger ones—would have a marked interest in making sure souls were going where they were supposed to.

The Death Treaty made Kane and his Reapers the mailmen of all souls, but that didn't mean that everyone else didn't do their own accounting. Trust but verify or something.

"Where did you get that?" Her voice was as sharp as her features, cutting through my sentence with ease. I didn't bother asking what she was talking about. We both knew.

"Yeah, that's what I was trying to explain—"

"Do you know to whom that belongs?" I almost rolled my eye at her *proper* use of the English language. Supernaturals get so specific. *Who* just sounds better, I'm sorry. Also, while we're on the subject, there's nothing wrong with ending sentences with prepositions—or starting them with "and".

"Azrael knows that I am...borrowing it," I replied after a moment of thought. "It's sort of on a world tour." If anything, my knowledge of the Angel of Death seemed to surprise her more than me carrying his sword.

"Does he know you're using it to interfere with a Holy Inquisition?" she demanded, taking a step toward me. "I could drag you to the Pit right now for obstruction of Justice." The way she pronounced the word, I could practically *see* the capital *J*.

Panic bloomed in me as I processed her threat. That sounded like a whole new way to end up in the very Bad Place I was working so hard to avoid. I didn't even know she could do that.

"This is the Hunt's territory," I told her, taking my own step toward a freaking angel holding a burning blade. Which might be one of the stupidest things anyone has ever done. But I didn't dare back down. "We have jurisdiction."

"Then where is the Hunter?" I tried not to wince at her frosty tone. My line of argument was *beyond* a stretch. Technically the Hunt didn't exist anymore after Polaris had disbanded it at the Constellation

Convention. But I was hoping this angel wasn't up to date on all the gossip about her nieces and nephews.

"He…uh, had another appointment. So he sent us instead." I gestured at Alex, who gave her a small wave, lifting his left hand from the front grip of his assault rifle to do it.

"Last I heard, he had been thrown into the hole of Tartarus and stripped of his title."

I felt my stomach sink as the angel tilted her head and studied me with cold eyes, white as the depths of winter. I guess that was too much to hope for.

"Your jurisdiction is not recognized."

My eyes narrowed as I studied her hostile face. She hadn't rejected the idea that I might have the right to intervene in this case, only that the Hunt still existed.

That meant the argument itself was sound, I just hadn't used the right credentials. I had a few other titles I could whip out; I was just a little hesitant to show all my other cards.

"Who are you?" I demanded, stalling for time. "White eyes and a fancy sword are a great trick, but if you're going to arrest me, I want to see a badge." The angel stared at me for a long moment, before looking around the room as if to say, *Did you not see me banish an Elder?*

I shrugged as if I wasn't impressed. Only an idiot wouldn't be, but that was fine. I was used to being correctly estimated. She rolled her eyes before making a gesture with her left hand. A bronze seal appeared from nowhere, filling the entirety of her palm. At the same time a burning glow began to shine above her head that I dared not look at for fear it would make me permanently blind.

I had seen its like once before, but smudged and dirty.

The seal was stamped with a crest that was also familiar: three arrows held by a closed fist. The two angels who had inspected my delivery of souls to Hell had worn armor stamped with the same image. I wasn't exactly sure what it signified but filed it away for later.

A name was etched into the top, written in markings I could not read. Yet even as I gazed upon it, I was filled with understanding of her name, like a stray thought I could not banish no matter how hard I tried. *Evangeline.* It sure looked legit, although I was hardly a subject-matter expert. I glanced at Alex to see what he thought. The Nephilim gave me a shrug; he seemed willing to play along.

"Okay, I'm convinced," I said, shaking my head to break eye contact with her badge. "Thank you, Officer Evangeline."

"Enough of these games," she replied with a snort, banishing her seal with the same gesture. "You're under Judgment."

"Just one more moment," I insisted, holding up my free hand to stop her. "If another Power sent me here to hunt down this group of death counterfeiters, would that be enough to unjudge me?"

"Depends on which one it was."

I sighed. I wasn't looking forward to explaining exactly *how* I was a living Reaper, but it was better than being dragged off to the Pit.

My scythe leapt to my call with great enthusiasm, filling my empty left hand with its chill, balancing out the warmth of Azrael's blade that still burned in my right. There was a flicker of something as the two kinds of Death within me reached toward each other, like old friends being reunited.

I opened my eyes to find Evangeline staring at me in slack-jawed disbelief. Her eyes flickered from Azrael's sword to the Reaper scythe and back, as if trying to make sense of seeing the two in the same place.

"I was tasked by the power of Death himself to hunt down those who would counterfeit his rightful power. Is that enough Authority for you?" Evangeline was silent for a moment longer, clearly caught off guard.

"I'm going to have to discuss this with my superior," she muttered at last.

CHAPTER THIRTEEN

AFTER CONVINCING EVANGELINE to not Judge me right on the spot, we gave the warehouse a final pass. The three of us worked in an uneasy partnership, scouring what Beatrice and the rest of her technomancers had left behind. I returned Orion's blade to its sheath, relying on my scythe's powers to help me hunt for the rotten, counterfeit death that they had been cooking up here.

Evangeline seemed a little appeased by my ability to do so, and I wanted to keep the avenging angel as happy as I could. The CFO of Hell once almost crushed me like a bug, and I had no desire to see how closely her own power measured up to Zagan's.

Farther inside the warehouse, we discovered an industrial foundry used to refine raw metal into ingots. There were more than fifty black metal bars sitting next to it, waiting to be used. Despite the fact that most of the crew escaped, I took a lot of pleasure in seeing how much corrupted metal we'd captured. But that pleasure was tempered with horror, remembering that each ingot required a human sacrifice.

"We believe they are making weapons out of this fallen material," I explained to the angel, trying to appear helpful, even if she already knew this.

"It is called Neodeath," Evangeline supplied absently, reaching out with her open hand to touch one of the ingots. I winced at the thought of physically touching so much of it.

"Souls taken by it are pulled out of the mortal world and taken via routes that are not monitored by Death Corp," I continued as if she had not interrupted me. A blinding light, similar to but more focused than the one she'd summoned to banish the Elder, erupted from her hands.

I staggered back a step, surprised by the burst. By the time I raised my hands to block its harsh glow, it was already gone. Blinking furiously, I looked in time to see the Neodeath crumble into a thousand pieces, turning from metal to ash.

Yet another good reason to keep on her good side.

"Warn a guy before you start blasting with the power of the sun," I complained, rubbing at my aching eyes. "I do *not* have insurance." Although maybe that was something I could get through my company. I made a mental note to check with Robin.

Evangeline grunted noncommittally, pawing through the ash, making sure every last inch of the stuff was destroyed.

"At least we got a lot of it off the streets?" I asked, arching an eyebrow at her back. "That's progress."

"I still don't know how they're making it," Evangeline replied, scowling. "They'll just go underground and set up a new laboratory, and we'll have to start the process all over again."

"I mean, it seemed like they were making some sort of connection or pact with the Nothing and the Elders." I shrugged as if that weren't *terrifying*. "If Legion can steal souls, I don't see why their master wouldn't have other ways."

"What do you know of the things that lurk in the Dark?" she hissed, turning to glare at me in suspicion. I glanced at the black scythe that loomed above us before looking back at her with a flat expression. Some of her tension eased but didn't completely fade.

"It shouldn't be possible," she murmured, brushing past me to continue her search of the warehouse. "The Veil is supposed to prevent any contact like that."

"But Legion is able to come here," I pointed out, trotting to keep up with the angel. "Surely it's not foolproof."

"Legion is twisted and corrupted almost beyond recognition, but they are still from this world. That is what makes them a useful tool for the Elders and the Nothing." A shiver ran down my spine as I grasped what she was saying.

If that was true, then something was seriously wrong, and I had a feeling that it was connected to the mission Kane had given me while I was his heir. Whatever Pluto and the corrupt Reapers under Jack had been up to was only the tip of the iceberg.

"Come," Evangeline said when we finished searching the rest of the facility. We destroyed their computers and equipment and every single tool we could find. I was certain they had backups, but I wanted to hurt their operation as much as I could. "We will see what I am supposed to do with you."

"Uh, where are we going?" I asked, hoping I didn't sound as pathetic as I felt.

"We need hallowed ground."

"Oh." I blinked in surprise. "I know just the place."

We took the angel to St. Sebastian's. She climbed into the back of Alex's van without comment, although the expression on her face said plenty. Alex stared at me for a full five seconds over the hood of the vehicle, making his own opinion known.

I shrugged, and after a couple of heartbeats, he returned the gesture. What was I supposed to do? *Run* from an angel? I couldn't hide from the demons; the other team had to be equally effective.

The only upside was that taking Evangeline to that particular church was going to help me scratch an item off my own to-do list. I might end up fully condemned by some scary angel boss after, but at least I would be able to show Father Gerald that we had accomplished something.

I texted the reverend that we were on our way and asked him to meet us there. He had plenty of time, since we had to come all the way back from Long Beach, a journey that was twice as fast now that it was late enough for the traffic to have faded.

We rode in stony silence. Evangeline's brooding was intense from the back seat, but mostly it made me nostalgic for Orion. She might have more of whatever genetic material makes up angels and demons flowing through her veins, but nobody looms larger than the Hunter.

An hour later, when we pulled into the parking lot of the squat little church, Father Gerald was waiting for us. His wire-framed glasses glinted off Alex's headlights as we turned past him. Even at a distance I could read the tension on his dark features. I hadn't told him who was in the car, just that it would be better if he met with them before we brought them inside.

Partly because I assumed that text messages are not a safe space to say, *We're bringing an angel to meet you,* and partly because even after doing this for the last two years, I still didn't know how to type that without sounding like a lunatic. So instead, I hopped out of the car and approached my friend with my own twisted expression. I wasn't entirely sure how this was going to go.

"We found Maria," I told him quietly, letting the tone of my voice convey what I meant. Gerald's eyes closed in sadness, and I gave him a moment with his grief. It was the least I could do.

"But we also found something else," I continued when the two brown pools of pain opened once more. The door behind me slid open, and I gestured over my shoulder. "This is Evangeline." Gerald's eyes widened in awe as he took in the woman.

He stepped past me, approaching the angel with a reverent wonder. I was oddly relieved that he could recognize what she was without me saying it out loud. Like he had passed some sort of litmus test that I couldn't really explain.

"Messenger," he said softly, inclining his head ever so softly. "I am honored by your presence." To my surprise, Evangeline looked suddenly uncomfortable, as if she was embarrassed to be what she was.

"Greetings, shepherd," she replied softly. "I bring you grave tidings of terrible woe."

Gerald took us back to his office by a side door. For once I was disappointed that we did not encounter Father Bryant as we walked. The petty part of me wanted to see if he could identify an angel at first glance. I'm not much of a betting man, but I would put some money down that the answer was no.

"Maria is dead?" Gerald confirmed as he slid into the thick leather chair behind his desk. He seemed to regain some of his strength as he settled into his natural habitat. The three of us stood across from him, towering over his seated form.

"She is," I confirmed. "I suspect that your theory is correct."

"What theory?" Evangeline interjected sharply, looking between the two of us with a sudden interest. Some of the ice in her expression had faded in the Father's presence. He had that sort of effect on people.

"Maria was coming to me for help," Gerald answered for me,

leaning forward to peer up at the angel. "She believed she was being pursued by demons that were trying to convince her to sign her soul away." Evangeline let out a grunt that might have been irritation. As if the contracts were a thing she knew of and had to accept but wasn't happy about.

"She maintained to me that she had no intention of doing such a thing. But she was afraid they might force her. She told me they had threatened to steal her soul if she didn't give it willingly. She spoke names she should not have known."

"How did these two get involved?" Evangeline asked, pointing at me with a long finger. "If what you say was true, why would you take it to these pups?"

"Well," I snapped, irritated by her condescension, "the same thing happened to me."

Evangeline went entirely still. Every single facet of her seemed to freeze, as if for a moment she existed outside space and time. I have seen a handful of supernatural beings express shock or surprise in such a way. Evangeline didn't move for a dozen heartbeats, until at last her head slowly turned so she could stare at me with her pure-white eyes.

I resisted the urge to sigh. I had told this story to more than one angel before, and the most interest I had ever garnered was mild suspicion. Usually, my tale was met with outright derision and mockery. I expected that Evangeline would only be more of the same.

"*WHAT?*" She leaned toward me with fierce focus. "Tell me."

I was so caught off guard that I didn't even know where to start. "You believe me?"

Her eyes narrowed. "I am not the first angel you have told this to." It was not a question. I shook my head, confirming her guess. Something dark flared on her face, a kind of anger I do not have a reference for. It was *Old Testament* in the fire-and-blood kind of way, and it terrified me down to my bones.

"It started a little over two years ago," I told her, not willing to miss my moment. I had the ear of someone who might be able to do something, and I wasn't going to let this opportunity slip by. "A demon named Dan found me in a movie theater..."

I gave her the broad strokes. I left out the part about dying and rescuing my sister's shade from Hell. I also didn't think it was important to bring up who I was betrothed to. Instead, I focused on the part about me and my missing soul. With each new sentence, Evangeline's face grew darker. I barely finished telling her about killing Lilith when the angel could bear it no more.

"Shepherd, we are going to need to borrow a room," she announced, turning to Gerald. She was practically vibrating with anxious energy.

"Of course," Father Pike replied at once. "Does my office work?"

"I am afraid you cannot be present. There are some things that can't be unseen." Alex and I traded uncomfortable glances behind her back. Apparently it was fine if *we* saw them.

"I understand." Gerald rose from his chair at once, a tight smile forming on his face. "But please, use my office. I insist. I will stand guard outside until you are done."

"Thank you, shepherd." Evangeline nodded as the reverend slipped out of the room, leaving Alex and me alone with an angel. She glanced between the two of us, a strange expression on her face.

"The Hunter—" the angel began, before catching herself. "Did he know?"

Alex snorted softly, amused by our mentor's long shadow.

"Oh, he knew," I told her. She nodded once, as if that explained his behavior perfectly. With her left hand Evangeline pressed two fingers to her collarbone and spoke as if she were talking into an invisible policeman's radio.

"This is Angelus Evangeline, Seal Five Oh Niner Seven Six One One Delta Oh, to PG command. Over." She paused, tilting her head to the side as if listening to a feed only she could hear.

"Copy PG, I have a potential Six-Six-Six on my hands. Requesting immediate superior attention." She cocked her head once more, listening as some sort of angelic operator replied. Alex and I exchanged incredulous looks over her shoulder. This was a bit much, even for me.

"Say again, PG?" Evangeline replied in surprise, her white eyes widening. Something in her tone made me even more uncomfortable. I was counting on her to be the professional here. There were already enough confused people in the party.

"Understood, PG—" she started, but she never got to finish the sentence. One second there were only three of us in Gerald's office. Then the world flickered.

A thousand things flashed before me, assaulting my mind with their vastness. Shapes I could not name or re-create. Creatures made of eyes with a thousand wings. No! Wings made of a thousand eyes. A series of concentric circles made of eyes and wings. My psyche shuddered under the weight of it all. It was like seeing the Elders, but everything was too bright instead of too dark.

Then we were back, but now there were four of us in the room. A pale blond woman with short, spiky hair sat in the chair that Father Pike had recently evacuated. She was broad-shouldered and strong. Power, both physical and not, radiated from her like heat. White eyes blazed like miniature suns as she took in the three of us standing before her. She was dressed in all black, from tactical gear to a long trench coat. The only color was a bronze seal depicting a fist holding three arrows pinned to both of her lapels. Something about her was familiar, but I couldn't quite put my finger on it. I felt like I was looking at a reflection I had seen before.

Her presence reminded me of Zagan's but magnified. The room suddenly felt *heavier*, as if something that was too big for the fabric of Reality had been jammed into this tiny space with us. I thought I could feel the ground shudder under my feet in fear.

Every fiber of my being screamed that I was in terrible, terrible danger. I understood now why Evangeline had sent Gerald away: Here was a megalodon, a creature of incredible and unknowable power. I was swimming in waters no mortal man was ever meant to see.

"Ma'am," Evangeline said without missing a beat, drawing herself up straight and thumping her fist against her chest in some sort of salute.

"Five Oh Niner Seven Six One One Delta Oh, you called in a possible Six-Six-Six?" the woman asked, arching an imperious eyebrow. She seemed like a parent humoring an overly imaginative toddler.

"I did."

"You requested a superior, and I have come." The newer angel spread her hands to take in the room, smiling in a dangerous way. Her attention slid from her subordinate to Alex and me. Her gaze was like a physical touch, hot and forceful. She was reading me like a book, learning all my secrets.

When she was done, she leaned forward, shrinking the distance between us by a few inches. Her presence was so distorting that it felt like the back of the room rose to tilt us toward her.

"I am Raguel," she announced, staring into my eyes with a terrifying intensity. "Why are you carrying Azrael's blade, Matthew Carver?" Beside me, Alex let out a strangled squeak.

CHAPTER
FOURTEEN

I SWALLOWED IN FEAR. The new, scarier angel knew my name. I don't want to sound like I'm bragging, but a lot of *things* know my name. It has never once worked out to my benefit that they knew it before I gave it to them.

"He knows I have it," I replied immediately, wincing at how pathetic that response sounded to my own ears. I might as well have said *I promise* at the end of it. "We are—or were—squires of the Hunter," I continued, gesturing at Alex beside me.

"The Hunter," she mused in a voice that was as neutral as milk.

"Yes ma'am," I replied, echoing Evangeline's earlier honorific. I know that I'm infamous for mouthing off to things that are bigger and stronger than I am, but if the other angel was being extra polite,

I figured I should be too.

"Last I heard he was locked up in that hole Tartarus," Raguel remarked, leaning back in her chair to study us closely. "My niece finally got tired of his flaunting of Justice." She sounded almost proud. I felt both my eyebrows shoot up as a puzzle piece clicked in place.

Octantis, the South Star, ran the prison that Orion had been sentenced to. She was a Nephilim, the descendant of a demon and a human, which would make her also theoretically related to angels as well. As I understand it, they're all the same genetic family, just going down different paths.

Octantis was blind, or at least wore a cloth covering her eyes, which I had always thought made her look like an aspect of Lady Justice. But as I gazed at Raguel's features, I saw the resemblance that had been hiding from me. A clue to whom I stood before.

My fear redoubled, but I couldn't help but feel a glimmer of true hope. Finally, after all these years, after all the things I had been through, I was talking to the right person.

"Forgive me, ma'am, but you will want to hear this story," Evangeline cut in, directing us back on track. "I am *quite* concerned about what he told me."

"Very well." Raguel leaned back in Gerald's chair, fixing me with a pointed stare. "I'm all ears." I most certainly didn't look at her sharp cartilage to check if that was true.

"You know that I have been assigned to deep cover on the false death case," Evangeline began, glancing at me as if wondering how much she should say in front us. Raguel nodded, gesturing impatiently for her to continue.

"Tonight my cover was blown when these two ambushed the warehouse that was being used to manufacture Neodeath."

Raguel's attention turned back to Alex and me with a newfound intensity, as if she suddenly was taking us seriously.

"Oh boy," I heard Alex mutter under his breath.

"And why were you two there?" Her question was mild, but even I could sense the danger lurking in it, like an alligator just below the surface. I cocked my head, studying Raguel, trying to understand *whom* I was dealing with.

I don't know exactly how the power rankings of the supernatural beings stack up. There's no handy guide or number system that really quantifies what someone is capable of. This is real life, not a video game. The difference between an immortal and an Immortal is vast, but that distinction barely scratches the surface.

I'm pretty sure Zagan outranks a diminishing god like dearly departed Pluto. But even that wasn't really helpful. Especially because I got the feeling that this particular angel was a heavy hitter, even for her own species.

I held Raguel's glowing gaze and extended my right hand, summoning my scythe with a thought. The physical shadow blinked into being, settling into my palm in a heartbeat. Its chill ran through me, keeping me calm. The senior angel merely arched an eyebrow at my theatrics.

"So. Kane knows," she said. "I wondered when he would finally wake up the rats that tunnel through his walls." Her attention flicked away from me to Evangeline. "That hardly seems like enough to summon *me* here."

"No ma'am," the woman at my side replied rigidly. "That's not the development that I wanted you to hear."

"Interesting." Raguel paused for a moment, considering the three of us for another heartbeat before nodding. "Continue." My heart was racing, high on a cocktail of fear and hope. It felt like I was running toward the edge of a cliff, preparing to throw myself off. I hoped there was water below—and that it was deep enough to catch me.

"I was one of Kane's first clues," I told her, banishing the scythe.

I knew I did not have the Authority to harm her with it and holding it felt rude, like a child threatening a mobster with a BB gun.

"Well, maybe not the first," I admitted at the skeptical expression on Raguel's face. "But one of the big ones. I think I was the blueprint."

"What do you mean?" The new angel's voice was sharp and demanding.

"Two years ago, Hell stole my soul, and I suspect my story has given someone else an idea of how they can get away with it." The room was silent as she stared at me, waiting for more.

For the second time that evening, I ran through the details. Once again, I focused on Dan and Lilith, not feeling the need to tell the rest of my tale. It wasn't really as relevant to what we were discussing here.

"I always hated that whore," Raguel hissed, leaping to her feet with such violence that Alex and I both jolted backward. "She was a terrible influence on *him.* Drove him to a new kind of madness." The angel began pacing, anger boiling off her like steam. It took me a moment to realize that she was implying that Lilith had corrupted *Lucifer.* I knew Lilith. She was trouble, but that was pushing it a little.

"You see, Evangeline? This is exactly why we are needed. Why *I* am needed." Raguel whirled to spear our angel with her irate gaze. "Look at what we have become. Apathy tears through our ranks. No one cares. Where is the protection of the innocent? Where is the *Justice*? Look at what is happening in our own house."

Alex and I traded wide-eyed glances. His expression showed me that he was just as excited by the angel's reaction as I was. Finally, someone was *listening.* A vision of Zagan being forced to tear up the contract and release my soul flashed through my mind, filling me with hope.

"That's why I knew you needed to hear this immediately, ma'am," Evangeline responded, still staring straight ahead.

"You were right to call me," Raguel panted, almost out of breath from her excitement. "Well done. Finally, we have our smoking gun.

Our *proof.* The others should have listened to me. I am needed." Her white eyes seemed to glow brighter, lit from the inside.

"Michael will be furious when he finds out," she added with a small smile that on anything other than an angel I would be tempted to call wicked. Then the world flickered, and she was gone. Her crushing presence vanished, and I inhaled deeply, suddenly able to get a full breath.

"Um, what about me?" I asked the now empty room. I felt suddenly deflated. Raguel had believed my story, but she didn't seem all that interested in helping *me.* I was the victim here, not her.

Evangeline turned to study me, her expression unreadable. "Fear not, mortal. I am on your case."

"Matt," I replied, extending my hand toward her. She eyed it strangely for a moment before slowly taking it in her hand. "My name is Matt," I explained. "That's Alex. Let me know if you need my government name or, like, Social Security number for your paperwork. Wouldn't want to end up with the wrong soul." The angel looked at me like she had no idea what I was talking about. I didn't either. I was babbling, saying anything I could to keep some fraction of my hope alive.

Evangeline was going to look into it. I was a case on the good guy's desk. All I had to do was be patient and this would all be sorted out. I wouldn't have to do an Impossible Task. I was going to be fine.

"Was that…?" Alex's question trailed off as the angel nodded.

"Who?" I pressed, glancing back at my friend.

"Raguel, the Archangel of Justice," he answered, his voice tinged with awe.

"Oh," I replied meekly, feeling the world spin a little under my feet. Even as a terrible Catholic, I knew what that meant. She was at the top of the angelic pyramid. No wonder she had referred to Lucifer and Michael in such a casual manner. They were her…siblings, if that was the word.

Terrifying.

"What's our next move?" I glanced at Evangeline, but the angel wasn't looking at me. Her white eyes were fixed on the wall, staring at something I couldn't see.

"'Our'?" she demanded sharply, snapping out of her own reverie.

"Do we go shake down Zagan? Can you do that? Do you need a warrant?" Her eyes narrowed at the mention of Hell's CFO. I forgot I hadn't mentioned his involvement yet.

"*We* are not doing anything," she reprimanded me. "I still have to hunt down the makers of Neodeath."

"What about my case?"

"It's on my docket. I'll get to it," she promised.

"Uh, well, there's like a time limit on it."

She shook her head, interrupting me. "We have an eternity to set it to rights." I tried not to shudder thinking about any amount of time spent in old Lucy's clutches down in my own personal circle of Hell. No matter what she might promise me, I knew that once I got there, I would never leave. El Diablo would rather unmake me than turn me over to my rescuers. That was not an outcome I was happy with.

"You need to solve the counterfeit death case before you can work on mine?" I pressed, leaning forward. "You might as well work with us. Three heads are better than one."

"You are not to get anywhere near—"

"Do I need to summon the scythe again?" I interrupted, crossing my arms. "Because I will do it." Somehow, I was less scared of this angel now that I had seen her standing before an archangel. I would mouth off to Zagan if he were here; why should she get special treatment? "Kane himself has assigned us to work on this on his behalf. You can't stop us." That was mostly true. Goodness, how many times had I fudged the truth to an angel today? Clearly, I've been hanging out with too many demons.

"Besides, we promised Father Pike we'd solve Maria's murder," Alex added.

Evangeline studied the two of us for a long moment before letting out an exasperated sigh. "Fine," she allowed. "But you will do what I say."

"Whatever you say, boss. We are very good at following instructions," I replied easily. Alex snorted. I grinned at my friend, glad to see his personality returning after our brush with Raguel. "What are our next steps?" The angel looked between the two of us, a sense of unease radiating from her, like we were dangerous in a way that she couldn't quite understand. Orion used to give us the same look.

"We wait," she growled, glaring at me. "Now that my cover is blown, they will know their operation is exposed. They will abandon all their locations and rebuild. It will take *years,* if not *decades,* to ferret them out of their holes. By the time I am ready to move on them again, you will be old and feeble." I resisted the urge to bring back up that in eight years I'd be in the hands of Hell.

"They used some sort of doorway to escape," I pointed out. "Do you know where that went to?"

"I do not, and even if I did, I would dare not follow them," Evangeline said grimly. "Not without the entire might of the Host behind me. These people are dangerous. You need to be careful."

"I noticed," I replied dryly. She ignored my comment.

"Give me your number," she demanded. "I'll be in touch. Try to get some sleep."

I pulled out my phone, and we exchanged contact information. She hesitated as she tucked her phone away in her pocket, a shadow of something crossing across her face.

"I know that this is not easy for a mortal to understand," Evangeline said, her tone much gentler than it had been before, "but that game is not over when you think it is. I swear to you, I will never stop until I see this set right. Justice is not always fast, but it always comes." Then the room flickered, and she vanished before I could protest.

For a moment, the world twisted, the shadows in the corners reaching out like claws trying to dig at me. I could have sworn a pair of glowing eyes opened up in the midst of the bookshelf next to me. *Not now*, I blinked my eyes rapidly, trying to banish my insomnia's warped reality, further proof that my mind was breaking under the strain of its sleepless stretch. Yet another reminder of the ticking clocks that hovered over my head.

A knock sounded on the office door. "Come in," I called, abruptly remembering that Gerald had been stranded in the hallway for the better part of twenty minutes. The older man peeked his bald head in, studying us with wide eyes.

"Is it over?"

"Oh no," I told him with a wry shake of my head. "I have a feeling we're just getting started."

CHAPTER
FIFTEEN

ALEX AND I barely spoke on the drive home. Over the last two years, we've developed a decompression ritual that both of us adhere to strictly. If someone tries to kill us, both of us need a breather before we start unpacking it.

That might sound like a mature and reasonable trauma response, but I suspect it is the opposite. Neither of us is capable of having a serious conversation while we're overwhelmed, so we just don't.

It's a simple rule, and it stays in effect until we get out of the car in our driveway. Then all bets are off. So I wasn't the least bit surprised when Alex broke the silence the second his door slammed shut.

"So that happened."

"That happened," I agreed, fishing for my keys. Something in his tone prompted me to push further. "How are you doing with it?"

"With what?"

"The angel part of it, I think?" I opened the front door. "Couldn't help but notice you were pretty quiet in there." Alex didn't answer me right away as we made our way to the living room and flopped down on our respective chair and couch.

"It was a lot," he admitted.

"Nephilim stuff?"

"Nephilim stuff."

"Want to talk about it?"

"I think I'm still trying to piece it together," he replied with a groan, lying all the way down. "I think it has to do with the fact that our bloodline is by nature demonic."

"I've never really understood that, by the way. Why aren't there like...angelic descendants?"

"Because doing the do with a human is a Falling-level offense." I felt my eyebrows rise in surprise at the still form of my friend. "Lust is one of the Seven Deadlies," he reminded me.

"I guess I should have made that connection."

"First-generation Nephilim are born without free will. They have no choice; they come out fallen. They just are what they are."

I nodded, remembering Orion explaining something like this to me what felt like a lifetime ago.

"Evangeline was nice enough to you," I pointed out. "As more human DNA gets introduced into the family, you get more free will. If I know that, she must."

"Sure, but then I'm just too weak to be interesting." Alex gestured wearily from his couch. "To the angels, a Nephilim is either an enemy or not worth their time. I'll give you one guess which category I fell into for them." I struggled to hide my wince as I crashed into the sore spot of the conversation.

"You're not weak," I told him, leaning forward to glare at his reclining form. He didn't turn to look at me, instead keeping his eyes on the ceiling as if he was trying to stare a hole through my roof.

"You and I have fought dragons—"

"Technically we died doing that." His tone was morose and heavy. I squirmed uncomfortably as the memories from the alternate timeline—the one in which we burned horribly—tried to break free from the box they were held in.

"Not the second time," I pointed out.

Alex grunted in irritated acceptance. Just because the Hourglass Constellation had to intervene didn't mean it didn't count.

"We also survived a Fae massacre."

"Okay, that one was pretty legit," Alex admitted, chuckling.

"You beat up Sagittarius."

"You know, Nika was a Sagittarius. In hindsight maybe that should have been a clue."

"You've been in LA too long," I chuckled. "Go charge your crystals."

"Don't forget the time I took Lazarus's whole lab hostage so they'd bring you back to life."

"Is that how you remember that one?"

"You were dead. What do you know about how it went down? I seem to recall I had to shoot the circle so you could start breathing." Alex sat up to glare at me with an amused expression. "There's no way you're trying to take that one from me."

"That last part happened." I felt something in my chest lighten as my friend's good mood returned. It is hard to walk in the shadow of the people we follow. I can't imagine having to do it for two hundred years. If we were back to arguing about things that didn't matter, then all was right with the world.

"Well, how did I have a gun to shoot the ring, if they weren't all my hostages?" Alex crossed his arms confidently, leaning back against the couch to fix me with a smug smile.

“Fine. I’ll give you Lazarus’s lab.”

“I’m pretty sure I killed more rats in the sewer than you, too.”

“We don’t talk about the rats.” I repressed a shudder at the thought of the rodent horde the Piper had sent after us. I could still see their beady black eyes shining in the dark.

“All I’m saying is my record speaks for itself,” Alex insisted with a sniff.

“All right, you’re the hero. I just work here,” I agreed, holding up both hands in surrender. Inwardly I was pleased that I had managed to distract him from his own self-pity so effectively. I’d gotten a lot of practice in the last few months. Maybe I should charge him for therapy along with rent.

Disaster averted, we watched some TV for a while, until I began to feel exhaustion’s razor-sharp fingers pulling at my lids. My body stopped pumping adrenaline hours ago, and now the crash was coming. I knew I wouldn’t be able to sleep, but my body craved what rest I could scrounge, like a man dying of thirst in the desert.

I stumbled upstairs and crawled into my large, empty bed. The AC kicked into gear as I cranked the temperature down for the night, giving me an excuse to use my thick comforter even in the middle of a mild California spring.

Trying to sleep with my dreams under lien made me feel stupid. The ritual of preparing for bed seemed awkward and silly. I was an outsider to the normal human experience, and as I lay in the dark, staring at my ceiling, I was almost swallowed by a sense of crushing despair. The stress grew like water pressure building behind a dam.

Then shockingly—mercifully—the darkness took me, and I slept.

I had just enough time to process that I was actually dreaming to remember that this was not a good thing. I was not welcome here. Lightning crackled in an empty, burned sky as my teeth fell out of my mouth in an endless wave, a waterfall of bone.

A thousand spiders of all sizes pursued me, driving me like a wolf pack. I fled from the nightmares that assailed me, running deeper into the kingdom of Somnus, the god of sleep. The features of the world bled away until I was on a glass floor that reflected the empty heavens above.

Mount Olympus, dark and brooding like it had been in the Underworld, loomed in the distance.

A million arachnid appendages clicked on the glass as they followed me. In the distance something approached, a black smudge on the otherwise empty horizon. As I raced toward it, it grew in size, moving to meet me.

As I got closer I began to be able to make out an army of corpses, little more than skeletons with scraps of rotten flesh and clothes clinging to them. They marched in unison, carrying a large dais on their bent backs. On it sat a giant throne made from skulls, with Somnus lounging on top.

Terror surged in me and I turned to flee, but I was surrounded on all sides by his spider horde. The only out was to meet the god of sleep. Reluctantly, I continued toward him, moving as slowly as I dared. The arachnids kept pace, herding me like a sheep.

His bone porters drew to a halt when we finally met, but they did not kneel, allowing him to float above me while he peered down his imperial nose at me in disgust. He was dressed in black, an echo of his dead relative Pluto. They say to dress for the job you want, and he looked every inch the part of a death god.

"Mortal," he greeted me in a rumbling tone. The sky flashed again with its lightning, and the world flickered as a twisted, many-eyed whale swam beneath the glass floor at our feet. It reminded me of the Elders. I shuddered, forcing myself to keep my attention on the god.

"You rang?"

"I warned you what would happen if you did not meet my demands," Somnus announced imperiously, his army of dead things watching impassively. They weren't real, just dreams manufactured to fit his desired aesthetic.

"It's been a *day*," I protested, feeling indignant even though I had very little leverage here. I had no illusions about my chances of standing up to a dream god in the sleeping world. I had barely been able to go toe-to-toe with Pluto, and he had been underpowered. I didn't know what Somnus's source of power was, but plenty of people still slept, so I doubted he was hurting for juice the same way his relative had been.

"And you failed," he sneered imperiously.

"I was *busy*. I'm pretty sure the world almost ended. That took priority. You should be thanking me, by the way. If Reality collapsed, I don't think there would be any souls left for you to put into Hades even if you managed to refinance it."

"It seems like you are not taking my threat seriously," he continued as if he had not heard me. "I am a *god*. You will obey me." Why was it that everything that I have ever met that names itself a deity has to shout it to anyone who will listen? It seemed like a little bit of compensation to me. Maybe the bigger dogs didn't feel the need to posture endlessly. I couldn't picture Zeus as a petulant child—actually, now that I finished that thought…that's the only way I could picture him.

"I am taking you very seriously, uh—sir," I replied, putting on my best customer service tone. "But you are asking for quite a thing. It will take some time. Plus, you're the one who is taking my sleep from me, which will only slow me down."

"Enough excuses!" Somnus shouted, interrupting my speech. "You will do as you're told, or you will *suffer*." The world twisted at his words. The glass beneath my feet shattered, and I fell. I think I screamed, but there was no sound, only horror.

I landed in another dream. Blood ran from the walls as things with no name and no form hunted me. When they killed me, I woke up in a boiling vat of lava, burning from the inside out. My ashes were sent to a new nightmare, where I watched my mother and sisters drown over and over.

Somnus might be the god of sleep, but he certainly seemed to have perfected the "tormenting" part of being a death god. Even some of the circles of Hell weren't as twisted as his dreams. Was this something deities had to study in college, or was he just naturally twisted enough for the position?

Time had no meaning. I was tortured for an eternity. Yet when I woke screaming in my bed, it had only been twenty minutes. My throat was raw and burning. Panting, I threw off my heavy covers, letting the cold air sweep over my sweat-drenched skin.

"Okay, okay," I said to the empty room. "You don't need to get all angry about it. I'll figure out how to get you a soul." I was pretty sure he couldn't hear me, but just in case I thought it would be good to at least sound like I was going to obey.

As I lay there, trying to catch my breath, I wasn't planning on getting him a soul. I was trying to figure out how to kill a god in my sleep. Technically, I hadn't killed any gods. I engineered the situation where Pluto died. At best, I could take credit for the trap that got him. I didn't stab the guy to death. I destroyed his Underworld while siccing an even more deranged goddess on him like a rabid dog.

But even if I knew where Aite was, I wouldn't dream of trying to play with her again. The Mother of Ruin was a herald of the Nothing, and I'd had more than my fill of that for a while.

My gaze slowly fell to Orion's sword, which was propped against the wall by my bedroom door, only a few paces from my bed. *If only I could figure out how to bring you with me.* A small smile worked its way across my face as I imagined the look on Somnus's smug face when I pulled the blazing blade on him.

It was only a daydream and not a real one, but it was enough to distract me as the long hours of the sleepless night ticked by.

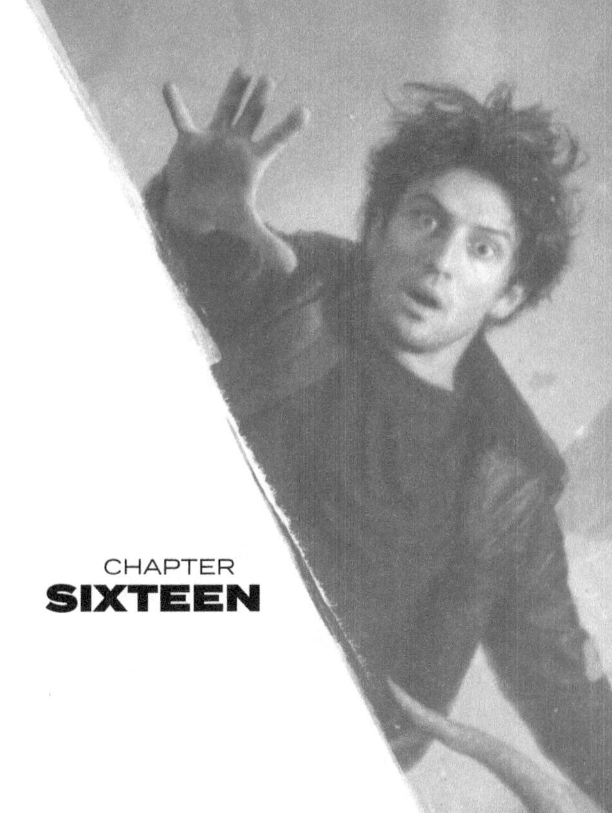

CHAPTER
SIXTEEN

MY PHONE RANG, startling me from my trance-like stare at the ceiling above me. I groaned, aching from my exhaustion as I reached for it. The clock on the lock screen read 9:01 a.m., and of course it was Robin. He waited until the exact moment working hours began.

"We have updates," he told me when I answered the phone with a grunt.

"On which disaster?"

"Our mole."

"We're on our way," I promised, hanging up the phone. With a world-weary sigh, I forced myself out of my bed to go wake up Alex. Everything around me felt heavy, weighed down by the growing mountain of my exhaustion. I didn't know how much longer I could carry this load without suffering permanent damage. Part of me fancied that I could feel the foundation of my psyche cracking under its weight. But until it snapped and the foundation collapsed, I was going to need a lot of caffeine.

It only took twenty minutes to get back to the MCIAW ETC offices. Alex pulled the minivan into a parking spot, and we hopped out. The most annoying part about having so many cases was having to battle our way throughout the city to keep all the plates spinning. There had to be a more efficient way to do this.

"Explain to me again why we're here," Alex said as we entered the empty lobby.

"Ash and Robin have a lead on that Douglas guy who is trying to torpedo my company," I answered between sips of my extra-large iced coffee. I could feel caffeine's sharp claws digging at my mind, trying to pull it out of its nosedive, but it seemed hopeless. We were going down.

"Oh, so it's your company now, is it?"

"Technically it's always been my company. I just didn't know it existed."

Leila, the receptionist we met last time, was behind the desk at the front of the office when we entered. I spared a tired glare at the cartoonish caricature of me on the door as I passed it. Now that I knew I was in charge, it was going to be the second thing I took care of. Right after I made sure I wasn't going to prison.

"Welcome back, sir!" she chirped brightly as we entered. "The president and COO are expecting you. Right this way." Leila led us through the open-air bullpen where the finance teams worked away investing internationally, or whatever it was that we did.

On the far side sat a conference room named BILLIONS, which had to have been Robin's choice. I shuddered to think what I had done to the world by giving him capital to play with. That was like inviting the monster in the front door.

Ash and Robin were waiting for us inside, sitting at a long white table. My betrothed wore a gray power suit and rose to greet me with a warm smile and long hug. I leaned in for a quick kiss, but she shook her head, scandalized.

"Not in front of the workers," she reprimanded me. "Do you know what HR would do if they caught us pursuing a personal relationship at work?"

"Uh, no?"

"Bad things." Robin shuddered, closing the door behind us. "Even I want no part of those people and their bureaucracy."

"Okay, where are we at with the corporate spy?" I asked, sliding into one of the empty chairs. The other three supernatural beings took their seats, and for a moment it felt like a real meeting at a real workplace.

"Douglas has rabbited," Robin announced matter-of-factly. "Somehow he knew we were onto him, or maybe he had finished what he came here to do."

"Any luck with figuring out how he cooked the books?"

"Still unraveling the damage, but so far, my initial guess seems close. Rather than paying our taxes, he funneled the money out into a series of foreign accounts."

"There's no way for us to get it back?" I asked, looking between the two of them. "If we call those banks…" I trailed off as both Fae shook their heads.

"That's rather the point of those kind of places," Robin explained dryly.

"What about showing the IRS that we were robbed?"

"Weirdly, it won't do much." Robin shrugged as if not even surprised. "Turns out you can't write theft off very easily. I guess that makes sense. Someone like me might abuse that."

"Robin, I have no idea what any of that means."

“The simple version is this: The IRS doesn’t really care if the money was stolen,” Ash interjected over the lawyer. “They want their pound of flesh, and proving that it was taken will not happen overnight nor will it solve all our problems. But we should start that process.”

“Joy.” I snorted, rubbing my face to try to wake myself up.

“Might I suggest we do something before we start sending up alerts that we’ve been robbed?” Alex suggested, leaning forward over the table.

“And what is that?” Robin crossed his arms, giving the Nephilim a glare down the bridge of his nose.

“You’re this Douglas character’s employer, right? You know where he lives. Let’s go take a look before the cops do, to make sure we find anything from our side of the fence before it’s lost.”

“That…” Robin started before pausing to think. “…is actually a good point,” he conceded after a moment of thought. Alex rolled his eyes at the surprise that filled the Faerie’s tone. The two of them appreciated their banter too much to be in the same room together for too long. They were like a pair of betta fish, ready to turn on their own kind first.

Huh, maybe I do need a fishtank.

“Get us his address, and we’ll go pay him a visit,” I told Robin with a nod at Alex. Mortal cops can be great at what they are supposed to do. But if this was one of my supernatural enemies making a play, those same cops might be well out of their depth. It’s hard to look for clues from a world you don’t know exists.

“Let me bother Leila,” the Faerie said with a smile, popping out of his chair and trotting out of the room. Ash glanced over at Alex, giving him a small, tight smile full of meaning.

“Oh yeah…let me see if he needs help finding the front desk,” my friend offered, getting to his feet. “I’ll wait for you—you know where we parked.” Then he fled the room, leaving me alone with my betrothed.

Ash chuckled slightly at Alex's nervousness, her expression changing from stiff to amused. Her smile warmed as she turned to look back at me, relaxing for the first time.

"Hi," she said.

"Hey, you." I felt my pulse quicken as I took in her expression. Ash and I were engaged for business reasons first. Before she died, Gloriana—her mother—had made that a requirement for helping me getting my soul back. I had to choose one of her four daughters to marry.

In the end I chose Ash, and with every passing day I grew more confident that I'd made the right choice, despite who her father is. But since I came back from being temporarily dead, the mood between us had changed—deepened perhaps. Before we were allies, but now we were starting to become something more…something real.

"I'm worried about you," she told me, breaking the silence. "You look ragged. When's the last time you got a good night's sleep?"

"Oh yeah." I winced, realizing that this was not going to be a fun conversation. I could get away with not talking about my rest habits with most people, but it's much harder to dodge a betrothed's question. She had too many hooks to catch me with.

"About that. I sort of can't anymore."

"Can't what, sleep?" Her green, human eyes sharpened as she leaned forward. If I knew anything about Ash, she had already guessed half of the situation. She just couldn't help circling me like a shark as she pulled the information out of me. She was a Faerie after all.

"Have you ever heard of a god named Somnus?"

"What. Did. You. Do?"

I sighed.

CHAPTER SEVENTEEN

ALL I'M SAYING is if you're going to be a while, I'd appreciate a heads-up so I can go get a snack or something," Alex complained as we rotted in peak rush-hour traffic on our way to check out Douglas's home. Ash had kept me for almost an hour, demanding to know every detail of my meeting with Somnus, the god of dreams.

"I didn't know she was going to grill me."

"Maybe you should just assume that she's smarter than you and knows everything that's going on with you from now on."

"Yeah." I sighed in defeat, leaning back into my seat. "I probably should."

"Just saying."

"You got the address, right? Where are we going?" I asked, desperate to change the subject. The last thing I needed was more people jumping down my throat. Ash had not been pleased that I had made a new enemy, nor did she like the agreement we had come to about when he would let me turn my lights out again. I tried to explain that there hadn't been a lot of negotiating, but she's a Faerie—that's an Impossible Task all on its own.

"El Segundo."

"Seriously? We have to go back down south?" I groaned. "We were just there."

"Yeah, honestly a major security flaw not having some native Angelinos working there," Alex remarked, crossing over into the HOV lane even though there was no break in the line. "Anyone who is from here could have told Robin and Ash that was a red flag the moment he started."

He's not wrong. LA has many jokes about friendships that don't cross highways or last when someone moves across town. They're not jokes. They're axioms. The City of Angels never ends. It sprawls for more than five hundred square miles.

Five hundred.

It can take hours to cross even on major interstate highways. Just because two people live in Los Angeles doesn't mean they live in the same place. El Segundo wasn't the farthest point that you could get from Northridge, but it was about as far south as you could go. A senior-level finance guy who was willing to spend more than two hours commuting was unusual.

"Well, I guess we will see what there is to see," I replied, glancing at my phone's GPS, which said we still had more than an hour to go. "Glad we waited until the start of the lunch rush to make the drive."

"Your fault."

"I know."

Seventy-three minutes later, we parked outside a home. Well, it *had* been a home. Now it was mostly just fire. The two-story building was consumed by an inferno that seemed insatiable. Flames jetted out of every broken window, raging that there was nothing else to eat. It was a miracle it had not spread yet, but I knew that was only a matter of time. This is California. It's dry.

"Well, at least we know it's the right address," Alex murmured as we stared.

"Come on," I called, unbuckling and leaping out of my seat. "Let's see what we can do."

"Um, Matt? Not to be a pessimist, but this one seems pretty far outside our pay grade," Alex called as he followed me, loyal even through his skepticism. I ignored him, trotting across the street toward the blaze.

Nervous neighbors watched from their driveways, several on phones, presumably calling the first responders. A few smart folks had their garden hoses out, spraying at the lawn, trying to prevent the inferno from spreading.

"Was anyone inside?" I shouted at one of them, gesturing at the building. They shrugged, looking helpless.

"Uh-oh," Alex said right before I made up my mind. "Please tell me you're not going to do what I think you're going to do."

"What do you think I'm going to do?" I asked, shucking my light jacket and passing it to him. He accepted it automatically, a concerned expression on his face.

"Run right into the fire and hope that your cool little Faerie spirit keeps you from burning alive."

"Oh," I looked at him with a surprised expression. "We gotta stop hanging out together."

"If you get turned into ash, your Ash is going to murder me."

"I'll be fine," I promised him with a wink as I broke into a jog toward the inferno. "I've survived way worse." It was true. Last year when Doyle had gone full-dragon and tried to turn Downtown LA into a pyre, I had taken a straight burst of dragonfire from him and been able to absorb it. No matter how intense it looked, this little house fire just couldn't pack the same kind of punch.

This was actually one of the least dangerous things I had done this week. Gritting my teeth against the heat, I lowered my head and raced to the front door. It was easy to kick open—the fire had already eaten away at it. Bystanders shouted in alarm behind me as I ducked inside, but I didn't let myself be distracted. I had to know what had happened here.

The moment I was inside, I summoned Willow, keeping low so that I stayed out of the worst of the smoke. My hands glowed with the familiar nimbus of the Fae Fire, warmer and brighter than the inferno that raged around me.

I pulled with the spirit, letting it eat at the flames that licked at me. To my surprise, I felt a strong flicker of power run through me as we consumed it. I had not expected it to be so potent. Willow was not a creature of the mortal world. They could not breathe while here unless they were connected to a power source. The way they explained it to me was that magic fire needed magic air to fuel it. I had expected that they would be able to keep the flames devouring this home from eating me too. I hadn't expected them to feed the spirit.

For a moment, I drew the flames in with all my might, trying to extinguish the inferno. Power flooded into me, but no matter how hard I pulled, I was not able to claim it all. It was already too large.

Wow, this is great! Willow's floaty, androgynous voice rang in my head. *You should get your house done like this so I can talk to you all the time.*

"What do you mean?" I asked as I made my way through the hallway and turned into the living room. It had been well furnished. A pair of couches burned merrily while a flat-screen TV started to melt. "Just set it on fire?"

Not with just any fire. It has to be delicious fire. Willow didn't have lips, yet somehow, I got the sense that they were smacking them.

"Oh, it's delicious fire, is it? Any idea what's making it so much better than regular, normal fire?" I made my way into the kitchen, drawing up short in surprise as I realized what was causing the spirit's excitement.

A figure stood in the middle of the inferno, a tall, lean woman who would have been of European descent, if she were human. She had short blond hair that fell to her shoulders and was dressed in a leather biking outfit. Only her catlike pupils and a series of electric-blue scales that ran down the side of her face revealed her for what she truly was.

A dragon.

She was standing over the body of a man lying on the floor. Fire already pecked at him, like a hungry army of ants. He was older, perhaps in his late fifties, wearing a gray suit. His face was slack, but his last expression had clearly been one of terror.

Hatred flooded through me as I looked from my murdered CFO to the creature that had killed him. Her face was not horribly disfigured by a reptilian snout like most of their grunts. Dragoons, I like to call them—not like the cavalry unit from the 1700s, but like *goon* and *dragon* put together.

From my so-far limited study, it seemed that the more lizard-like one of the reptiles looked, the lower on the totem pole they were. I wondered if it had something to do with how ravaged they were by their species-wide curse. Whatever the cause, the grunts were unmistakably monsters, but she was not one of them. She more closely resembled Doyle, the now dead Dragon Don, looking mostly human except for a few wayward scales and those spooky eyes.

For a moment we stared at each other, silent in the middle of the blazing inferno, both of us waiting for the other to make the first move.

The dragon broke our fragile peace, exploding forward, right hand shifting as her fingers turned into a vicious claw. I twisted, dropping back to stay out of range of her swipe. At the same time, I raised my hand and triggered a concussive blast with Willow's power.

Now, I just so happen to know that it's pretty hard to outfire a dragon. Whatever flame burns inside their bodies is in a category of its own. I think the sun is hotter, but I'm not sure what else is. But thanks to this woman's liberal use of her dragonfire to set Douglas's house on fire, I was packing more of a punch than normal.

A furious orange orb of fire formed in front of my hand before detonating like a bomb. The force of its explosion sent the dragon tumbling end-over-end as I caught her off balance. A vicious smile crept across my face as I charged after her, trying to catch her before she was back on her feet.

The creature was far too quick to be such easy prey. She leapt up from the ground, eyes burning with hatred as they fixed on me. A shiver of fear ran down my spine at the expression on her face. No matter how confident I was, I was still trapped in a small enclosure with her. I'd probably be better off being in a swimming pool with a great white shark.

This was a dragon. A dragon. A living, breathing dinosaur with untold years of wisdom and cunning. The curse their entire species was under might keep them from being able to achieve their true form, but that didn't mean that they weren't about as dangerous as it gets.

Yet I've stared down a god of death. I've stood in the Nothing and seen the Elder things that wait on the edge of Reality. I have killed a Dreadknight and retrieved its horde of souls from the dark.

It gives a man a different sort of perspective on fear.

"Foolish mortal," she hissed, just loud enough to be heard over the inferno. "You should have brought the sword." She was almost certainly an Immortal, with the capital *I* and everything. Bullets wouldn't be enough to kill something like her. You needed something with a little more *oomph.*

"Eh," I replied with a halfhearted shrug. "I think I'll be okay."

She didn't bother speaking again, instead feinting forward, trying to draw out my flames. I merely smiled and shook my head, happy to keep hoarding the power that Willow was accumulating by feasting on the fire around us.

Frustrated by my patience, she lunged forward recklessly, confident that I had no way of hurting her. I threw out my right hand again, triggering another blast. This time she kept her center low to the ground, taking the blow to the chest. The force of my attack tore her leather jacket to shreds, but she was able to stay on her feet and press her assault.

A jolt of panic ran through me as I saw how close she was getting. I threw out of my left hand, sending another supercharged fireball at her. She caught this one on her crossed elbows, using them to shield her face. Willow's power pushed her back a couple of feet, but it did not knock her down.

When she looked up, she smiled at me with sharp, serrated teeth. A distinctively sharklike promise. Some of my earlier confidence began to fade. However much dragonfire she had used to create this blaze, it didn't seem like it was enough for me to harvest and funnel back at her.

Well, crap.

I took a couple of steps back, coughing as my lungs grew more irritated by the horrible smoke. Willow could protect me from the fire, but I couldn't stay here much longer. I needed to either win this fight or get out.

Fortunately, I had one more trick up my sleeve.

The blue dragon's eyes tracked me with a hungry gaze. My hesitation was a sign of weakness. I looked like a foolish human who had just realized how out of his depth he was. To a predator like her, that was a siren call she could not ignore. The monster crouched low, her movements reminding me of a cat preparing to pounce on a mouse. Then with an explosion of muscle, she launched herself at me, claws outstretched.

It took every ounce of self-control I had to keep a smile off my face she dashed toward me. I hadn't been backing up because I was afraid; I was just trying to make sure I had enough room to swing.

In the brief seconds before she leapt, I banished Willow, replacing their warm power with a cold one. Death flowed out of me, filling my hand with its terrible chill as my scythe manifested as a physical shadow.

It felt more frigid than I remembered, a side effect of me still being warm from Willow perhaps. I twisted with my hips, swinging the weapon like a baseball bat, hoping to cleave her right out of the air. The world seemed to slow down as I swung.

I had enough time to see her eyes go wide with shock before she twisted, warping herself with impossible control to dodge the scythe's blade in midair. The dragon slammed into the wall behind me, crashing through the weakened structure like a wrecking ball.

I spun, readying myself for her counterattack, but it didn't come. I looked through the hole, watching as she got to her feet and looked at me with true fear. *That's right, I don't need the sword.* I smiled.

With a hiss of irritation, the dragon dashed to the side, running away from me. I heard the crash of glass as she burst through a window. I let out a curse and gave chase through the hall, but by the time I ran into the living room, she was already gone.

"Did a dragon just run from me?" I asked the burning room in shock. Only my own coughing answered me as I sucked down more smoke. Right, I was on the clock here. I banished my scythe, trading its cold power for Willow's warm protection.

Moving with urgency, I raced back to where Douglas's body lay. The older CFO's throat was slashed, probably cut by the same claws that I had dodged. He was dead; there was no doing anything about that.

But maybe he could tell me something. I dropped to my knees, rooting through his blazer pockets. It would be just too convenient if he had died with a little note in his pocket announcing who he was working with and why he'd robbed me.

But I never get to do things the easy way, so of course he hadn't.

Something crashed on the far side of the house, and I leapt to my feet, terrified that the dragon had returned with reinforcements. But it was only the house beginning to collapse as the dragonfire ate it from the inside.

It was time to go.

I raced toward the front door, only to find my path obstructed by a fallen wall. Cursing, I turned, trying to find another exit. I coughed, choking on smoke as the inferno grew. Even through Willow's protection, I could feel the heat growing.

It was a race to see if the house would collapse on me before the smoke and fire killed me. As if summoned by my concern, a section of the roof crashed down to the floor a few feet ahead of me.

I yelped, covering my face with my arms as fragments of burning wood and drywall flew everywhere. Despair filled me as I surveyed the damage. There was no path out now. I couldn't breathe; there was only smoke, no air.

Gritting my teeth, I reached out with Willow, trying to contain the fire by subsuming all of it. I knew I would not be able to extinguish the entire home, but maybe I could create a path to escape. But the inferno had grown even larger since I'd first tried. No matter how much I pulled in, there was more, spreading at ravenous speed.

Something creaked dangerously overhead. My head snapped up just in time to see the supports around a huge beam in the living room give out. Above me, a massive chunk of the ceiling broke free as the house began to collapse. My hands snapped up to shield my face, but in the back of my mind I knew it wouldn't matter. I was going to be squished flat like a bug under a shoe.

Then the world froze.

The raging sound of the fire around me vanished. Slowly, I lifted my head to stare at the rubble falling toward me, which was frozen in midair. I turned to take in the tongues of flame around me that were not dancing or giving off heat.

Everything was still. I was the only thing that moved. Was this a dream? Had Somnus tormented me so greatly that I no longer could tell waking from sleeping? The god had warned me that my mind would crack; I just didn't think it would be this soon. A low cough sounded behind me, trying to capture my attention. I whirled, raising my fists to protect myself from my tormentor. Only it wasn't Somnus waiting for me.

Horologium, the Constellation of the Hourglass, was dressed in his usual modern clothes, dark-washed jeans and a black shirt. He wore a tan robe that hung open, dangling to his ankles. His beard was neatly trimmed, and there was a disappointed smile on his face as he inclined his head in greeting. Compared with most Nephilim, he looked almost mortal. Only his pointed ears and solid-black eyes hinted at what he truly was.

"This marks the third time I have saved you from dragons. From here on out, I'm going to have to charge you," he told me with a wry twist of his lips. His expression soured slightly as he looked me up and down. "When's the last time you slept? You look like a wreck."

CHAPTER EIGHTEEN

CAN I AFFORD your rates?" I asked, panting as I caught my breath. Being outside time is a strange thing. There was still oxygen, but it was blessedly free from smoke. I don't know where it came from, but the clean air was too delicious for me to ask too many questions.

"We'll see." He smiled again. It almost sounded like a threat. Like he knew I was going to be fighting dragons again. I suppose that wasn't exactly a hard prediction to make. This feud had predated me by a couple hundred years.

"It's been a while." The last time I saw the Nephilim, he had saved Alex and me from being burned to a crisp by Doyle in his super-dragon form at the Constellation Convention. "To what do I owe the pleasure?"

"Oh"—Horologium smiled in a way that was deliberately disingenuous—"I was in the neighborhood. Saw the place was on fire. Assumed I would know someone who was involved."

"Seriously?" I arched an eyebrow at him.

"I knew Dracaena was in town." He shrugged as if that was all I needed to know. "Dragons are not welcome here." His voice had a familiar ring of steel in it. "Orion doesn't have a monopoly on hatred of the lizards. Thought I'd do him a favor while he's otherwise occupied."

I thought for a moment—well, sort of. Technically there were no moments while the world was paused. But even so, there was a lull while I considered his words. I'd never understood why he had helped Alex and me during the convention. This shed some light on his motivations. "Thanks."

He accepted my gratitude with a shallow nod. "The question is, young squire, why you keep allowing yourself to be caught in their traps." He crossed his arms as if disappointed.

"Well, I didn't know there were dragons in town," I answered, realizing after the words were out of my mouth that it sounded like I was making excuses. "I've been busy making new enemies, so I guess they got jealous."

"What do you mean?"

"It seems like the dragons have decided to try to financially ruin me—"

"No, the part about *new* enemies."

"There's this whole thing going on with someone trying to manufacture a counterfeit death that lets them steal souls from the gaze of Fate." My explanation trailed off as the son of Time stared at me with rigid intensity.

"It's called Neodeath and—"

"Where?"

"They had a warehouse in Long Beach, but we took care of it. There was an angel named Evangeline who helped us—"

"The angels know about this?" His whole face tensed as he leaned forward. Why that concerned him so much, I could only begin to guess. "I thought you smelled of angels."

Confused, I took a whiff of myself, but all I got was the faded scent of house fire. "Do you want to hear my story or are you going to keep interrupting me?" I crossed my arms and gave him my best Orion glare.

The fashionable Nephilim stared at me blankly for a couple of heartbeats before his lips quirked in amusement once more, and he relaxed. "My apologies, young squire." He gestured for me to proceed.

"Thank you." I sniffed in mild indignation before telling him the events of the night before. I left out the meeting with Raguel, which felt like something that you don't just share lightly. I trusted Horologium well enough; the guy had saved my life three times now. But that didn't mean he deserved access to all my secrets.

"Fools," he murmured, shaking his head in disbelief when I finished. "They risk undoing everything, for a few moments more." I blinked in surprise, suddenly remembering something Kane told me when he was giving me my Reaper orientation.

Souls were the fuel of the universe. They powered Reality and held back the Nothing. Death said that if human beings became Immortal and stopped dying, the Underworld would run out of souls and eventually collapse.

Neodeath was—among other things—a form of stealing. It was taking the souls and preventing them from being ingested into the machinery of the universe. Right now, it was a rather small number compared with the trillions of humans who have lived and have yet to come. But how many of them had to be embezzled before it started to be a problem?

"Oh no," I breathed in understanding. This wasn't just a crime against the individuals that were being abducted. This was a danger to us all.

"You have learned much since the last time we met," Horologium told me, arching an eyebrow in my direction. He seemed surprised that I had followed his concern.

"Fear is a great tutor."

He glanced around the burning wreckage of Douglas's home, frozen in time, as if to ask why I had ignored its warning and come here. I could only shrug. Just because I had gotten smarter didn't mean I was perfect.

"We destroyed one of their labs," I told him. "But that's only one piece of the operation. I don't know where the souls are going. Or how they're being transferred without going through the Veil and into the Nothing."

Horologium was silent for a moment, pursing his lips in thought. "Are you sure you should be getting involved in this?" The question was gentle but firm.

I winced as if he had struck me. When I looked back into his black eyes, they were kind. Like a parent watching his toddler trying to stand up for the first time. "Orion would." I didn't bother to mention that Kane could have forced me to get in the middle of it too. Truthfully, it wasn't relevant. I had been the one to call Death and report it. I would have done that even if I wasn't an employee on leave.

"He would," the Nephilim replied with a sense of amusement. He didn't need to point out that I was not the Hunter. The comparison was echoingly obvious for anyone with eyes. I cannot try to be him. I can only try to be like him, to follow the path he showed me.

"If you were trying to stockpile or sell the most valuable item in the universe, and you were trying not to get caught, where would you do it?" I asked him.

His eyes narrowed. "Be careful," he warned me, giving me one more chance to walk away.

"Not in the job description."

"I know of no such sanctuary. But if it were to exist, it would be in a forgotten place." His expression sharpened as he studied my face. "A fallen world." The key that was always in my pocket suddenly felt heavier, and I kept my face blank.

I knew the kind of worlds he was talking about. There were doors to hundreds of them in the Between, the office hallway between worlds that had been made by a pair of Roman gods before they vanished to wherever deities go when they're done.

Worlds without souls were inevitably crushed by the Nothing as they lost the power to hold back the darkness. I had been in such places. Lazarus had used crumbling Elysium as a safe place to talk without Death being present. Mother Ruin had emerged from the door of another. It was only too likely that there were more bolt-holes spread out in the dark.

Horologium saved Alex and me when my key had been blocked by some Power that prevented us from fleeing Doyle. He had to know that I possessed it. And yet, I was loath to admit it. His smile only grew, as if my silence confirmed everything he needed to know.

"Thanks for the tip," I told him.

"What will you do about the dragons?" His question was mild, but I caught a sense of the anger burning in his black eyes. Whatever his reasons for hating the reptiles, I got the feeling they were as good as my own.

"They're next on my list."

"But it seems you are first on theirs."

"I'm on a lot of lists. Trust me."

"Draco has been released," he commented softly, eyes narrowing to watch my reaction. I swallowed against the sudden lump of fear that grew in my throat. Part of the sentence against Orion had been that his mortal enemy, the god of the dragons, would be released. Draco had languished in Tartarus for hundreds of years after he murdered the last Hunt.

"Oh? I hadn't heard." I was proud of how little my voice shook.

"Yes, the cycle for Tartarus has come and gone. The Hunter has been taken, and the beast has been released." The bitterness in his voice echoed my own feelings.

"Well, that is certainly good to know."

"What would you do, young squire, to have him back?" Horologium's voice was soft, as if he was afraid of being overheard even here, outside time.

Despite that, my heart stopped as I cataloged his request. I might never have been given a more dangerous query—not even by Dan. "Is this a real question or just for fun?"

"Would you trade a favor for a favor?" Horologium's eyes twinkled with the black void of the Nothing, and my fear spiked. I was less afraid to hear that the draconic god had been released than I was of this. I have too many Fae for mentors to ever be comfortable when someone asks for a favor.

Suddenly I wondered if the son of Time had really saved me or if he was just waiting for the right moment to corner me for his own gain. Mentally I probed at the spot in my mind where my powers of fire and death sat, but they were not here. The blue dragon was right. I should have brought the sword.

"What are you asking?" I demanded, taking a step toward the Nephilim.

"Tartarus is a prison outside time, much like we are now," he told me, not looking the least bit intimidated by my approach. I tried not to let that get under my skin. "It can only be accessed by someone in the right time and space. I have one piece of the puzzle." He gestured at the frozen world around us. "You have the other."

Once more I felt the key's weight in my pocket. I licked my lips, suddenly nervous. This felt like very, very dangerous territory. "What kind of favor?"

"There is someone that I need help saving. Don't worry," he assured me, seeing the wary expression on my face. "Orion would approve." I hated how much that assuaged my fear. Something told me he wouldn't dare lie about that endorsement.

"And in exchange, you'll help us bust him out of Tartarus?" I felt my pulse race as the pieces of a plan began to fit together.

"I will operate as your driver," he interrupted, holding up his hand. "I will get you to and from the prison world. What you do in it will be up to you and whatever team you can put together."

"Deal." The words were out of my mouth before I'd even thought about what he was saying. For a chance to get Orion back in my lifetime, I would risk everything. If Draco really was free and hunting me and my friends, we were going to need the Hunter. "Who are we killing?"

Horologium's smile widened, not in a smug or cruel way, but genuine amusement. "It is not yet the hour," he admonished me. "When it is time, I will find you."

"Okay." As my excitement began to fade, I couldn't help but find his words ominous. But I've made deals with worse people before. I would survive this one too. "Now what?"

"If you'll just duck under the burning wreckage and make your way to the front door, I can return us to the present." He gestured at the beam that had almost crushed me before he arrived. In all my excitement, I had forgotten about its existence. Almost dying wasn't that exciting anymore.

"Sure thing." I followed his instructions, climbing over the pile of burning rubble. It didn't shift under my weight despite clearly being structurally unsound. The solid flames didn't impede my progress either;

I parted them like they were holograms, made of nothing.

"Oh hey," I called, pausing to look back at the Time Constellation from the top of my little hill. "You wouldn't have any tricks for dealing with an angry dream god, would you?"

The amused Nephilim shook his head. "Sorry, Matthew, sleep is a place on the edge of time," he told me with a shrug. "That's a bit outside my purview."

"Ah well. I thought I'd ask."

"Matthew," Horologium paused for a second, a rare look of hesitation flashing across his face. "When they offer you three, choose two."

"What?" I asked, clueless to what his cryptic statement could mean. But the Nephilim only shrugged.

I waited for another moment, feeling suddenly awkward. We were the only two beings awake in this moment outside all other moments. I wasn't sure what the etiquette about saying goodbye was.

"Be seeing you," I told him, jumping down to the other side of the pile, relieved to see a clear path to the front door before me.

Then the world flickered, and the fire returned to its dance. I staggered under the force of the heat and smoke that slammed into me as time kicked back on. Alone, I stumbled out of the inferno.

CHAPTER NINETEEN

DRAGONS," ROBIN SAID flatly from across one of the conference tables in MCIAW's office. His face twisted in distaste, but that might have been because I reeked of smoke.

"Don't pretend like that's a new thing," I groaned, leaning back in my chair. "I'm so tired." My brain felt like it was in a fog. No matter how much coffee I drank, I was *slow*, unable to keep up at my usual speed. Somnus's lien was a weight on my cognitive ankles, dragging me down.

The two Fae were dressed in their sharp professional attire, dark-gray suits with gold accents. They looked like they came from the same tailor. Meanwhile Alex and I were really pushing the definition of "business casual" with our combat boots and jeans.

"So Draco wanders the world again," the lawyer continued, ignoring my complaints. "We knew it was only a matter of time, but I thought it would be another cycle before all the paperwork was done."

"Polaris must have expedited it," Ash remarked from the head of the table, her eyes distant and thoughtful. "Another punishment." I felt my lip curl in hatred for the North Star, the corrupt head of the Constellation Convention. That certainly sounded like something he would do.

"Tell them the other thing," Alex pushed, seated at my right. He still wore a shadow of the same shocked look he had given me when I told him what had happened inside the inferno.

"What other thing?" Ash's voice was sharp and suspicious, like she didn't trust me not to get into more trouble when I was out of her sight. I'd have been more offended if it wasn't true.

"They're going to yell at me," I protested, which only made the look on her face grow more suspicious.

"I still might yell at you," Alex replied with a snort. "Making deals without—"

"You would have said yes too," I interrupted, sitting up so I could lean forward and stare at my best friend. "Look me in my eye right now and tell me that you wouldn't have made the exact same agreement." Alex's lips compressed into a thin line before he looked away, frustrated by how right I was. The Hunt might not legally exist anymore, but the three of us were bound by fire and blood. There was no world where I could have done anything else, and we both knew it.

"You made a deal?" my lawyer asked tightly. I glanced at the two Fae to find them staring at me, spines ramrod-straight. They looked like a pair of sharks, intrigued by all the blood in the water. I shot Alex a glare before slumping in my chair. There was no getting out of this now.

"Horologium had a suggestion," I began, not making eye contact with either of them, instead staring at the wooden tabletop. "About how to get Orion out of Tartarus a little early."

"Oh gods," Ash murmured in despair.

"Tartarus," Robin repeated in the flat tone.

"Apparently it can only be accessed by someone who has the right intersection of time and space—"

"Tartarus. The supernatural supermax prison that exists outside of Reality, overseen by the South Star, the Constellation of Justice."

"Yes, that one."

"Tartarus, a place so secure it makes Hell look like a public park. Where monsters that could eat Cerberus in a single bite walk free. Where the Titans died. Where no mortal has ever trod and survived."

"I think so?" My voice went up an octave as I answered his rhetorical questions. Those details had not been in the brochure.

"*Tartarus,*" he continued, irritation boiling over into his voice. "Where the Furies wait and hydras patrol like trained dogs to make sure that no prisoner escapes."

"Are there two Tartaruses…Tartari…Tart-Tart—"

"There are not," Ash replied in an icy tone. I winced without looking at her. Afraid of the dangerous anger that would lurk on her face.

"Well, then I don't know why Robin is asking questions *he already knows the answer to*!" I snapped, fixing my lawyer with a murderous gaze. "Yes, it is the Tartarus where Orion, our master, our mentor, our *friend,* is held. Where Alex and I will be going to rescue him and bring him home."

I paused for a moment, suddenly unsure of myself. "You are coming, right?"

"Yes, Matt," Alex sighed. "I'm coming to Tartarus."

"Just checking."

"And what price did you agree to pay for this most *Impossiblest* of

Tasks?" Robin asked, golden eyes narrowed. I couldn't tell if he was more annoyed that I made done a deal without him or that I had made a bad one.

"Uh, we have to help him save someone. Probably kill someone to do it."

"Who?"

"I don't know," I admitted with a wince. I should have done better on that part. "He told me Orion would approve."

"You idiot." Ash leaned forward, burying her head in her hands.

"He would do the same for me."

"*And that is why he is there.*" Robin's tone was cutting and dismissive. Anger flooded through me, and I fixed the Faerie with a glare. Beside me, I could feel Alex doing the same. Robin blinked in surprise, then sighed as if he needed to explain himself to very young children.

"The Hunter is a most deadly foe," he admonished. "But he has never been clever. The bull never wins the fight; he ends up in a cage or dead. Polaris played him like a fiddle, and now he pays the price."

"We all do," Alex said softly. Robin's condescending expression softened slightly. Despite being the most cynical Faerie, there was the hint of a heart lurking inside his chest.

"Yes," Ash agreed after a moment, in the same gentle tone. "We all do."

"That seems like a tomorrow problem," Alex pointed out now that the shouting had finally paused. "We have a few more pressing issues to deal with first. Then we can all get mad at Matt again."

"Oh, I'm sure we will," Robin huffed, but he nodded his assent. "If Draco is really back and the dragons are coming after us, we're going to need to do something."

"Realistically, how much stronger is Draco than Doyle was after he took the serum?" I glanced between the two Fae, hoping one of them could tell me something useful.

"I wasn't born when last he roamed free," Ash told me with a shake of her head. "I've heard stories, but I do not know what is myth and what is truth." She glanced at Robin. "Do you…"

"Much stronger," the lawyer replied with a sour expression. "Doyle was an awkward teenager, still getting used to his new body. Draco has had centuries of practice." I tried not to let a shudder of fear run through me at the thought of a bigger, badder version of the Irish dragon hunting me.

"We should get the lance out of storage," I murmured to Alex, who nodded.

"Does it strike anyone else as odd that he hasn't actually attacked us, just maybe tried to financially ruin me?"

"No, that makes total sense," Robin replied with a dismissive wave of his hand.

"How?"

"He's going after your hoard."

"My what?"

"There's nothing those scaly bastards like more than being rich. Remember all those legends about dragons curling up on giant piles of gold? They're real and, if anything, wildly understated in the modern retellings," Robin told me. "The dragons coming after your wealth is the greatest act of humiliation they could commit. To them, they are stripping you of the thing that gives you any sort of credibility. It would be like if someone came and claimed Los Angeles as their territory from the Hunter."

My mouth made a small O as I processed the layers to that. For a minute there, I had been feeling a little grateful that they hadn't been trying to murder me. But apparently, I had not been taking this as personally as I should.

"Okay, well, let's figure that out," I said, blinking to catch back up. "Douglas is dead. What other options do we have?"

"Not as many as I would like," Ash replied grimly. "We can report the embezzlement, but I can only imagine how poorly that will go."

"Why?" Alex asked, arching an eyebrow.

"Fraud is always an exhausting and painstaking process," Robin answered for the Lady of Autumn. "But mortal authorities tracking down the Dragon Dons? I wouldn't hold my breath."

"So what are our other options?" I rubbed my eyes, desperately trying to force some energy back into my brain. Exhaustion lurked in my skull, growing like a tumor to squeeze out every other thought.

"We find enough money to pay our debts," Robin replied as if that was simple.

"Okay, great. If we find seven million dollars lying around, we'll be sure to bring it back home."

"Don't be petty, Matthew. It is beneath you," my lawyer sniffed as if hurt.

"Why can't we just, like, get a loan?"

Robin and Ash exchanged glances, their faces unreadable. I let out a sigh of irritation before they turned back to me. It is never a good sign when they do that.

"Matthew, in order to explain it to you, I will have to use words like *leveraged assets, EBITA, inflation,* and *interest rates.* Do you really want me to? Or would you rather trust me that this is not a road open to us at this time?" Alex mouthed *EBITA* over Robin's shoulder at me, his eyes twinkling with amusement.

"We're more likely to find success bringing in an outside investor, although that will mean losing some control of the company," Ash added, trying to soften Robin's condescension.

"I'll trust you, I guess," I muttered, fighting off the urge to yawn. "Just tell me if there's a bank we need to rob. Alex and I have to get to work anyway."

"Where do you two think you're going?" Ash asked, arching a red eyebrow at me, which I've learned is how a betrothed traditionally displays a warning before striking.

"Oh, you know, the usual. Just wandering through dying worlds, looking for a place to hide from Death."

CHAPTER
TWENTY

THE KEY OF Portunus looked like it had been made in ye olde days. It was big and blocky, with teeth that had been carved by hand instead of a precise machine. A large smiling mask, like one from an old mummer's play, was set into the bow. Across the Veil, that smile would turn upside down, signifying that it would open the place Between Underworlds instead of just worlds.

Despite looking nothing like the lock in the conference room doorknob, it slid in easily, clicking into place as if it was made for it. Ash watched with narrowed eyes as I unlocked the closed door and swung it open to reveal the mustard-yellow walls of the Between. She wasn't happy with my plan, but she understood it. As a daughter of the previous Queen of All Fae and sister to the current one, she knew a thing or two about obligations, and I didn't really have a choice.

"Didn't Evangeline ask us not to do something like this?" Alex asked me as he dropped a duffel bag full of weapons on the table. We hadn't felt comfortable openly carrying them through the office, even if I was the boss. The last thing the IRS needed to hear was that I was stockpiling guns. That's how you get passed over to the ATF, and that never ends well for anyone.

"We're not doing *anything*," I pointed out. "Just a light scouting mission, testing a theory. Besides, technically I answer to Kane, not her, and I'm pretty sure this falls more under Death's jurisdiction than Heaven's. She's just scary enough that we should be polite when she's around."

"Well then, once more unto the breach," Alex told me, patting me on the shoulder as he stepped through the door into the Between. I paused for a moment, holding Ash's green eyes with my own. A thousand unspoken thoughts swirled through my exhausted brain.

I had no illusions that I was a perfect partner, or even a good one. Most of my time was occupied putting out fires I had no business sticking my nose into. Ash too kept her own counsel. She ran a House of the Dandelion Court, after all. In our personal lives, we were beyond independent.

But despite our distance, every step seemed to bring us just a little closer. When I first chose her, I did it out of desperation. She seemed the least terrible choice. But now I chose her, and she chose me. There was a difference, and it scared me—but was also intoxicating.

I'm sorry. I'll be back. Try not to miss me. Look on the bright side, if I die then you don't have to marry me. I condensed all of these thoughts into a tired smile, which after a moment Ash reflected back to me.

"See you soon," she said, a threat lurking in her tone.

"See you soon," I promised. Satisfied, she finally released me with her gaze, allowing me to follow Alex into the faded hallway built by missing gods. I didn't look back to see if she was still watching as I closed the door behind me. I needed to keep my focus for the journey to come.

On the surface, the Between is deceptively simple. It looks like it is a single office hallway that runs eternally in either direction. Old fluorescent lights buzz in the ceiling, adding a low hum to everything. Some flicker, desperately holding on to the last moments of their life like dying fireflies. Peeling mustard-yellow wallpaper covers the walls. White wood doors with frosted glass are equally spaced out on either side.

"What are we looking for?" Alex asked as we started down the hall, going to the right out of habit. I'm not sure if this place is truly infinite, or if it just eventually loops back on itself. The doors appear to be placed randomly; whatever logic drives them completely escapes my understanding.

I froze as I suddenly had the overwhelming sensation that I was being watched. Slowly, I turned to scan the hallway behind us. It was empty and barren as always, but the feeling only grew. My eyes widened as the lights behind us began to dim, fading until the space was pitch black. Soft mocking laughter seemed to drift on the air, teasing my ears like a faint wind. A dozen pairs of glowing white eyes stared out at me from the shadows. I glanced at Alex, but he took no notice of it. This wasn't real. Somnus's lien was eating at me once more. With a force of will, I shook myself and turned my back on my hallucinations.

"Honestly, I have no idea. I'm sort of hoping we will know it when we see it," I admitted, studying the door to my right without turning all the way to see if the nightmare was still following us. A thick black chain bound it to the wall, preventing it from opening all the way. The sign next to it read BENBEN (DEVOURED). A shudder ran down my spine as I remembered Aite emerging from a similar door whose chain had been broken.

"So we're just winging it?" Alex's voice was unreadable.

I paused, turning to stare at my best friend with an unamused expression on my face. "When was the last time we weren't winging it?"

"Two Tuesdays ago."

"Oh?"

"It was Taco Tuesday, and I made tacos, which you said were the best you'd ever had." I grunted, turning back to start walking. They had been pretty good, but I didn't want to give him satisfaction. Besides, I thought I had made my point.

The truth was that Horologium's tip gave us a direction, but it didn't really narrow down the search area. There were hundreds of worlds connected to the Between. Even after using this place for the last two years, I doubted I had even walked past all of them.

The Time Constellation might as well have told us to go search for a specific grain of sand and recommended we head to the beach. Sure, we weren't looking for it in the snow now, but that didn't make things much easier.

If only my brain didn't feel like it was in a fog.

"Horologium thought that they might be using a forgotten or falling world," I mused out loud, hoping to use some of Alex's brainpower as a replacement for my own. "As far as I know, the doors marked DEVOURED are gone-gone. Which means we can probably exclude those. We want something like the Faerie Lands that is just hanging on by a thread. Look for doors that are dingier than the others."

"If a new world gets devoured, who puts up the sign and chains? Is there some sort of maintenance staff that's responsible for keeping up with the place?" Alex eyed a section of wall where the paper was heavily peeling. "Because if there is, you should fire them."

"Me? Why would they work for me?" My protest sounded silly

while I carried the key to this little pocket universe. But it hadn't occurred to me that I might technically own the place. I had been thinking of it more like borrowing.

"Maybe there is," I admitted after another moment. "I haven't thought to do a complete catalog of all the doors before now. I don't even know if any of them have been devoured since we started coming here." It seemed so obvious now, but it was too late to go back.

"So we go off vibes." Alex sounded almost relieved.

"You watch the left, and I'll watch the right. If you see something, say something."

We walked in silence, each inspecting our half off the hall. I read many of the names without knowing them. I felt like my own education was a tiny piece of driftwood in an ocean of knowledge. ALFHEIM. HAWIKI. URDHVALOKA. XANADU (DEVOURED). ALATYR. Some names were familiar, but most were places I had never even heard of.

"This is harder than I thought it was going to be," I admitted after a few minutes. Any of them could be where the makers of Neodeath were hiding. We had only passed a dozen doors but might have already missed them, or maybe the world they lurked in was a hundred farther down.

"Don't give up," Alex reprimanded me, still walking. "We haven't even done a full pass yet. Might as well get the lay of the land."

"Maybe it's Kvenland," I offered, pointing at the sign with a sense of defeat. There were too many places. This clue was just a new way to waste our time.

"I think Muspelheim would be more likely," Alex offered, pointing at a couple doors down.

"You know what it is?" I asked in surprise. I had been kidding.

"Some sort of Norse place, I'm pretty sure." I eyed the door he had chosen. It certainly matched the archetype of what we were looking for. Its white paint was peeling, and spots of black mold were spreading across it. There was no motion through the glass, no hint of anything waiting on the other side.

"Sure," I said with a shrug. "Might as well start somewhere." I pulled Portunus's Key from my pocket and slid it into the doorknob. Its loud *click* echoed through the infinite hallway like a gunshot. Mentally, I tried to picture a secret place. Somewhere a person might go to trade things they should not. The magic of the Between was not rocket science—it too mostly worked off vibes, but it was all that I had.

"Here goes nothing." With a shove, I pushed the door open and poked my head into a new world.

Heat assaulted us. It emanated from everything. I staggered under its oppressive power. The air smelled of sulfur and char. Volcanic rock spread out before us, carved by rivers of what looked like flowing magma. Trees of blackened wood dotted the landscape, embers glowing in their boughs instead of leaves. In some ways, it looked more like Hell than Hell had.

"Great choice," I told Alex as we stared in horror through the open doorway.

"So we're saying no?"

"I mean..." I glanced around the burning expanse before us, looking for anything that might be a black market. All I could see was a crushing blackness that began like a fog, swallowing the land. There were no lights beyond it or stars in the sky. Just as the door had shown, the Nothing was devouring this place.

"It's certainly the right kind of world," I admitted slowly. "We could take a quick little peek just to fully write it off our list."

"Why not." Alex did not sound enthused.

"This. Was. Your. Idea," I hissed, taking my first step into the burning lands of the Norse. I didn't even know they had fire in their mythology. I thought it was all snow and ice. Maybe when your society comes from the coldest part of the planet, you dream of a place like this.

I stepped out of a wooden door hung on rusty hinges that the Between had hijacked for our purposes. Volcanic rock crunched under my boots. "Don't close that behind us," I told Alex, eyeing the door distrustfully. I didn't know how many more swings it had in it. Besides, we weren't going far.

Despite the distant roar of the magma and overall intensity of the place, Muspelheim seemed remarkably calm and quiet. It felt like it had gone to sleep. It wasn't dead—there is a difference. I could not say how I knew it was one and not the other, but I did.

I walked half a dozen paces from the door, aware that Alex followed in my wake, covering my rear. There was a hunger to this place, like the cave of a bear that has been hibernating but will soon wake. It seemed a little too on-the-nose for me.

"See anything?" I asked my more keen-eyed friend.

"Not really. It looks like the whole world is maybe a square mile or two before it falls into the dark."

I grunted, satisfied that we had seen all there was to see. "HELLO?" I shouted, my voice echoing off the sharp hills of black rock. "Is anyone here stealing souls?" The only response was my own voice coming back to us. Whatever slumbered here was not yet ready to wake.

"I really hate it when you do that," Alex grumbled.

"I get results." I turned back toward the entrance in time to see the whole world move. Behind the rock hovel that we entered from, a dark form shifted, rising from its slumber. I felt my jaw go slack in awe as the massive being sat up, towering above us like a building.

The massive man's flesh was coated in soot and ash. His beard was bright red, and his dark eyes glittered with malice as they settled on us.

"I know that look," Alex said, still staring at me, unaware of the thing that stirred behind him. "He's right behind me, isn't he?"

"Yup. Time to run." My voice was at least an octave higher than usual. Maybe two. I think it kept going up as the giant rose to its full height, towering above us. Calling him tall would be a disservice to the word. Giraffes are tall.

This thing was *gigantic.* Too late I remembered that among the key races in Norse mythology are giants.

My mouth worked soundlessly as I stared up hundreds of feet at the distant face of the Norse monster. A deafening hiss rang through the shrunken world as he drew a sword that was longer than most football fields. It burned with red fury to match the sun. My rifle hung limply in my hands, forgotten in my shock. Given his mass, our bullets would be less than bee stings to him.

The giant let out a roar that shook the world, startling Alex and me into motion, like a pair of foxes chased from their hiding spot. My feet pounded on the volcanic rock as I followed the Nephilim through the still-open door and back into the Between. I took some comfort in the fact that even the giant's pinkie finger was too big to follow us.

The world behind us thundered as the monster stomped in rage at our escape. I watched in awe as the entire building on his side exploded under a heavy foot, severing the connection between the worlds. The door was still there, but there was nothing on the other side now, just a wide expanse of familiar yellow wall. Slowly, I let it close, unsure if I would be able to open it again, or if we had just destroyed the last connection to that falling world.

"I've never seen a guy too tall to play in the NBA," was all my scattered brain could think to say.

"I'm pretty sure that was Surtr," Alex told me, as if that was supposed to mean something to me. I stared at him blankly until he remembered that my education is much worse than his.

"Norse fire giant guy who's supposed to kill one of the gods during Ragnarök and then set the world on fire."

"He does seem to match that description," I replied in an acerbic tone. "You remember his name but you forgot where he lives?"

"Whoops." Alex had the good grace to look chagrined as he shrugged.

"I don't suppose he's supposed to be asleep until the big apocalypse, is he?"

Alex's eyes narrowed in thought. "I don't remember."

"Well, I'm sure that waking him up will have no negative consequences." We traded a long, depressed look. The two of us had been doing this for too long to fall for that one. I just hoped that Surtr was someone else's problem and not a cleverly concealed trap that had been personally laid for me.

"Okay, I'm changing my vote to one against our vibes strategy. Someone could get hurt," I announced. Alex snorted but didn't protest. It's hard to argue with logic like that. Slowly, we resumed our walk, eyeing the doors on either side with more reluctance.

The curiosity that normally burned in me, the kind that got cats killed all the time, had gone out. I had no idea what LONGMEN was, but I had absolutely no desire to open its door and find out for myself.

I felt useless, like I had a bunch of tools that I wasn't qualified to use. What was the point of being entrusted with all these things if you couldn't use them to save people? If Orion were here, he would know what to do. Instead, Alex and I could only fumble along until we made things worse or got killed.

"Do your Reaper powers work here?" my friend asked, interrupting my pity party.

"Yes, why?" I was instantly alert, twisting to look over my shoulder, hands curling, prepared to hold my scythe. Had something followed us out of Muspel-what's-it? Just because it had held a giant didn't mean there weren't smaller things in there too. The waking terrors that plagued my sleep-deprived mind still followed me, keeping me on edge.

"Well, I'm just wondering if your supercool ability to sense this counterfeit death might give us a hint on which door to go through."

I was so shocked at my own stupidity that I froze in my tracks. "Why didn't I think of that?" I closed my eyes against the harsh yellow fluorescent light. I wasn't in danger of falling asleep, but even so the darkness felt welcoming, like a much-needed hug. I stayed there, soaking up the comfort, until I felt strong enough to continue.

"Are you okay, bro?" Alex's eyebrows were condensed into a sharp V of concern.

"Nope." I shook my head, taking a step forward to break my line of sight to his expression. "It's probably going to get worse too. So if you could keep thinking for me, that would be great."

"I already do every day."

"I'm too tired to contest that obvious lie. Now be quiet, and let's see if Mr. Grim Reaper paid for the deluxe version of this bad boy." I let out a long exhale, closing my eyes once more as I sank into a different dark.

The cold power of Death coursed through my veins like a shock of ice water. Energy flooded through me, and I fought the urge to laugh in delight. If sleep is the small death, the younger, weaker brother, then who was it to tell me I was tired? Reapers do not sleep. Nominally that is because they are dead, but maybe there was more to it. Our boss was bigger than the lord of dreams.

I shook myself free of the cold's comforting embrace and pushed my awareness outside me, letting it sweep down the hallway in both directions. I saw the world in shades of gray. There were no living things here other than Alex and me—nothing for it to sense. But to my surprise, the doors were not able to hold everything back. Death could not be contained by them, and its presence leaked through the cracks like a dark light.

Empty, devoured words were gray, as uninteresting to Death as they were to us. Other places, ones that were still rich and vibrant, were bold and black. But that was not what I was looking for either. I took a deep breath, pushing my senses even further, looking for the same rot I'd found in Los Angeles. I could feel the strain building, but I forced myself to keep going, digging deeper.

Just when I began to despair, I caught a whiff of something in the distance. A door that burned with an oily aura. I felt the sickness rising inside of me as I stared at that twisted, counterfeit presence that leaked through the cracks into the Between.

"I have something," I said with a gasp, letting go of Death's hand and blinking against the sudden harsh light from the fluorescent bulbs above. "Farther ahead."

"Well then, let's go that way," Alex murmured with a toss of his head. I nodded, still trying to catch my breath from pushing myself so hard. Death was powerful but not kind to a living body.

Silently we worked our way down the hall, walking past more sealed worlds. I ignored them, focused instead on the horizon, trying to gauge how far we had gone. My mind felt clear again, as if Sleep's curse had been banished by his older brother for a time.

"Whoa." Alex's voice stopped me in my tracks. I turned to see what he had found, only to be presented with a blank section of wall. The place where the door should have been was empty; even the frame was missing. There was only a bare patch of yellow wall. A sign hung in the space that read: TARTARUS (UNAVAILABLE).

For a moment the two of us stared at that closed passage, no doubt thinking the same thing. Our master, mentor, and friend was on that side of the wall. In physical miles, we were no closer to him than we had been before, and yet the distance suddenly felt very small. If only we had sledgehammers, maybe we could carve our way to him.

If the door was here, no power on earth could stop us from barreling through it. But the prison world was cut off from the rest of

Reality in its strange cycle. Horologium had promised that he would help us cross the path, and we would have to wait until then.

"Soon," I promised the blank wall, turning away with a heavy heart. "We'll be back." Alex didn't move for a few more seconds, staring silently at the empty space. I left him with his own thoughts. As much as we were like brothers, his bloodline gave him his own path to walk in terms of his relationship with Orion.

I pressed forward, looking for the door that stank of Neodeath. We passed MANU, ALTJIRA, ATLANTIS (DEVOURED), and MEROPIS. Reluctantly, I slipped back into Death's grasp, sending my senses sweeping before me.

We were close—our target waited half a dozen doors ahead of us. I banished my Reaper powers back into their dark corner of my mind and slipped forward, feeling my tension rise. Excitement thrummed through me as I stalked toward the closed door.

It was unremarkable. A dingy white door identical to the entrance to where Surtr had slept. The sign that hung on it read LAND OF DARKNESS, which only heightened the thrill in my bones.

"Well, that's a bit on-the-nose," Alex murmured, eyeing the placard with distrust.

"Know anything about it?"

"Never heard of it." His suspicious expression deepened. "That sort of makes me *more* nervous. We could be walking into anything."

"That's never stopped us before," I pointed out, jerking my thumb over my shoulder at the door we'd left behind.

"Even Evangeline was reluctant to follow them here," he reminded me. "She said they were dangerous."

"Isn't there a poem about men 'rushing in where angels fear to tread'?" I joked, cracking my neck to relieve some of the tension that I could feel rising. "Sounds like a job for mortals to me. What were they, heroes or something?"

Alex didn't answer right away. My hand settled on the knob as I guided the key into the lock. I took a deep sigh and pushed, swinging the door open into the Land of Darkness.

"Fools. He said they were fools."

CHAPTER TWENTY-ONE

THE FIRST THING I noticed about the Land of Darkness was that it was…aptly named. An oppressive shadow hung over everything like black ink. This ink wasn't cold and hungry like the Reality-eating emptiness of the Nothing. It was a different thing, a smaller sibling to it.

"Trippy," Alex remarked as we stepped out of the doorway and into the night. Even the ground was hidden. Cobbled streets of white stone seemed to float before us, but it was only because the surface was so dark that it blended in with the air. I have walked through a dozen worlds and the spaces between them, yet this was one of the strangest things I had ever seen.

Despite the cave-like feel of this place, it was vibrant and packed.

Bright lampposts shone, carving out tiny spaces in the oppressive dark. People streamed by, moving with purpose, dressed in all kinds of colors. I saw a man in a toga and a woman in a burka. This seemed to be a melting pot, a place where those who had needs came.

We stepped out the door of a low, single-story building and into the crowd of what seemed to be some sort of market or bazaar. Small huts and tents dotted the area, thrown up haphazardly, with no real sense of order.

I turned in a slow circle, taking in the breadth of this place. Several hundred people moved through my line of sight, browsing the wares. How long had this place existed? Humans and supernaturals glanced at us curiously as they passed us, but no one seemed distressed by our presence. This was a market, and customers had to come from somewhere. I found myself wondering how many different portals led to this place.

Despite my earlier apprehension, I felt my fear lifting from my shoulders. This was far less dangerous than I had been expecting. Evangeline had warned us against following the Neodeath makers into their lair, but this was clearly not it. This was a communal area. But perhaps it would give us some insight into where to follow them next.

"Okay," I muttered at Alex as we took in our new surroundings. "Now what?"

"I guess we shop." His voice had a hint of the same stunned emotion that I was feeling.

"With what money?" I grumbled, turning to follow the flow of people down the cobbled path in the dark. A few denizens eyed our weapons warily, but most of the folks here were armed. This didn't feel like a tame place. It reminded me of a market in the Wild West, on the edge of civilization.

Alex and I strolled down a row of stalls that sold a random mishmash of things. I couldn't discern any sense of organization or theme.

It was overwhelming, but despite that, I found myself fascinated by the things that were available.

"Come, mortal," hissed a woman shrouded in a long black cloak. "Feel the finest silks from worlds long gone." She brushed her clawed hand along a row of fabrics, as if to entice me to try them. They came in bright colors and patterns that were not familiar to me.

"My prices are very affordable," she assured me. "I promise not to bleed you dry."

"Vampire-killing kits! Get your vampire-killing kits!" a short, squat man dressed in armor thundered from across the path. I glanced over my shoulder to see him glaring daggers at the woman with the fabrics. She hissed at him but did not speak further. I shuddered, moving past her cloth without pausing.

"You sense any of the weird stuff?" Alex murmured as we navigated the crowded street. No one seemed to be listening to us, but too many of these creatures could hear far too well.

"I haven't tried yet," I admitted softly. I was hesitant to reach for Death's power here. What if someone else around me could feel me using it? I did not want to reveal myself too early. "Let's keep looking."

"Sure, I got nothing else to do," Alex replied easily. We turned at a crossroads, moving parallel down another stretch of stalls.

"Fancy a potion, young masters?" a crone cackled in a thick Russian accent as we passed. A cauldron before her boiled with a purple liquid. "Love. Hate. Death. All of these are within your grasp." I swallowed against a lump in my throat, making sure not to make eye contact with her.

Magic gives me the creeps. That might sound stupid given who I hang out with and what I do, but there's a difference. Orion's prowess can be explained by science and DNA. An old woman making something to break the rules of the world doesn't sit right with me.

"This is insane," I said to Alex, scanning the sea of stalls that we still had not been to. "How long has this been here?"

"Longer than you or me, I suspect," my friend said grimly, nodding his head to where a bleached and faded skull rested on the ground next to one of the ever-present lampposts burning brightly. A few longer leg and arm bones were scattered around it, suggesting that it had been there for quite some time.

"Yeesh." I made a disgusted face at the remains, stepping past them as quickly as I had the witch. Maybe we should have listened to Evangeline.

We passed another dozen stalls that sold strange things. One man offered custom-built siege engines for any occasion. He had a pair of small catapults set up that would fire flour into the air, staining the black ground around him white, like a small patch of winter.

Another man sold swords, but none of them seemed to be on fire, so I wasn't that impressed. Alex stopped to inspect a wicked-looking knife set with a dark stone in its hilt, and I hovered over his shoulder, idly scanning the crowd.

That's when I saw her.

I hissed in surprise, turning away sharply to look down at the blade in my friend's hand. His head snapped toward me, but I motioned for him to keep his attention down at the weapon.

"Damn. Damn. Double damn." I felt a spike of panic bloom in my chest.

"What?" Alex hissed, trying to scan the market out of the corner of his eyes. "What spooked you?"

"Wait," I growled, not willing to answer while she was this close to us. Despite my fear, I couldn't stop myself from lifting my head slightly to watch her. She was a taller woman, with dark skin and white hair that fell to her shoulders.

I'd never seen her before, but I knew a demon when I saw one. The solid-black eyes were a dead giveaway. She moved with purpose through the crowd, which parted for her as if people could just sense that it was in their best interest to get out of her way.

"Ten o'clock," I murmured to Alex when she had moved a little past us. My friend slowly raised his head, taking a surreptitious glance as he placed the knife back in its holder.

"Dark Abyss," he swore when he spotted the infernal. "That can't be a coincidence."

I nodded, thinking along the same lines.

What were the odds that we'd met an angel investigating the origins of Neodeath only to immediately encounter a demon hovering around the same thing? Pretty good actually. I got the impression that the two sides liked to be all up in each other's business, like estranged siblings that weren't ready to go fully no-contact.

What else could she be doing here? What could this place have that someone like her would need that she couldn't get elsewhere? It was obvious that this was some sort of black market. But it's not like Hell had rules and regulations. Which meant she sought something that could only be found here. My stomach curdled at the thought. This wouldn't be the first time Hell tried to steal souls.

"We're going to follow her, right?" Alex asked, taking a step in the direction that the demon went.

"How could we not?" I replied with a reluctant sigh. The last thing I wanted was get to know more demons on a personal level. But she was here, and people's souls were being stolen. So I didn't really have much of a choice, did I?

My heart pounded in my chest as we strolled in the demon's wake, following her progress through the crowd with ease. The ripple her passage created was still stitching itself back together as we cruised behind her.

Alex peeled off to inspect the wares of a stall on our left, trying to blend into the crowd. I copied his idea on the right, forcing myself to meander, hiding my interest in the demon's movements. But she did not turn to the left or right, instead continuing her forward progress at a calm, unhurried pace.

"Excuse me, sir." A grave voice interrupted my study of a set of silver spoons, each engraved with a different Celtic rune. Startled, I turned to face a squad of four security guards standing behind me, looking at both of us. They looked human; any hint of Nephilim blood they might have was so faint that its influence was not immediately apparent.

They wore gray body armor over their matching fatigues. Each had a pistol on their hip. None had drawn their weapons, but their hands rode the grips in an assertive manner. The other people around us barely reacted, giving us a wider berth as they streamed by.

"Can I help you?" I asked, my mouth suddenly running dry. *Don't make a scene,* I told myself. *Maybe she won't turn around, won't see this.*

"You two need to come with us," the dark-skinned leader said in the same serious tone, nodding his head at where Alex lurked on the other side of the path. He sounded like a law enforcement professional or former soldier. From the way he and his team carried themselves, I had no doubt that his services were expensive.

They eyed the weapons strapped over our shoulders with a mild disinterest, not intimidated by the fact that we were armed. It made my skin crawl to feel their casual gazes tracking our movement. I knew that the lazy appearances were deceptive. If either of us reached for one of our guns, this street would explode into violence.

"Oh, uh, why?" I was desperately trying to stall for time, to let the demon get farther away before we caused a scene. Mentally, I reached for the warmth of Willow lurking in the back of my mind. The Faerie spirit would be more useful in this situation.

"Boss wants to see you," he responded flatly. "He's being polite, but he doesn't have to be."

"Who's the boss?" The four guards only stared at me flatly, hands still on their guns. Alex and I traded unhappy glances. After a moment, he shrugged, and I copied his motion. Might as well find out.

"Sure thing, let's go see the boss."

The guards moved to surround us like the corners of a box, closing us in as they marched us through the inky blackness of the Land of Darkness. We garnered more attention now that we were being escorted, but it remained mild. People here did not seem to be on edge, as if they knew that danger was being held at bay. Probably by the men carrying all the weapons.

"How long is it going to take us to get there?" I asked the guard who had done all the talking. "I need to use the little mortal's room."

"Not far, sir," he replied calmly, ignoring my banter. His eyes were professional and cool, watching everything around him without quite glaring. I felt my estimation of his team's experience rise. These people knew what they were doing.

We threaded our way over the cobblestone paths, moving past more stalls. Many of the things in the bizarre bazaar looked entirely normal. One guy was selling flat-screen televisions. One of them was playing a scene from *Braveheart*, which felt a little on-the-nose to me.

"Where is he getting electricity from?" I remarked to Alex. So far none of the other worlds I had visited had AC or DC power. Shoutout to Benjamin Franklin and Nikola Tesla. Humans might not live forever, but at least we had air-conditioning. On second thought, I guess I could see how a TV and some sort of Blu-ray player might seem like magic to someone who had never been to earth.

"Portable generator," one of the guards behind me answered with a cheerful tone. "They bring diesel and everything. One of the weirdest things I've ever seen in this place. Right next to the guy selling magic crystals that actually work." One of the other guards chuckled, just as amused by the strange world she found herself in.

Their friendliness relaxed me a little. I glanced at the leader, but he didn't reprimand them for speaking. They were attentive but not on edge. Maybe I wasn't being marched off to get shot in a dark alley.

"It's a lot to take in," I agreed amiably. "Pretty sure I saw a vampire a couple streets back."

"Ah, you met Lama," the friendly one said with a knowing warmth. "Friendly advice? Don't go out drinking with her. She means something different." The female guard laughed again. I risked a glance over my shoulder to give them both a warm smile. The chatty guy was a head shorter than me, with close-cut blond hair and a relaxed smile. The girl was the same height, with brown hair pulled back into a tight ponytail.

"Thanks for the tip. I bet you guys have a lot more. This is a weird place."

"Eh, it's not that different," Chatty said. "After about six months you don't even miss—"

"We're here," the leader interrupted, his voice taking a bit of an edge for the first time. I glanced at him out of the corner of my eye, but his face betrayed no emotion.

We emerged from the chaos of the stalls and tents to a little clearing. A white, concrete building rose out of the black ground. It was windowless but blazed with artificial light that had to be running more of those imported generators.

I felt my suspicion spiking as I studied it. It stuck out like a sore thumb, with all the hallmarks of earth design about it—equal parts fortress and airplane hangar. Steel beams reinforced its walls, making it a little more imposing.

Our escort took us to the large metal door that slid to the side, gliding on rails as we approached. Another pair of security guards waited just inside, holding assault rifles and more serious expressions. I felt Alex shift next to me as he noticed the increased tension inside the compound.

Maybe they only sent the friendly guards out to interact with the population. My mind's hand hovered just shy of where Willow's power burned brightly, like a gunslinger prepared to draw at any moment. If this was an ambush, I was going to go down shooting.

The heavy door slid shut behind us, humming softly as its electric gears turned. Bright LED lights were set in the ceiling, casting down pure white, banishing any trace of the shadows of the world.

I blinked against the sudden glare, taking in my surroundings as my eyes adjusted. The interior of the compound was surprisingly well decorated. I had expected something more spartan and martial—a holding cell that was easy to hose down.

Instead, we were in a waiting room that felt more like a den. A thick brown carpet covered the floor; I could feel its plushness under the soles of my boots. A pair of potted trees rested in the far corner of the main room, their lives green and bright.

"This way," the leader said, nodding down a long hallway. He led us past mahogany-paneled walls that made me feel like we were heading to someone's study, not a boss's office. The other guards stayed back at the door.

"Enter," a strong voice called when our escort knocked. The guard popped the door open and stuck his head through, blocking our sight.

"We have the two men you asked to see, sir," I could just faintly hear him say.

"Send them in."

"Sir." The leader withdrew his head and pulled the door open all the way, nodding at me to enter. "The boss will see you now."

"Do you want us to leave our guns outside?" I couldn't stop myself from asking what felt like an obvious question, even though it made me feel like a student reminding the teacher they forgot to assign homework. It was just too weird. I couldn't believe they were going to let us just walk into the head honcho's office carrying assault rifles.

“Shouldn’t be a problem.” The guard gave me a smile that had a little bit of teeth in it, as if he knew the exact calculus that was running through my head. What exactly was waiting for us beyond this door?

My heart rate spiked as I slipped past him and into the office. It too was heavily paneled with dark wood. Packed shelves full of old books ran across all three walls, making it feel more like a library.

A man sat behind a matching desk. He looked up at our approach, something dangerous glinting in his cold blue eyes. He was a little older than I am, a man just beginning to leave the prime of his life. His rich blond hair was starting to go white at the temples.

His arms were muscular, straining the rolled-up sleeves of his white button-down. A discarded suit jacket was hung over the back of his chair, leaving a pair of shoulder holsters visible. His horn-rimmed glasses glinted under the lights as he studied us.

“Matthew Carver.” He greeted me warmly, gesturing for us to sit in the plush leather chairs waiting for us. “You’ve certainly seen better days. I hardly expected to see you so soon. But showing up uninvited does seem to be your gift, doesn’t it?”

Uh-oh.

CHAPTER TWENTY-TWO

OH STOP," I said, sliding into one of the chairs as Alex sat next to me. "You're going to make me blush."

"I think you will be fine." The man smiled thinly, his blue eyes cutting me like knives. "If it were possible for someone to die of shame, you would have done so by now."

"Did I do something to you?" I blurted, unable to contain myself. "I don't usually make a great first impression, but this seems really focused. Usually it takes a couple of meetings to get someone to hate me this much."

"Trust me, it doesn't get better," Alex offered from beside me. I shot my friend a glare that said *NOT HELPING* in all capitals. He shrugged. He knew that already.

"No, Matthew, we have never met." The man leaned back in his chair, tapping the clicker of his pen idly on the surface of the desk as he studied me. "But I am more than familiar with your...exploits."

"Okay, well, I don't know what you've heard—" I began, feeling incredibly off kilter. This was somehow bothering me more than when Raguel had known my name. I don't think I like being *known.* I may have grown up in LA, but I have no interest in fame. I've seen enough of its price up close.

"Like I said, I am more than familiar," he cut in smoothly. "I have no interest in the *why* of your exploits. I have only one question for you, and that is, *What are you doing here?*" His voice took on an edge, and he fixed me with a sharp stare.

I was missing something.

Probably many things. I am not known for my efficiency or my accuracy, just my unquenchable stubbornness. He clicked his pen another half a dozen times as he waited for my answer. That was a tell of some sort. The man who ran this Land of Darkness was on edge at our presence. But why? There was a lot about me not to like. I was a member of the technically defunct Hunt. I was a Reaper. But perhaps most important, I was an enemy of Hell, and there was at least one demon just wandering around the place. My eyes narrowed as I studied him, trying to guess which of my many messes he was a part of.

I still couldn't shake the sense that I was missing something. I needed more information, and the only way I was going to get it was if I got him talking. Fortunately, that might be the one thing I *am* good at.

"I'm sorry," I said pressing a hand to my chest in demure apology. "We seem to be getting off on the wrong foot. You already know I am Matt. This is Alex, in case you're not fully up to date on my dossier." The man's cold blue eyes flickered toward my friend for a fraction of a second, but he said nothing. It was hard to read the look in them behind the lenses of his horn-rimmed glasses.

"This is usually the part where people say their own name, and then we all know each other and can communicate well," I prompted after an uncomfortable silence.

"You may call me the Overseer. I am the founder of this marketplace," he said at last, still not shifting in his seat. His pen clicked a few more times, a sign of his latent irritation. My discomfort only grew. Maybe I had met this man before. I racked my brain trying to find the moment. But elusive thoughts are like stray cats. The harder I chased it, the more it fled.

"Okay, Mr. Seer, it's lovely to meet you." I powered forward, forcing a false smile onto my face. This was like pulling teeth from a vampire. Painful and hard not to get bit. "Does that mean you're responsible for this whole…area?" I gestured with one of my hands in an all-encompassing manner.

"I am."

"Well, this is our first time visiting, but it seems lovely. I just love a good sale. You can ask Alex. We go to flea markets all the time. It's like every Saturday morning; I knock on his door—we're roommates by way—I knock on his door and am just like, 'Let's go to Melrose!', and he's grumpy, but we go. So you can only imagine how excited I was to learn about a place like this." The Overseer's expression only grew more dour as he listened, as if he were a bull and every word was a red cloak being waved in front of him. The pen clicked a few more times. I resisted the urge to smile at his frustration.

"Why. Are. You. Here?" He repeated his question slowly, a dangerous edge in his tone that had not been there before.

"I don't understand the question." I exchanged a dramatic, confused look with Alex. "Why is anyone here? To barter and exchange currency for goods and services. That is what a market is for, is it not?"

"What are you here to buy?"

"Oh, you know, this and that."

"I'm afraid, Mr. Carver, that you two did not enter Abaddon Market by any of the approved security checkpoints. Which means that you are not here as *Guests.*" There was an implied threat in the last word. In the supernatural world, being a Guest offers a sort of inalienable right of safety. If you brought someone into your house, they were a part of your family until they left. Even monsters like Doyle wouldn't dare to harm a Guest.

It also explained why everyone had been so relaxed while they wandered around the market. If entering the Land of Darkness required you to become a Guest, it basically guaranteed that no one would dare hurt you. Or if they did, the repercussions would be immense.

It was actually kind of brilliant, now that I thought about it. I wondered if they charged a membership fee to become a Guest, like a cover charge to access the market. Given how many people were coming through, that would certainly be a profitable enterprise. Reminded me of some supermarkets back home.

"Oh," I replied, looking embarrassed. "I am so sorry. I didn't know there were formal entrances. We must have stumbled across one of the side doors. I promise we didn't mean to come sneaking in. It's our first time at…Abaddon Market." My eyes narrowed as I tried the "official" name on for size.

"We're happy to become Guests, if that will make everyone feel safer." I chuckled, as if relieved that we had uncovered the source of tension. "We're not here to cause trouble."

"Somehow I doubt that," the Overseer remarked dryly, tilting his head to study me further. The lights flashed off his horn-rimmed glasses, blinding me for a second. After a moment of thought, he sat up abruptly, pulling a sheet of paper in front of him and setting his pen to it.

"We might as well get you on the roster," he said with a sigh. "I have your names and address." I tried not to shiver at that casual declaration. Whatever organization ran this place clearly had fingers in many pies.

"However, I will need to know," he murmured, pen scratching as he filled out the form, "the nature of the goods that you are looking for. We have different vetting processes for different types of purchases."

"Really?" I blinked in surprise. "I sort of assumed the point of this place was to have as little...ah, regulation as possible."

"We certainly encourage a free economy," the Overseer said with another thin-lipped smile that did not reach his eyes. "But we have partners who put themselves at significant risk to provide valuables of a certain caliber. In consideration to them, we provide a thorough background check on anyone trying to acquire more unique items."

"You're a fence," Alex grunted in understanding.

"Auctioneer," the Overseer corrected gently, still wearing his fake grin. "Now, if you would be so good as to give me the categories you are interested in?" I paused for a moment, trying to organize my thoughts. Obviously, I had to lie. Neodeath wasn't something you could just walk up to the concierge and ask about. Especially not if this guy knew my connection to Kane and real Death.

"Norse," I said as an idea sprang into my mind. "We're looking for some Norse artifacts." I could feel Alex's confused gaze from my side, but I ignored him, matching the insincere smile of our host with my own mask.

"What kind of Norse artifacts?"

I hesitated, and the corners of his lips twitched as if he was pleased by my discomfort. I had already avoided his question too much. I knew I had to give him something to sink his teeth into.

"I'm in the market for an apple of Iðunn. I heard this might be the place to find one." To my surprise, both the Overseer's eyebrows shot up in genuine shock. He studied me for a moment, as if seeing me for the first time. Satisfied by whatever he found, he leaned back down to the page and spoke as he wrote.

"Immortality supplements." I opened my mouth to protest, but Alex shook his head. I closed it, sighing inwardly. Sure. Close enough, I guessed.

"There, that's done," the Overseer said when he'd completed the paperwork. He leaned back in his chair with a smug look on his face. "I'm glad we could resolve this issue without any excessive unpleasantness."

"Oh yeah," I agreed enthusiastically, as if I was just as relieved. "We didn't mean to cause any trouble. Just on the hunt for something rare."

"Of course." He didn't sound liked he meant it. "I will just need your signature on this page." He slid the paper and pen toward us. "It creates your Abaddon One account and will enter you into our database. Since you're already inside the market, it will also count as the beginning of your Guest rights. They will last until you leave. Next time, you will need to come through one of our security checkpoints, where your ID card will be waiting for you, and you can renew your Guest status."

"Sure…" I replied slowly, a little overwhelmed at the amount of information that was being thrown at me. I scanned the document, making sure that it more or less looked like what he said it was. I have a little bit of PTSD when it comes to signing things.

The top line read ABADDON MARKET NEW USER SIGN-UP FORM, which made me feel a lot better. Well, actually it made me feel weird. But it did reassure me that I wasn't accidentally signing my soul away to a new, third party.

I scribbled my name at the bottom before passing it to Alex, who repeated the process. Despite the oddity of the entire thing, I felt some stress lifting off my shoulders as we completed the process. We were Guests now, which meant people weren't allowed to just shoot us at will.

"Thank you for your cooperation," the Overseer said, accepting the paper back from us and tucking it away in his desk. "Welcome to Abaddon Market, Reality's best source of lost and rare antiquities."

"That's it?" I asked in surprise. "We can just go shop again?" I jerked a thumb over my shoulder pointing out of the guard station.

"Please do." The Overseer's mouth stretched into a wide, real smile—his first since we'd arrived. "This place is expensive to maintain."

"That was weird," Alex murmured to me as the electric door of the concrete fortress slid shut behind us. The guards who'd collected us were nowhere to be seen, but the two on duty had watched us with solemn expressions as we left.

"Beyond weird." I agreed, sticking my hands in my pockets and scanning the market ahead of us. The demon would be long gone now. I felt my irritation grow at losing sight of her.

"Did he look familiar to you?" I asked, turning to stare at him. "The whole time I just got this feeling that I had seen him before. I don't know how to explain it."

"I see why you say that," Alex replied thoughtfully, his own blue eyes narrowed in thought. "Maybe he just has one of those faces." I thought about that for a second, trying it on as an answer to my problem. It didn't fit.

"Nah," I said, picking a random cobbled path and beginning to walk out into the darkness. "Nothing we do is ever that easy."

CHAPTER TWENTY-THREE

SURELY WE'RE NOT going to find the You-Know-What just lying out in the open," Alex complained after we had browsed what felt like a hundred stalls. I had seen everything for sale, from holy relics the pope would kill to get his hands on, to cursed objects pulled from realms that no longer existed. It felt surreal to be in this black world that was made of shadows instead of light. People go to dark alleys to make their illegal deals in bad fiction. This was another level.

"I know," I admitted reluctantly. "It's probably time to start getting a little more advanced." For some reason, I was still hesitant to call upon Kane's powers here. The name Abaddon Market had me walking on pins and needles. Land of Darkness wasn't very welcoming either.

It felt like danger was lurking around every corner, and I was hesitant to do something to spring the trap.

"What's the worst that could happen?" Alex asked. We exchanged amused glances before both laughing. Historically speaking, the worst that could happen was pretty freaking bad. At least when it decided to happen to us.

"It just feels like toeing the line," I said, finally zeroing in on the source of my current discomfort about using my ability. "Not exactly very Guestlike to bring Death into someone's home."

"I see that. But given what we know they are selling here, Death is probably also invited. Or at least the cheap knockoff version. If you can buy a fake, why would the original not be allowed?"

"Because then everyone can tell which one is the counterfeit really easily?"

"I see your point."

"Regardless, I don't think we have much of a choice." I sighed, jamming my hands back into my jacket pockets. "We've got a job to do. At a certain point, we can't let being polite stop us from rescuing Maria."

"Rescuing?" Alex's eyebrow arched in surprise. "You know she's still going to be dead when this is over, right?"

"That's not the kind of rescue I meant," I told him grimly. "Wherever her soul was siphoned to is not where she wanted to go. If we can get her to where she belongs, that would be better than nothing. I cannot offer salvation, but I can try to make sure the mail gets delivered to the right address."

"A fair point."

We fell silent as we stopped to peruse a stall full of skulls—human and otherwise. One was made of black bones radiating a dark power that made me feel sick to my stomach.

"Do you seek the power of the Elders, mortal?" a wizened old woman asked me, noticing me staring at the inhuman death's-head.

"With this, you can call them to your aid."

"No thank you," I told her, taking a step back and looking at it with wide eyes. "I'm trying to cut back."

"Stop stalling," Alex scolded me when we streamed back into the flow of traffic. "I'm getting hungry, and I don't think I want to eat anything they make here."

"I'm with you on that one." I licked my lips, trying to calm my nerves. He was right. I was hesitating, and I just needed to throw myself off the cliff. We were never going to find what we were looking for otherwise.

Slowly, I eased past the burning presence of Willow in my mind to grab the inky black of Death. Made of true night, it was even darker than the Land of Shadows. I did not summon my scythe, but instead slid into the power's cold embrace, letting it fill my senses.

The world shifted into a series of gray tones, like an old black-and-white movie. I let out a long breath, sweeping my consciousness out into the wide expanse of the Land of Darkness. There was no Death here, I noticed quickly.

There also seemed to be no life here other than the people who had come to shop. I sensed no ants crawling along the dark ground. No flies in the air. It was a sterile, empty place. It felt like the rest of us were intruding on a quiet rest.

Part of me wondered if that was a deliberate choice. Lazarus had once taken me to the ruins of Elysium because Death and his Reapers were not present there. It had been a way to try to hide from Kane's eyes as they plotted to send me to invade the Veil. Maybe whoever ran this place had a similar plan in mind.

Unlike when I scoured LA with these senses, I was not overwhelmed by the sensation of creatures dying all around me. But that only meant that the Neodeath had nothing to hide among, so it burned like a beacon.

There was so much of it. Its dark, oily energy was overwhelming. I felt my stomach twist as a wave of nausea swept over me. The warehouse we had destroyed in Long Beach had only held trace amounts compared with the stockpile that was hidden here.

"That way," I gasped, releasing my grip on Death's power and extending a finger in the direction I had sensed it. "It's not far."

Alex didn't say anything, just nodded as we set off. A shared tension spread between the two of us. A familiar bond that comes from having gone into too many dangerous situations together. We didn't need to talk; we each knew exactly what the other was going to do.

Confident in the direction we were going, I navigated us through the white-stone streets, marked in sharp relief against the inky ground. Merchants called at us as we moved past, hawking their wares, but their words were a blur. I was an arrow flying toward my target, and nothing could distract me from my purpose.

"Is that it?" Alex asked, speaking for the first time as we drew to an abrupt halt. Another long, low building made of concrete reared out of the darkness. Like the one that the Overseer worked from, it was part fortress, part warehouse.

A dozen guards in the same gray body armor stood guard around the facility, armed and alert. A chain-link fence ran around the perimeter, making the only avenue of approach right under a squad of four.

"Oh, definitely," I said, studying it for a long moment. Something tugged at my memory, another hint of that familiar feeling, but I ignored it. It would come to me later. "Let's see how friendly they are."

Alex and I strolled up to the checkpoint, rifles slung over our shoulders. I could feel the eyes of the guards on us as we walked across the flat, open land. I try not to be a betting man, but I would have put down a decent chunk of money that there was a sniper hidden somewhere with us in their scopes. There's a certain kind of itch that you only feel when someone's observing you through a magnifying lens.

"This area is off limits, sir," one of the guards told me. His voice was flat but amicable, just a man doing his job without any rancor. Like the ones who had pulled us into our meeting, they appeared to be vanilla mortals. I saw no sign of pointed ears or inhuman eyes.

"Sorry," I apologized, giving him a warm smile. "First time, so just wandering around, getting the lay of the land. What is it?"

"Escrow, sir." The man surprised me with a real response. "Vendors and clients can store things here to guarantee their safety until delivery or sale is completed."

"Oh, well, that's rather useful," I said, exchanging a glance with Alex. The Neodeath that was in there was on its way out into the world. If we were going to stop it, we'd need to figure out where it was going and who sold it.

"If we wanted to make a purchase that was similarly protected, what's the process?" Alex asked the man, doing his best to look like a serious collector.

"You'd negotiate it with the vendor, who would have the channel to request our oversight." The guard smiled easily. I could feel him and the men around him beginning to relax now that we were showing no signs of hostility. Answering our questions and sending us on our way was a much easier job than getting into a fight with two armed men.

"And we'd have access to the facility ourselves to be able to do final inspections?" I tried to copy Alex's level of professionalism.

"Yes, sir, that would all be detailed in the agreement. There is a standard contingency process to make sure you're satisfied before the finances are all transferred."

"Lovely," I murmured to thin air, reluctantly impressed at how well this institution was run. It was if someone had taken the peak of human innovation and efficiency and brought it to the supernatural world. Kane would be delighted.

I smiled as brightly as I could at the guards before giving them a wave and turning away, heading back toward the sea of tents. Alex followed at my shoulder, a concerned expression on his face.

"Why do you look like you're about to do something stupid?" he asked.

"Probably because I am. Sounds like we gotta buy something super expensive, doesn't it?" But how? The damn lizards had embezzled all my funds. The IRS was already after me for a cool seven million. I didn't exactly have deep coffers at the moment.

"That seems like an Impossible Task all on itself."

"It won't be easy," I admitted reluctantly. "But I'm not sure how else we might get in there. We can't exactly just break in. We're Guests, and that would be breaking some rules that I don't think we're ready to."

"Agreed." Alex shivered. He's less mortal than I am, which means things like that have their hooks deeper into his bones. I didn't think anything would happen to me on a *metaphorical* level if I broke the rules of Guestdom. I'd just die when the big scary things no longer had to play by the rules.

"Even if we put something in escrow and they let us into the warehouse, then what? It's not like we can steal the Neodeath without the same problem."

"But we'll get a chance to see what's going on in there. Right now, we don't really know who is making it or who is buying it."

"Outside of Bellerophon and Beatrice being involved."

"Well, yes, but that doesn't tell us who they're working for. If the Neodeath is moving through Abaddon Market, it might be our only chance to figure out where it's going."

"You're hoping we'll see a delivery address on the boxes?" Alex's voice was incredulous. "Maybe they'll be nice enough to write down their name too."

"I don't know, man." I let my shoulders slump. "I'm not a real private eye, just pretending to be one. It's right there." I turned to look over my shoulder at the fortress warehouse in the distance. "But we have no way to get at it."

"Unless..." Alex's voice trailed off, making me look up. My friend's blue eyes were narrowed, focused on something in the distance. "Unless we find another way."

"What are you thinking?" I tried to follow his gaze to where he was looking, but my stupid, human eyes weren't nearly as good as his.

"This place is a market, right? A place for things that have been lost to be bought and sold. A place without too much oversight."

"It feels like a corporate smuggler's den," I agreed.

"Then there must be something around here that one of our rich sponsors would want." His lips quirked into a self-satisfied smile as he began to get excited about his own plan.

"Like what?"

"We'll know it when we see it."

"Maybe you will," I said with a scowl. "I don't recognize half of this crap."

"Sounds like I'm useful for once. So buckle up and follow me," he murmured, striding into the bazaar once more with purpose. I followed, scanning the stalls for something that would get Alex excited, but I didn't see any comic-book posters anywhere.

We worked our way back through the market, looking for something we could pitch to one of our contacts. It was almost too bad that I had killed Lazarus. His bottomless pocketbook would have come in handy here. Granted, he definitely deserved it, but he might have been the richest person I knew.

An hour went by, and my enthusiasm began to wane. It was one thing to be excited about the idea of finding a lost treasure in a flea market, but actually doing so was another thing entirely. Most of these places were picked over. None of these trinkets would get us the kind of deal we needed to make.

Just when I was getting ready to abandon our plan, something changed. "Dark Abyss," Alex swore, starting in surprise. "Is that who I think it is?" I followed his gaze to a nearby stall full of weapons, but I saw nothing that looked remarkable.

Alex didn't explain, instead marched up to the collection, which was spread across a series of racks that showcased a wide variety of armaments. Heavy mauls stood vertically next to razor-thin rapiers. The wickedly spiked head of a mace dangled from a black chain. The ball glowed with an angry red as if it were made of burning coal.

"This is quite the collection," I admitted to Alex, scanning the weapons with a critical eye. "But I don't know what—"

"Welcome, far travelers," a man's voice trilled as the vendor stepped out of the back of his stall and approached us. I blinked in surprise as I realized he was a Faerie. He had tan skin and brown hair, but his solid-gold eyes and sharply pointed ears were a dead giveaway.

"You're Esras." Alex's voice was soft. It wasn't an accusation, just a statement.

"Nowadays I go by Ezra," the immortal replied with a half-smile. "Easier for everyone to spell."

"Or easier to hide from Constellations asking you to make them weapons?" Alex sounded equal parts amused and awed to be speaking to the Faerie. For my part, I was just confused. My Greco-Roman knowledge is passable at best. But outside of Shakespeare, my understanding of Fae lore gets sparse. I should probably do something about that, it being my own heritage and all.

"Something like that." The man's eyes crinkled in the corners, a slight wince. "I don't suppose I can count on you not to be bothering an old Faerie to craft something to kill a god?" It took every ounce of my self-control for me to keep my mouth shut.

"I won't ask you to make me something," Alex promised, his own lips quirking up in a smile. "But we do want to buy some of your work."

"Well, I would be happy to make a sale." Ezra's smile grew in relief, and he stepped back to throw his hands out in a wide gesture encompassing his wares. "Let's see if I have something that sings to you, young Nephilim."

"The spear." Alex pointed over Ezra's shoulder to a plain-looking thing that was leaning against a rack. I was surprised he even noticed it. It was a simple weapon with a wooden haft and a bright triangular head made of an almost bronzish metal. Compared with most of the other weapons, it looked positively *normal.*

"Oh, that old thing?" It might have been my imagination, but I thought the man's face paled slightly at Alex's request. "I fear that wouldn't do you much good, my friend. It is meant for Fae hands."

"Oh, I know." Alex's voice sounded triumphant. "You should talk to him." He jerked his thumb at me. The Faerie's golden eyes swept over me, and a slight frown grew on his face.

"Hi, I'm Matt," I told him, extending my hand for him to shake. After a moment, he took it, his palm rough and callused. He was eyeing me with the air of someone who knows he is falling for a trap, but he doesn't know what it is yet.

"What house are you, Ezra?"

His eyes narrowed further, and he licked his lips before answering.

"Autumn, although it has been many years since—" The smile that grew on my face interrupted him. It was not a kind one. This was a Faerie on the run, someone who had fled after Ash had taken over her house, abandoning her to ruin.

"Autumn," I said brightly. "Me too." His head cocked sharply. Maybe he had been gone too long—he was giving away far too much information. Robin would have a field day with him.

"You're a mortal," he protested slowly.

My smile was bright as I raised my right hand and summoned Willow. The fire spirit burst into being as a red nimbus around my fist. Ezra staggered back a step, his eyes going wide in surprise. After a moment, I banished the flame, trying to show him that I wasn't threatening him.

"It's true, I am a mortal. But dear old Dad left me some funny genes. Maybe you know him. Have you had the misfortune of encountering Damien Fireheart?" The corner of my mouth twitched at having to say that stupid last name.

"You're Damien's son?" Ezra's voice was sharp with disbelief. "I knew he ran off with a mortal woman, but I never thought he would have children."

"He had three actually," I told him with a shrug. "Well, two now, I guess. It's complicated and not important. Tell me about the spear."

"Unfortunately, young man, the Spear of Lugh will be of no use to you. Your friend has a keen eye. It is one of the lost treasures of the Tuatha Dé Danann. The bearer of this weapon has never lost a battle." My eyes narrowed as I studied the increasingly nervous Faerie. Honed by two years with Robin and Ash, my instincts were going wild, certain there was blood in the water. There was more to this story; I just needed to dig a little deeper.

"Tuatha Dé Danann," I said slowly, my mouth stumbling over the unfamiliar words. "That's the *olde* name for the Fae isn't it?"

"Did your father not teach you?" A look of shock passed across his face as I snorted in derision. He was aware of Damien, but clearly, they did not know each other well.

"I grew up mortal, so I'm still catching up a little bit. When you say it is lost…what do you mean? Because it looks like it's right there behind you. How could a weapon be lost when it's in your possession and for sale?" I was not surprised to see the worry lines in Ezra's forehead crease deeper.

"There are different kinds of lost. Many of our kind have been searching for it for a long time. I have not." I couldn't help but notice that it was suddenly *our* kind.

"Interesting." I kept my voice neutral as I studied the weapon with more interest, trying to make the smith crack. He had clearly been gone from Goldhall for far too long.

"The Spear of Lugh is worthless to you. It is tied to the Path of Air. You would need to be bound to Sylph, not Willow, for it to accept you." There was a note of panic in his voice, as he tried to dissuade me from the weapon. I threw my head back and laughed, sending a shocked expression across the smith's face. I understood exactly what Alex's angle was now. It was brilliant.

"Why have you hidden it for so long, Ezra?" The Fae's shoulders slumped in defeat. He looked down at his hands, fiddling with his longer fingers for a moment before he answered.

"I feared what that kind of power would tempt Gloriana to do in the twilight of our race. So I took that which I made and left, unwilling to be a party to her atrocities." I arched an eyebrow in surprise. Fae cannot lie, which is why they abhor blunt answers. He could only speak so directly if he meant it with every fiber of his being. Having met the old Queen of All Fae, I could understand why he would.

"It was *Gloriana* you hid it from?" I asked, pressing him on the point.

"Yes, she cannot be trusted with its power."

"Well, I don't know if you've heard, but there's been a change in leadership in the Dandelion Court." Ezra's eyes widened. I guess the news hadn't made here to the Land of Darkness.

"We have a new queen now."

CHAPTER TWENTY-FOUR

"WHY ARE YOU calling?" Evangeline answered before the first ring. "I told you it would take time before we were ready to move again."

"I have news," I said, rolling my eyes as hard as I could in the hope that she would hear it over the phone. "I found a lead that you're going to want to hear." I was back in my living room, on earth. Alex and I had used a convenient door to slip out of the Abaddon Market and return home after convincing Ezra to wait for us to return. I needed cell reception for the next part of this plan.

"I told you not to—"

"Listen lady—er angel—ma'am, we need to clear up this whole jurisdiction crap. I'm getting tired of having my toes stepped on in this dance."

"Who is dancing?"

"Never mind. The point is, I don't work for you. I don't answer to you or your boss, or maybe even your boss's boss. Don't quote me on that. I don't really know how anything works. But Neodeath falls under the purview of good old regular Death."

There was a loud, angry silence from the other side of the phone.

"Now, I am more than happy for us to have a joint task force working to stop this horrible atrocity. However, if you're not willing to play ball, I've got a boss too. His name is Death, and he is very scary. So either we coordinate our investigations, or I am gonna go do what I gotta do to keep the Grim Reaper from being upset with me. Does that make sense?"

"Fine." Evangeline sounded almost defeated. "What do you have?"

"We found where they're selling Neodeath."

"*What?*" Evangeline was so startled, she didn't even try to hide it. "Where?"

"It's a place called Abaddon Market, hidden inside a world known as the Land of Darkness."

"Tell me everything." Oh, sure, *now* I was useful. Somehow I bit back the desire to sass the angel more than I already had. I think that's called maturity. Mostly it just seems to be boring.

I gave her everything we had. Lying to an angelic investigator seems like a bad idea. Doing it to the cops is a felony; I have no idea what lying to someone from the upstairs office might be classified as. A Hellony maybe.

"I'm requesting a strike team," she announced. I blinked in surprise. Despite my lecture to her, I had expected her to want to come see the evidence for herself before she got all smitey. "You're sure that you could find the source again?"

"Easily," I promised. "It's part of the Reaper package."

"Stand by," she said tersely, and the line went silent. For a moment

I thought I'd been hung up on, but then the music started. A chorus of voices erupted in perfect harmony, singing "Joy to the World," which it wasn't even the season for, but sure.

"How's it going?" Alex asked, walking into the living room. He had a mozzarella stick hanging from his mouth and two more still in their wrappers in his hands. I hadn't even waited to get a snack before calling Evangeline.

"I'm on hold." I raised a hand, and he tossed me one of the cheese sticks with a sigh. "But she did say she was going to assemble a strike team."

"Damn, I'd love a chance to see the Heavenly Host operators in action," Alex mumbled around his cheese. He wasn't peeling it into little strings, just taking giant bites out of it like an animal. "Even Orion said those guys were the real deal."

"It sounds like we'll be riding along," I told him with a grin. "So you just might get a chance."

"Becoming your best friend has been a full-time job," Alex said, swallowing his cheese in one gulp like an alligator. "But there are perks."

"Matthew." Evangeline's voice cut through the carols with an abrupt violence.

"Yeah, I'm still here," I told her, pausing mid-bite. "That was fast. Is it go time?" The angel was silent for a long moment. Something about her hesitation gave me a bad feeling.

"I was denied."

"What?" Why?" On the couch across the room, Alex sat up, a concerned look on his face.

"Because the Abaddon Market is owned by a mortal."

"Why should that matter—oh. This is a free will thing, isn't it?"

"Yes." The irritation in her voice could have been used as sandpaper. Free will is a prickly subject for the immortals and their like. It goes something like this: Humans have souls, and as such they have the right to free will. We get to make our choices and live with them. Angels and demons can't interfere with humans who do not give them permission. That was rather the whole kerfuffle around the whole soul fraud thing. I was totally allowed to sign my soul over to the Devil. They weren't allowed to take it without my permission.

If the owner of the Abaddon Market was a mortal, that could make things murky. Even if Neodeath was just being sold there, that didn't mean the angels could just go smash up the place. That would be intruding in a space where they were not allowed. It was an interesting limitation on unfathomable power. I could only assume it was frustrating to be capable of doing so much yet forced to do so little.

They say that's why Lucifer fell in the first place.

"Did you run it all the way up to Raguel?"

"It was she who told me that Abaddon Market was off limits."

"Is it normal for you to be denied like this? Feels like this is a pretty big deal to let get by on a technicality." The silence was longer than it had been before.

"It's not unheard of," she replied at last. "There are rules that cannot be ignored."

I frowned, trying to force my sluggish, sleep-deprived mind to work. It felt like the gears were gummed with tar, resisting my will with their immense weight. It took an age, but slowly, they began to turn.

"Is there any wiggle room in those orders?" I asked, a thought occurring to me.

"What do you mean?"

"If a human owns Abaddon Market, it shouldn't matter as long as we only target Neodeath, right? Someone is shattering the Death Treaty. How far does that have to go before Heaven can intervene?"

"I wish it was different. I tried my best. But it's not my call. I *must* respect the chain of command." Resentment filled Evangeline's voice. I believed that she truly wanted to help. But I could also hear the resolve to obey. It was the sullen anger of a well-adjusted teenager who is angry at their parents' rules but will follow them. "But the non-mortals are fair game."

"So if I can figure out who the non-mortals involved with Neodeath are while inside the Abaddon Market, you can go after them?"

There was another long pause on the other end of the line. "Yes," she said at last, her voice suddenly thoughtful.

"See, this is why you needed us the whole time."

"What do you mean?"

"I am not barred from messing up the market. I can go in and figure out where the shipments are going. You whack them, I'll handle the mortals who are involved, and we'll use them to take down the source together."

"You'll take care of the mortals...?" There was a note of hesitancy in her tone now. Too late I remembered that one of the Ten Commandments is *Thou shalt not kill.* I should probably be more careful about how I talk to a member of the Heavenly Justice Department.

"I'm a legally licensed deputy of Death," I reminded her. "Mortals are our business." Evangeline was silent for a time. I stood stock-still in my living room, mozzarella stick forgotten in my left hand.

"Very well," she agreed at last. "We will do this together."

"I'll be in touch," I promised.

"Well?" Alex arched an eyebrow from the couch, a knowing expression on his face. "How much harder is it going to be than we thought?"

"We'll see," I said with a sigh. "It depends what kind of mood Dawn is in." I pulled up the Queen of All Fae's number and pressed CALL. It was time to cash in on that favor.

———×———

atthew, darling, at last." Dawn waved lazily at me from her seat as Alex and I walked up to the table. "What have you

doing? You look positively *bedraggled.*" We were in a fancy Italian restaurant in the heart of Beverly Hills. It was one of those places that makes me feel underdressed no matter what I'm wearing. All the wait staff wore immaculately matching uniforms that were half suit, half apron. My leather jacket and jeans were fashionable but not up to the same level.

The room was spotless, made of marble from the Old Country. Piano music floated over the sound of running water from the indoor fountain. The tables had too many utensils and glasses for one man to use. A manager in a three-piece suit wandered the room watching everything with a critical eye.

Of course this was the kind of place where Dawn demanded we meet her. The Queen of All Fae would never schlep to Northridge. If I wanted an audience, I had to go to her, no matter how nice she was on the phone. She also was wildly out of place dressed in a bright-blue designer sweatsuit, her blond hair coiled tightly in a bun that looked both casual and complicated. Still, she *reeked* of money in a way that would guarantee she was never turned away.

"Sorry," I told her as I pulled out a chair and joined sat across from her. "We had a long trip."

"Alexander, delightful to see you," Dawn said, ignoring my excuses as she leaned forward to clasp one of my friend's hands with both of her own. "Where have you been? I haven't seen you grace my court in ages."

"The last time I was there, you called me 'the help,'" Alex replied with a skeptical look on his face.

"That is only because you are so helpful." Dawn dismissed her own behavior with a casual gesture. "It was a compliment if you think about it."

"I do feel complimented," Alex managed to say with a straight face. Dawn chuckled, a hint of her real personality leaking through as she released his hand and leaned back in her chair. I deliberately didn't look at Alex. The last thing I needed to see right now was him mouthing the words *brothers-in-law* while Dawn gushed all over him.

"Regardless, I am thrilled you are here. You're so much more fun than Matthew, and we simply must have a chaperone to keep my poor sister from thinking something untoward is going on between us." She flashed me a saucy wink that did not make me feel any better. I was about 75 percent sure she didn't mean anything by it. She just liked to see me squirm. I did my best not to give her the satisfaction, but it was hard.

"Now, I am eager to hear all about whatever it is that you two are cooking up, but not until we order." She raised her hand to flag down a waiter. "The queen needs some carbonara."

I ordered the chicken Parm—or, more correctly *pollo alla parmigiana.* I am nothing if not consistent. Dawn insisted that we each have a glass of red wine. "It's a *crime* to eat Italian food without *vino,* darling."

When the waiter was finally gone, the Queen of All Fae raised her glass and held it out for us to cheers ours against. "To my most loyal and useful subject and his best and *helpful* friend." I rolled my eyes at her but accepted the toast.

"You're in a mood," I said over the rim of my glass after I sipped the wine.

"Everyone is always in a mood, Matthew," Dawn scolded me, her false blue eyes sparkling with mischief. "That's how life works. Although knowing you, I'm sure that by the time this lunch is done I shall be in a different one."

"That depends," I replied airily, glancing off to the side, enjoying holding some of the cards for once. "Do you have any interest in the Spear of Lugh?"

Dawn's expression warped in an instant. The amused socialite was gone, replaced by the cold marble statue of the Queen of All Fae. I felt my smile grow wider as I processed her shock.

"Is that a yes?"

"Matthew." Dawn said my name in a clipped, dangerous tone. "Do not play with me. You are my favorite, but I will destroy you." Of all the possible responses I thought she might have, anger had not been one I had anticipated.

"I am half Faerie," I replied amusedly, remembering something Robin once said to me before my birthday massacre. "I do not play." Dawn glared at me as if somehow she could hear the lawyer's tone in my words.

"He's telling the truth," Alex told her, coming to my aid.

"You really found the Spear of Lugh?"

"We found Ezra." I leaned back in my chair, swirling what was left of my Chianti in its giant glass. This was more fun than I thought it would be.

"Who is that?" Her expression clouded in confusion.

"He used to be called Esras," Alex offered.

Understanding bloomed in the queen's expression, and she leaned forward hungrily. "The master smith himself? That traitorous thief lives?"

"He does," I affirmed, unsure how deep Dawn's hatred of the Faerie might go. "He had issues with your mother and her policies—"

"Join the club," Dawn murmured to no one in particular.

"—but he is interested in returning to the fold now that there is a new regime in place."

"Well, if he gifts me the Spear of Lugh, I will consider pardoning him for his crimes," Dawn said magnanimously. I winced, unsurprised that her starting position was so unreasonable. If this was going to work, Dawn would have to be willing to play ball.

"About that," I said slowly, gathering my thoughts. "We actually had something else in mind."

"This sounds suspiciously like my own vassal is working against me, *Matthew.*" Dawn's blue eyes narrowed in irritation and suspicion. "You know how I feel about being schemed against." This from the woman who kept two of her sisters bound in golden obedience collars.

"I am not working against you, Dawn," I assured her, giving her my most winning smile. "But you did offer to help me with one of my problems..."

"A moment of weakness, I assure you." Her eyes flashed with annoyance, but she did not protest further. She couldn't; she was a Faerie, and her word was binding, even when given lightly.

"Just listen," I begged. "We have a plan that gets you the spear. It just has a couple extra steps to it."

"Why do I get the sense that these extra steps will be expensive?" Dawn's suspicion was still written across her face.

"A little," I admitted. "But they come with a whole lot of theater. And you and I both know how much you love playing a part."

"I'm listening."

I told her my plan. She tried to pretend like she wanted no part of it, but the wicked light in her eyes only grew brighter as I explained her role. She would hem and haw, but she would do it. Because deep down we both loved the same sort of cruel justice.

"Very well, Matthew," she said at last, sniffing haughtily as if I had asked the world of her. "I will participate in your little show."

"Participate? I'm going to make you a star."

CHAPTER TWENTY-FIVE

NOT WILLING TO be outdone by dragons and soul-stealers in being a pain in my ass, the IRS decided now was the perfect time to remind me of the danger I was in.

Agents Peters and Wong lurked outside the Beverly Hills restaurant. From the way they stood out in the open, it was obvious they wanted me to notice them. A chill ran down my spine at the sight of the two of them on the sidewalk, waiting with all the patience of a pair of spiders. Wong carried a manila folder with her that I had no doubt was full of things I didn't want to see.

"Oh my, it's the Feds," Dawn murmured from behind me. "I will be taking the back exit. They're still after me for the estate tax on my mother's passing."

"You're kidding. How do they even think they have a claim to that?"

"On Gloriana's US accounts, silly boy." Dawn gave me an affectionate pat on the cheek, like I was a very smart toddler that she was very proud of. "But what are they going to do? Arrest me? Ha!" Chortling, she strode off to leave me to face the wolves alone.

"You gonna run too?" I asked Alex, giving him an unamused stare.

"Matthew, I have faced down ghouls and monsters with you."

"Yes."

"Don't forget the giant scorpion."

"Wish I could."

"*Plus,* a dragon." I already knew where this was going.

"Dragoons and dragon, to be specific," I corrected unhelpfully.

"I would like to sit this one out if I could." Alex gave me an embarrassed look. "My fake ID isn't really up to federal scrutiny."

"Ah." For what it was worth, I actually understood that one. Alex was more than two hundred years old but looked like he was in his mid-twenties. In order for him to function in the modern world, he had to have paperwork that made sense. Which meant his identity probably had to be reforged every couple of decades.

"Do you have a Social Security number?" I asked him, suddenly struck by a thought.

"Several, technically."

"...are you collecting retirement checks?" Alex's lips compressed into a tight, unyielding smile. I sighed, rubbing my hands over my face to try to banish some of my stress. "Yeah, on second thought, you stay here."

"I owe you a drink."

"You owe me at least several."

"Deal." He held out his fist and rapped my knuckles against it, taking comfort in the ritual even as my tension began to rise. I would rather face Doyle in all his draconic glory once more than the agents of the Idiot Revenue Service. There was just too much math going on for me to feel comfortable.

I squared my shoulders as I crossed through the atrium of the restaurant and stepped out the door, adopting what I hoped was a surprised expression on my face at the sight of the two sunglassed Feds waiting for me.

"Mr. Carver," Agent Wong called as I emerged. She held up her hand in a way that looked like it could be a greeting, but was more like a crossing guard commanding me to stop. Together they moved to interpose themselves between me and the rest of the sidewalk.

"Agents, I had no idea you were fans of Italian food," I said, stepping toward them as if I weren't afraid of them at all. It was important to look like I had nothing to hide. Especially since I had enough secrets to bury me.

"Quite an expensive restaurant for a man who's under investigation for tax fraud," Peters remarked threateningly, like I owed him money personally.

"Wasn't on my tab," I told him with a tight, flat smile. Say what you will about Dawn and her megalomania, at least she picks up the check for her lavish meals. "To what do I owe the pleasure? I thought we were sort of up to speed since you dropped by my home the other day."

"Are you familiar with a Roger Douglas?" Wong asked, opening her manila folder to pull a photo from the stack of documents inside. A shudder ran down my spine as I recognized the photo of my former CFO in a pre-burned state.

"Only vaguely," I replied honestly. "I'm not as involved with the day-to-day operations of Matthew Carver Investment Agency Worldwide *Et Cetera* as perhaps I should have been. Why?"

"You haven't heard that he was murdered yesterday?" Peters's voice was incredulous.

"Murdered." I repeated the word slowly, looking between the two agents. I did know that. I had been there right after it happened. But I didn't think that Matthew Carver, law-abiding, normal citizen of these United Mortal States, should know that.

"He was killed in his El Segundo home, which was then set on fire."

"Wow," I said in what I hoped was a stunned tone. "Do you have any suspects?"

"We are the Internal Revenue Service. Homicide falls under the jurisdiction of the local police force. They will lead the case unless for some reason it becomes part of our fraud investigation." Wong's voice made it clear that her sentence was a threat.

"Ah, I apologize. I'm not really up on all the intricacies of law enforcement."

"No reason for you to be," Wong agreed. Something about the way she said it made me nervous. "Do you have any reason to think that his death might be connected?"

I hesitated, looking between the two unsmiling agents, trying to figure out how I needed to play this. Yes, I did have reason to think that. Because that's exactly what had happened. Douglas had been working for or compromised by the Dragon Dons, and when we began to follow the lead, they cauterized it.

But I had no idea how to say that without sounding insane—or guilty. As far as I knew, this was a case being run by the mortal side of the IRS. Dawn had made it clear that there was at least some part of the organization that knew to shake down supernatural beings for their wealth, but Wong and Peters had made no acknowledgment of it.

When I had been accosted by Agent Richter from the FBI, he had made it clear from the moment I met him that he was in the know. There's just no good way to ask someone if they're open to blaming the dragons for a murder. Once you go down that road, you can't take it back and seem at all sane.

"I'll be honest: I'm not sure," I said after a moment of thought. "I know that my office was in the process of going through the books after your shocking news the other day. They told me they were concerned by some strange patterns they were uncovering, but that it was in no way definitive yet."

Wong nodded as if unsurprised by my response. I guess IRS agents deal with sentences like that all the time. It was remarkable how out of my depth I felt. This was the first purely mortal problem I had faced in a long time, and I was daunted by how little I knew. Thank the Fates I had spent so much time dealing with annoying Fae.

"Were you close with Mr. Douglas?" Peter's voice was mild, but I could tell that danger lurked in this question. The only safe answer was the truth.

"I saw him once or twice, but we never spoke."

"Do you have any theories why LAPD has witnesses saying that a man matching your description was seen running into the fire that was set at his house shortly after his murder?" I struggled to swallow over the sudden lump that grew in my throat.

"A guy matching my description?" I asked, arching an eyebrow. "A tall, white guy with brown hair. In LA? What are the odds." Neither of them laughed. "Okay tall-ish." I'm six feet. It counts.

"Mr. Carver, I don't think I need to tell you that this is serious," Wong scolded me, ignoring my comments. "If Roger Douglas's murder is connected to this case, you need to tell us immediately. Otherwise, things may go very poorly for you as your case expands from fraud to something more severe."

"Are you implying that I'm a suspect?"

"You are a known person of interest, with an FBI folder that is far too thick to be ignored," Wong replied, which was neither a confirmation nor a denial. Inwardly I cursed Agent Richter for his incompetence. "You've also yet to respond to the deadline for your payment plan for your outstanding tax balance."

"Deadline?" I asked, my mouth going a little dry. I had missed that part. Hopefully the rest of the home team was on top of their game. I did pay a million dollars a year for representation, after all.

"You have until the end of the week to file your plan, or you may be subject to more fines or arrest." Peter's tone was rich with anticipation, as if begging me to give him an excuse.

"Should I be having this conversation with my lawyer present?"

Neither of them responded, which I took to mean a resounding *yes.* Robin was going to kill me.

"Let me say for the record that I had no knowledge of my taxes being unpaid. Anything that I have learned since then is new knowledge. I want to get to the bottom of this and get it resolved just as much as you do. If there is a conspiracy going on, I am the victim, not the perpetrator."

"You're the victim," Peters repeated in a flat tone. "Not the dead guy."

"Well, he may be *a* victim," I allowed, feeling a little stupid. "But like you said, we don't even know if that is connected yet or just really odd timing. There can be more than one victim; I'm not trying to claim a monopoly here. Pretty sure you guys arrest people for that too, don't you?"

"No sir, they don't arrest people for monopolies," Wong told me, her expression unreadable. For a second, I was tempted to point out that I was too stupid to run this scheme, but I decided to keep my mouth shut. I was pretty sure they already knew that anyway.

"As I mentioned, my team is investigating our financials with a fine-toothed comb. We intend to comply with you all as much as possible in a gesture of good faith. I have no interest in robbing Uncle Sam, I assure you. My team and I will get the paperwork filed before the deadline."

"We're glad to hear it, Mr. Carver," Agent Wong said, tucking her manila folder under her arm as she and her partner turned away. "We'll be in touch. Don't try to leave the country."

"I wouldn't dream of it," I told her with a straight face.

CHAPTER TWENTY-SIX

YOU REALLY HAVE to do something about the wallpaper," Dawn lectured me for the dozenth time as we walked down the long hallway of the Between. She had traded her blue sweatsuit for a sharp white pantsuit. Three different necklaces of gold hung from her neck, the jewels set in them matching the smaller ones set in her demure tiara—well, demure for Dawn, anyway.

"I don't think I do," I replied, giving her a wry glance. "We're the only people who come here."

"You have no shame," she sniffed, lifting her chin like a proper member of the elite class. "There are royals who walk these hallways."

"I don't think I could change the decor even if I wanted to."

“Plus, you have no idea how to install wallpaper,” Alex commented from Dawn’s right. “You’re about as handy as a toddler with a toy tool belt.”

“Yeah, well, I didn’t exactly have one of those dads who taught me those lessons,” I grumbled, giving him a glare. “Damien was more of a hands-off kind of guy.”

“Can you imagine?” Dawn mused. “Damien Fireheart doing chores around the house? I cannot even begin to picture it.” Her golden eyes glinted with humor.

“Well, that’s because it never happened.” We fell into a companionable silence, walking past the white doors that go everywhere.

“So many worlds,” Dawn breathed, eyeing each of them with interest. Like her sisters, she had been kept cooped up inside the Faerie Lands for a couple of centuries while Gloriana had begun her descent into madness.

Part of me suspected that was why she was so often out and about in the mortal world. She was reveling in a freedom she had not enjoyed for some time. I’d probably do the same thing.

“Will you take me to one sometime, Matthew?” I twisted in surprise at the earnest tone in her voice. There was a soft expression on her face, making her look a lot less like the Queen of All Fae and a lot more like Dawn. “Just one adventure.”

“You mean other than the one we’re on right now?”

“Oh, this hardly counts,” she snorted. “I’m doing you a favor.” I tilted my head, studying her. Ever since she’d called me the other day, she had been acting different. If I didn’t know better, I’d say she was being nice. Dawn is not cruel or evil, but she isn’t nice. Alex shot me a confused look over her shoulder, telling me he was just as puzzled.

“Sure, Dawn,” I said after a moment of thought. “We can go on an adventure.”

“That would be lovely,” she murmured, a small, genuine smile growing on her face. That only made me feel weirder. Something was off, and I needed to know what it was before we set food in Abaddon Market.

"Are you okay?" I asked, stopping mid-stride in the middle of the hall. "You don't have, like, Faerie cancer or something, do you? Why are you being like this?"

"Being like what?" Dawn held a hand to her chest as if shocked by my improper question. "Can't a queen dote on her friends?"

"Okay, now I'm on Matt's side," Alex remarked, taking a step back from the Faerie as if she might be rabid. "Since when would you admit we are friends?"

Dawn laughed softly, her shoulders lifting as she closed her eyes for a moment. When they opened, her eyes had faded from the solid gold of her Faerie persona to the blue shade she wore when she wanted to blend in among mortals. It made her look almost human, except for the ears.

"Is it that obvious?" she asked wryly. Her response sent a spike of fear through me. Exhaustion clawed at the edges of her face, like dark shadows reaching for her. For the first time ever, I saw Dawn struggling under the tremendous weight of her crown.

"Are you going to tell us what it is?"

"It is simple," she finally said with a tired smile. "My sister has vanished."

"Mav?" I took a step toward her without meaning to. "I thought you said—"

"No, not her," Dawn shook her head. "I still have my most dangerous kin's leash well in hand. It is the other one. She who killed our mother."

"Tania." I paused, surprised by the discomfort I felt at this news. Mav was terrifying. While I wanted to kill her with my whole heart, I also would be happy to do it unfairly. Crossing blades with the Lady of Winter was asking to get stabbed.

Compared with her violent sister, Tania, the Lady of Spring, wasn't nearly as intimidating a figure. But she was the one who had been seduced by Samael, who had conspired against Gloriana and killed her.

She had been the most aggressive of the sisters in trying to marry me when I was being forced to choose among the siblings, but I was convinced she would have been the worst option.

"What do you mean, 'vanished'?"

"There is no sign of her, which means one of two things." Her lips twisted in frustration. "She escaped, or she was taken." I blinked in surprise at that second one. I assumed that Tania had finally made good on her desire to be free of the responsibilities of her station, but Dawn seemed skeptical.

"How long has she been missing?" I paused, struck by a sudden thought. "Are you keeping an eye on me?"

"Don't flatter yourself, Matthew," Dawn scolded, some of her old bite returning as she breezed past me, resuming her stride down the Between's long hall. "I'm using you as bait."

"Ah, yeah, that makes sense," I grumbled, following after the queen. "You think she's going to come after me?"

"It was you who foiled her plot. If she's alive, you have to be high on her list."

"Kind of. You were involved too. So was Ash. But if she really wanted revenge, couldn't she just kill you and become queen herself?"

"She could try." Dawn purred with destructive energy. It was worth remembering that the former Lady of Summer was no slouch either. Her connection to Sylph and the Path of Air made her dangerous.

"Why didn't you just tell me this in the first place?" I hated the thought that I had yet another enemy lurking in the dark, stalking me.

"Alexander, please explain it to him," Dawn said with an almost disappointed sigh. "I grow tired of being a tutor."

"It's a Fae thing," my friend offered with a shrug. "If she came to you about it, she would be asking for help. Now it's more of a conversation about mutual benefit."

"So you had to play mild-mannered until I got worried enough to ask about it before you were free to talk about it?" I asked incredulously, turning to glare at Dawn. "Does Ash do this too?"

The blond woman gave me a look so condescending, it felt like a physical pat on the cheek.

"I knew there was something wrong," I protested, my pride a little stung. "I just didn't know what. You're never *that* nice."

"Matthew, there is no need to say such rude things out loud." Dawn sniffed like a British noble, indignant at my terrible manners. "No matter how true they may be."

"Well, thanks for telling me eventually," I said with a sigh, resuming my walk toward the distant Land of Darkness door. "I'll add that to my list."

"List? What list?"

"Oh, you know which one. It goes: Get my soul back, finish three Impossible Tasks, find something for Ash's birthday..."

"That might as well be four Impossible Tasks," her older sister interrupted, a note of irritation in her voice. "That woman is beyond difficult to shop for."

"Trust me—I know. If you have any ideas about what she might like..."

"I'll give you my gift for a favor."

"I'm desperate, but not that desperate."

We spent the rest of the walk debating about who was a better gift-giver. Secretly I had to agree that Dawn had the edge. She had the resources of an entire kingdom behind her. How was I supposed to compete with a chain of diamonds that sang when the sun set? My best idea was one of those fancy coffeemakers that brews an entire cup from a little pod.

Sure, I was objectively rich. Well, not after I paid the bill I owed the government, but getting handed five million dollars a year was nothing to sneeze at, even if it was all somehow gone. And yet, even if I still had every dollar, I wasn't Dawn's kind of rich.

"This is it," I announced when we arrived at the door. Something had updated the sign that hung on it. It now read: LAND OF DARKNESS (AKA ABADDON MARKET). A shiver of fear ran down my spine at the sight. I know that a god made this place, but seeing it take care of itself made me worried that it was more prescient than I was comfortable with.

"Are you ready?" I asked, glancing at Dawn.

She rolled her solid-gold eyes. "The day I need time to prepare myself to perform the most basic of roles is the day that someone should take my crown from me, Matthew Carver."

"You are a Faerie," I reminded her with a sharp-toothed grin. "The day you do is the day someone *will*."

"I would have it no other way," she replied with a dangerous smile.

I took that as permission to start and pulled out my key. Dawn's expression sharpened as she spied the gift her mother gave me shortly before she died. While she could do nothing but honor Gloriana's wishes, I had no doubt she would've loved to have it for herself.

I held the key right up to the edge of the lock and closed my eyes, trying to visualize exactly what I was looking for. The Between wasn't GPS-guided, but it did its best to send me where I wanted to go. It was a tricky language to learn, but I had made a lot of progress over the last year.

Whatever power Portunus put into his weird hallway didn't think like a modern human being. It had its own way of categorizing the places in its library, and as with a programming language, I had to learn how to describe what I wanted in a way that it understood.

Mentally, I pictured the kind of place I wanted to go. An opening, a welcoming. The beginning of the other world. I tried to visualize it like a mudroom, a spot for outsiders to enter and become proper before they were admitted into the rest of the home.

After a few moments of manifesting, I slid the Key of Portunus into the lock and turned it, unlocking the door with a *click.* Opening my eyes, I gave Dawn and Alex a look, double-checking that they were ready. This first part of the plan was up to them.

Dawn frowned and gestured in my direction, waving her hand in an imperious motion. I felt a breeze flow over me, tussling at my brown hair as it danced by. The world distorted briefly, as if I were looking through a cloudy mirror.

"Whoa," Alex sounded legitimately impressed. His voice was condensed and distant, as if coming down a long tunnel.

"What?" I glanced down to look at myself, but for the most part I looked the same. I knew Dawn had done *something,* but it didn't seem that impressive.

"You're just gone," Alex told me, narrowing his eyes to stare at where I was. "I know you're there, but I can't see you. There isn't even a seam or any fuzziness."

"Fire might be fun, but it doesn't have all the tricks I do," the Queen of All Fae gloated, a proud smirk on her face. I wasn't sure exactly how, but she and her air spirit were bending the light around me to make me vanish.

"Here goes nothing," I muttered, pulling open the door and stepping through without hesitating. The last thing I wanted was to blow my cover by having Alex trip over me. I emerged from the Between into the familiar decoration of the Land of Darkness.

We emerged from a short, squat building made of the same bright concrete as the rest of the Abaddon Market's structures. The black ground spread in every direction, blending in with the empty night sky.

The path before us was cobbled with the same white stones, which led toward a long gate and what could only be described as a bus terminal. A large, backlit sign read: WELCOME TO ABADDON MARKET. A second sign underneath indicated that existing members should go right, while first-time shoppers should go left. A long line snaked in the latter direction, full of people waiting to be processed.

"Hmmph," Dawn announced with a sniff when she read the sign and saw the crowd ahead of us. "Well, that is something we will not be doing."

"Uh, I don't think they're going to let us in without—" Alex began, playing the role of her staff.

"Alexander, you must remember that I am *royalty*," Dawn lectured, stepping forward without looking back to see if we followed. I floated in their wake, hoping that she remembered to maintain the working that made me invisible. "I have my own world. I will not be waiting in line like some mortal at an amusement park." She led us down the right-hand path, which was empty. "Besides, you already have one of these accounts, do you not? We shall tell them that you are acting as my emissary."

"If you say so." Alex sounded skeptical.

"Oh, cheer up, Nephilim," she scolded him good-naturedly. "For a few hours you're gainfully employed. When's the last time you actually had a real job?"

Alex muttered a response under his breath that might have been "Nineteen sixty-five," but I was too far away to be sure. Although given what I knew of his history, that sounded about right.

Together we threaded through the empty zigzag of the returning-customer line, drawing steadily closer to the row of ticketing windows waiting at the front. A human in the same gray livery as the guards sat behind bulletproof glass in each section, calling up people to talk one by one.

It reminded me of the DMV—the Department of Mortal Valuation—where the souls of the departed were sorted on the other side of the Veil. It also reminded me of the mortal Department of Motor Vehicles, but I hadn't been there as recently.

We stopped at the front of the line, waiting for one of the kiosks to open up. It seemed that they pulled from both lines but gave priority to ours. Or at least I hoped they did before Dawn blew a gasket.

The Queen of All Fae was playing her part perfectly. She crossed her arms and huffed in annoyance, glaring at the staff with an impatience I could feel, even lurking behind her shoulder. Well, I thought she was playing. There was a chance that this was the real Dawn. It was always hard to tell.

"Next," a voice called down the line, echoing from a speaker set into the wall above the thick glass. What kind of beings was that meant to stop?

"Come along, Alexander," Dawn said primly, striding through the open space in front of the long line to get to the waiting kiosk. I followed behind, staying close enough that no one else would step on me, but trying to stay out of the way of the visible members of our party.

"Welcome back to Abaddon Market, what's your account number?" the woman behind the glass asked without looking up from her monitor.

"I am Dawn, Queen of All Fae."

Click, click, click, went the woman's keys as she typed in Dawn's response. "I don't see an account for you. You'll need to get into the other line," she replied abruptly, finally looking up from her screen to point where the masses waited. She did not seem to be too impressed by the royalty she was dealing with.

"My vassal has an account that will suffice," Dawn managed through gritted teeth.

"Very well, what's his account?" The woman sounded skeptical.

"Uh, it should be under Alex Johson?" My friend leaned forward, trying to seem confident. "I actually was just signed up by the Overseer himself, so I don't have my card—"

"I have you." Somehow the woman's voice became even more clipped as she scanned the items on the page. "I do see you are a brand-new account." A printer on the side of her desk began to whine; a moment later, a freshly laminated card popped out of its side, glinting under the office lights.

"Here's your ID." She slid it through a tiny gap under the glass. It reminded me of the old movie theater setups, where you'd buy tickets from an actual human instead of on your phone.

"What about my, uh, liege lady?" Alex asked, picking up the orange membership card and slipping it into his pocket. "Is there a way I can get her on my account for this trip?"

"She'll need to wait in line to get her own." The woman gestured once more at the mass of people behind us.

"But she's royalty," Alex protested weakly.

"Darling, do you have a manager I can speak to?" Dawn asked, her voice dangerously composed. I resisted the urge to step in; that would ruin everything. I wasn't here. That was the whole premise of the plan. But Dawn was going to draw attention to us that we did not want. We could wait in a little line.

"I am the shift manager." The woman's eyes were flat as she looked up, settling herself into the defensive stance of a soldier in the trenches.

"And who is your manager?"

"Corporate."

"Is there someone from Corporate I could speak to?" Dawn's voice became sweeter with every syllable, like she was actively trying to counter the poisonous rage that was filling her.

"They're off-site."

"What about the Overseer?" Alex asked, probably sensing the

same impending disaster that I did. "Could he make an exception? As I said, he already personally handled my account."

"I see that, sir, but I cannot make exemptions for anyone. There are plenty of nobles already waiting in the line behind you."

"Nobles! Do you think that is the same—" Dawn began, but she cut herself off abruptly as I coughed in irritation. I couldn't help it. She was going to bring this whole thing burning down. The three of them exchanged confused glances as the woman behind the glass tried to understand where the sound had come from.

"Excuse me," Alex said flatly. I could hear the tension in his words.

"Bless you," Dawn said through gritted teeth.

—— × ——

"At least the line seems to be moving quickly," Alex remarked quietly after we had been standing in it for more than an hour. Maybe a dozen groups had been processed since we'd joined, which meant we still had several hours to go.

Dawn didn't reply, but she didn't need to. She was still fuming with outrage that was loud enough that every soul in this terminal could hear it. There was a gap on either side of our party in the line, as if the bystanders around us were wary of getting too close. I hadn't needed to cough again, so I thought my message had been received.

"Oh, look, I'm pretty sure that's a god," Alex offered, pointing at a lion-headed man standing twenty spaces ahead of us in line. "Arimanius or something like that. Actually, now that I think about it, Orion might have killed him. Maybe that's his son. Demigod still kinda counts."

Dawn sniffed.

"All I'm saying is, if they're making gods wait in line then it's not really that rude…"

Dawn sniffed louder.

I kept my mouth shut, shuffling closer to the irate queen, trying to make sure the people around us didn't bump into me by accident. At least her anger was giving me some breathing space.

"Let's play a game," Alex offered after a while. "I spy with my little eye, something black."

Dawn gave him a withering glare. The two supernatural beings stared at each other for a long moment, neither one blinking or moving.

"The ground," Dawn growled after Alex refused to back down.

"Nope."

"The sky."

"Nope."

"Your eyes."

"What? No, they're blue."

"They won't be in a second."

"Did I say it wasn't the sky? It was the sky. I must have misheard you."

Dawn growled in satisfaction before turning away to glare at the distant kiosks. I shook my head, but no one could see me.

The hours crawled by as the line shuffled forward inch by painstaking inch. I half suspected that the marketplace would close for the day before we got to the front, but I didn't really think that likely. Evil black markets don't seem like the type of place to have a healthy work/life balance.

After an eternity, we reached the front of the line. Dawn's anger had grown quiet, more focused, like a hunter readying herself to pounce. She was just looking for someone to take her irritation out on. I could only hope we didn't get the same agent.

So of course we did.

The woman didn't look up as she slid a familiar sheet of paper through the little gap in her window. "Welcome to Abaddon Market, please fill this out for review."

Dawn said nothing as she took the sheet, ignoring the pen that was provided and producing a white feather quill from somewhere within her pantsuit. I didn't ask any questions. The queen's scowl grew deeper as she filled out the form, which only filled me with more dread.

"I think you will find that this is more than sufficient for your highest level of service," she said as she slid the form back under the glass. I blinked in surprise. The Overseer hadn't told us there were levels to the membership. I wondered which one we had.

"Unfortunately, ma'am, I cannot offer you a full Abaddon One account," the woman said as she scanned the results. "We'd be happy to give you a provisional Abaddon trial membership to see if your spending is a good fit for our—"

"Listen here, you petty little bureaucrat," Dawn interrupted in a voice ringing with true fury. "I am the Queen of All Fae. I own a world that puts even this one to shame. You will treat me with the respect I deserve or so help me—"

"An Abaddon trial membership can be elevated to One status at the choice of the Overseer and our executive staff," the woman continued as if she had not been interrupted. "The major factor considered in those cases is the amount of spending done in a fiscal year. In the meantime, you are still eligible to collect Abaddon Points on every purchase, which will also contribute toward your status. There is a shorter line available for our Gold, Platinum, and Medallion Members."

Dawn's fist thudded against the glass with such violent speed that I twitched in shock. The woman behind it didn't even blink. I had a feeling this wasn't the first time someone had reacted like this. The Queen of All Fae hissed in pained surprise, jerking her hand back like a toddler touching a hot stove.

"Ironglass?" she demanded, sounding insulted beyond measure. I could understand why. Many if not most supernatural beings were allergic to iron. It didn't kill all of them, but it could burn them something fierce. For a place like this, run by mortals, to build it into their design was a loud statement about power and who was in charge here.

"Unfortunately, this is the only way we can keep up with demand and serve all of our clients adequately," the manager continued without a pause. She was clearly a veteran of customer service. "We look forward to reassessing your account in the future. Thank you for trusting Abaddon Market."

The printer next to her whined and printed out a white, laminated ID card for her. I saw Alex's eyes narrow as he noticed that hers was a different color than his. I was sure that wouldn't come up at any point at all.

"Take these cards and show them to the guards around the corner," she instructed, the matter already resolved. "Once you are scanned in, you are a Guest of this place until you cross back over our borders. Do you understand the implications of that?"

"Of course," Dawn snapped, insulted to even be asked.

"Excellent, enjoy your time in the universe's best free market." A fake smile flashed across her face as she gestured to Dawn and Alex to leave. The Queen of All Fae glared at her rival one more time before turning on her heel to stomp away.

I flowed in her wake, feeling my heart rate beginning to spike. This was the hard part. So far there had been very little scrutiny on us. Well, there had been plenty of eyes, but we hadn't actually tried to cross the security line yet. I was about to attempt the supernatural equivalent of sneaking through TSA, and I could only pray that they couldn't detect Dawn's spirit at work.

True to the manager's words, a checkpoint waited around the corner, surrounded by the same cement as the rest of the terminal. A thick yellow line was painted on the ground, signifying the border between the Land of Darkness and the Abaddon Market. A narrow gateway of thick iron bars stood open and inviting.

A trio of bored-looking guards stood in front of the line, assault rifles slung over their shoulders. They watched Dawn and Alex's approach with the idle attention of someone with nothing better to do.

"IDs please," the leader said, holding out a gloved hand when they got close. Dawn stepped forward, placing her white card into his hand. He glanced at it for a second, his gaze flickering between the card and her before he nodded once.

"Thanks for your membership," he told her, gesturing that she could move on. I slid past Alex, hovering at her back, barely daring to breathe. I just needed to make it a few more steps, and I would be in. Dawn paused, a normal traveler waiting for her companion to be approved.

Alex offered his orange ID, and the guard's eyebrows shot up as he scanned the information. He must have found whatever he was looking for, though, because he smiled as he handed it back to my friend.

"Thank you for your Abaddon One loyalty, sir. On behalf of myself and the entire team, welcome back. There is a new lounge in the southwest node that I highly recommend. Their buffet is delightful." Dawn's glare could have melted steel beams.

"I will be sure to check that out, thank you," Alex replied in a carefully neutral voice as he took the ID back and slid it into his pocket. His hand might have shook, but I wasn't sure if that was from amusement or fear.

"You are officially a Guest of the Abaddon Market." The guard made the same encouraging gesture to Alex, indicating that he could cross over the line. "Please behave in a polite manner to your host during your time here, and all will be well. When you depart, use one of the five major exists and present your IDs again so you can be removed from the rolls."

"Understood," Alex said with a stiff nod. "Thank you for your help."

"Anytime, sir." The guard turned his attention to a group of veiled women coming up behind us. "IDs please!" he called.

"Here goes nothing," Alex muttered, stepping close to sandwich me between him and Dawn. My pulse was pounding in my ears as we moved through the entrance. This was going to be either brilliant or monumentally stupid. I dogged the queen's heels as she stepped over the line, in case there was some sort of infrared camera trained on the spot. Hopefully our heat signatures would overlap.

None of the guards reacted as we entered the market, which seemed anticlimactic. I would have preferred it if an alarm had gone off or maybe some sort of green light dinged, marking us safe. We wouldn't know if they were onto us until it was too late.

"Oh my," Dawn said, taking in the dark expanse of the Abaddon Market before us. "You boys do take me to the most interesting places. I *love* shopping."

CHAPTER TWENTY-SEVEN

THE HARDEST PART about navigating the crowded Abaddon Market while being invisible was that no one had any respect for anyone's personal space bubble. The beings that flowed along the cobblestone paths were there to find things that they could not get anywhere else. They had no compunctions about running over someone to get a good deal.

"Sorry," I whispered to Dawn for the umpteenth time as I stumbled into her, dodging past someone who'd cut too close on her heels.

"Shut up." She growled her irritation at me and not the pressing crowds. "You are so loud even Alexander could hear you." I didn't have to look at my friend to sense his annoyance. But I obeyed, holding in my complaints, cramming up against Her Royal Majesty, the Queen of All Fae, sister of my betrothed, like we were dancing in a club. It was beyond awkward, but I didn't want to die, so I persisted.

I was under no illusions about what would happen to me if our duplicity was discovered. The first time that Alex and I had snuck in here, we had been treated very kindly, all things considered.

I still wasn't sure why the Overseer had given us premium memberships or why he seemed so familiar. But I've been around the block long enough to know that it wasn't charity. The best theory I had was that he was too busy to pick a fight with us, and by getting us into the system he would prevent us from sticking our nose too far into the things he didn't want us to see.

But even that felt like it was missing something.

Confusing motives aside, I was breaking an *olde* kind of faith. The kind of people who still dealt in Guest rights were using a set of manners from a time long past, when strangers were dangerous and brigands roamed more often.

We don't really have many of those in the civilized world anymore. In the Wild West, they started calling them outlaws or gunslingers depending on whether they were popular or not. But the term *brigand* hadn't been used much since then.

By skirting the Guest checkpoint, I was invading. There were only two ways to come into a place like this: invited or uninvited. Well, technically there was a third, which was in ignorance. But we had already burned that card last time. In fact, now that I thought about it, that bit of theater might have been *exactly* that. The Overseer knew that we'd be back, so he went to great lengths to make sure we knew the rules. Since I had refused to become a Guest before entering, that was a tacit confession that I was here to do mischief. Which was fair. I was. If he killed me for it now, not a single person could cry foul. I was committing this crime knowingly and willingly.

The only exception in the entire world to breaking and entering might be Santa Claus, but he's not real.

"Alexander, darling, we simply *must* look at these rugs," Dawn announced, abruptly halting at a stall full of ornate floor coverings. "I haven't seen ones like these since Mother bought a bunch when Nibiru went under."

"Uh, well, I did tell Ezra that we would meet him…"

"Hah! He stole from my mother and fled our home. He can wait a little on my pleasure." Dawn's voice was savagely amused as she reached out to brush a thick carpet full of beautiful colors that looked like the Persian kind from back on earth. "I've been thinking about redoing the east wing of my estate."

I growled as faintly as I dared in her ear, from where I was pressed behind her. She chuckled. Even now, in this place, she had to remind me that she was in charge.

The shopkeeper greeted her in what I assumed was Farsi, and Dawn responded immediately in the same tongue, startling the peddler. The two went back and forth at a rapid clip, clearly negotiating.

Dawn's tone grew outraged as the conversation progressed. She kept poking the rug, repeating the same phrase, while the woman she was arguing with shook her head vehemently.

"Have it your way," the queen snapped at last, her blond hair dancing as she gesticulated. "Good luck selling these to the Devil himself, because who else could afford these ridiculous prices?" She turned to storm off, and I shifted, following her movements to stay out of the way and undetected.

"Dawn?" A woman's voice interrupted her theatrical exit. Every fiber of my being seized up in shock and terror as we finished our combined turn to face the newcomer. I knew that voice. I heard it in my nightmares sometimes.

The woman was standing in the middle of the cobbled road. The crowd continued to flow around her, but they did so with a wider berth than they gave the Queen of All Fae, despite the fact that she was shorter and smaller than Dawn.

She had pale skin that was a stark contrast with her chin-length black hair. She wore a charcoal business suit with a white blouse. But it was her eyes that were the most striking. They were solid black, infinite pools of night that had no beginning or end. They were the only things I had seen dark enough to blend in with the abyssal night of this world around us.

She was a demon—a fallen angel. Her name was Samael, and she was a member of el Diablo's inner circle. His Dark Whisper, who spread his lies. In many ways, I was more afraid of her than I was of Zagan. The CFO of Hell was tricky and conniving, but compared with Samael, he was a blunt object. It was she who seduced Tania into killing her mother.

"Samael, darling, is that you?" Dawn's voice contained no trace of anger, no hint that the woman she faced had been responsible for her mother's death. For a moment I saw the two immortals as fencers, striking their guards. Of all the beings I have ever met, there are few I would trust to match edges with the Dark Whisper more than the Queen of All Fae.

"It has been too long," Samael replied in the same cheerful tone. "Give me a hug." Terror pulsed through me. Angels and their true counterparts operate on that part of the power graph where things get fuzzy. Dawn had successfully hidden me so far, but there was a difference between slipping through a casual inspection and being under the direct scrutiny of a fallen angel.

Thankfully, the unspoken bubble of space that existed around Samael encompassed us as Dawn moved to embrace the shorter woman. I withdrew a couple of steps, letting the demon's arms pass by me but still managing to stay out of the path of traffic.

My heart wasn't pounding. I was starting to suspect it was frozen.

I had seen a demon in the Abaddon Market before, but I had not expected this.

"How have you been?" Dawn asked, pumping her royal charm for all it was worth. "Has the Dark Star still got you going wherever the wind blows?"

"Oh, you know how it is," Samael replied with an airy smile. "Always traveling. There's always a fire that needs to be built. The Faerie Lands one day, earth the next. It's exhausting. I'm looking forward to using my paid day off next century. I think I'll go sit by the water in Atlantis."

"You mean *in* the water of Atlantis," Dawn corrected, chuckling.

"I suppose it's hard to find a dry spot anymore," Samael agreed easily. "How about you? I never thought I'd find you skulking around this place."

"I'm doing a major renovation," the Queen of All Fae replied proudly. "We're making our first expansion in a few centuries. But I can't trust any of my staff to have good taste."

"An expansion?" Samael's inky eyes flashed as something grew sharper within them. "Dawn, have you started collecting souls again?" I felt a flash of fear run through my guts as I turned my head to study the queen in a new light.

I hadn't heard anything about an expansion. The Faerie Lands were a small, paltry remnant of what they had been hundreds of years ago. Gloriana had essentially put the place into maintenance mode, hoping to keep it stable for as long as possible on the souls they had. They had been closed for business ever since. But Dawn could not lie. If she was in the market for souls again…could I trust her?

"Oh, not yet." The Queen of All Fae made a dismissive gesture. "I'm sure you'd have heard something if we had gotten that far. Just a first step. You didn't think I'd be content to sit on a throne in the midst of my mother's ruins forever, did you?"

"I suppose not." The demon's voice was thoughtful as she studied Dawn. They were about to become competitors: The Queen of All Fae had just declared herself a rival to Hell.

Only a finite number of people live and die, leaving a limited number of souls to be claimed by the Underworlds on the other side of the Veil. The Fae had not been taking any of the harvest, so to speak, for quite some time. But now they were planning to come back and make a play for some of the pie. It was a zero-sum game. Every soul that ended up in Annwn was one that couldn't go somewhere else.

"Well, I'm sure we're excited to see what you come up with," Samael said at last. "There will be many eyes on your new venture."

"You know I love the attention, darling."

"Perhaps there is a way we could work together. There are quite a few subsidiaries that have seen tremendous benefits by joining our larger enterprise." There was an edge to the fallen angel's expression now. I've received more than enough threats to know one when I see it.

"I've never been good at following someone else's vision. Besides, I don't think our relationship is one that particularly promotes trust. The last Faerie princess who worked with you ended up a mother-killer and a slave." Dawn's voice was just as sharp, a master duelist matching her opponent stroke for stroke.

"Be careful, Dawn. You're a big fish in your pond, but these are deeper waters than you're used to." A dark smudge began to glow above Samael's head, pulsing with a steady, irate beat. I was no longer afraid Samael would notice that I was here. I was more worried about her trying to kill Dawn while I stood next to the queen. The streaming crowd around us was still present, but the bubble of space doubled. I was surprised by their lack of reasonable fear until I remembered that she was a *Guest.* Man, that came in handy.

"Threats? From you? In this place?" Dawn's laughter was cutting, as if this alone meant she had won the exchange. Perhaps in some way it did. “Maybe you should take that day off. You’re losing your touch, darling.” The Queen of All Fae turned abruptly, ending her audience with the Dark Whisper of Hell. Startled by the sudden movement, I bumped into her, trying to close the distance before we were back out in the fray.

“You. Nephilim.” Samael’s cold voice stopped me in my tracks, and my head whipped around to find the fallen angel glaring at Alex. “Tell Matthew Carver that we will be seeing him soon.”

“Tell him yourself,” Alex retorted, his voice braver than mine would have been.

The demon studied him for a moment, her head cocking to the side like a bird studying a delicious bug. “Maybe I will,” she said at last. I could not tell if her black eyes tracked toward the invisible space where I was hiding.

Then we were free, swallowed by the masses of the crowd like fish joining a school. Neither of our visible party members spoke for a long time as we walked, putting distance between us and the predator we’d left behind. I kept throwing fearful glances over my shoulder, but there was no sign that the demon was following us, or that she had tipped off the guards to my presence.

Most of my focus was taken up by trying to keep in step with Dawn’s long, aggressive strides. What little brainpower I had left focused on dissecting the conversation that I had just been a witness to. The thing about creatures like Dawn and Samael is that they are never just having one conversation. I have learned a little of the art of double-speaking from spending time with the Fae in my life, but I am a student of something they’re fluent in.

While I was certain Dawn had just declared herself a competitor to Hell, I couldn’t shake the feeling that more had been said that flew over my head. I could feel its shadow like an owl flying overhead at night, but I couldn’t see it.

"Alexander, take me to see Ezra," was the only thing Dawn said when she finally broke her silence. Her tone was sharp. "I have a feeling I will have need of what he has."

The master Faerie smith was parked where we left him. His racks of weapons were on display, each one stranger than the last. The mace with a glowing red head sat next to a sword that looked like it had been made from the moon. I saw a glass knife and a hatchet of gold.

But those were not what we were here for.

Of the Spear of Lugh there was no sign. It was no longer propped up against a wall, hiding in plain sight. Esras, or Ezra, spotted us as we emerged from the crowd, and his tan face grew pale at the sight of Dawn.

"It's true," he whispered in awe as the new Queen of All Fae stood before him. He raised a hand to his mouth, and I was surprised to see it was shaking like a leaf in the wind. Tears appeared in the corners of his eyes, and for a moment I thought he would start weeping. Dawn is an imposing figure, but that seemed a bit ridiculous.

"I am so sorry," he moaned, burying his head in his hands. "I am so sorry!" For a moment I forgot I was invisible and tried to exchange glances with Alex. To my surprise he was looking in my vague direction, a similarly confused expression on his face.

"Why are you sorry, Master Maker?" Dawn's voice was cold and harsh like a judge waiting to pronounce sentence.

"I feared what your mother would do with the spear," he moaned into his hands. "I knew she had aspirations that were beyond what we Fae had become. I thought she would be consumed by the power." A chill ran down my spine as I considered the conversation Dawn had just had with Samael. That particular apple had not fallen far from the tree.

"So you took her greatest protection from her," Dawn mused, that dangerous ice still lurking in her words. "You stole the mightiest Faerie weapon and hid it. When the wolves came, they found her undefended."

"I did."

"She loved you." Dawn's tone was softer, but the edges were still sharp. Ezra flinched as if struck. I felt my jaw drop at that revelation. Gloriana's dating life had many layers to it. Each of her daughters had a different father, chosen for his power, but I had never heard of the deceased queen *loving* anyone.

"She loved what I could do for her."

"Her love was conditional, it is true. No one knows that better than one of her daughters." Dawn laughed harshly. "But conditional love is still a kind of love."

"I loved her enough to stop her."

"And what of me?" The new queen took a step forward, her gaze pinning the somber Faerie in place. "Will you also stop me?"

"I should."

"Can you bear it again? To see one of your sister's daughters killed, torn to pieces while she is without the power of her people?" Dawn's voice was cruel, whipping at him like a scourge. I could see every single syllable sink into his flesh. Inwardly my mind was racing at the realization of who exactly this Faerie was. I had known he was old and important. There was no other reason for him to carry the Spear of Lugh. But he was Gloriana's brother! That would make him a prince of the realm or something similar. A lord at least. I didn't know how the Dandelion Court's titles worked for siblings.

"I will if I must." Ezra raised his head from his hands and stared at Dawn with a defiant but tearstained gaze. "There can never be peace while the Spear of Lugh is taken to war."

"Oh, Uncle," Dawn said, her words becoming soft, almost fond, for the first time. "You have been gone for too long. There is no peace to be found. The Great Correction is coming, and your people are without their teeth."

The two Fae stared at each other for a long time, their golden eyes dancing with a conversation I could neither hear nor understand. I may be almost half Faerie, but I am mortal in all the ways that count.

"It is time to come home," Dawn announced at last, extending her hand toward the old man. "Goldhall welcomes you back, and so do I. All you need to do is accept." Ezra was silent for a long time, battling with some internal choice, torn between duty and family, unless I missed my guess.

I understood his hesitation. Gloriana had been like a shark. She was a cold-blooded predator who would hunt and eat anything she could. If the Spear of Lugh truly was as powerful as they were acting like it was, I could see why he had chosen to keep it out of her hands.

Dawn was her daughter through and through, but there was a little more humanity in her than her mother had ever had. Maybe she got it from her father—and now that I thought about it, I still did not know who that was.

Tania's father had been a wealthy mortal of some sort. Ash's was well known to me, enemy number one and all that. Mav's sire was Ullr, the Norse god of winter and ice.

Thematically speaking, Dawn's progenitor had to be someone related to the wind, but that didn't really narrow it down. I resolved to ask Ash about it the next time we were together. That seemed like something I should avoid being surprised by at a later date.

"I accept your kind offer," Ezra said at last, his shoulders slumping with relief or defeat. "I am ready to come home."

"Oh, Uncle, you've made me a happy girl," Dawn gushed, stepping forward to embrace the old Faerie. His thin form looked like a stick in her arms. "Our family has grown too small over the centuries. It is nice to add to its number for once instead of only subtracting."

"Do you want the spear?" Ezra asked when they parted. "It's just in my tent. I could get it for you..." Alex coughed pointedly, giving Dawn a direct stare. The Queen of All Fae sighed, straightening her spine like she was about to suffer terrible punishment.

I suppose in some ways she was. The Fae love to bargain and negotiate. For her to pay for something that was hers by right had to skewer her to her core. I'd probably have found some amusement in that if this weren't so damn serious.

"No, Uncle, I insist you let me pay for it," she managed through gritted teeth.

"What? Why would you—" Ezra began, stunned by her offer.

"Because this is a strange place, Uncle, and there are rules I *need to follow.*" Her emphasis only made his eyebrows go up higher. It was clear he knew there was another game afoot. I was not surprised that he was quick on the uptake. He was Gloriana's brother after all.

"Well, we can negotiate a fair price," he offered amicably, clasping his hands in front of his waist. A bit of life seemed to come into his expression as he settled into the thing that his kind love the most, making a deal.

"I must also require that we make use of the Abaddon Market's escrow process," Dawn announced, refusing to make the first offer.

"Surely you are not worried that I would give you a fake?" Ezra laughed indignantly, placing a hand against his chest in mock outrage. For a moment, it was crystal-clear that they were related. His demeanor was a mirror to her own.

"I *must* require it," Dawn repeated, leaning into the word with gusto. A look of understanding flashed across her uncle's face before it was gone.

"Very well, we can make sure that it goes through the proper channels," he agreed amicably. "But first there is the matter of price."

"I rather thought that restoring citizenship to the Dandelion Court was priceless beyond measure," Dawn admitted dryly.

"A million florins," Ezra responded without hesitating.

"A million? Ha! Why not ask for the sun and the moon while

you're at it." Dawn laughed. "What use is ancient gold? Surely your tastes have evolved with the times."

"I do accept several cryptocurrencies."

"Dark Abyss," Dawn swore, a look of genuine irritation spreading across her face for the first time. "Not you too."

CHAPTER TWENTY-EIGHT

SOMEHOW THE NEGOTIATION between Ezra and Dawn took longer than any other stage of the plan. The two Fae seemed to be both enjoying the competition and unable to stop, like a pair of eagles holding on to each other's talons, locked in a death spiral.

I felt my own irritation coming to a head. I was tired of being trapped in my distorted world. Fortunately, Alex was there to be the voice of reason—there's a first time for everything, I guess.

"Your Majesty, in my professional opinion a hundred thousand pounds sterling seems a reasonable price for such an artifact," he said when I thought I could not stand another round of haggling. Dawn's head snapped around to fix him with an irate stare.

"Oh, does it?" she demanded, a fury building in her voice. Her gold eyes looked like two suns, burning bright enough to give off heat. "It's your professional opinion that I empty the coffers of Goldhall and leave my sisters and me destitute? Tell me, Nephilim, by what metric could you possibly think that is a reasonable price?"

"Well, there's the *time* to consider," Alex replied through gritted teeth, not backing down from the furious queen. "The longer you spend on this project, the less value you're actually getting out of it. Time is money after all."

"How *mortal* of you," Dawn mused, making it sound derogatory. But a thoughtful look swept across her face, as if she had just remembered something important. I resisted the urge to laugh from within my invisible cocoon. When there is blood or gold in the water, immortals lose their minds.

"Fine," she snapped after a moment of deliberation. "Your terms are acceptable, Uncle. Call the extra a welcome-home gift, something to make up for missing several centuries' worth of your birthdays."

"That is *most* kind of you, Your Majesty," Ezra replied sardonically, placing a hand on his chest. "I am flattered that you remembered."

"I always do," she sniffed, drawing herself up a little taller. She hadn't gotten me a gift for my last one, but I didn't feel the need to correct her. She could not lie, so there must be some sort of loophole there. Besides, Dawn was finally on task, and I saw no reason to distract her.

"If we are all in accord, can we proceed with the process of putting this in escrow?" she asked her uncle.

The intake process into the escrow facility was going to take a while, so the staff recommended that we kill time in the Abaddon Market One lounge, which was not far from the warehouse that held all the items in review.

It turned out that Alex was able to bring in a plus-one with his membership, so they admitted Dawn after making her fill out several forms, including some sort of nondisclosure agreement not to divulge the identity of any members she saw in there to the outside worlds.

The Queen of All Fae's irritation was palpable, but she behaved well enough that no one stopped us from entering. I slid in on her heels, no longer having to sidle up against her now that we were out of the press of the crowd.

The lounge was so far out of my price range, it defied quantification. A giant aquarium-slash-terrarium dominated the center of the massive room. A pair of live bears wandered around the main island of the exhibit next to where a series of thundering waterfalls poured into a massive fake lake full of salmon and what looked like a genuine crocodile, or maybe alligator.

Crystal chandeliers in the shape of constellations sparkled from the ceiling, casting twinkling light everywhere. A massive, never-ending buffet spread from one side to the other, while waiters carried around trays of hors d'oeuvres.

"Wow," Alex muttered as he took in the scope of the room. "This is pretty wild."

Dawn snorted in disgust, eyeing the room like it had killed one of her family members. "They're not even grizzly bears," she commented to no one in particular. "Just brown ones. And those aren't real king salmon."

"I didn't even know there was a King Salmon," Alex replied, looking surprised.

"That does not surprise me," the queen replied with a sniff, heading toward the food. My stomach rumbled inside my distorted field of invisibility. It had been hours since I'd last had a snack. But eating someone's food was a sign of accepting Guest rights, so I didn't dare even try to smuggle a bite. I should have brought some of those cheese sticks from home.

I tuned out their bickering, scanning the room to see if I recognized any of the other VIPs who had been allowed in. The room was busy but not crowded; it had clearly been designed so that even while people were using it, they would have space from one another.

I suppose if everyone lives long enough, they all get into everyone's business and learn to hate one another. Many of the supernatural beings in the room looked human, a natural defense that many of them had adopted at this point. Some might even have been mortals themselves once.

There were a couple of monsters. Two humanoids that could only be werewolves lurked in a far corner. I was grateful to be invisible, because I stared at them in shock for a long time. Somehow, they had never come up in my training. I had rather thought they were one of those things that fell on the myth side of things.

Everything is real, but that doesn't mean it is true. I shook my head at how prophetic Alex's first lesson had turned out to be. Maybe I should listen to him more often.

Nah.

Reluctantly, I tore my gaze away from the werewolves and continued my inspection of the room. Most of the creatures kept to themselves, their heads close together as they conversed in low tones. It reminded me of my high school lunchroom.

Just as I began to turn my attention back to my companions, I noticed a familiar-looking older Asian woman sitting at a table with two other mortals. Her white hair had been dyed black, but the roots had begun to grow out. I did a double take as my brain remembered the two places I had seen her before.

Once when I went to visit Megan with my father while she was catatonic and under Lazarus's care, I had run into the old woman as she exited the building. Her hair had been white then. That had only been a passing moment, and I had forgotten about it until now.

The second time, her hair had been freshly dyed black when she handed Don Doyle the case that held the serum allowing him to go full dragon. She was an agent of chaos, a fell creature who worked either with or for Lazarus before his demise, and it seemed like no accident she was here now.

A large, golden ring glittered on her finger. I couldn't make it out at this distance, but for some reason I could not take my eyes from it. It pulled at me with undeniable gravity. I needed to study it. It was a part of something that I had to understand.

My feet moved of their own accord as I drifted toward her, trying to get a better glimpse of who she was with and what she was doing. A surprised hiss sounded behind me as Dawn noticed me move, but I ignored her protests. They weren't as important as this.

In a daze, I walked the path between the tables, eyes locked on the ring. It flashed in the light as she moved her hands. My heart was thudding in my ears, its sound the only thing not diluted by the barrier of air that separated me from the rest of the world.

At last, I got close enough that when she shifted, I could make out the symbol on her finger. I froze where I stood in the middle of the walkway, overwhelmed by shock. The gold ring was set with a pale-green stone that seemed almost poisonous. I do not know what sort of mineral it was, only that I finally understood what it represented.

I had seen it before but hadn't realized what it was until I had encountered its sibling. The one I knew wasn't set with a green rock; Kane's had been a milky white, like the pale horse of Death, but there was no denying they had been made by the same hand.

The woman's sigil proudly proclaimed that she was one of the Powers of the world. Ever since my Impossible Task told me that I had to kill several of them, I've been doing my research.

The Four Seals of the Apocalypse—sometimes called horsemen—are known to most of us: The fire and blood of War. The creeping starvation of Famine. The cold embrace of Death. But the last is the wasting sickness, the toxic corruption that eats us from within.

Pestilence.

I knew without a shadow of a doubt that I had found another of the Four Seals.

My hands curled around thin air as I started to reach for Death's cold power. If the rest of the Horsemen were like Kane, then they were mortals who bore some aspect of the pain and suffering of the world.

According to my research, no one knows exactly what the Powers are, what their purpose is, or how they came to be. The best explanation I've read was some dead philosopher's thesis that claimed they were the things that made us mortal. All of them were pathways that led to the grave.

War. Famine. Pestilence. Time. And Death itself, the greatest of them all. The King of the Powers. I didn't know why Time wasn't one of the Horsemen, but there was some sort of distinction. Maybe I'd get the chance to ask Horologium sometime. It didn't matter right now.

Kane was a mortal who had been given his Authority to wear like a cloak. I suspected the rest of them were similar avatars. The point was that although Pestilence was very old, she was not the kind of immortal that would prevent me from killing her with my Reaper's scythe.

Attacking her would jeopardize our mission to find the source of Neodeath, but at that moment, I did not care. I was thinking only of myself and my Impossible Task. I might never again have a chance like this to save my soul.

"Do. Not. Move," Dawn hissed in my ear as she stepped between me and Pestilence, bending over to help herself to a lovely-looking tomato bisque soup on the buffet line just in front of me. Her face was placid, but the fear in her voice was palpable.

"I—" My explanation didn't have a chance to form before she snapped to glare at me with *furious* golden eyes.

"I know exactly *what* you are thinking," she admonished me, her words short and clipped. "But you are being foolish. Tan Yunxian is not some gentle immortal who will tolerate your irreverent games. You will die horribly, bursting from the inside as her diseases consume you." Slowly, I leaned to the side so I could peer over the queen's shoulder, investigating the woman called Pestilence.

"But—"

"No." She stared right into my eyes, pinning me in place. As the manufacturer of my invisibility, she was evidently able to see me just fine. For the first time, I considered what it took for the Queen of All Fae to be scared. When her sister had staged a coup and murdered her mother, Dawn had not hesitated for a moment to throw herself into the fray. She had not blinked when I asked her to smuggle me into the Abaddon Market. But here in the sight of Pestilence? She was terrified.

A smart man might learn something from that. If only one was around. A sense of my resolve must have flashed across my face, because Dawn's expression hardened like a parent glaring at a disobedient toddler. I gathered my strength, preparing to throw myself past the queen and at the Seal of the Apocalypse, when we were interrupted.

"Pardon me, Your Majesty, but your goods are ready in the escrow warehouse," a smooth voice announced as a security guard appeared out of nowhere. "I have been sent to collect you."

You gotta be kidding me.

"Wonderful," Dawn announced, placing her untouched bowl of soup down on the buffet table, already forgotten. Her gaze did not break from mine until I looked away, accepting that the moment had passed. Whatever narrow chance I might have to kill Pestilence only got slimmer when Abaddon Market staff members were around.

Reluctantly, I followed in the queen's wake, casting one long glance back over my shoulder at Pestilence, who continued her conversation, unaware at how close to death she had just been. I had only seven years left to finish my Impossible Task; how would I find her again? I'd need help hunting her down.

Good thing I knew a guy.

Promising myself that I was being wise even if I didn't really believe it, I ghosted along in Dawn's footsteps, preparing myself to plunge back through the crowded streets of the Abaddon Market.

"This way, please," the man said, surprising me by not leading us to the door through which we'd entered. "There is a more direct path for Abaddon One members." He took us out another exit, which was a staircase that descended a floor to a bright-white concrete tunnel under the Land of Darkness. The four of us trooped down the sterile hallway, free from the press of the regular shoppers above.

"I must say I could get used to this," Dawn remarked to Alex after we were about halfway through the passage. "It was far too crowded up above."

"We like to take care of our loyal customers, ma'am," the guard responded in a professionally friendly tone. He barely seemed to be paying attention to the conversation as he walked up to a sealed metal door the size of the hallway.

"Begging your pardon, this is cold iron," he warned, pulling out a gray ID and tapping it against a sensor on the wall. "Please be careful if that is something for you to be concerned about." The door groaned as it began to pull apart, revealing a second staircase on the other side.

"No problem here," Alex offered agreeably. "But we might want to wait a moment for Her Majesty." Dawn sniffed but did not deign to comment.

When the gap was wide enough that there was no danger of Dawn touching the cold iron, the guard waved them through, following on our heels like a sheepdog.

We ascended the flight of stairs, emerging in a dimly lit warehouse. The building wasn't much different from the one that the technomancers had been using in Long Beach to make Neodeath. But this place was clearly used to store precious things.

Everything about the interior spoke of a degree of wealth that was on another level. The floor was not hard concrete but thick, plush carpet. Instead of rusting metal, the storage racks were made of polished wood. The temperature was perfectly climate-controlled. A hint of classical music floated through the space. It seemed more like the basement of the Getty Museum, full of priceless paintings and art, than a black market's illicit storage facility.

This was it. I was in. My heart began to race in my chest as the adrenaline and excitement coursed through my veins. I couldn't believe that it had worked. It seemed like a good idea when I pitched it to Dawn, but Matthew Carver plans *never* go how they're supposed to.

"Right this way," the guard said, setting off to the right with confidence. "Several of our on-staff historians are waiting to give you their inspection." True to his word, he took us to a small conference room nestled among the wooden storage racks.

For a moment, I debated splitting off from them, using my Death sense to find the supply of Neodeath, and getting to work. But I didn't dare risk setting an alarm off while Dawn and Alex were still here in Abaddon Market. I still had some time to kill, so I decided to follow them and wait for my moment.

The experts were waiting in a plain white room, nicely furnished. Potted trees sat in each corner. A man and two women sat across a conference table, pleasant expressions plastered on their faces. Before them the Spear of Lugh lay on a black velvet cloth.

"Please come in," the older woman said, beckoning Alex and Dawn with a gesture. She was dark-skinned with a shock of gray, curly hair on her head. "I am Dr. Adebayo. I will be leading the inspection of your item today."

"I am Dawn, Queen of All Fae, and this is my vassal Alexander.

He is the bearer of the Abaddon One account, so you may direct any questions about that to him." She managed not to sound too bitter about her membership status.

"Doctor, do I detect a hint of Cambridge in your accent?" Alex asked. His grin was a little forced, but he made an effort to warm up the room.

"You do," the woman replied with a pleased smile. "I received two of my doctorates from their programs."

"An Englishwoman to tell me about my Irish relic," Dawn mused, showing more than a hint of her cutting, dangerous side. Her eyes narrowed into slits as she studied the panel of experts. "How typical." Dr. Adebayo had the good grace to let her smile wilt ever so slightly.

"I am only one of the members of the inspection panel, Your Majesty," she assured Dawn.

"I am all ears for what they have to say," Dawn replied, sliding out one of the chairs across the table from them and sitting down primly. "Tell me the good news."

"Dr. O'Connor?" The dark-skinned woman gestured at her male co-worker, whose red hair and last name seemed very on-brand. I wondered if he was always going to be the first one up, or if Dr. Adebayo was trying to appease Dawn's prickly sensitivities.

"I suspect that there is very little known about the Spear of Lugh that you are not already aware of, Your Majesty," he began, gesturing at the weapon on the table between us. His voice bore an uncanny similarity to Doyle's, which made the back of my neck itch.

"Carbon dating suggests that this spear is roughly two thousand years old, which would have it being made in the right era to overlap with when we believe Lugh lived."

"Has it truly been two thousand years?" Dawn murmured to no one in particular. "Mother would be horrified." I shot her a wry glance that she ignored. As far as I knew, the queen was only a couple hundred years old. But she did love an audience.

"Likewise, we ran it through a series of tests to identify whether or not it is imbued with something beyond normal parameters," O'Connor continued. "It gives off an electromagnetic signature similar to other relics that have innate power."

"Give it to me straight, Doc. Is it the real deal?" Dawn seemed amused by this dance. She already knew it was, but there was something funny about a group of mortals lecturing her about a lost piece of her heritage.

"The Spear of Lugh has not been cataloged by modern science before now," O'Connor replied with a halfhearted shrug. "That means it is impossible for me to make a direct match, but if it is not what the vendor claims, then it is something within a reasonable approximation of what I would expect the spear to look like."

"So your official stance is 'probably,'" the Queen of All Fae said with a wide smile, turning back to Dr. Adebayo. "I do hope that this fee gets me something better than that."

"Next is Dr. Quinn, our expert on ancient weaponry." The younger woman, with brown hair and green eyes, rose as O'Connor returned to his seat. She held a manila folder in her hands, which she opened to pull out a series of black-and-white images.

"First we ran the spear through several different forms of X-ray to study its internal structure, checking to see if it was flawed or compromised." She held up one of the negatives so we could stare at it through the light. When I was a kid, I broke my arm, and the doctor showed me the dark line in my bone where it had fractured. I saw nothing that looked like it here. The weapon appeared to be solid, with no cracks.

"We found no sign of structural damage, nor did we find any internal sources of power, which further indicates that the electromagnetic signals Dr. O'Connor's team found are inherent to the Spear of Lugh rather than inserted in an attempt to create a counterfeit."

"So more probably?" Dawn arched an eyebrow at the younger woman, who blushed and nodded before sitting down.

"Your Majesty, Abaddon Market is confident within a 90 percent certainty that this *is* the Spear of Lugh," Dr. Adebayo promised. "We are happy to keep it under observation while payment is processed between you and the vendor. During that time, we will submit it to a battery of deeper tests to try to find any discrepancies."

Dawn opened her mouth to make what was no doubt a scathing comment, but Dr. Adebayo continued gamely on, not giving the queen a moment.

"Given our certainty, we will also be happy to offer a lifetime warranty on the spear. If at a later date you are able to discover that it is indeed counterfeit, we will buy it back from you for the price that you paid for it."

"A buyback guarantee," Dawn mused, leaning back in her chair to exchange an appreciative glance with Alex. My friend had the hint of an exasperated expression lurking in the corner of his eyes, but he played along with Dawn's theater.

"Very well, I am satisfied," the Queen of All Fae announced after the silence stretched for several moments. "Run your battery of tests. I will speak to my treasury and have them deliver the payment."

"Wonderful," Dr. Adebayo's face lit up in what almost looked like a relieved smile. I could understand. Working with Dawn could be tricky if you weren't used to dealing with things that bit. "We're thrilled that you trusted us to oversee this transaction for you. Our office will be in touch when the inspection is completed, but I am confident that we will be able to deliver this artifact to you without any issues."

"Lovely."

"Now, if you are satisfied, please allow us to escort you back to the market or to one of the egress points?"

"I have what I came for, an exit would be preferred."

"Of course, Your Majesty, we have one here in this escrow facility. Please come with me." Dr. Adebayo rose, gesturing for them to proceed her out of the conference room. My heart rate spiked as I realized this was my moment. Dawn's eyes followed me as I slunk along the edge of the room, staying out of everyone's way. I gave her a grin and a thumbs-up before slipping away from my friends and heading alone into the dark of the escrow warehouse.

It was time to do what I did best.

Cause trouble.

CHAPTER TWENTY-NINE

MOVING QUICKLY, I wound my way through the luxurious warehouse, looking for someplace out-of-the-way and forgotten. My invisibility would only last a little longer, and I needed to prepare to return to the land of the visible.

I spotted a perfect gap in the storage racks on the ground level—an open spot waiting for more purchases to come in for escrow and assessment. I'm still not entirely sure what *escrow* is. Every time I ask, everyone just rolls their eyes at my incompetence but doesn't explain. I'm starting to think no one knows, and everyone is just too embarrassed to admit it.

I slipped inside the darkness of the gap, being careful not to brush against what looked like a large painting wrapped in brown paper and sealed with a rough string. I had no idea whose work might be underneath, but if it was in this place, it was certainly worth more than I was.

The classical music continued to play, adding a lighthearted soundtrack to a scene that was actually quite intense. Thanks to the sound distortion of the air bubble I was in, it felt weird and almost alien. The more I listened to it, the more unsettled I felt. In a moment, I would truly be on my own in a strange world. I was under no illusions about the reception I would receive if I was discovered.

But I was an agent of Kane, a Reaper tasked with maintaining the sovereignty of the Death Treaty. That might sound like a bad thing. Death is rarely welcomed, even by the wisest of mortals. But I have walked the places beyond the Veil and seen the alternatives. Everything else is much, much worse.

My heart raced as I ignored the impulse to reach for my dark power and began searching for the Neodeath that was being stored here. It had been driving me nuts all day, resisting the temptation to even peek at it, because I was *certain* that frequency was being monitored by some sort of supernatural surveillance. If I were an enemy of the Grim Reaper, deliberately manufacturing a counterfeit death to steal souls from him, the very *first* thing I would do is figure out how to detect if his Authority was being used near me.

I hadn't worried using my Death senses the last time we were here because the Powers That Be already knew I was in the market. There was no point in being subtle. But since I snuck in today, I didn't want to tip them off until the time was right—and it almost was.

I just needed to wait for one more thing.

The sound of Beethoven—or whoever it was—suddenly snapped back to normal as the invisible bubble of air around me burst. I thought I heard a faint *pop*, but that might have been my own dramatic imagination.

I froze, remaining crouched in the shadows, waiting to see if anyone reacted to my sudden appearance. My heart thundered in my chest. Its pounding echoed in my eardrums at a tempo the old music could never match.

I forced myself to wait ten seconds, then twenty, then a minute. With each passing moment, I felt some of the tension in my shoulders release. I hadn't been discovered. I almost certainly would be soon. There was no way this place wasn't monitored in every conceivable manner. But I just needed a little more time to accomplish my mission. Now that Dawn and Alex were gone, I was free to move on to phase two.

You see, the order of operations today mattered a lot. Being a Guest is a funny thing. As with everything else in the supernatural world, there are a thousand rules, and they are precise and specific.

The trick was if I acted out now that I was alone and unsupervised, I couldn't be held to the standard of breaking the Guest rules because I had never been one. And since Dawn had left the world, she was no longer a Guest herself and couldn't be either.

It was thin. It was based on a series of technicalities. But then, what isn't?

The bubble that surrounded me popping meant that she and Alex were gone. It was our agreed-upon green light, and I was eager to make use of it. A grim smile spread across my face as I reached for the bundle of darkness that I carried in the back of my mind.

Death's Authority leapt to my call, like a hound eager to hunt. I let its coldness sweep through me, chasing away my fear and excitement. I held the peace for a moment, marveling at how poised I felt. Was this what Orion felt like all the time?

Then I sent out my senses, searching for the oily scum of Neodeath. The moment I did, I started a mental timer. I had no way of knowing for sure, but I was positive they would sense my actions somehow.

My enemies were too resourceful for me to assume that their

incompetence would allow me to do what I wanted. I had gotten lucky making it this far, but that didn't mean my good fortune would continue. I had to act as though right now some alarm was blaring in a security office somewhere, alerting them that Death had come.

Fortunately, I didn't have to look far to find the evil I had come for. It was right here in the building with me. My senses zeroed in on it immediately—it stank like rotten garbage from the far corner of the warehouse, which meant I would need to navigate through the building to get to it.

Now that I understood where I needed to go, my eyes popped open, and I leaned forward, scouring the row to see if any guards were patrolling. But my section was empty, so I slid out of the shadows and began to move with purpose.

I held my Grim Reaper power lightly in my hand. It would only take a simple flick of a wrist for me to summon my scythe. It felt like the correct weapon to bring on this mission.

Evangeline had been forbidden from coming, and I took that as a hint that this wouldn't be an appropriate time to use Azrael's sword, so I'd left it at home in my gun safe. Man, I really wasn't a Californian anymore, was I? All it had taken was getting my soul stolen.

Coming to a crossroads, I again leaned out, looking for a squad of armed security hunting me. I spotted a pair of guards walking toward me, their shoulders relaxed. They didn't seem to be particularly alert, just on a standard patrol around the facility.

Moving slowly, like an alligator going below the water, I ducked back into my aisle, tucking between two large crates in one of the shelves, burrowing in the dark. I was pretty sure the large pools of shadow in the warehouse caused by the hanging cone lights were designed to make it feel intimate and luxurious, but they also made it easy for me to skulk around undetected.

I held my breath as the two men strolled by. Their heads turned as they passively scanned the room, but their low conversation didn't break. They were professionals—but bored professionals. Only a madman would dare to strike here.

My eyes drilled into their backs as they continued their patrol, walking past my row as they headed farther into the facility. I made myself count to a hundred, slowly. Still worried that they might be too close, I counted another thirty seconds before at last slipping out from my hiding spot and checking to see if the coast was clear. I found nothing but the darkness waiting for me.

I dashed across the intersection and made my way down another long row, gazing at the endless sea of crated-up wonders. What would I find hidden here if I had the time to peruse? I suspected that many "lost" artifacts lay all around me.

I could tell I was getting closer to the priceless section of the warehouse when the layout suddenly changed. A thick chain-link fence ran up the width of the path from floor to ceiling. A metal gate with a keycard reader was set into it, barring my path.

I eyed it in frustration for a moment before shrugging and summoning the scythe. The physical shadow formed in my hand in an instant, its icy cold numbing my palm. I hefted the weapon and slashed at the wires, making three quick cuts.

The scythe cut through the metal as if it were smoke, and a triangle big enough for me to crouch through opened as a section fell onto the thick carpet with a quiet *plop*. It would have been a lot louder if the floor was a more standard cement. Once more the luxury of this place worked against its security.

I banished the weapon as I ducked through the hole and picked up my pace as I moved through the more secure section. I could only assume that the things on this side were more precious—or dangerous. A massive crate twice my size bore the label LIVE ANIMAL—DO NOT APPROACH—OMEGA PROTOCOL stuck on its side. The entire box hissed and shook as something slammed against the wall at the sound of my footsteps.

I felt the hairs on the back of my neck stand on end as I studied the container. I am a pretty obstinate guy. I don't like being told what to do. But whatever was in that box scared me. I felt absolutely no desire to get closer.

Forcing myself to focus, I summoned my senses, letting them guide me toward the Neodeath. I was close. Another row over and just a little farther down. The darkness burned wrongly, calling to me. I cut through the next intersection and drew up in surprise at what I found waiting for me.

Gone was the quiet luxury of the Abaddon Market escrow warehouse, replaced by harsh efficiency. The carpet ended abruptly, segueing into dirty concrete. A row of half a dozen shipping crates like the ones they use on ocean liners faced into the walkway, their metal mouths open.

POSEIDON OCEANIC SHIPPING said a big sticker on one of them, worn faint by years at sea. A red trident was painted horizontally underneath the sign. I felt a chill settle over me at the sight. I'm not a big believer in coincidences anymore. Not after the things I've been through. I've had too many run-ins with the Olympians for this to be anything other than a big clue.

Technically, Pluto and Somnus were Roman, while Poseidon was Greek. While some of the original cast came back for season two, I didn't know if the same guy reprised his role as Neptune in the sequel or if he had to break off into a solo career.

No matter which of the ocean gods he was, it struck me as important that Poseidon's name was on the shipment. Hades was broken. Pluto was dust. The position of Death god in the Roman pantheon was up for grabs, and one of the elder gods of that pantheon was helping to smuggle Neodeath. Maybe it was a coincidence. Maybe he didn't know.

Or maybe it was a plot against Somnus.

Tentatively, I took a few steps forward to peek in the open door of the first shipping container. My stomach fell as I found exactly what I'd expected. Box after box full of the dark metal ingots, stacked and ready for shipping. There was even more than I expected.

When Alex and I helped Evangeline take out the technomancers who were actually making the stuff in Long Beach, there had only been a few ingots in the warehouse. I had never considered that their production might be more expansive than that. Having a few weapons like the athame that was used on Maria was enough to commit atrocities. Murder is a horrible thing, one of the worst things that can be done.

But this? This was enough to commit a genocide and then steal its fruits.

My mouth was dry, and my heart pounded as I raced to the next one, glancing in to confirm that it was the same. The third and fourth were also stuffed to the brim. But to my relief, the fifth was only half full, and the sixth sat empty, like a starving whale, waiting to swallow a ship. I don't know if they do that, but it felt appropriate for the branding.

I wasn't sure what to do. I didn't have the angel's ability to fry the dark metal, so my plan had been to steal all the Neodeath and take it back to her. Depleting their supply and figuring out where it was going would have been a huge win. But this was too much. I could never even put a dent in this.

Panic threatened to set in, but I ignored it, leaning into Death's cold power, trying to keep my mind clear. This was so much bigger than me. This was world-ending stuff. That sounded dramatic, but I didn't think it was.

When I "died" for a brief moment and made my way to the DMV in the sky, I had been given a number and told to get in line. My number was far too high. It was off from the numbers held by the other people in line by *billions.* At the time, I took it as a good sign, a clue that I would escape my predicament and get my soul back. That I wouldn't die in the next seven or so years but live for a long time.

Now I wasn't so sure that was what the number had been telling me.

Stop panicking and look for clues. My training shouted at me, with an inner monologue that sounded suspiciously like Orion. I guessed that was only fair; he had been the one to hammer them it into me anyway.

I couldn't steal all of it, but I *could* try to figure out where it was going and who it was going to. Unlike most of the time that I was operating, I didn't have to solve all of this myself. I had some big scary friends I could call up to do the smiting. It would be a race between the Angel of Justice and the Grim Reaper for who got their hands on these idiots first.

Suitably scolded, I raced back into the first container, looking for a manifest or a shipping label. Anything that might tell me who was buying all this Neodeath. I pulled my phone from my pocket and used it to snap photos of the crates and the containers. I made sure to get a shot of the POSEIDON label too. Just in case.

I could see the remnants of stickers that someone had peeled off each box, hiding the identity of the recipients. I moved to the second container, running my hands along the boxes. My heartbeat was still pounding in my ears, and I was all too aware that my time was slipping away.

There was nothing in that second container, or the third. Just stacks and stacks of the counterfeit death ingots, waiting to be forged into weapons that could be used to steal the souls of mortals. My anger grew like a storm cloud as I pondered that.

Who dared?

Seriously. *Who* dared?

I have a pretty dim view of humanity as a whole. It's okay; I'm allowed. I'm a card-carrying member of the species. We are arrogant and selfish. We burn bright and char the things around us. We cut down forests and leave our weak to starve.

But that is not all we are, just some of our great failures. We also love and make music and have babies and heal. We care for the sick and build wonders that the supernatural monsters that skulk around us can only look at and marvel.

We are the ones with souls. Reality is for us, not them.

Who dared?

These monsters were going to learn exactly the price of such hubris. I was going to see to it that they were erased, *unmade,* sent into the darkness and forgotten. There would be no mercy for an act like this. I only hoped Kane would let me watch as they were cut down.

"Attention, intruder, this is the Abaddon Security Force, we have you surrounded." A voice from a bullhorn broke through my furious monologuing. I looked up at the ceiling of the fourth container in surprise. They had snuck up on me.

"Come out with your hands up."

I chuckled. Even in another world, some things stay the same.

"Sorry, no can do," I murmured, more for myself than for them.

I had no desire to get shot by a bunch of tense guards, so I decided to make my own exit. With a thought, I summoned my scythe, using it to carve through the back of the steel shipping container like it was butter. The metal screamed in protest but parted without resistance.

A section fell to the ground with a loud clang, but I didn't wait to see if the guards realized what I was up to. I leapt out the back, running around the rear of the rest of the containers, heading deeper into the secure section.

I wasn't that worried that I had been discovered. All I needed to do was find a door, and the Key of Portunus would do the rest of the work for me. I'd be gone before they even realized I had a way out.

"There he is!" a voice shouted. Gunfire erupted behind me, causing me to duck in surprise as some of the bullets pinged from the crate next to me. I didn't think they'd start shooting in here. There were too many valuables that couldn't be replaced if they were hit by a stray round.

I guess they took security *very* seriously. I mean, I would too if I was hiding the kind of secrets they were. I ducked low, cutting back to the front of the container and using it as a shield as I dashed forward, running toward the next intersection.

Despite their threat that they had me surrounded, it seemed they actually had me corralled. I understood the reasoning. Why bother stopping me from running deeper into the facility? That would only give them more time to catch me.

I cut to the right, running down one of the parallel rows, scanning the room for a door. There were plenty of offices and conference rooms in the rest of the warehouse. I was certain there would be some here. I just needed to stay a little ahead of these guys, and I would be gone—

I slid to a stop, stunned by the glint that I caught out of the corner of my eye. I could hear the guards shouting threats behind me, but their words were distant, muted. My jaw dropped as I turned to stare at the orange glow.

Ten familiar-looking cartons designed to hold giant, tennis-ball-sized spheres were stacked on metal shelves. Most of them held at least a couple. Some were full. Each one glowed with an inner orange light.

They were souls. The vessels used to transport and carry mortals on the other side of the Veil. They most certainly should not be *here* on the living side of Reality.

For a wild moment, I debated grabbing one. This was exactly what Somnus was demanding in order to release the lien on my sleep. All I had to do was give him one of them, and he would not be my problem any longer.

But that wouldn't be right. These souls were stolen, taken from where they were meant to go. I hadn't been the one to take them originally, but I'd be no better if I used them for my own ends.

"There he is!" a woman's voice shouted, snapping me out of my moral quandary. I don't know what I would have done if I stood there much longer. Temptation is a rot that eats away at even the strongest foundations. But I had no more time for it to do its dark work.

I tore myself away from the stolen souls and raced toward the end of the row, feeling a sense of relief as I spotted exactly what I was looking for, a door set in the far wall. Laughing with adrenaline, I stuck my hand in my pocket, fishing for the Key of Portunus.

"Sorry, everyone, I am supposed to be elsewhere," I shouted over my shoulder as I stopped at the door. "Hate to go so soon, but don't worry, I'll be back."

I reached for the handle, and my world went black.

CHAPTER
THIRTY

I SLEPT.

For the first time in *months,* I floated in perfect, formless sleep. There was nothing but infinite darkness that wrapped itself around me like it was swaddling a baby. It was a different kind of abyss than the Nothing, despite looking similar. There was no all-encompassing hunger here. Instead, it was almost peaceful. If sleep truly is the little death, then the main aspect they share is that of rest.

Dimly, I was aware that I was dreaming. My consciousness stirred just under the veil of the water, not quite breaking the surface tension but making it bow as it moved. I wasn't lucid, only slowly seeing beyond the façade that held my mind.

There was something troubling me, but it was a slippery thought.

The more I tried to squeeze it, the more it slipped from my grasp, sliding along ahead of me. I chased it, burrowing through the formless void of sleep, but no matter how hard I pursued it, it remained just out of reach.

I told you, a voice whispered in the darkness.

I paused, my quest interrupted. There was nothing to see, and yet I was waking up. I was alone in the infinity of sleep, and yet I knew someone else was there. Their intrusion was like a splinter in my mind.

YOU BETRAYED ME, it thundered. Its rage shook the darkness. My mind broke free of its cobwebs as it was jostled by the fury of the thing that invaded my dreams.

Somnus. It had to be.

NOW SUFFER YOUR REWARD! it thundered, and the void exploded. A mouth larger than any whale's emerged from below, open wide to devour me. I screamed, but I had no body or voice with which to cry out.

The god must know that I had chosen not to steal a soul for him. That seemed impossible. I was in another world, far beyond his grasp. Perhaps he managed to peer through my eyes after slipping into my mind in my dreams. I had no true understanding of what he was capable of.

But somehow, he knew.

Terror ravaged my mind as I was swallowed whole like that Jonah guy. Light crashed from every direction, blinding me. I felt myself twist as I was crushed by invisible forces. It was agonizing, and I felt things crack in me that did not seem like bones.

"Please!" I managed to croak; somehow the pressure had condensed my consciousness back into the form of a body. I had limbs and lungs again, and I made use of them. "I did not betray you. I can still help you accomplish your goal." The mighty jaws paused, as if intrigued by my promise.

How? the voice demanded, speaking without moving. I was grateful for its ventriloquism, given that I was trapped between a pair of the thing's molars. I did not know how much more of its crushing power I could take.

"There are others who move against you," I gasped. Why did I need to breathe in this place?

What others? There was a note in his voice that caught my attention. It sounded like panic or paranoia. They're cousins, much like sleep and death. I paused, drawing out the tense silence for a moment as I tried to remember what I had seen.

Somnus was looking for a promotion. He wanted to become the death god of his pantheon. That meant he wasn't trying to upend the apple cart. If I completed his task, he would begin to rebuild Hades and fill it with souls to the best of his ability. I'm not sure how many mortals still follow that particular path, but that was all well and good. As far as Kane was concerned, it would fall under the Death Treaty.

That told me he probably *wasn't* involved in the Neodeath conspiracy. It wouldn't make sense for him to play both sides. Stealing souls from being delivered was actively against his best interest. But it was very telling that one of his sort-of sibling's names was on the shipping containers. Why would the Greek version of the oceanic god move to block his elevation? If he had been replaced by Neptune, maybe he thought this was his chance to get back in the band playing a new instrument?

"It's Poseidon," I told the god of dreams at last. "He's working with those who are trying to cheat Death. I think he's trying to take your spot." The tension in the dream spiked sharply. My words had found their mark.

The world rocked, and I rattled around in his mouth, but the teeth did not resume their grinding. A stinging sensation swept over my face, but I ignored it, focused on this moment.

POSEIDON? Somnus's omnipresent voice voiced hissed in surprise. *You've found that washed-up has-been?* How about that: Matthew Carver, accidental genius.

The world shook again, and the stinging on my face grew sharper. I gasped in pain. It felt like someone had just slapped me with all their strength.

"We could work together," I offered the silent god. "Death wants what you do. Poseidon and these others break his treaty and threaten his peace."

Perhaps. Together we could—no!

Everything shook a third time, and the dream shattered, pulling me free.

My body flailed as I returned to it. I heard myself gasp in shock and pain. My head was turned to the side, my cheeks stinging in pain from the blow. I tried to raise my arms to defend myself, but they were bound behind me.

"I'm awake!" I screamed, panting as adrenaline and fear coursed through my veins. "I'm awake!" I swung my head in an arc, taking in my surroundings. Everything I saw filled me with more dread.

I was in a blank, concrete room, bathed in a spotlight from above. It looked like some empty portion of the warehouse, tucked away from where the customers came to review their purchases.

My hands and feet were bound tightly to a metal chair. I jerked my limbs, but none of them could move more than an inch. A black ring was set in the floor, surrounding me.

Three gray-garbed guards and the Overseer stared at me with cold expressions. Two of them were mortals I didn't recognize, but I knew the third. Bellerophon. The scarred Nephilim glared at me from beside the door.

The man who'd just finished hitting me took a step back, crossing the ring to stand on the opposite side. That more than anything filled me with a chill. I have a couple of tricks up my sleeve, but they wouldn't work in here. Willow's fire couldn't cross the circle's borders to burn them to a crisp, and Kane's Authority couldn't reach me inside. My captors knew their business and were taking no chances. As I adjusted to my new surroundings, I began to understand what must have happened.

Before I could escape through the door, Somnus had lifted the lien from my exhaustion and pulled me into the dreams. It is not normal for a human to stay awake as long as I had. I could only assume that his banishment somehow propped me up to exist beyond what should be possible, like a cinder block under a car's axle in place of a missing tire. Once he pulled out the support, I fell. My sleep debt was so immense that no amount of caffeine or danger could keep me awake. Only the curse of a god would do the trick.

"Sorry, I think I passed out for a second there," I said, adding a yawn that started out as fake but turned real as I opened my mouth. "Hope I didn't miss anything important." The Overseer watched me for a long moment, his mouth formed in a frown. His square horn-rimmed glasses glinted in the harsh lighting of the interrogation room.

There was still something eerie about him that I hadn't figured out. He seemed disappointed by me at every turn. Was he one of my high school math teachers? I narrowed my eyes as I studied him, but he clearly didn't resemble Mrs. Bowman at all, and I honestly couldn't remember what any else of them looked like. So maybe that was it.

"I must say, I really expected more, Matthew," he said at last, crossing his arms to stare down at me. "Breaking the Guest rights?"

"Whoa, whoa, whoa," I interrupted, my hands jerking against their bonds as I tried to wave them in front of him. "I am going to have to stop you right there, bucko. I *absolutely* did not do that."

"You entered—"

"Sneakily. The guards on your borders state that you are only a

Guest once your ID is scanned into the market." The Overseer stared at me for a long moment, as if surprised by the loophole.

"We shall have to fix that then," he murmured softly. I didn't like that response. It seemed far too composed and dangerous. My least favorite enemies are the ones who can keep themselves together.

"Well, since you've confirmed you are *not* a Guest," he continued, as if no longer bothered, "that means we have a certain amount of freedom in how we conduct this negotiation." I managed not to gulp audibly at the darkly pleased expressions that passed across the face of the three guards hovering behind him.

"Are you sure you want to do that?" I asked, drawing myself up straight in my seat and trying to look unbothered. I still wasn't sure if the Abaddon Market people were involved or just infrastructure that Bellerophon, Beatrice, and the rest were using. "You know some of the people I represent, but maybe not all of them. Some of your clients are meddling with things that will bring *judgment.* I would not recommend making enemies with—"

"Let's see if I can save us some time. The Hunter is in Tartarus, and Death is not welcome here." The Overseer listed off my allies with the bored air of a man who knew everything. "Have we gotten to the end of your list?"

Well, crap. At least I had one more ace in the hole to play.

"I was actually thinking of calling someone of the *smiting* variety," I replied, wiggling my eyebrows to make sure that he got the full context of the threat. I've never seen what it looks like when the Heavenly Host conducts a raid on a bunker of evil, but I can't imagine that it is fun.

"The angels?" The Overseer laughed in amused disgust. "I have no fear of them coming down from their lofty heights to chase shadows and rumors. They are perfectly happy to let us contain the chaos and keep it under control." So that was why Evangeline had been forbidden from coming here. This place was a honeypot, just crooked enough to be useful to all sides.

"But the Neod—" I started, only to be interrupted again.

"I must say, after everything I knew about you—all the stories, the headaches, the problems—I really expected you to put up more of a fight, Matthew."

"You keep talking to me like you know me. But mister, we've never met." An expression of genuine surprise flashed across his face, before turning into delight. It made my stomach turn sour to see it.

"Remarkable," he mused, tilting his head to look at me closer, like he was looking for the lie written in my face. "I was right, wasn't I?" He seemed relieved, as if he had doubted himself until this moment.

"You were?"

"You truly do not recognize me, even though we once knew each other very well?"

I shook my head in confusion.

"I would have thought that killing me would have made me hard to forget." The corners of his mouth turned up in a wicked smile. I had no clue what he was talking about. It seemed to me like the dear Overseer was a few sales short of a full flea market. I had never seen him before in my life.

"If I killed you, then I did a pretty poor job of it," I remarked, arching an eyebrow, trying to make him sound like even more of a lunatic than he already did. "Seeing as how you're alive and all."

"Come now, Matthew. It's right there in front of you. All you have to do is reach out and take it," the Overseer chided me, tilting his head again, as if he was stunned that I could not connect the dots.

"Listen, I already thought you were crazy for going after Kane. But now you're really selling it. I don't know who you are. I definitely haven't killed you. Are you sure this is the guy you guys want running this thing?" I asked, looking past him to the three guards who watched this exchange with flat, professional eyes. "Surely there's some sort of protocol to remove a manager from his post? You're picking a fight with the *Grim Reaper.* Nobody ever gets out alive."

"I told you that we were not equals," the Overseer said. His eyes had taken on a distant, spaced out look behind his glasses.

"You, uh, what?" I asked, my throat suddenly dry.

"I said that I *owned* you." His expression was dreamlike, as if he was revisiting a fond memory. Terror clawed its way up my spine. I remembered those words. They were among the last ones of a man I did kill.

"Dark Abyss," I swore in horror. My mouth hung open as I stared at the abomination before me. He was right, it had been in front of me the whole time, but I hadn't been able to see it. Now that I did, it was shocking that I'd missed it.

"Do you understand now?" The Overseer's voice was low and pleased. He was delighted to have been here for this moment, to see the realization and the fear dawn in my expression. We were enemies, he and I. We had been for a long time.

"You're Lazarus," I said, staring into his cold blue eyes.

Kane told me that the old man had split his soul into two pieces. My Death Tax had been to deliver a half soul to Death. No more, no less. I had assumed this meant the other half was already gone. That he had done something to destroy it. But he hadn't, not at all.

His other half endured. The reason he looked familiar was that he was the same man, just several decades younger. Age had not yet worn down his face and bent his back. He didn't need a cane to walk.

Beatrice and Bellerophon and the rest of the technomancers weren't outcasts scrambling to rebuild their cabal after their leader's death. This had been planned for since the beginning. It was entirely possible that the two Lazaruses…Lazari? It was entirely possible that the *two* of them had been working in tandem on separate projects. The man who wanted to defeat Death had gone and made his own.

"If you can't beat them, join them, huh?" I asked, feeling my features darken.

"Oh, you mean the Neodeath Project?" He laughed as he crossed his arms, amused by my anger. "That development is entirely thanks to you, actually."

"What?"

"When you returned from the Veil, you told the elder me something before you killed him. Do you remember what it was?"

I frowned, trying to remember the conversation. I had been desperate to protect Megan, to convince him to leave her alone.

"I told him—you—that Reality keeps expanding." The words came out of my mouth without prompting. A numbness swept over me as I saw the dominoes that fell after I'd revealed this. "I explained that we will always need people to die, to keep everything from collapsing."

"You did." The younger Lazarus nodded, spreading his hands wide, gesturing at what I assumed was the warehouse behind us. "And thanks to your insight, we have begun a project to solve this dilemma." I felt like I was going to be sick. The murders, the stolen souls. Maria. It had been me that sent them down this path.

When I told the original Lazarus about the nature of Reality, I had hoped it would convince him to change his ways, to abandon his disastrous plans for the human race. I had been looking for an excuse to spare him—to defy Kane's Death Tax.

He hadn't given me one.

The lesser Lazarus and I stared at each other, our eyes striking at each other like knives. There would be no peace, no quarter. The term *mortal enemies* is used to describe two men whose very souls are opposed. It implies that the parties involved are mortals. I wasn't sure if that still applied to him, but I felt the animosity all the same. As long as I lived, he would never be safe.

I hated Dan and Zagan and the rest of the supernatural beings who have crossed me. But that felt paltry and small compared with the anger that built in me as I glared at the man I had already killed once. Just because I had paid off my Death Tax didn't mean I couldn't get ahead on my next one.

All I had to do was figure out how to get outside this circle. I licked my lips, trying to wriggle my wrist surreptitiously as I searched for a weakness in the cords that bound me. But no matter how I twisted, they held me tightly.

"So what's next? Where do we go from here?" I demanded, looking back at Lazarus. It felt strange to use his name for the Overseer, but now that I knew the truth, I couldn't help but see it etched in his features. His jawbones were the same shape, though a little sharper, not yet sanded down by age. It was Lazarus, just as I had never known him.

"Given your current alliances, I knew that our confrontation was inevitable," he admitted. "I had hoped that making you a Guest of the market would delay our clash, but I should have known there is no peace you can't disrupt." If I weren't in so much danger, I might have taken that personally.

"We could kill you," he continued thoughtfully, as if still formulating his plan as he spoke. "But that has its own complications." My eyes narrowed until I realized what he meant. If I died and proceeded to the Veil, I would be able to tell Kane everything I knew.

A terrible feeling began to curdle in my gut as I realized where this was going.

"There are some parties who would be most upset if your soul were to vanish." He cocked his head, watching me, enjoying seeing the fear growing in my eyes. "But they will get over it, I think. Especially given the circumstances."

Neodeath. He was talking about using his counterfeit product on me in order to keep me away from the Grim Reaper. It meant I wouldn't be ferried to Hell. But why would they get over it? Maria told Father Pike that Zagan had threatened her. Was that why Samael and other demons were here?

Like I said, world-ending stuff.

"I can feel it, you know," he remarked conversationally, enjoying living in this moment.

"Feel what?"

"The agony. My other half suffers even now in the depths of the Pit. I believe you're familiar with the facility." My eyes widened as I realized I might have guessed that. Megan had suffered similarly while half of her soul had languished in Hell.

"I did have a brief tour," I admitted, giving him a smile that was all teeth. I wasn't sorry in the slightest. "Which circle did they get you a time-share on?"

"Treachery."

"Oh, all the way down on Level Nine." I let out a low whistle of appreciation. "Chilly down there as I recall." The entire floor had been frozen over, with the prisoners buried in the ice. It was perhaps not the *worst* thing I had seen on my tour of Hell Industries, but it didn't look like much fun either.

"So cold that it burns." Lazarus was no longer smiling, as if speaking of the horrors that half of himself was experiencing sapped some of the joy from the moment. Good. I hoped it did. I hoped that occasionally they dug him up just so he could feel a hint of warmth again before they buried him in the ice once more. Maybe I'd suggest that to Zagan next time I saw him.

"Marco." Lazarus held out his right hand, snapping his fingers like a dog trainer to get the attention of one of his guards. The man responded by producing a sheathed blade from behind his back, passing it to his boss.

My eyes fell on the Ka-Bar-style knife. I understood what it was even before Lazarus drew it. Made from the same dark metal that was stored in Poseidon's shipping containers, it was darker than condensed shadow. An almost perfect match for the scythe that was worthless to me now.

My heart raced, and, despite my desire to be brave, I twisted in my chair, desperately trying to break free. The four men watched me with coldly dispassionate eyes, watching a cornered animal panic in its final moments.

Unbidden, an idea on how escape came to me, a path shown to me by Dawn. I did not think this was the scenario she had in mind when she'd told me I could give up my soul and become immortal, but if it kept me from being smuggled off into the dark with the lost and their monsters, it would be worth any cost.

"I wish I was a Faerie," I said softly into the room. The rest of the guards ignored me, but I thought I saw Bellerophon's eyes narrow in suspicion. Perhaps he was the only one old enough to guess what I was doing.

Dawn told me that I would need to speak it three times for it to become true. This was only my second time. If my end came abruptly, I didn't want to risk only being able to get it out once. But even as I said it, a sense of determination began to grow in me. I didn't really *wish* that I was a Faerie. I wanted to live! I wanted to be human and to experience life. Giving up my soul was a form of surrender, and I wasn't ready to do that.

Lazarus twisted the weapon slowly in his hands, eyeing its darkness against the bright light. "What a strange thing we have made together," he mused, his words soft, eyes unfocused. "I am sure you know that the immortals say they cannot make art because they do not have souls." I'd been told the same thing. But I let him continue to monologue, preparing myself for what was to come. If I wasn't going to give up my humanity, then there was really one way I was going to get out of this alive.

"I suspect that is true," he continued, not actually waiting for my input. "But it is man who has created this, guided and shaped its purpose, not *something* that set it as the constant of the universe. Does that mean it is an art? I think so. This is the new era of Death, and it is beautiful and poignant instead of an empty thing that we try to paint meaning on." His lips curled up as he turned to study me once more. "You'll see what I mean soon enough."

Terror gripped me as he stepped into the ring.

The half-souled man eyed me warily, clearly wondering if my abilities were strong enough to reach him, even as restrained as I was. He knew what Lazarus knew, which was a lot but not enough—not by far.

The ring cut me off from my Reaper powers. They were an external gift, and it acted as a border, preventing them from reaching me. I could still sense the cold Authority, just out of my reach, like it was behind a thick pane of glass. Willow was present; I carried the spirit inside me wherever I went. But their fire was rather directional, making it hard to use while I was still bound with my hands pointed at the floor. I didn't think we had enough juice in the tank to turn the entire circle into an inferno. He was right to assume that he was safe from an immediate attack. All my other options got a little stupider and more reckless.

Fortunately, stupid and reckless is sort of my thing.

Lazarus took another step toward me, treating me like I was truly dangerous. I appreciated the respect, but not enough to spare him for what he'd done. I locked eyes on the abomination and smiled, which caused him to pause. He was more scared of me than I was of him, I realized.

With a nudge, I summoned Willow, and the Faerie spirit burst into being around my hands, burning bright and warm. Lazarus tensed but relaxed slightly when I wasn't immediately able to burn myself free of the bindings.

"We use fireproof ropes here," he told me with a disappointed chuckle. "It will take you a long time to—" I didn't bother letting him finish his sentence, instead using Willow like my father taught me.

Flaring both hands wide, I pointed them at the floor and triggered a concussive blast at an angle. The force of the burst launched me into the air, sending me flying forward like a missile. My chair spun, flipping end-over-end as I slammed into something with enough force to crush a watermelon—or someone's skull, it turned out. I could only hope it was Bellerophon—as we landed in a tangled heap. For half a second I lay on my back, stunned by the force of my landing. Then everyone started screaming, and I reacted purely on instinct.

Free of the circle, Death's power flared to life in my brain. I summoned my scythe, using my will to twist it and bring it forth at an angle. The curved blade erupted into being, growing out of me, cutting through chair, the ropes, the floor, and the poor guard beneath me as if they were smoke. If he wasn't already dead, he was now.

I was free.

Roaring in anger, I leapt to my feet. The ruined chair was split down the middle, the front legs still tied to my ankles. They restricted my movement but not enough to stop me from standing.

The guard next to me was raising his rifle, and I gestured with my left hand, sending a burst of Willow's fire out in an underhanded toss. The glob of fire hit him in the chest and attached to him like napalm. He fell to the ground screaming as the inferno swept over him, ravenous beyond anything normal.

"No! Use the Neodeath!" Lazarus screamed from behind me before I could be gunned down where I stood. "We can't send him to the Veil."

Bellerophon's expression grew tighter as he slowly lowered his gun and reached for his own Ka-Bar made of black metal. I grinned evilly at him, advancing with my scythe extended to prevent him from coming close to me. The two halves of the metal chair rattled in my wake. I cut them free with a backward slash of my scythe.

"Not as cocky now, are you?" I asked the Nephilim with a cold voice. Death's power had chased away any of the warmth that lived in me, but I didn't mind. This one had it coming.

The scarred man didn't respond, only backed up, falling into the circular steps of a skilled swordsman. He settled into a low stance, holding his Neodeath knife in a reverse grip. I had the advantage, but I would be a fool to forget who he was. Just because he hadn't gotten the Hunter's job didn't mean he wasn't very, very dangerous.

"I'll be right with you," I promised Lazarus with a glance over my shoulder. "I know we have unfinished business, but I owe Scarface." A shadow of fear passed across the lesser's expression, which only made me smile. He seemed shaken by the prospect of facing his death—again. Perhaps knowing for sure what waited for him on the other side only made him more afraid.

I know it did for me.

I lowered myself into the springy crouch of a swordfighter and followed the Nephilim through his circle. My scythe flashed out in a series of quick strikes, probing his defenses. Bellerophon caught them on the edge of his black knife, directing them away but not trying to counterattack.

I watched Lazarus out of the corner of my eye as we moved, concerned that he would seize the moment to sneak up on my unprotected flank. But I need not have worried. The man was a lot less brave now that he was down to half a soul.

The moment my attention was pulled from him, he spun on his heel and sprinted into the darkness of the empty warehouse. His footsteps echoed off the concrete as he fled.

"Fine by me," Bellerophon growled. "Now I have you all to myself."

"You sure know how to make a guy feel wanted," I replied with a flutter of my lashes. "Keep that energy as things get worse for you."

"You talk a big game, little pup," the scarred Nephilim growled, continuing to lead me in our circular dance. "But big brother isn't here to keep you safe."

"Yes, he is," I told him, showing him my teeth. "I carry his instruction with me, to use on evil like you."

"You'd better pray that you were a good student." Bellerophon whipped forward, moving faster than I could ever hope to keep up with. His black knife hissed as it cut the air, coming far too close despite the advantage of my reach.

My stomach flipped as I darted to the side. *He's so quick!* I had only ever seen the Nephilim run from true conflict, which had perhaps colored my opinion of him slightly. He supposedly once killed a chimera—a nightmare creature made from a lion, goat, and serpent. Depending on the organization of those three creatures, that could be a pretty deadly combo.

No thanks.

It was my turn to give ground, widening the space between us. The Nephilim followed me, trying to stay in killing range, but my scythe carved through the space between us, claiming it once more.

When Kane first made me one of his Reapers, I had no idea how to fight with the long, curved weapon that his agents carried. But it had been months since then, and I'd been practicing. Now that I had room to work with again, I stepped forward into a heavy swing that would cut my opponent in half.

He cursed, ducking to the side. I bailed out of the strike immediately, resetting myself into a comfortable stance so that I didn't leave myself open for his counteraggression. His speed was so tremendous that a single mistake could lead me to a quick end.

"You've learned some, pup, but you're not the Hunter," Bellerophon snarled, crouching low. "Let's see what you can really do." He lunged forward, a dark streak against the concrete ground. Primal fear spiked in my brain as I twisted, trying to cut off his assault. He seemed more like a wolf than a man, hunting me as they hunted my ancestors.

His speed meant that I missed my opportunity to cut him with the blade, so I reversed my grip, swinging the heavy butt of the weapon up to crash into his jaw. I saw his black eyes widen in surprise before he twitched to the side, flashing past me just out of striking range.

I sent a burst of Willow's fire after him, forcing him to move even farther away to avoid the ball of flame that smashed into the floor. It burned merrily for a few moments, eating at the very concrete.

I lowered my weapon again, beckoning for him to try that again. I was ready this time. Bellerophon ground his teeth, glaring at me with true hatred now. I couldn't help but feel a glow of pride in my chest as I faced down one of the most dangerous killers ever to live. Maybe I had been a good student after all.

"Is that all you got?" I taunted the scarred Nephilim. "I thought you were supposed to be scary."

Bellerophon opened his mouth to snap back at me, but his words were overridden by the squealing sound of an alarm klaxon that blared to life, filling the warehouse with its warning.

"ALERT! CONTAINMENT BREACH! THIS IS AN OMEGA-LEVEL WARNING. ALL NON-EMERGENCY PERSONNEL MUST PROCEED TO THE NEAREST SECURE ZONE."

I glanced up at the ceiling, trying to parse what that actually meant. It sounded serious, but I didn't know if it was just for normies or for people like us. When I looked back at Bellerophon, I was surprised to see that he had gone pale, his face full of fear. As I watched, he took a step farther from me and then another. When I made no move to chase him, he turned on his heel and fled without a word, sprinting across the empty warehouse toward the distant wall.

"Well, that's not a good sign," I muttered.

CHAPTER THIRTY-ONE

THIS IS AN OMEGA-LEVEL WARNING," the voice blared again, the canned recording echoing over the mind-numbing sound of the alarm.

"ALL NON-EMERGENCY PERSONNEL MUST PROCEED TO THE NEAREST SECURE ZONE."

"Yeah, yeah," I grumbled, banishing my scythe with a thought. It would be easy enough to summon again if I needed it. "I'm pretty sure I'm part of the emergency, but I can take a hint."

Slowly, I began walking across the now-empty warehouse, following the path that Bellerophon took. I wasn't sure exactly what I was planning. I could escape—all I needed to do was find a door, and my original plan would still work. On the outside I could regroup with

Alex and Dawn before making a report to Evangeline.

That seemed like the smartest play. I'd already learned so much. Lazarus was alive and involved in the manufacturing of Neodeath. Most important, *he wasn't a real mortal.* With that information, surely it would be easy for us to get a warrant—or whatever the heavenly equivalent of that was—and bring the Host down on his head like a hammer.

Or if the *good guys* didn't want to play ball, I was pretty sure Kane would be more than happy to send a task force of his own. They might not be angels, but a crew of Reapers is pretty effective too.

The question was, what should I do next? I couldn't help but feel like it was a mistake to leave now. I was alone and unsupervised behind enemy lines. A perfect opportunity to see what else I could uncover. Sure, Bellerophon had gotten scared by whatever this alarm was and run away, but he did that, like…all the time. At this point I was starting to not take it seriously. Promising myself that I'd keep my eyes open for a door I could use to get to the Between, I followed in Lazarus's and Bellerophon's footsteps, back toward the main part of the warehouse.

The alarm still blared, but it was now more muted, reduced to a dull, warning throb. I slipped through a door, noting its location, that took me back into the client-facing portion of the escrow building. I padded along the carpet, wishing it was plush enough that Lazarus had left footprints as he fled.

I didn't know what I was looking for. This was the man's private world. He had a small army of employees and tons of dangerous toys that he could use against me. He could be anywhere, with a force that outnumbered me by a significant amount.

But I owed Maria to see this through. When I reported back to Evangeline, I wanted to have everything I needed to see Lazarus hung.

The warehouse was deserted, and I walked boldly down the center of the main aisle. I might be outnumbered, but they were scared of me. Little old Matthew Carver had become something to fear. I was the omega-level threat. An impish delight grew in my chest, something born out of exhaustion and excitement, and I began to whistle amicably as if I didn't have a care in the world.

The aisle took a turn, and I followed it, stopping in surprise at the sight of what was waiting for me there. A stone statue stood in the middle of the thoroughfare. It was a woman in a startled pose. It seemed familiar, but she clearly wasn't the *David,* which was the only statue I could think of off the top of my head.

I paused for a moment, impressed by the detail of it. I could make out every wrinkle of her clothes. Whatever artist had hewn this had been a true master. Was this some lost work of Michelangelo? That didn't feel right. I'm no art expert, but I thought he worked with marble. This statue was made of a gray stone that seemed more common, like granite.

I studied it for another moment, appreciating the work, trying to solve the mystery of its origin. It was so life-like; every detail of her feature was captured with perfection. Now that I looked closer, I knew the artist had to be someone more contemporary. The woman in the statue was dressed in a modern outfit.

Whoever had been transporting it must have abandoned it the moment the alarm went off. A pity; if they weren't trying to kill me, I would have loved to ask about it. One more mystery that would have to remain unsolved. Maybe Dawn would know.

I began to turn away from the statue's face, but a sudden noise froze me in place.

A clicking sounded from behind me, like the slow rattle of a snake. Cold fear flooded through me, its clarity showing me why the statue seemed familiar. It wasn't one. It was a perfect replica of Dr. Quinn, the third expert who had inspected the Spear of Lugh.

She had been turned to stone.

The clicks echoed again as something stalked me. The hair on the back of my neck stood up, and my instincts went wild, begging me to turn and face whatever was hunting me. If I hadn't just realized the kind of thing I was being hunted by, I would have.

And I would be dead.

One thing I've learned since I started studying is that a surprising number of creatures can turn their prey to stone with a look. Of course there's Medusa. I've met one of her sisters, and if Lazarus had somehow conscripted one of the Gorgons, I didn't stand a chance. Outside of the famous snake-haired lady, the big two are the basilisk, which needs no introduction, and something called a cockatrice, which is much scarier than it sounds.

Click, click, click, went the thing hunting me. My heart pounding in my chest, I risked a quarter turn, trying to face away from the monster. I froze as the faint outline of something entered the corner of my eye.

I forced myself to keep breathing as I staved off panic. Was I still able to move? My eye was burning. Was that because it was being hurt by the thing's gaze, or because I hadn't blinked? If I blinked and it moved in front of me, would I die?

Focus! I snapped to myself, squaring my shoulders, settling into a fighting crouch even though I wasn't facing my enemy.

"THIS IS AN OMEGA-LEVEL WARNING," the automated system reminded me distantly.

"Yeah, no kidding," I grumbled. I guess it wasn't about me after all.

As if triggered by my voice, the monster hissed and launched toward me, head low to the ground about waist height. A cockatrice then. Squeaking in fear, I squeezed my eyes shut and threw both of my fists at the ground, triggering a blast of Willow's fire.

The explosion launched me in the air, vaulting me up over the thing's charge. Mentally, I tracked my rotation as I flipped, grateful that my sister had convinced me to practice this movement with a blindfold. It had seemed stupid at the time, but she told me that Father Dearest swore by it.

I hate to say it, but he was right. About this one thing specifically.

My eyes popped open as I completed my turn away from where the cockatrice charged, guiding my feet into their landing and dropping into a roll to bleed off my excess momentum. The creature let out an angry hiss from behind my back, prompting me to break into a sprint down the long hall.

It screamed in something that sounded like delight, leaping to chase me. Every instinct I had developed over the last two years cursed me for being an idiot as I ran. One of the most fundamental laws of the supernatural world also applies to the animal kingdom: Don't turn your back on predators. Don't run from them like prey. There's also a second one which says: Get out while you can, but I'm bad at remembering that one.

But in my defense, that advice doesn't work as well when the thing can turn you to stone if you make eye contact with it. It's hard to stare down a thing you're not allowed to look at. We were operating under unusual circumstances here.

As I raced, I scoured my brain, trying to remember what I knew about the cockatrice. The thing was some sort of Frankensteinian monstrosity made out of a chicken and a snake. There might have been a bit of a lion in there too; I couldn't remember. Really what they ended up looking like was a more anatomically correct velociraptor. You know, one of those dinosaurs with feathers that are way less cool than the ones in *Jurassic Park.* I don't care if they were birds; the truth is lame.

But bottom line was: It didn't really matter *what* the thing looked like, since I would never get a chance to take a gander at it. I'd have to trust the artist's rendering on this one. I also seemed to remember that the creatures were pretty hard to kill. I thought there was something about using roosters to take them out, but I was currently short on farm animals, so that was mostly unhelpful.

My scythe might pack enough punch to bring it down. I had no idea if this thing counted as an immortal or an Immortal. Monsters might have their own power scale that I was unaware of. All the rules were more like guidelines anyway.

The safer bet seemed to be finding a door. Then I could just throw myself into the Between and hope that I had enough time to close the door behind me. Leave the monster to Lazarus, who was probably the guy who'd let the thing out in the first place.

I liked that idea the most. I really didn't want to fight it. I'm an idiot. I'm forgetful, and I get overwhelmed easily. It was easy to remember not to look at the cockatrice *right now,* but if we got into an actual fight, I just *knew* I was going to forget and stare at the thing right in the eyeballs. Next thing you knew, I'd be on display in Lucifer's study as a piece of Matt-ern art and that somehow sounded worse than getting my own personal circle.

"*Screeeeee!*" The thing let out another hunting scream behind me, which sounded a lot like a twisted eagle's cry. I could tell, even without looking, that it was getting closer. Whatever horrible creature had given it their legs, they were *strong.* I wasn't going to get out of this by running in a straight line.

Of course I wasn't.

I never get to do things the easy way.

There was still no sign of a door anywhere. Even if I found one this moment, I didn't have enough space to use my get-out-of-jail-free card before the cockatrice caught me and got revenge for every drumstick I had ever eaten in my life.

Which meant that if I was going to live longer than the next thirty seconds, I was going to have to do something dumb. It's funny how that works. You'd expect doing something monumentally stupid to be what gets you killed. But in my experience, being an idiot was the only thing that kept me alive.

Spotting an intersection ahead, I held out my right hand, letting it trail to the side, making sure that I had space to summon my scythe. Slowly, I turned my head to the side, trying to catch a glimpse of the monster chasing me out of the corner of my eye.

The moment I spotted a flicker of movement I jerked away, confident that I understood how close it was now. I was going to have to time this just right.

Too late to overthink it. We were here.

I hauled a right at the intersection, darting around the corner to break the monster's line of sight on me for a handful of heartbeats. The second I was under cover, I summoned my scythe, holding it out to the side. As my left foot came down, I pivoted into a spin off it, pouring all my momentum into a wild slash behind me.

I closed my eyes at the last possible second, trying to guide my weapon to the right height to cut off the thing's head. In the darkness behind my lids, I heard the cockatrice let out a shocked scream of anger—and maybe fear?—as my weapon swept through the air. My heart dropped as I completed the spin without feeling any impact.

I missed.

For a moment I froze as if I had been turned to stone. That had been my one idea, and it had failed. For a second, I debated opening my eyes. If I peeked now, I might be lucky enough to turn to stone before the thing tore me to shreds. But despite the cold logic of that idea, I couldn't make myself do it. So they stayed screwed shut, protecting me from the thing's mineralizing gaze. My entire body was taut, braced for the rending claws.

But no attack came.

Cautiously, I scrunched up my face and cracked open my right eye, just a hair, as if my lashes might somehow save me from becoming granite. My vision was dark and blurry, but I saw no sign of the cockatrice.

The intersection before me was bare.

Slowly, skeptically, I opened both of my eyes, scanning for the thing that had to be waiting for me. There was no sign of the monster.

"Okay. . . ." I said slowly, feeling more creeped out than relieved. Where had it gone? Why had it gone? Was it coming back? I had a bad feeling I wasn't going to like the answers.

I stared at the dark form of my scythe, wondering if somehow, I had caught the thing and just not felt the impact. What other explanation could there be? The shadowy edge seemed clean, although I didn't even know if cockatrices bleed blood in the first place.

"THIS IS AN OMEGA-LEVEL—"

"Was!" I shouted, drowning out the automated alarm's warning. "*Was* an omega-level warning. Don't worry, I took care of it for you." There was only silence. "Don't everybody say thank you at once," I grumbled, taking a step toward the intersection.

"*Screeeeee!*" In the distance, the cockatrice screamed from the direction I was about to go. My head whipped toward the sound before I remembered the *one rule.* Dark Abyss, I really could not be trusted. Fortunately, it was not yet in sight, or I would have become permanently stoned—and not in the Californian way.

Somehow the thing had gotten ahead of me. Maybe its eyesight wasn't so good, and it didn't notice me take the sharp turn. That actually sort of made sense. If it didn't have some limits on its vision, it would just dwell in a world of stone. That's pretty much what happened to my buddy Midas. There were *no restrictions* on his golden power, and it had been super annoying.

I guessed the cockatrice had run past me and only begun to double back once I was dumb enough to talk out loud. That was fine, I could work with that. Now all I had to do was remember to be quiet *and* not look it in its eyes. Just two things. Surely I could do that.

Surely.

I was feeling a lot more hope about my chances of surviving. The creature had a weakness I could exploit.

"*Screeeeee!*" cried the cockatrice off to my left. I froze in my tracks, all that hope fading from me like the lights had just been turned off.

"*Screeeeee!*" came another from behind me.

"*Screeeeee! Screeeeee!*" two more sounded from my right.

There wasn't one cockatrice on the loose, but several. They apparently ran in packs. A thing that *would* have been a good thing to know. The first one didn't lose me—it went to get reinforcements. Even monsters recognize when they are threatened with the power of Death.

"THIS IS AN OMEGA-LEVEL WARNING."

I ran.

All thought fled from my brain. My prey instincts kicked in, sending me scrambling. The pack's cries echoed through the empty warehouse as they closed in on me. Sometimes they clicked back and forth, as if communicating their hunt.

I didn't think I was going to survive this.

I threaded through the different aisles of the escrow building, using the cries as warnings about which paths to avoid. But after a few minutes, I began to have a bad feeling about this plan.

My path was steadily being guided away from the walls, back toward the center. Every time I had a chance to break free, a *screeee* would sound ahead of me, causing me to take a different route. If I didn't know any better, I'd say I was being herded.

Surely cockatrices aren't that smart.

Surely.

But when I encountered poor Dr. Quinn's statue for the second time, I knew it must be true. They had brought me back to this place on purpose.

"*Screeeeee!*" came the cry before me.

"*Screeeeee!*" echoed from behind.

"*Screeeeee!*" called from my left and right.

There was nowhere left to run. I was ringed by at least four of the monsters. For some reason, my panic chose that moment to finally fade. Now that there was no more hope, I was calm. If this was to be my end, then I was going to go down with my head held high.

Well, metaphorically. In reality, I stared at the floor a few paces in front of my feet, determined not to become a lawn ornament. I held my scythe in both hands, my grip tightening on the handle as I waited for the hunters to come.

They clicked to one another as they stalked forward. It might have been my imagination, but it felt like there was an amused tone to their communication. Almost as if they were co-workers laughing around the watercooler about their hunt.

Did you see the look on his face when he realized there was more than one of us, Dale?

I thought he was going to look you right in the eyes, Bob!

I forced myself to exhale, bleeding off some of the nervous energy. Any second now their shadows would sweep into my vision, and it would be the time.

I stared at the staff of my scythe, wishing that there was something else I could do with it. When I had born the title of Death's heir, it had given me much more control over the properties of my weapon. I had been able to grow it or shrink it at will, which would have come in handy right about now.

No, the only other thing I could do was use it to open a path between the living world and the Veil, which was only useful as a—

I was so stunned by my own stupidity that I couldn't even form a new thought for a few heartbeats. I didn't *need* a door. I could carve my own. Although the Veil wasn't the safest place in the world for an alive mortal to be, it certainly couldn't be as bad as this. In fact, the more I thought about it, the more I knew it was exactly where I needed to go.

I needed to speak with the big man about some important issues.

Click, click, one of the cockatrices behind me called. It was so close, I felt like it was whispering down the back of my neck. No more time for thinking. It was do or die.

My heart raced, and I braced for the feeling of them leaping on me as I reached out with my senses, feeling for that paper-thin shred of something that existed between Reality and the Veil. It was a little seam, no more noticeable than a tiny bump on the fabric of the world around us.

With a practiced gesture, I reached out with the tip of my scythe, hooking the razor-sharp shadow on that seam and slicing effortlessly. A dark tear in something—maybe it was the time-space continuum ripping open before me.

"*Screeeeee!*" one of the cockatrices cried. As if it knew I was escaping. I didn't turn around to look.

As soon as the hole was big enough, I threw myself into the waiting darkness, flinging my scythe behind me, hoping that its sharp edge would delay anything that tried to follow me through long enough for me to close the exit up behind me.

For the second time in my life, I passed through from the living world and into the Veil.

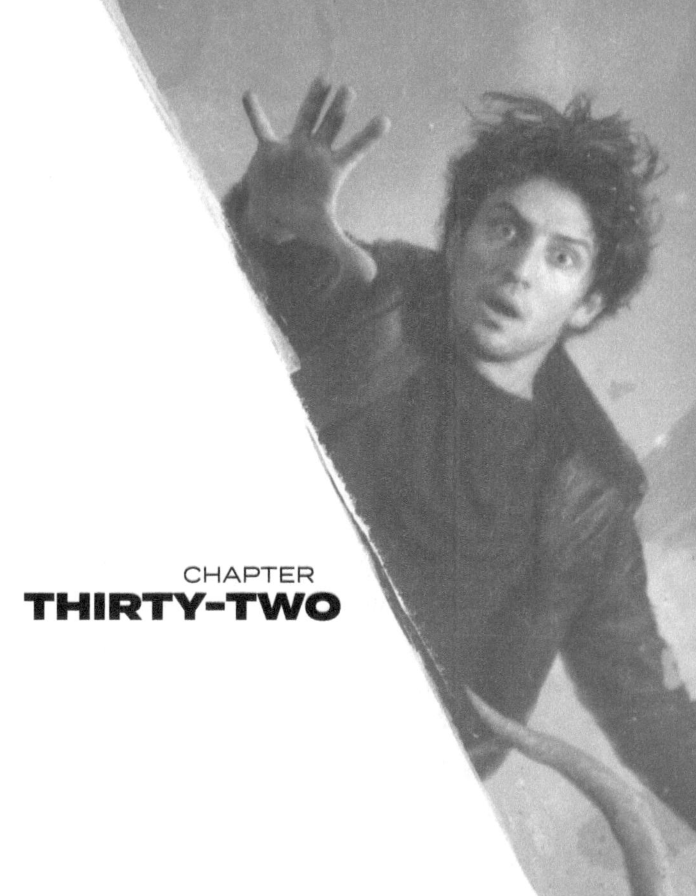

CHAPTER
THIRTY-TWO

I TUMBLED OUT OF the rift between the worlds, landing in an awkward heap on the floor of the hallway that the Reapers have marked off for arrival and departures. I released my hold on the tear in Reality and could faintly hear the enraged scream of a cockatrice start before it snapped shut.

The familiar white of the Veil burned at my eyes, causing me to squint after being trapped in the dim warehouse for so long. The air smelled slightly of antiseptic and lemon. Maintenance must have just mopped. Hopefully none of those guys would see my scuffing up their freshly polished floors.

"Ack! Who the blazes are you?" a man shouted from the side, leaping to his feet in surprise at my sudden appearance. He was a pudgy, older man with a white handlebar mustache. I'd never seen him before, but he wore the black uniform of a Reaper of Death Corp.

"Sorry to startle you," I said, groaning softly as I rose to my feet. "I don't think I was supposed to come back so soon." Everything about this place felt familiar but also *different.* The lights were too bright, the smells too sharp. The last time I had been here, I had only been a spirit. Even though my mind had interpreted everything as if I had a body, I guess it wasn't quite as good as the real thing.

"I've got the schedule, and you are not on it," Mustache said, his voice growing angrier by the second. "You need to declare yourself right this moment or—" I turned to stare at the shorter man, and his rant abruptly cut off mid-sentence. I don't know what he saw in my eyes, but it unsettled him.

Wordlessly, I summoned my scythe, letting it tower over the two of us like an umbrella of doom. "My name is Matthew Carver," I told him. His expression grew pale. Maybe he knew the story, or maybe he was just enough of a rookie to find a more senior Reaper intimidating. "I've been…undercover."

"Undercover?" he half whispered to himself. "I didn't even know we did that."

"You must be new."

"I am, sir. Still going through orientation." I tried not to chuckle at the thought of this man who had lived many more years than I had calling me sir.

"Are you *alive*?" he asked, sounding scandalized. Now that he mentioned it, I did seem to be more…vibrant than him. It was as if my image was just a little sharper than his. We both looked real—but I was *more* real, somehow.

"What's your name?"

"Teddy."

"Well, Teddy, welcome to the job. It sucks. Do you know where

I can find Wilbur?" Impossibly, Mustache's face grew even paler. He must be *really* new.

"The—the heir?"

"Tall guy? Pretty skinny? Country accent?" I held my hand up a few inches above my own head to indicate my friend's height.

"If you've been undercover, how do you know he's the heir?" Teddy's eyes narrowed as a new suspicion grew on his face. "He only got that job recently."

"I know. I gave it to him."

When Teddy finally calmed down enough to be useful, he told me that Wilbur was in his office and gave me directions. I tried not to be a little bitter. When I wore the ring, it didn't come with an office. I knew that technically he had held the title longer than I had—especially on this side, where Time moves differently. But still, why didn't I ever get a space of my own? I had been jammed into the smallest cubicle with the tall Reaper during my tenure here. Then again, Kane told me he always knew that I wasn't truly dead. Maybe he didn't feel the need to let me get comfortable when he knew I would be heading back to the other side soon enough.

Whatever. It didn't matter. It just hurt my feelings a little.

Green-uniformed janitors eyed me warily as I moved through the halls. I saw plenty of familiar faces, but they all shrank away from greeting me. I suppose I did look a little out of place—I was clearly alive and wearing mortal clothing instead of the usual Reaper uniform. Also, the last time I was here, I accidentally let the prophet of the Nothing into the Veil. I could see why some people might feel uncomfortable, like my arrival was some sort of sign of bad times.

A Harbinger, if you will.

I jammed my hands in my jacket pockets and adopted a bright whistle, striding boldly through the sterile white halls as if I belonged there. Technically, I was still an employee, so despite the unusual fact that I had a heartbeat, it wasn't a lie. If Kane didn't want me here, he could have taken the scythe from me.

I had every intention of going to see Wilbur first. I needed to tell him what I had discovered about Neodeath and who was behind it. But as I made my way to his office, I was struck by how *good* I felt. The cloud that had been hanging over my brain had vanished. I was clear of the fog and could suddenly think clearly for the first time in months.

I wasn't tired.

Somehow by traveling to the Veil, I had gone beyond Sleep's reach. This was the land of Death, and he had a superior claim over the little brother. I let out a relieved laugh, marveling at the freedom I suddenly felt. It was suddenly so easy to think.

I paused, struck by a sudden burst of inspiration. Something about being back in this place reminded me of the other pieces on the board. I had been too narrow in my focus, acting like I didn't have options, but that's because I was exhausted and still wasn't used to who I had become. I had forgotten about the Dreadknight.

There might be a path I could walk to fix the problems that hung over me like a headsman's ax. Neodeath and the lost souls. Somnus and his sleep debt. But there was only one person who could make it happen. Good old Matthew Carver.

Death Corp might be different from most companies on earth in that everyone who worked here was dead, but heartbeat or no, bosses are the same everywhere. They love it when you have a plan they can approve that requires no input from them.

Which meant that if I was a smart employee, I'd take my time in filing my report. If I had a solution ready to go, it might just be easier to convince Kane to follow my plan instead of concocting one of his own. I had no doubt that a guy whose business card read THE END wasn't afraid to deliver some serious *judgment*.

Whistling even more brightly, I slipped down the hallway toward cold storage, walking the same path that several of Jack's cronies had lured me down to try to kill me what felt like a lifetime ago.

Deeper in the industrial side of the Veil, the lighting grew sparser. It was as if management felt like they were saving money by not keeping this section as brightly lit. Maybe it was out of some sense of respect, not forcing the souls that were stored down here to be under eternal sunlight, so they could get some modicum of rest.

Metal double doors on either side of the hall were marked alphabetically by the range of mortals they held. I passed STORAGE AB–AC with a small smile, remembering the showdown I had fought here. It had been a moment of growth, I realized now. Cornered by a famous killer and his gang, I had refused to back down, and because of it I'd helped Kane bring down at least part of the conspiracy that was stealing souls.

Now I was back to do the same thing. My whistling faded now that I was alone. It felt rude here in this quiet resting place. I made my way down the long, long hallway, passing STORAGE KA–KE, which meant I still had a fair bit to go. Even after having spent so much time here, the sheer volume of souls waiting for delivery was still daunting.

But they weren't what I was here for. Finally, I passed the set of doors marked STORAGE ZY–ZZ. My heart rate picked up slightly in anticipation of what was waiting for me. I wasn't sure that it would be here, but my faith in the system was being rewarded. There was one more pair of doors at the end of the row, and the sign above it read simply: LOST AND FOUND.

I slipped through the unlocked doors. The room on the other side was much smaller than the other warehouses. It was the size of a large closet, and everything inside was labeled individually.

My heart skipped a beat as I surveyed the treasure trove that I had found. After seeing so much rot and corruption, I had half expected this section to be forgotten. But instead, it was fuller than I dared to hope.

I felt my already high respect for Kane rise. You can say a lot about the guy, but he did care. When you're running an enterprise that spans the entirety of human existence, it would be easy—understandable, even—to miss some stuff, to let some things fall through the cracks in order to keep the majority of the machine running smoothly. But that was only if you lost sight of the value of what Death was being entrusted with. Each of the trillion pieces was priceless, and Kane made sure each was treated as such.

"Okay," I told the empty room, rubbing my hands together. "Let's see if you have what I need."

—— × ——

Teddy told me that Wilbur's office was next to Kane's, but he had undersold it a little to me. The entrance to the Grim Reaper's space had been redone. Before, it was an open entryway into a small foyer where Atty, the eldest Fate, kept her desk.

That room had been expanded. Where once there was a single dark door leading to Kane's office, now there was a second, for Wilbur's. It was fine. I never wanted the job anyway. It just seemed like I had been replaced *quite* easily.

Atty, who looked like an older woman, sat behind her desk, typing away with her stenographer's keyboard. She had another, more accurate name: Atropos. The famed crone from the trio with her daughters, the maiden and the matron.

She was not sending emails or writing memos. No, she had a more final duty. It was she who wrote the lists of names of those who would soon depart the mortal plane. After she was done, they would be handed to the Reapers like me, who would be sent to collect their souls.

"Why hello, Ms. Atty," I said as brightly as I could. The Fate was rather terrifying, and she didn't like me very much. The last time I saw her, she had been trying to stab me with a pair of black scissors that would have *unmade* me. Despite my confidence that Kane still wanted me to be here, I couldn't help but feel a sharp spike of fear at the sight of the old woman. She was dangerous in a way that even a pack of cockatrices wasn't. I had no desire to find out what would happen to me if she managed to stab me with her black scissors.

"Carver comma Matthew," she replied coolly, turning from her little typing machine without pausing at her work. Her fingers flew across the strange keyboard without pausing. "It is a good thing that you're alive."

"That's the nicest thing you've ever said to me," I replied, pressing a hand to my breastbone as if truly touched. "Nope, not dead, the old heart is still very much ticking."

"Because if you were dead early again, I'd rend you myself." I felt my stomach go sour at the thought of being cut into little pieces by her. She sniffed, turning back to her work.

"No tricks, I'm here on official business," I promised, raising my open hands in a gesture of surrender. I hoped she wouldn't notice the bulge of my jacket pockets. Just because I was playing for the home team didn't mean I couldn't get in trouble.

"How go the tasks? Eaten any golden apples lately?" I couldn't help the scowl that started to form at the corner of my lips at her mocking tone. As one of the Fates, she had been required to approve the Impossible Task that Midas had created for me. I strongly suspected she had helped make it extra-impossible, just out of spite.

"I've got seven years," I told her, hating how defensive that sounded. "I'm saving it for a special day."

"Leviathan still breathing, is he?" Atty murmured, her cruel smile deepening. Her keyboard click-clacked softly as she continued writing the list. She knew the answer to the question. The crone was just enjoying how deeply her words cut.

"Is he in?"

"Which one?" Atty actually paused to raise a finger and point at the doors behind her. "Death or his heir?"

"Kane is here?"

"No, he's in session with the Death Board. They're always meeting and—"

"Yes, I know," I interrupted testily. "Wilbur is fine for now."

"Let me see if he's free," the crone began, starting to rise from her chair, but I cut her off, breezing toward my friend's door without waiting.

"That won't be necessary. He'll want to hear this." I had enough time to hear Atty hiss in annoyance behind me, then I pushed open the door to Wilbur's office and stepped inside.

The tall heir of Death startled from behind his desk, looking up at me with wide-guilty eyes. It was a remarkably human expression, and for some reason, it filled me with relief to see him still be so jumpy. This place has a tendency to turn people cold. A large tome sat on his desk, open to a page blotched with a light-gray color, as if someone had painted the whole thing with a roller.

"What are you doing here?" he demanded, staring at me with wild shock. Then a look of concern passed across his face. "Are you—"

"Alive? Yes." I cut him off smoothly. It must really stick out like a sore thumb to the dead. I could tell that there was a difference between us, but I really had to look for it. "I have news that can't wait."

His expression paled. "What news?"

"I found out who is making the Neodeath."

"Already?" Both of his blond eyebrows shot up in surprise. "I didn't really think it would be that easy."

"What can I say? You gave me quite the gift." I told him the entire story: the warehouse in Long Beach, the Land of Darkness and Abaddon Market, and Lazarus's other half who was working to manufacture the Neodeath.

With every passing second, Wilbur's eyes grew wider, as if he couldn't believe the depths of the conspiracy that I had uncovered. When I finished my tale, he stared at me for several seconds, blinking as he processed all the information.

"I believe you," he breathed after a few moments. His gaze tracked up above my shoulder to focus on the air behind me. "It's safe."

"Huh?" I started to ask, completely thrown off by his strange behavior. But even as I did, I felt a PRESENCE unveiling itself, like an eye opening out of the darkness. Slowly my head turned to the side so I could watch as the Grim Reaper appeared behind my right shoulder, where he does for every man.

A deep, abiding coldness swept through the room, chilling me to my bones. It felt far more powerful than I had ever noticed before. But then, I had never physically been in his presence before.

Kane was a tall man with dusty skin and dark eyes. His brown hair was cut short, and he seemed to be ageless, except for heavy bags under his eyes that spoke of an eternal weariness. A golden ring with a white stone sat on his finger, a sibling to the one Pestilence wore.

"Hi," I said softly, staring at him with an uneasy feeling in my stomach. Having Death himself lurking in my blind spot was not the most comforting thing that had ever happened to me. How long had he been behind me? Had he followed me on my errand to the Lost and Found? The weight in my jacket pockets seemed to grow heavier in his presence.

"Tell me the truth, Harbinger," he commanded sharply, staring at me with distrusting eyes. "Is now the time?" If I didn't know better, I'd say that he was equally uncomfortable in my presence. It almost felt like he was afraid.

"The time for wha—oh." I felt my eyes widen in shock as I realized what he was talking about. He knew about my Impossible Task. He thought I was here to kill *him.*

Death.

My stomach flipped itself in knots as true fear blossomed in me. I had walked in here so confidently and casually, not realizing that my movement was almost a declaration of war. But those were the rules of the game. If I ever wanted to get my soul back, one day I would have to kill him.

I wanted to reassure him—the Grim Reaper—that I was not here for his soul. That we were allies, on the same side of this serious issue. But a different question popped out. "Is that why you didn't come when I summoned you?"

Kane didn't respond, only watched me flatly. I understood now. He had feared that the circle would be a trap he would never leave. A way for me to limit his power and kill him with ease. So instead, he had sent Wilbur to scout it out. That explained the nervous expression on my friend's face.

Despite the seriousness of the moment, I couldn't help but be a little disappointed. I understood what he was worried about—I was contractually obligated to try to kill him at some point. But I also thought we understood each other. Sure, we had both used each other for our own ends the last time we met, but we had also worked toward similar goals. If we weren't on the exact same team, we were at least *allies.* My feelings were hurt that he thought so little of me.

"No!" I snapped, tired of this awkwardness. "I am here to save the Death Treaty. I am not here to break your seal, whatever that means. I swear it—I'd swear on my soul if I am even allowed to."

The tension flowed out of the room in an instant. Kane's shoulders relaxed. He studied me for a moment, then nodded sharply in agreement. He slipped from behind me to stand behind Wilbur's desk with his arms crossed. My friend mouthed the word *Sorry* to me when his boss couldn't see his face anymore. I responded with the tiniest of nods. I couldn't blame the guy; it was the job.

"It's Lazarus," I told Kane, unsure how much he had heard. "He's making the Neodeath and stealing souls."

"I wish I could say I was surprised."

"You told me to kill him."

"I told you that you owed me half of a soul and that there were three you might find. The fact that two of them belonged to the same man was not important."

"Okay, well, that was still deliberately obtuse!"

Kane shrugged, unbothered. He had told me what he wanted, and I had done it. By most supernatural rules, that was as fair as a deal ever got.

"I am more concerned about *how* they are making this Neodeath." He struggled with the word as if it were in a foreign language.

"Yeah, you should be," I told him, letting some of my irritation bubble through my tone. "I had a front-row seat to the show, and it was not good. They're summoning a weird version of Legion from the Nothing and sacrificing mortals to them while the Elders watch."

"They're *what*?" Kane's voice was so primal that the room shook around us, reacting to its master's rage. My heart didn't so much skip a beat as it started to beat very gently, as if afraid to remind Death that it was here.

"Um, they made a circle, killed a mortal, and then these things that look like Legion but bigger and with half of their body turned into twisted crabs came through. I'm not sure what was supposed to happen next, because we started shooting, but after the circle broke, something tried to shove a *very* big tentacle through the hole, and an angel had to stop it." I paused to take a breath, only then realizing how quickly I was talking.

"That's impossible," Death breathed. His dusty skin was paler than usual, as if he'd seen a ghost. "The Veil prevents the Lost from passing through. The Elders cannot reach the living world."

"But Wilbur and I were attacked by Legion on that side," I protested.

"That is different, Legion is of this Reality. They have been recruited by the Elders to cross over on their behalf. But the actual masters are not able to leave the Nothing."

"Well, this one definitely got a couple of inches through," I told him, feeling much more concerned than I had when we began this conversation.

"The only way that would be possible is if there were damage to the Veil. If something had created a gap that they could squeeze past"—Kane shook his head in disbelief—"and they cannot harm it." I remembered the massive tentacles of the Elder that chased me out of the Nothing slamming into the white border of Reality with no effect.

The only thing that had been able to pierce the Veil at all was my scythe when I used it once to anchor Yuki and our driver to the surface. *Uh-oh.*

"Surely you'd notice if there was a gaping hole in the wall," I said, hoping Kane would confirm it easily and assuage my growing concern. But Death hesitated, seeming suddenly unsure of many things.

"It would not need to be large. You know that the Nothing isn't real like the other side is. Even a tiny gap—a small cut—would be enough for their power to begin slipping through."

"How small?" I managed not to squeak the question—but only barely.

"Something the size of the eye of a needle would be enough," Kane replied, his eyes narrowing. "Why?"

Waves of panic swept over me, threatening to pull me to the ground. I knew what was happening. Worse, it was my fault.

Slowly, I reached into my pocket and pulled out a pair of glowing orange soul orbs. Wilbur's eyes widened in shock at the sight of them, but Kane only watched me coolly, waiting to pass judgment. Given who he was, he'd probably known they were there the whole time.

"I'm going to leave these right here," I told them, placing them on the heir's desk. "So we can keep them safe until we have time to circle back on the other plan I have. But first, we've got another problem to deal with. I know where the rip in the Veil is."

CHAPTER THIRTY-THREE

KANE WAS FURIOUS with me.

“Why did you not report that you cut the Veil?” he thundered, storming ahead of Wilbur and I as we trotted to keep up with the Grim Reaper through the sterile halls of the Death Delivery offices. The man’s long legs could really eat up the distance. Why did everyone so strong have to be so *tall*? “You damaged the Veil and didn’t think it important to *mention*?”

“In my defense, I didn’t know I could do that, and I was a little busy at the time, being chased by an Elder and keeping the rest of my team alive,” I protested. Unless something else more horrifying had happened, we were pretty certain that *I* had caused the damage to the Veil.

When Kane sent Yuki and me out to hunt for the missing shipment of souls, we were ambushed by an Elder, a terror of the Nothing. The thing awoke in the deep dark and chased us all the way back to the Veil. It even broke the Rainbow Bridge, knocking us into a free fall in the void.

I'd managed to save our lives by using my scythe to grapple onto the surface of the Veil, doing what I thought at the time was only cosmetic damage to the wall that spanned the infinity between Reality and Nothing. But now I feared my blade had created the gap that was allowing this great hungry power to slip through.

"How did I even manage to cut the Veil?" I demanded. "Shouldn't that be way harder to do? Otherwise, it seems like you could have a new hole every week!"

"Technically there aren't exactly weeks here," Wilbur pointed out unhelpfully.

"You were my *heir*," Kane hissed, stopping in place and turning to face me with a snarl. "You cut it with my Authority. It is the *only* thing that can harm the Veil."

"That was not in the safety briefing!"

"Your greatest priority as a Reaper is the protection of Reality and the souls that come from it!"

"You never actually mentioned that," I snapped, getting tired of being blamed for something that was definitely sort of my fault.

"What?"

"My orientation was all soul sorting and delivery. You never mentioned protecting the Veil or watching it for damage even once. In fact, when that Elder that almost splatted us into a thousand tiny bits showed up and hammered the border, no one even seemed bothered. If this was such a big deal, shouldn't some of the other people with me have brought it up?"

The tension in the hallway spiked as Kane and Wilbur exchanged knowing glances. I felt my heart still as I realized the meaning of that look.

Someone should have.

But they did not.

I dimly remembered Yuki's panic as my scythe bit into the surface of the Veil. The other Reaper had been terrified by the damage I caused hooking us to the white surface. She clearly knew the potential repercussions of what I had done. From the dark look on Kane's face right now, he had the same thought.

"Where is Yuki?" I asked softly, looking between the two men. The Japanese Reaper had helped me fight off Jack and the rest of the corrupt Reapers when Aite stormed the Veil. She had also been a member of the smuggling cabal but underwent a change of heart after being overcome by guilt.

She should have been one of the good guys, trusted by both Death and his heir, yet both of their expressions were troubled. Had she gone back to her ways?

"She is gone," Kane replied at last, his face unhappy. "She was part of a convoy that was attacked by Legion and destroyed. All the Reapers that were escorting the delivery fell and were consumed."

I felt a momentary flicker of guilt for suspecting my friend of a moral failing. Who was I to doubt someone just because they had lost their way? The world—the real one or the supernatural one, whatever you wanted to call it—was so much bigger and more overwhelming than we mortals knew.

Yuki was not the first person, nor would she be the last, to be crushed under the gears of its massive industry, forced to make impossible choices, left with no hope. I could only hope that whatever waited beyond the darkness after being unmade gave her a modicum of peace.

"That still doesn't answer the question of why she didn't report it," Wilbur probed gently. The tall boy's face was scrunched with concern.

Yuki had helped save his life too. I was certain he wasn't enjoying these thoughts any more than I was.

"How long ago did she fall?" I asked, knowing it was a worthless question. Time on this side was almost nonexistent. Robin once explained to me that the Veil was the dam where time's reach ended, and it crashed against the wall like a wave, coming and going. Time didn't flow here, it swam.

"It would not have been long after you returned to the living world on your side," Kane replied with a shake of his head. "But it was a long time here. She had ample opportunities to make me aware of the danger."

I nodded, my mouth dry with something like fear. I wasn't scared for me, but I was afraid of losing the legacy of someone I counted as a friend. Yuki might be gone, but she was still a member of my tribe. Depending on what we found out, I might lose her again.

"First, we will patch the hole," Kane announced with a sigh, turning to resume his march. "Then we will go rat hunting." Something about the finality in his tone sent an icy shiver down my spine. Even the Hunter could not have said it better.

Eleven Reapers were waiting for us in the hangar where convoys of souls were loaded up. The great double doors were wide open, covered by a thin layer of translucent orange power that was a filter keeping the Nothing from pouring in and devouring us. It felt like being on the deck of a starship, preparing to launch out into space.

I scanned the sea of faces, surprised at how few I recognized even in passing. While I was working here full-time, we lost a few Reapers, but that seemed to be an unusual thing. From the grim expressions on many of their faces, I got the feeling it was far more common now. Given the non-linear way that Time ran here, many of them could have already clocked more hours than I did during my stint.

"Who's the new guy?" a tall woman with blond hair shaved into a buzz cut asked. She stepped forward at the head of the squad to meet Kane with an expectant air. She must be the new Rex, I surmised. She had a fighter's build, with broad shoulders and a nose that had been broken more than once.

"I've been deep undercover," I told her without missing a beat. It was starting to sound less ridiculous every time I said it. I thought I saw Kane give me an almost amused glance out of the corner of my eye.

"Matthew is a senior Reaper who has been on…assignment," Death agreed after a moment. The skeptical looks on the rest of the crew's faces didn't lessen; if anything they seemed to grow sharper as the group studied me with new eyes.

"He was the heir before me," Wilbur offered with a small shrug, as if embarrassed. A couple of raised eyebrows was all I got. A different reaction from the last time I was introduced with that title. However "new" these guys might be, something told me they had been through the wringer already.

"Boss, is he alive?" The tough woman's eyes went wide as she realized what she was looking at. "The Squids are gonna go nuts if we go out there with live bait." A couple of the others nodded in disgust, eyeing me with naked jealousy.

"He is the only one who knows where to look for what we need to fix," Kane rumbled, overriding their complaints with his inevitable Authority. I tried not to wince at how that made me sound. Sure, it was technically my fault, but that didn't mean he needed to tell *everybody.* "Gear up," Death added, eyeing the thirteen of us Reapers with a weary gaze. "You have a hole in Reality to patch."

"You're not coming with us?" one of the skinnier guys asked, his voice going up an octave. He must be green still. I understood his hesitance. Some of the Lost things that waited out there were bigger than cities. No matter how hard we stabbed them with our scythes, they wouldn't even feel it.

"I cannot," he told the terrified Reaper with a sad shrug. "I am bound to this place, unable to pass it until THE END." I remembered him telling me something very similar once before. Back then he had said it was because he had never died.

"Hey, question," I said, raising my hand. Kane glanced at me, a knowing darkness welling in his eyes. "I'm alive. Can I..." I let my question trail off as I gestured at the inky void waiting on the other side of the soul air lock.

"I guess we'll find out," Death told me, his expression firm. I nodded, doing my best to swallow over the lump of fear in my throat. As much as I wanted to protest, I knew I didn't have much of a leg to stand on. My mistake had jeopardized—well, if not *everything,* then something like *most* things. Neodeath was a rot that would eat the universe out from under us. Depending on where those stolen souls ended up, it might even lead to the decay and collapse of Reality itself.

As much as I wanted to play it safe to protect my own soul, that was being selfish. If I was going to play the big game, then I would have to take the big risks. "Understood," I told Kane, giving him what I hoped was a stiff nod.

"Let's get this done, people," the tall woman snapped, turning to stare at her ten Reapers. "I want you suited up and ready for action in five!"

"Yes ma'am," they grumbled back in something like military unison. I felt one of my eyebrows arch at that. When Rex had been running this team, it had felt more like a gang than the army. Maybe Kane had improved his recruiting practices.

"I'm Matt," I told her, extending a hand for her to shake. She eyed it like it was disgusting, and after a moment I pulled it back, embarrassed. I'm not entirely sure what would happen if a living man touched a dead Reaper, but I did not want to be the case study for that particular science experiment.

"Joan," she replied, crossing her arms. A large gothic cross was tattooed on her right biceps. I narrowed my eyes as I studied her, suddenly concerned about who exactly I was—

"Not the same one," she said, answering my unspoken question with a slight roll of her eyes.

"Sorry," I replied, holding up my hands in mock surrender. "There was a guy here named Jack who actually was—"

"I've heard."

"Cool." I struggled to find something to say as the conversation slipped away from me. I'm not a roguish charmer of mythical proportions, but this was going poorly, even by my standards.

"What's the plan, boss?" she asked, turning to look at Kane directly.

"Your team will escort Matthew and Wilbur out onto the Veil," he ordered. "They will identify the location of the damage to the structure and then help defend the site until it can be repaired."

"Who has operational Authority?" Something tensed in her jaw, as if she already knew she wasn't going to like the answer to the question. Kane turned his head to Wilbur, who shrugged, sending Death's heavy gaze to settle on me.

Ah crap. Why was it always me?

"The new guy?" the woman asked, as if giving him a chance to change his mind.

"Don't worry, Joan, he's been here before," Death promised.

"H*e's been here before,*'" I muttered under my breath a few moments later as I stood at the head of thirteen Reapers, preparing to launch myself back out into the hungry dark that was the Nothing.

"What was that?" Wilbur asked, coming to stand next to me.

"Nothing."

"Here, I got you a few more," he said, holding out two pairs of

Reality Anchors dangling from their necklaces. Each of them held an orange sphere that had been charged with a soul's power, enabling it to create a buffer of Reality around me, stopping the dark from chomping on me.

No one was quite certain if it would be enough to hold it back from devouring me, the *living* guy, but it was the best tool we had. I was more than happy to throw on a few extras just in case.

"Thanks," I grumbled, slipping them over my head. I tried not to let my bitterness seep into my voice. Wilbur was my friend, and he was just trying to help. As Death's heir, he was the most powerful person we could bring with us. I hoped he had been practicing with all the Authority that he had under the hood, because I had a bad feeling we were going to need it.

I was just nervous about what would happen the moment I stepped out of this doorway. The worst-case scenario was that my body would implode like I had been exposed to the hard vacuum of outer space, and I would die in silence. The best case was I'd fight some sort of battle with Legion and the other lost creatures that lived in the dark while trying to seal up their access to the living world.

Safety not freaking guaranteed.

"We're ready, *sir,*" Joan called from behind my left shoulder. There was just a hint of bitterness in her tone, but I chose to ignore it. What was the point in getting all snotty now? I was maybe gonna die in the next thirty seconds. If I did, I might as well make my final words a little more pithy.

I glanced behind me to make sure I knew what we were getting into. Two of the Reapers were positioned behind what looked like a personal-sized cement mixer from the living side. It hummed as it blended a sterile white goo that was apparently the material the exterior of the Veil was made of.

The rest of the strike force was circled around our cargo. A couple of them carried long-handled brooms to aid in the application of the mixture when the time was right. All we had to do was find the hole, get the machine to it, and then protect the rest of the team long enough to patch it up.

That's it.

How simple.

"Okay, follow me. Uh, if I drop dead, I'm pretty sure it was that way." I gestured in the direction I remembered racing from when I made my mad dash to the hangar. My heart pinged in sadness for Yuki, regardless of her faithfulness. I wished she were here to help me remember.

It was time. I didn't bother with a countdown; that would only give me time to get scared.

"Once more unto the breach!" I said and launched myself forward.

The orange light of the barrier between Reality and Nothing swept over me like a warm, summer wind. Then the unending cold of the abyss bit into me with the force of a thousand winters.

It was worse than I remembered. My body locked up as my senses were overwhelmed with pain. The cold crushed me from every side; I could feel it trying to burrow its way through the orange nimbus that shielded me. One of the Reality Anchors around my neck flickered, its light going out for a moment before coming back, but weaker.

This is it!

Inwardly I braced for oblivion, but it did not come.

The pain did not fade, but the darkness did not take me.

"You good?" Joan asked sharply. I had a feeling she was less worried about me and more concerned about the org chart, but I managed to shake myself free of my stupor enough to get moving.

"Come on, we're wasting time," I snarled, not looking over my shoulder as I shifted my body underneath me so my feet sank toward the flat surface of the Veil. It was disorienting, changing my perspective by ninety degrees. I was now standing on what had been my wall a few moments before. The white surface felt warm beneath my soles, a hint of Reality bleeding through it.

I paused for a moment, trying to get my bearings. My vision was full, but there weren't many landmarks other than the orange door we had just emerged from. At our feet, the wall—or floor—of the Veil extended in every direction in an infinite, flat plane. Above us, the empty dark of the Nothing filled everything else, like an eternal, starless night sky.

Behind me, the rest of the Reapers emerged from the air lock, floating with ungainly movements as they followed me, dragging the mixer. This close to the border, the Veil offered some gravity, but it was incredibly low. I'd guess it was less even than what could be found on the moon.

I hunched my shoulders and leapt forward, setting the pace for the rest of my team. I didn't know how long I could stay out here without attracting the attention of things I did not want to see. Aite, the mad goddess who was bound to the Nothing, once told me I was marked. They might know already.

Together like a murder of crows, we swept across the blemish-free surface of the Veil, hunting for one mar on its surface. My tension rose as we searched. I'd hoped this would be simple. In the frantic scenes of my memory, we hadn't run very far after I hooked us onto the surface.

But we'd been terrified, and fear's wings are the best of them all. It was hard to judge how far we had traveled now, when I was *less* afraid.

"Does this look familiar?" Wilbur asked from my side as we leapt ahead of the slow-moving pack. Joan and the rest were escorting the mixer, making sure it stayed safe until I could point them to their destination.

"I mean…all of it does." I sighed, gesturing at the wide, white expanse in front of us. It was like standing in a desert that stretched from horizon to horizon. All we were missing was a little mirage in the distance. "Not in a helpful way, though."

"I get it." Wilbur's southern drawl was oddly comforting here in the crushing dark. It sounded just a little more alive than any other accent. I didn't know why. The movies, probably.

The weakest orange bulb that hung from my neck flickered out again. This time it did not come back. Despair tickled at my heels, driving me forward. We were running out of time. Soon the rest of my anchors would fail. Aite and her mad hunters would come for me.

I only had a little while longer to make this right.

Fortunately, the same uniformity that made searching the Veil a nightmare became our salvation. A flicker of something, a dark smudge in the distance, caught my eye, and I drew up short.

"Is my mind playing tricks on me, or does that look suspicious?" I asked Wilbur, pointing at the blemish. My tall friend squinted, trying to make it out better.

"Hard to say," he admitted after a moment. "It certainly seems different from everything else."

"That's it," I said, feeling a rush of hope building in my guts. The location felt right. What else could it be, unless there was more than one hole in the Veil? I shook my head, refusing to even think about that.

"Come on!" I called to the group following in our wake, I gestured at the distant blemish like I had a clue of what I was doing. "Let's get this patched up and go home."

"Uh, Matt?" Wilbur called from my side, staring in the direction of the blemish. "I think it's moving toward us."

CHAPTER
THIRTY-FOUR

IT TURNED OUT that the blemish wasn't a gaping hole in the Veil.

That would have been far too easy, so naturally that isn't what happened at all. When the blob was close enough that I could make out the individuals in its herd, they were the twisted bodies of Legion. The only good news was that their presence was probably a sign that we were barking up the right tree in this flat expanse.

The Elders must have sent their troops to guard the extraction point. I didn't mind carving through a pack of the soul-stealers on my way there. Of all the things I have killed, they are the ones I have found the most satisfying. There is no moral gray cloud attached to their deaths. It's not a question of self-defense. They are monsters of the most irredeemable variety. Killing them is not only right—it is required.

I appreciate the straightforwardness of the relationship.

"Stay together!" I shouted over the rushing silence that coursed around us as our murder launched forward. Wilbur and I no longer raced ahead of the rest of the group; now we led our tight pack like the tip of the spear. I summoned my scythe and welcomed the coldness that flooded through me. It was just as hungry as the Nothing, but somehow it felt more *real,* as if it were the only true thing.

Our wedge shot toward the approaching horde, and I felt my excitement rise as I could make out the ever-changing faces of our enemies. There were more of them than I could begin to count, but I was not afraid. I'd slain a Dreadknight. What could these weak shadows do to us?

Most of the aspects of Legion looked like the first one I'd faced in the clearing defending Mason's body. They were large and bulbous, riddled with tumors that distorted their bodies into horrors.

Their faces changed with the beat of their black hearts, switching between the souls they had devoured. Nothing about their bodies conformed to their different heads, making them seem even more repulsive. For a moment one of them wore the anguished face of a pale, blond woman, another an old black man; then they changed. The first was now a young Indian man, and the second carried the head of a baby.

Their visages filled me with existential horror, yet I did not slow down my headlong rush toward them. Instead, I pulled on the darkness that lurked in me, the cold gift of Death, letting it soothe my fear.

I was a part of the Inevitable, here to carry out His will.

Not even the eldritch horrors of the Lost could stand against me and my flock. I felt a few of the Reapers behind me begin to panic as the distance between us closed to less than a football field.

"Do not fear the dark, my friends," I barked, trusting in the Nothing to carry my words to those who followed. I remembered something that Kane once told the Immortals who sat on the Death Board and stole it for my own use. "Today you are servants of Death, and all things die."

"All things die!" Wilbur bellowed at my side, igniting something in the rest of them.

"All things die!" they screamed back at me.

I was the bleeding tip of our arrow, and I slashed wildly, taking advantage of the open space in front of me as our lines crashed together. The first aspect of Legion split in half, carved by my Authority as if he were paper. I felt the familiar warmth as its stolen souls swarmed into me, pulled from its corpse as I destroyed it.

Then we were among the Lost, and there was only chaos.

Something massive slammed into my shoulder, knocking me off balance. I spun, staggering to the side to keep my feet as I bled off the momentum of the blow. A Reaper dashed by me, scythe ripping as they passed the Legionnaire that had checked me.

A dark line appeared across the creature's upper torso, but it didn't subsume. This one was bigger than most of the others in the front line and had clearly gorged itself on stolen souls. Its flickering head turned to track my ally, and I took full advantage, swinging my weapon around and up to bring it down in a devastating overhanded blow. The tip of my blade bit into its chest greedily.

Die, I commanded through gritted teeth.

I felt a tug of resistance as whatever foul thing that possessed its body tried to resist, to press its Authority back against mine. I was no longer the heir, I did not speak with the voice of Death, but I had borne his mark for long enough. My will crushed his like a paper bag, and I let out a satisfied growl as I felt its stolen souls rip free. They flew into me with delightful zips.

A shadow spread above me and despite my earlier admonition, I glanced up in fear, only to find Wilbur hovering over my head, borne on a pair of black wings, like a bat's. His face was scrunched in a roar of pure hatred, and as I watched, his scythe surged, growing to five times its normal size.

With a single swipe he reaped a quarter of the field, carving through the back line of Legion with ease. Orange lights erupted from a score of corpses, rushing to him like fireflies. I felt my jaw drop as he landed next to me. The surface of the Veil seemed to pulse like water reacting to the weight of his impact.

"What?" he asked, giving me a surprised look. "You were the heir. You did stuff like that too."

"Oh yeah," I lied, turning to launch myself back into the fray. "All the time."

"Come to me, little Reaper," a cursed voice chanted as a slim aspect of Legion leapt into my path. Its fingers ended in long, wicked points like talons. "I will feast on the souls you have stolen from me and be reborn!"

"No," I promised it, accepting its challenge gladly. "You will join your fallen in the dark." I dashed forward, letting my scythe trail behind me like a fox's tail. With a sharp step, I cut to the side, using my shift in momentum to carve a diagonal slash at the skinny monster.

It danced out of my range, moving far faster than the bulkier versions of itself I had already faced. One of its long, branchlike arms shot forward, trying to spear me while my weapon was to the side. I ducked underneath its thrust, gathering my wits quick enough to send a retaliatory strike at its limb. It yanked its arm back fast enough to avoid my cut.

Dark Abyss! This thing was *fast.*

It leapt forward, arms windmilling at me as I tried to keep up with its frantic tempo. We exchanged a dozen blows in quick fashion, moving at a pace that left no time for thinking, only reaction. If I had been able to spare the brainpower, I would have had another moment of thankfulness for the mentor who had drilled these lifesaving—life-taking—skills into my muscles.

Dimly, I was aware of a space around us opening up in the melee, as if the rest of the fighters were giving us deliberate space to finish whatever it was that we were doing. Orange lights blinked in the air around us, souls that had somehow not made their way into new vessels to carry them.

Their presence filled me with fear. We could not leave them exposed to the empty Nothing for long. I knew from firsthand experience that they *called* to the things like Legion that lurked in the dark. It was like chumming the water for sharks.

I had to end this now.

My fear made me decide to take a risk. I rolled my hips, feinting a lunge before throwing myself forward in a wild swing, my scythe describing a wicked arc as it carved through the air. The move left me completely open, but to my surprise, Legion fell for it.

"Go into the dark!" I screamed as my blade cut through its chest. The twisted, tumorous thing staggered back, staring down at the black line carved along its torso. For a second, its flickering face froze in an expression of shock. Then a wave of wicked cunning flashed over it, and I felt a thrill of fear as it looked up at me with a victorious light burning in its stolen eyes.

"Foolish mortal, I was *made* in the dark!"

An *implosion* erupted from the monster, like a black hole sucking in everything around it. I staggered forward, bracing my feet against the steady presence of the Veil, trying to hold myself in place. I glanced around to see the rest of my Reapers doing the same. Whatever was pulling us toward the skinny aspect of Legion wasn't enough to overwhelm our strength.

But it was more than enough to gobble up the floating, glowing specks of souls that drifted in the void around us. I gasped as a streak of orange shot past my ear, zipping into the black wound in its stomach like a bee returning to its hive.

A heartbeat later a dozen more followed, weightless and free. Terror bloomed in me as I watched more come to its dark call. I didn't know exactly how many souls Legion needed to evolve to his next stage. Kane told me that the Dreadknight I slew was carrying more than a hundred thousand within it. I doubted this was close to hitting that threshold, but I also had no concept of how many souls were lying around our battlefield. I had no desire to actually find out what it was going to turn into.

"No!" I screamed, launching myself forward, letting the thing's dark gravity pull me forward faster than I could have managed on my own. Legion's frozen face registered another moment of shock as I flew toward it, my scythe drawn back for a beheading blow.

But before I could strike its head from its shoulders, the ritual was complete.

Black lightning struck with no sound. The force of its impact sent me flying head-over-heels in the low gravity as the twisted pull coming from the monster vanished. I swung myself around as I drifted down onto the Veil, barely managing to get my feet under me before I landed.

My heart hammered in my chest as I rose to stare at the new aspect of Legion that stood before me, reveling in its change. It was still tall and gangly; if anything, it had gained another foot of height. More disturbingly, it had grown a set of skin, like a fleshy set of wings, that it held close around itself like a robe.

Spurs of bone erupted from its skull like a crown, and it sprouted a second set of arms underneath the first. Its face was no longer stolen, but clearly its own, a twisted horror of sharp teeth and hatred.

"I am reborn in the dark!" it screamed in triumph, throwing back its arms and spreading its wings. "Cower, mortal, for you suffer in the presence of the first Dread Bishop in millennia!"

"You gotta be kidding me. Are all your variations named after chess pieces?" The Bishop did not answer my pressing question. Instead, it flickered forward, limbs moving with sharp purpose like a massive praying mantis. My fear was displaced with revulsion. I hate bugs.

I screamed, retreating under the thing's vicious assault. There were too many blades for me to block; I could only dodge. "Wilbur!" I cried.

The heir answered my call, slashing in from the side as he flew across the field, the full-fledged avatar of our master. His eyes were black and cold. There was no warmth or humanity left in him; it had all been squeezed out by the hunger of the bottomless pit that is Death.

The Bishop screamed in challenge, catching Wilbur's large scythe with two of its appendages. The dark blade stopped short, unable to cut through the nightmare's arms. I felt a tremor of true fear trickle through me at the sight of that. Even the Dreadknight had knelt before the Grim Reaper's Authority when I wielded it. What power did this new horror have that it so easily shrugged off Wilbur's?

"Joan! Find the hole," I screamed, looking over my shoulder at the waning fight. It had to be around here somewhere. The rest of Legion was faring poorly, falling in droves to my murder's scythes. I did not know if we would be able to kill this new thing, but we did not have to. We only had to keep sight of our mission.

Neodeath must be eradicated. The dike must be sealed. Even if I died and my soul was lost to the abyss between worlds, I would see it done. The broad-shouldered woman turned at my shout and nodded once, her face tight with strain.

Turning swiftly, she gathered a pair of Reapers and began moving the cart toward where the Lost had been waiting. I put my faith in her and turned my back on them. I was no handyman.

I was a disciple of the Hunter. My master did not teach me to build but to kill. Squaring my shoulders, I slid into place next to Wilbur, adding my strokes to his as together we tried to corner the nightmare that contested our wills.

"You are not the only one with a patron, mortal," the Dread Bishop screamed, its voice a curse upon my sanity. "Would you like to meet mine? She is not bound like yours." The thing did not wait for our reply.

It danced back half a dozen paces, movements fast and jerky like an insect. With its two underarms it slashed its own chest, driving the talon-like nails of its fingers into its body until its wounds welled with dark, rotten blood.

"Attend to me, Whore of the Night!" it screamed. "Answer my call, Priestess of Despair!"

I lunged forward, too frightened for words. The world was slow, heavy, as if a mighty force warped the very gravity and time around us. I knew no matter how quickly I moved, I would not be in time to stop the Lost from summoning her.

"Come to me, Mother of Ruin!" the Dread Bishop screamed, its voice a blend of pain and ecstasy.

Silence swept over the battlefield. Every Reaper and Lost halted, struck dumb with terror.

The Bishop had called into the night, and a nightmare answered. I understood now why it had retreated, not to hide from Wilbur and me, but to give its mistress center stage. She stood in the midst of our scene, clad in a black toga. Her purple eyes roiled with madness, her heavy gaze settling on me with a hunger that would put even the grave's to the test.

Aite, fallen goddess, murderer of Pluto, Mother of Ruin, threw back her head and laughed. Every peal was like the ringing of an ominous bell calling the faithless to a midnight Mass.

"At last," she cawed.

CHAPTER THIRTY-FIVE

FOR ONE ETERNAL moment, the battlefield lay in silence.

I was the only living mortal present, but my heart did not beat. My blood did not flow. Whatever dark power makes a god a god was on full display. Kane once told me that Aite had left the Romanic band to give herself to the Nothing and become its prophet. If her brother Pluto had been at the seat of his power in Hades, then this was the arena of Aite's Authority. She wielded it like a sledgehammer, beating us all with it.

"I was beginning to think that you were too wise to return to my web, mortal." She sighed in pleasure, staring at me with her roiling purple orbs. The heir of Death stood beside me, but she cared for him not a whit. She only had eyes for me.

"I see now that I merely *overestimated* you," she chuckled. "I thought you must know about my masters' dark gift to your mortal enemy. That you were cautious, unwilling to be pulled into the trap that was built for you. But now I see you were merely *blind.*" Her voice warped with anger and delight. She seemed madder than I remembered. Perhaps the months in the dark had pushed her deeper into insanity.

"I don't understand," I managed, forcing my jaw to break free from the silence that held me like a vise. It resisted me but eventually shattered like a dropped mirror. My heart beat. My blood flowed once more.

"Clearly," she said, laughing. "You do not yet know what you are, do you, Harbinger?" Her taunt scraped its way along my spine. Only one other had ever named me such: Kane, my master lurking within the Veil at my feet. Had this whole thing just been a trap to lure me back across the Veil? What did she know that I did not?

"I am your enemy." I raised my chin in defiance. "I have foiled you once and will do so again."

"Foiled me?" Her shriek of delight pierced my ears. "You *freed* me. You are a delight to me. More precious than blood." I felt something crack within me. As if her truth had done physical damage to my resolve.

That wasn't true, was it?

I opened the door to the Between in the Veil, which had let her enter it. From there, I had lured her into the second hall and into Hades, which had then been destroyed. Aite was a goddess of ruin—another word for "entropy." Had I done her work in destroying the Underworld? Wasn't that what the Nothing wanted, to devour everything? I remembered her anger at Pluto for letting it fall into ruin, but perhaps that had been a piece of her that was not yet consumed by her madness.

Anger flooded through me. Perhaps I was her tool. It would not be the first time that an ancient being took advantage of my ignorance for their own ends. But each of them had learned a lesson. Lilith and Pluto both rotted in graves, Immortal no longer.

Aite could be educated too.

"Well, I'm here now," I snarled, pulling on as much of Death's Authority as I could. It too was cold, merely a different flavor. I missed Willow's warmth. If only we could have this conversation on the other side of the Veil. I would be happy to introduce them to the mad goddess. "Let's see this trap I have heard so much about."

"As you wish." Aite smiled, her plump lips thick with wickedness. The power that stifled the battlefield like a smothering banquet vanished, and my Reapers and her Lost threw themselves at each other with abandon.

Only four of us stood apart from the melee. Wilbur and me against Aite and her Dread Bishop. Out of the corner of my eye, I saw Joan and her escorts pushing the cart forward, their presence forgotten. I did not need to defeat her to win. All I had to do was last long enough to fix my mistakes.

Even when I was the heir, I did not have the power to stand up against Aite. I had survived by treachery and foolishness, my two greatest assets. Out here on the flat surface of the Veil, there was no room for subtlety—only Death.

"Are you with me, brother?" I asked Wilbur, settling forward into a crouch.

"Nowhere else I'd rather be," he drawled, matching my pose. The country boy's voice was sharp with iron, and I felt a small smile to hear the spine. It seemed that in his second life he had grown into being the man he should have been in his first one.

"Together then." As one we launched forward, a pair of crows looking for their next meal. Aite and her Bishop responded in kind, launching themselves toward us like arrows sent to bring us down.

I dropped a foot and dodged to the side, letting the goddess flash past me. My scythe licked out, catching her as she shot by. The hooked blade bit deeply, and I let out a gurgle of surprise as I was yanked off my feet, like a fisherman who had caught a whale.

Aite pulled me in her wake without slowing; I was nothing to her progress. A piece of plankton easily devoured and forgotten. Gritting my teeth, I banished my scythe, releasing myself from her force. I landed lightly in the gentle gravity, re-summoning my weapon with a flick of my wrist. Wilbur and the Dread Bishop clashed to my right, and I hissed in frustration, unable to help my friend.

The goddess laughed as she turned to face me. There was no strain in her expression as she mocked me. This wasn't a fight. She was toying with me. But why? What did she need from me? I tried to think, but my mind was shrouded by fear, and I could not see what lay before me.

"My turn," she murmured, almost adoringly. There was a flicker as she blurred forward too fast for my mortal eyes. Distantly I felt an impact, as if it was on someone else's body. Then the world was spinning as I landed on the Veil, bouncing like a rock skipped across a lake.

My eyes struggled to focus as I clawed my way to my feet. She was so fast that the pain was only now beginning to register. Aite watched me from a dozen paces away, an amused smirk on her face. The second Reality Anchor around my neck flickered and went out. The eternal cold of the Nothing pressed, delighting that the barrier between us was growing thinner.

Dread made my limbs heavy as I rose to face her. I could not beat her. I knew this. Even if I found a way to cut her, I was running out of time. I didn't know how long my final anchor would last. But if this was to be my death, then I would sell my life dearly.

"Not bad," I told her as I raised my weapon once more. "Zagan hits harder, though." The flesh around her right eye twitched slightly at the mention of the fallen angel. No one liked the CFO of Hell.

"We'll see if you think so in a minute," she promised, gathering herself like a baseball player going up to bat. Why did I have to open my mouth?

The goddess blurred again, and I lost track of time as she slammed me into the ground with enough force to rattle every bone in my body. It was a miracle that I did not break into a thousand pieces. I think the only reason I didn't was because I was more *real* than the surface I crashed into.

When I regained my feet, I glanced down at the last anchor, which still burned brightly. *Hang on,* I pleaded with the soul that powered it. *We're not done yet.* I didn't think it could hear me. Whatever soul lent some of its power to the relic was safely inside the Veil, unaware of the danger that it shielded me from.

Aite was on top of me before I could summon my weapon once more. This time she did not give me the space to recover. Her granite-like fist crashed into my stomach, lifting me off the ground. A second blow slammed into my back, smashing me into the Veil. Once I was down, she began to kick me with her sandals. Each blow felt like I was about to shatter into a thousand pieces.

I crumpled against the Veil and curled up into a ball, protecting my organs from the wrath of the Mother of Ruin. What hubris I'd had to think that I could even stand against a goddess! She was relentless, kicking me as I cowered at her feet.

Yet—something was wrong.

She was more powerful than I was, by several orders of magnitude. I was less than a child in her hands. So why was I still in once piece? She had defeated me without breaking a sweat.

Do gods sweat? Now that would be an old spice.

The point was, I was surprised she hadn't done more damage. The beating hurt, but I have hurt before. She could have broken me like a dry twig and yet hadn't. Why?

The mystery eluded me, but at last it seemed that she grew bored.

Aite bent down and lifted me from the ground with casual strength. Her left hand was wrapped around my neck as she held me up.

"A pity," she murmured lovingly into my eyes. "I rather thought that your friends valued you more than this, Harbinger." Her purple eyes bored into mine, searching for something.

"*Ack, uck,*" I replied, trying to say something smart through her vise-like grip. Her smile grew mean as if she understood the intent well enough. Perhaps she did. She was a goddess, after all.

"It has been too long since I enjoyed something as *real* as you, mortal." Her eyes fluttered in something like ecstasy. "If nothing else, thank you for being delicious." She raised her right hand and traced it toward my guts, black nails sharp as blades.

I wriggled in her grasp like a fish trying to escape to the river. Distantly I wondered if my guts would fall in the low gravity and stain the Veil forever, or if they'd drift off into the abyss. Her claws burned with hot fire as she sliced my stomach. I tried to scream, but no air could make it free from my throat. The last anchor hanging from my neck throbbed as it pulsed, desperately trying to hold back the Nothing.

In the distance, I saw Joan and the other Reapers working on the Veil. One of them used a long-handled broom to sweep the white goop over a portion that must be where the hole was. Triumph flared in my heart even as I prepared to die.

This was a worthy death.

"RELEASE HIM," a voice demanded from behind me. For a second, the darkness of the Nothing was as bright as day. The flickering orange light around my neck grew steady, and the cold retreated. Aite's nails froze, and her features flashed in triumph.

Oh no.

"As you wish," she purred, dropping me like a forgotten sack of potatoes. I landed on the soft surface of the Veil and turned to stare in disbelief at the interloper.

He was tall and thin, reminding me of a knife. His blond hair was cut short like a soldier's. But it was his white eyes that blazed like the sun that marked him for what he was. Azrael, Angel of Death, had come.

"There you are," she purred.

A cry sounded in the deep.

True fear, unlike anything I had ever felt, trickled down my spine as I remembered that sound. The waking of an Elder, that strange, twisted thing that Legion served. A moment later a second joined it, and a third.

Azrael's head whipped to the side, and he stared in the dark for a moment in pure surprise.

"We have been waiting for you, *messenger*," Aite cackled madly. "My masters wake from their slumber and desire to be fed. You shall do nicely." Her head cocked as she studied the angel with a predatory gaze. "A pity you do not have your sword."

Suddenly I understood the depths of the trap that I was bait for. The layers of the game that was being played around me. Aite and her masters had given Lazarus a taste of the darkness. They had given him the ability to create Neodeath to steal from Death and the Underworlds.

They knew that eventually Kane would discover this, and that he'd have to react. It was too great a threat to the Death Treaty and to Reality itself. And who would the Grim Reaper send to stop the mortals who trifled with Death back in the real world?

His one living Reaper. Good old Matthew Carver.

When my path led me back to the damage done to the Veil, a place where Kane could not tread, they would be ready to capture me and draw out their true prey. Aite had already killed a member of the Death Board, depriving the Grim Reaper of one of his trusted allies. It made sense that Hell's ilk had gladly cooperated with this dance.

For if the Angel of Death was gone, who would oppose Zagan?

"What will you do, messenger?" Aite taunted. "Things older than you stir in the dark, and they are hungry. Fly before it is too late." As if to echo her sentiment, the things in the void roared once more. They seemed closer now. If space even truly existed in the Nothing.

I coughed, rubbing my almost crushed throat as I scanned the horizon, terrified that I would see the great wriggling tentacles and madness-inducing shapes. But there was no sign of the Elders yet.

"I need no sword to deal with you, wretch," Azrael spoke at last. He raised his hand, and a blinding light coalesced above his head, a perfect ring that blazed like the sun. A halo, some might say.

"Poor messenger," Aite murmured, eyeing Azrael's display of power with narrowed eyes. "It seems that somehow you have forgotten that pride *is a sin.*" She raised her own left hand and snapped her fingers.

The sound echoed in the abyss, cutting through everything else like a sharp knife. A patch of darkness slipped into being, like someone had pulled its cover off. Horror jolted through me as I realized that we were standing in the middle of a circle that had been hidden on the surface of the Veil, like an alligator biding its time.

Black lines ran in intersecting directions, piercing the circle in the shape of a five-pointed star that was drawn to be the opposite of a pentagram. Harsh writing traced the sharp angles. I almost thought I could hear the words whispering in my mind even though I did not know how to read the script.

Azrael's burning light abruptly winked out as if the power line had been cut. For a moment, everything was brittle and still. Even the Angel of Death seemed stunned. He froze in the manner of Immortals, as if he had turned to stone.

"Now," Aite purred, taking a step toward the suddenly bound angel. Unlike Azrael, she still seemed to have all her power, as if the trap had been set to cut off one source while leaving hers intact. I glanced at the scythe that still sat heavily in my hand, realizing that Death's touch was also not blocked.

All these steps had been put into place just to lead to here. In the distance Joan and her team of Reapers worked to repair the damaged Veil, their efforts ignored by the few aspects of Legion that remained. The rift had served its purpose and was already forgotten. Wilbur and the other Reapers gathered on one side, watching us with nervous eyes. Being more spirit than flesh, they could not cross the boundary any more than the Lost that huddled in Aite's shadow.

"Matthew, I am afraid that I am going to have to advise that you run," Azrael murmured from beside me. His white eyes were half lidded, like the sun beginning to descend below the horizon. "I will not be able to protect you here."

"Yes, flee, little mortal," Aite cackled, drawing closer. "You have served your purpose wonderfully. We will see each other again, you and I."

"I won't leave you," I promised the angel, hefting my scythe. Azrael was my mentor's mentor—my hunting grandfather by the most basic of math. The Angel of Death was not my friend per se, but he had come to save me. Orion would never think about retreating, and neither would I.

Aite's mocking laughter scourged me. "Oh, little mortal, you have killed a few weak things and somehow convinced yourself that this means you have grown teeth. But you will break them if you try to bite me."

"Don't worry, Matthew, this is rather in the job description. Run," the angel insisted, not looking in my direction. His gaze was still locked on the predator that was circling toward him, watching it with the lazy patience of a dangerous creature. Even though he was trapped, he showed no fear, only the boundless confidence of a man who could kill anything. I had a feeling that more than one being that called itself a god had found him waiting for them when their time was up.

I glanced over my shoulder to see the helpless expression on Wilbur's face. Death's heir watched from right on the line, unable to reach us. He had enough power to threaten the Mother of Ruin, but he was trapped.

"I will not offer you this escape again," Aite called from behind me. "Flee now while you can. You have fixed your master's fence. Anything that happens after has nothing to do with you." In the distance, the Elders' haunting cries sounded again as they stirred in the dark. I wondered how long it would be before they came to feast on what Aite had caught for them.

Azrael nodded once sharply, part permission, part command. With a heavy heart, I lowered my scythe, accepting his wishes. Slowly, I began to back toward the waiting Reapers, watching the two Immortals locked in the angel trap warily.

Just because she said she was going to let me go didn't mean I was going to turn my back on her. But with each step, I cast my mind around the flat expanse of the Veil, hoping to find a way out of this mess.

I stepped across the line of the circle, feeling no change as I joined my fellows on the outside. I hovered next to Wilbur as together we watched the Mother of Ruin stalk the powerless Angel of Death.

"I have waited for this for eons," Aite chuckled, licking her lips like she was about to gorge herself in a feast. "Entropy always wins. That is one of the laws."

"You haven't won yet," Azrael murmured, still standing stock-still. He did not turn to track her movements, merely watched her as she paced. "Will you wait for your masters? Or are you brave enough to do the work yourself?" A heavy groan sounded once more in the abyss, underscoring his words.

"Brave?" She cackled. "What bravery is required in plucking an apple from a tree? You are helpless, angel."

"Am I?" I could hear the small smile in his voice. "Are you so sure?" Without another word he moved, taking a single, firm step toward the goddess. Aite froze, purple eyes narrowing. A dozen emotions flickered across her face too quickly to track. Anger. Madness. Fear. Sadness. Hunger. Fear. Rage. Desire. Fear.

Azrael took another step. The fallen Olympian flinched, retreating a step. A chuckle ripped itself free of my lips as I watched her give ground. Aite was terrifying, but the problem with setting a tiger trap is that sometimes you catch a tiger.

"What is the matter, *goddess*?" Azrael's voice was sharp enough to cut. "Surely you need not fear me here, at the height of your power? I am but an apple. *Come and pluck me.*" Aite's face paled slightly, and she retreated another step.

For a moment the two Immortals stared, their solid eyes scouring each other, fighting in a way that I could neither sense nor understand. But then a flicker of confidence burst across Aite's face, and I felt my fear return.

"You lie," she hissed and launched herself at the angel like a missile. Azrael tried to leap to the side, but he was too slow. The Mother of Ruin caught him with a wicked blow to the chest that sent him flying, only to crash against an invisible wall of power that contained him within the ring.

Before he could recover, she was on top of him, fists flashing as rained blow after blow down on the skinny man. I watched in horror as he tried to shield himself from her fury but was not able to drive her back. His confidence had been a shield, but the goddess had seen through it.

"Dark Abyss," Wilbur murmured in horror from my side. "We have to do something."

Screaming with rage, Aite grabbed Azrael with both hands and flung him across the length of the ring, smashing him into another invisible barrier. I felt a jolt of fear as the Angel of Death glanced in my direction. He looked bleary-eyed and stunned, but that was not what filled me with terror.

It was the trickle of blood that ran from the corner of his mouth.

An Immortal was bleeding. I knew then that Aite could kill him. That her trap had the teeth to kill one of the most powerful beings in the known universe—and that I was the only person who could cross her circle to stop it.

I took one step back toward the ring, but Azrael's eyes sharpened, and he speared me in place with a fierce glare. I froze, pinned in place by his irritation. His power could not reach me through the barrier, yet I was unable to move. He seemed annoyed with me, like he was waiting for me to do something. I recognized the look; I had seen it on Orion's face a thousand times.

"Elder!" screamed one of the Reapers behind us, her voice full of fear. I cast a glance over my shoulder in time to see the faint outlines of something horrible and wrong wriggling its way toward us. It was massive, the size of Downtown Los Angeles. I tore my gaze away from it before it could burrow into my mind. I could not afford a distraction now—Azrael's time was running out.

If only there was some way to break the circle! In rage, I hammered my scythe against it, but there was nothing I could cut. The trap was well laid, bound to a surface that was impenetrable. It could only be cut by the Authority of Death himself—

I understood.

My heart hammered in my chest as I turned toward Wilbur, catching his eyes with mine. My taller friend looked apprehensive, as if he could sense the madness that rested in my eyes. I banished my scythe, hoping that made me seem less threatening.

"Do you trust me?" I asked. He studied me for a second before nodding once, slowly.

“With my life.” He grinned faintly. “Such as it is.”

“I’m going to need you to remember that,” I replied, holding out my right hand. It shook like a leaf. I knew what I was about to ask him to risk. I was pretty sure that he did too. “I need the ring.”

Wilbur stared at my outstretched palm for just a moment, steeling himself. Just when I thought that he wasn’t going to do it, that it was too much to ask, he nodded. With a smooth gesture, he banished his own scythe and reached for Kane’s signet. The cheery death’s-head seemed to wink at me as he grabbed it.

“Are you sure?” I asked, causing him to pause.

“Of course not.” He gave me what looked like a brave grin. “But I’m only still here because of you. Would be pretty small of me not to repay the favor.”

“Thank you,” I whispered softly. Wilbur took a deep breath and jerked the signet ring of Death from his finger, stripping him of his enhanced Authority. For a heartbeat nothing changed; he simply reached out and placed it in my hand, closing my fingers over it. I shuddered at its familiar chill.

Then his face clouded, and he staggered to the side, clutching at his side. When Jack and his cronies had tried to kill me, my tall friend had saved me. But in so doing, he had taken a mortally wounding blow. Only the power of being the heir had kept his wound at bay. Without it, Jack’s blow would have long ago eaten him into nothing.

“Easy! Easy!” I gasped, catching Wilbur with my free hand before he could fall to the ground. “Help me!” I snapped at the other Reapers, who watched us with wide eyes. One woman opened her mouth to protest, but I slid the signet ring onto my finger and glared at her until she obeyed.

“Please don’t dally,” Wilbur managed to whimper through gritted teeth. “This is most unpleasant.”

"On it," I promised my friend, turning my back on him to face the ring once more. Azrael was still being pummeled. Aite stood above him, cackling as she rained kicks on his prostrate form. I winced in sympathy. Even if she had been holding back when she did the same thing to me, I knew firsthand how little fun it was. The Angel of Death looked terrible. His blood stained the white of the Veil, and he was powerless in the trap the Lost had set for him.

Time to do something about it.

Steeling myself, I reached inside to the darkness that lurked in my mind, immersing myself in it before reaching toward the cold ring that rested on my finger, using it as a straw to pull even *more* power into me. My own Authority had grown as I used my piece of Death, but the progress I had made was laughable against the torrent of insatiable hunger that poured into me.

I summoned my scythe. It was darker than I remembered. So black that it stood out against the lesser abyss of the Nothing that surrounded us. I had been worried Kane would not approve of my plan, but something about the amount of strength that flowed into me told me otherwise.

Inside the ring, Aite paused her beating, her head whipping around in surprise at whatever she sensed roiling in me. "You dare to challenge me?" she called, standing above the prostrate form of Azrael. "Be careful what you do with your master's power, mortal." The distant Elder screamed again, adding its mocking insanity to her threat.

"Oh, don't mind me. I'd never dream of interfering in whatever this is." I smiled brightly at her, confident in my path. "But I am out here to do a little maintenance, and it turns out, there's something the boss wants cleaned right away." Aite's face had just enough time to go pale before I slashed downward with my uber-scythe, carving cleanly through the Veil and whatever they had attached to it to make their angel trap.

This was the cleverness of the trap. The Veil could only be cut by the power of Death. Only the Grim Reaper himself, or his heir, had the Authority to do it. But the circle had also prevented the power of a dead Reaper from passing it. That meant that only an heir who was also mortal and *alive* could break it. Good thing I was here, then.

The circle shattered, and then there was only judgment.

Azrael did not get up. One moment he was bleeding and prostrate. The next he was flying, hovering a foot off the ground as he towered over Aite. The mad goddess's purple eyes grew wide as his halo began to glow once more.

For a brief moment, the dark became light. The empty abyss was bathed in daybreak, and it was awesome and terrible. I closed my eyes against its tremendous power, too slow to be spared a glance from the approaching Elder, whose non-linear shape only hammered at my psyche more when I could see it clearly.

The light crescendoed, searing me with its harsh, unforgiving power. I gritted my teeth and curled up against the Veil, cowering before the wrath that Azrael unleashed. Distantly I heard screams of terror as the rest of Legion reacted to the angel's retribution.

Then it was over. The light was gone in a moment, and as I slowly rose to my feet, blinking owlishly as my pupils tried to adjust to the return of the crushing dark. Azrael stood in the middle of the ruined circle, alone except for a handful of dark smudges on the far side that had to be the Lost that had waited.

There was no sign of Aite or the Elder.

"Did you fry her?"

Wilbur let out a pained whimper at my feet, and I turned away from the skinny angel before he could answer. With shaking hands, I ripped the ring from my finger and handed it to my friend. Wilbur's face was pale, and he was breathing heavily, but as the death's-head signet slid onto his digit once more, he let out a sigh of relief. I looked up from my friend to find the angel studying me, a strange expression on his face.

"Curious," was all Azrael said when I arched an eyebrow. "No, Matthew, I did not 'fry' Aite. The Mother of Ruin will return to haunt our steps once more."

"Why?" I demanded, feeling a surge of anger that she had escaped. She and her monsters had taken so much from people. If ever there was a crime that deserved *judgment,* it was the stealing of mortal souls.

"Because unfortunately, I too have rules." Azrael smiled softly as if he understood the outrage on my face but had already made peace with it. That only made me madder. I glared at the Angel of Death once more before turning my back on him to check on Wilbur.

"You still with me?" I asked, offering him my hand.

"Let's try to avoid that in the future," he grunted, rising to his feet. "Everything went black and white for a moment there." I glanced at the pale surface of the Veil at our feet and the darkness of the expanse above us. "Even more," he replied with a roll of his eyes.

"Fair enough." I clapped him on the shoulder. "We just need to have Joan and her team patch up this new hole that someone made, and then we can get out of here—"

Naturally that was the moment that my last Reality Anchor chose to give out.

CHAPTER THIRTY-SIX

I'M NOT SURE how long a human can exist in the vacuum of space without a sealed suit and oxygen. It can't be long. I'm pretty sure there's some complicated stuff that happens to your lungs when you're exposed to the void that makes you either implode or explode, depending on whether you hold your breath or not. I also heard your eyeballs freeze?

I don't know. I'm not a scientist. I'm barely even a college graduate.

The Nothing is *not* space, as far as I can tell. Space is real. The Nothing is not. But it's probably the closest analogy that we have in our realm to the thing that I was trapped in when my anchor gave out.

The experience was not pleasant. If not for the fact that I was being escorted back by a literal angel, I might not have made it. Everything burned with a cold that was hotter than any fire. The tips of my fingers and toes turned a little black, as if they had been nibbled on by frostbite. Wilbur told me the same thing happened to my nose, but I didn't look in a mirror. I was too afraid of what I would see.

We gathered in Death's office to debrief. The pair of glowing orange souls that I had pulled from the Lost and Found sat on Kane's desk, which was not where I had left them, but I took that as a sign he was at least willing to talk about what I wanted to do.

"You cut the Veil. Again," Kane stated, staring at me with a heavy, blank stare.

"We fixed it right away," I protested, gesturing at Azrael and Wilbur next to me. I wanted to feel more confident, but I was wrapped in a thick thermal blanket, trying to get feeling back into my body after my experience in the Nothing. It didn't make me look very imposing, but it was comfy. "I don't know why you're getting all snappy at me. Mission accomplished. No more Neodeath can be manufactured. Aite and the Elders didn't get to eat a freaking angel. Everyone is welcome."

"It could have gone a lot worse," Wilbur agreed, which wasn't exactly the rousing backup I was hoping for, but I would take what I could get.

"It seems our enemies grow bolder," Kane replied at last, leaning back in his chair. He had a long-suffering expression. The corners of his dark eyes were pinched with tension and exhaustion. For a moment I could see all of his long, long years fully written on his face.

"The counterfeit production may be broken, but that does not mean the supply is gone," he continued darkly. "There is still work to be done to purge it from the mortal realm, and its makers cannot go unpunished." His heavy gaze settled back on me.

"Let me guess, that's on my to-do list?" I grumbled. The Grim Reaper didn't bother to respond. Other than Death himself, I was the only fully living mortal in the room. There weren't a lot of other candidates around to do the job. I let it go with a quiet shrug. I had a bigger question that needed answering.

"What about the souls that were taken? What about Maria?" This had all started because of one woman, and even if we had stopped Lazarus from being able to make more Neodeath, it didn't mean the job was done.

"The Nothing is infinite, and there is a finite number of Reapers," Kane said with a note of sadness. "We will never stop looking for her, but it will take some time."

"What about you guys?" I asked, giving Azrael a challenging stare. "Why don't you just find them or tell us where they are?"

The Angel of Death frowned, giving me a tight-lipped shake of his head. "I will do what I can but—rules."

"What rule could possibly—"

"Free will, Matthew," Death interrupted softly, his voice far gentler than I expected. "This falls to me, a mortal, to solve."

"*Free will*," I sneered, taking in the two powerful beings with a sense of disgust. "What does free will matter when people like Maria suffer and have theirs taken away? What good is this?"

"That, I fear, is rather the point," the angel replied cryptically. His face was extra smooth now, an expression I was learning to recognize from Immortals who were treading carefully on the limits of what they were allowed to do. There might be more he wanted to tell me, but he physically couldn't.

"We will never stop looking," Kane promised me again. "We have an eternity to find her. One day we will bring her home. I swear this to you, upon my own name. I am Death, and I will deliver her." I cocked my head in surprise to hear his words echo Evangeline's promise. The room reverberated with the power of his oath. Even I, a lowly mortal, could feel the binding that had just happened here. I stared at the Grim Reaper for a moment before nodding in understanding.

"In the meantime, we will do what we can to make sure this does not continue to happen," Azrael echoed, not quite a promise, but pretty good. But now I had another mystery to solve.

"Why?" I asked, looking between Kane and the angel. "Why is this happening?"

"I named you Harbinger," Death reminded me grimly.

"Which means what, exactly?" Aite's mocking laughter burned in my ears.

"It means you are a disruptor." Azrael sighed softly. "A canary in the coal mine that warns of coming disaster. There has been tension brewing for millennia, but the pot is finally coming to a boil." I paused, trying to sort through what I knew. From the moment my soul had been stolen, people had warned me that there would be *implications* to my story being true. It had been a big part of why Alex and Orion had agreed to help me in the first place.

"It has to be Hell doing this, right?" I looked at Azrael for support. His counterpart Zagan had always been more than happy to oppose anything Heaven wanted to do; I could only hope the sibling rivalry went both ways. "I mean, not to put *too* fine a point on it, but they're the bad guys, aren't they? Or at least some of the bad guys? Stealing souls is sort of their move?"

"Lucifer would not dare." The Angel of Death shook his head grimly, looking concerned but convinced. "He has no need to *steal* them, Matthew. He already has a successful Underworld. There is no benefit to him breaking the laws that govern—"

"Really?" I asked flatly, somehow daring to interrupt an angel. "You're going to look me in *my* eyes and tell me that the Devil doesn't steal souls?"

Azrael sighed, acknowledging my point with a shrug. "This is different, even than what has *allegedly* happened to you." His expression told me that the disclaimer was more of a legal thing than what he actually thought—or even knew. That warmed my heart a little, to know that he did believe me…probably.

"Stealing a soul from another Underworld is a serious crime," Kane agreed solemnly, his expression dark. "But it has happened and has been dealt with in past eons. Stealing from me is another thing entirely."

"But it has to be Hell behind this." I looked between the two of them with desperate intensity, trying to force them to believe me. Who else would be so bold—so cunning? Is the Devil not the Prince of Lies?

"Do you have any proof?" Kane asked me gently, giving me an opportunity.

"Maria said that Zagan himself came to threaten her to sign the contract."

Azrael's lips twisted in irritation. "Just because something *said* their name was Zagan doesn't mean that they actually were him," he pointed out. "That's hearsay, not evidence."

"Samael!" I gasped, snapping my fingers as I recalled another point. "She was there."

"You saw the Dark Whisper with the Neodeath?" Azrael's voice grew sharp, as if I had finally gotten his interest.

"Well, not exactly," I admitted reluctantly. "But she was in the Abaddon Market, which is where they were keeping it."

"And everything else under the sun," Kane pointed out.

"But—"

"It's not even close to good enough, Matthew," Azrael told me gently. I sighed in defeat. I was no less certain that I was right, but I couldn't prove what I knew in my heart.

"But there is one who we do know is involved," Kane growled ominously, "and there is no doubt."

"You think that this is just Lazarus and his people trying to take advantage of the chaos?" I asked, surprised. This felt like something far bigger than that. "Where do the Elders and the Lost fit into all of this?"

"Their hunger is mindless." Kane waved a dismissive hand, as if they hadn't almost just destroyed a flock of his Reapers. "Entropy always seeks to devour that which exists, it is the way of things."

"You really think that a group of *mortals* cooked this up on their own?" I let a little of my frustration bleed through. The two Immortals before me both seemed convinced that they understood the situation, but the more I learned, the more out of control it felt to me.

"Lazarus didn't even know how the Veil operated before he sent me down to infiltrate it," I told Kane. "In less than six mortal months, he's learned about the Lost, taken their power, and used it to make a new type of Death? Doesn't that seem like a really condensed timeline?"

Kane let out a grunt of acceptance but did not comment.

"I mean, call me crazy, but that seemed rather mindful and organized," I murmured, glancing between Kane and Azrael. "It sure looked like the whole thing was set up to kill an angel." Death paused for a moment, considering my words. "Last time I was here, Aite had recently managed to kill another of your allies. All I'm trying to say is that it's not Zagan who almost got his wings pinned out there in the dark."

A long silence stretched among us. Kane and Azrael shared a look full of meaning. What were those two Immortals thinking? What did the metaphorical chessboard look like from their ancient perspective? I was certain there was a heavy hand guiding some of the players dancing around us, but whose? Was Lazarus really the top of the pyramid, or were there more empires trying to eliminate their opponents under the cover of chaos?

"I'm sorry, but I'm not following all of this," Wilbur inserted, raising his hand. Poor guy; he had a lot to catch up on. Somehow even more than I did.

"The boss thinks someone is looking to make a big play. Carve up the pie in a new way." I stared at Kane as I tried to explain. "But he also thinks it's not one of the usual power players. It's someone new, someone smaller. They don't want to be the poster boy for the fight and get everyone's attention. So they're making moves on the side while people are distracted."

"I guess that makes sense," Wilbur said after a moment. "It's like a shell game. I used to pull those on street corners all the time. Get people to watch the cups, and you can steal all the balls you want." He gestured at the pair of glowing orbs on Death's desk.

"Should I be concerned that you took it upon yourself to raid my larders without speaking to me?" Kane murmured, turning to me with dark eyes.

"I'm speaking to you now." I gave him my most winsome smile. "I just needed to do some research before I brought you my pitch."

"What kind of research?"

"I needed to know what we had in the coffers. I recently came across an investment opportunity, and I thought it would make a lot of sense for us to get in on the ground floor." I felt my smile grow. "And if you'll trust me with some of our precious cargo once more, I think I can negotiate a deal that gets us all what we want."

It took both more and less effort than I expected to convince Kane to let me leave with the two orbs. On the one hand, I was a little insulted that he trusted me so little, even if I had ripped two different holes in the Veil. On the other, I was also a little horrified that he let me just wander off with two human souls. All I had to do was sign them out from the manifest, and I was their keeper. It felt too entirely normal. I didn't pay my taxes, but somehow I had two little pieces of Reality in my pocket like it was no big deal.

"Well, I guess this is it," Wilbur said sadly as he walked me back to the far side of the Veil. I didn't need to carve my way out this time because I was alive. So instead of relying on my Reaper powers to get me home, I was just going to stand on the living half and use Portunus's

Key to get into the Between.

"Oh, I doubt it." I sighed, glancing at the somber heir. "I think you and I are going to be seeing each other plenty."

To my surprise, my friend's face brightened. "Really?"

"Do you honestly think this is the last disaster that's going to happen?" I arched a single eyebrow. "I'm pretty sure this Harbinger thing is like a weather forecast of bad times ahead."

"I guess you're right." Wilbur shoved his hands into his pockets, hunching his shoulders in sadness. "Just with you gone and Yuki...I don't have a lot of friends left here. People get uncomfortable hanging out with the heir."

"I remember," I snorted. When I wore the ring, he was too afraid to hang out with me. Being Death's right hand was a lonely path, but it also needed a good man to walk it. I knew it was hard, but I trusted him to be a good steward.

"This should be far enough," I told him, judging off my mental map of the Veil. I fished into my pocket for the god's key that was bound to me, checking to make sure that Portunus's laughing mask was present instead of Janus's somber one.

"Well, keep safe," Wilbur said awkwardly, looking like he wasn't sure if he should offer a hug. "I'd hate for the next time I see you to be when I'm there to, you know...collect."

"Yeah, let's avoid that," I laughed, surprising him by giving him a firm embrace. He felt a little too soft, as if he wasn't fully *there.*

"You can always just call me just to say hi." Wilbur's face brightened at the thought. "You're pretty good at circles." I didn't have the heart to tell him that Alex had banned me from any more summons.

"I'll see what I can do," I promised him, clapping him on the shoulder once more and reaching for the door with the god's key in my hand. "You be careful out there too," I ordered, pointing an accusatory finger in his direction. "If you get yourself unmade, I will never forgive you."

"Deal!" he called, as I stepped out of the Veil and into the real world. This time I did not bounce off an invisible wall but passed through easily. I gave Wilbur one more small wave before I closed the door, leaving him behind.

For a moment I stood there in the eternal hallway, frowning at the door to the Veil. There was a part of me that didn't feel right about this next step. Free of my deadlines, I had a moment to let my bold façade fade as I wrestled with my blows of doubt. The moment I walked out of this place, I was going to have to make a lot of decisions that I could not take back.

Was I doing the right thing? I thought so. At the very least it was the *most* right thing I could do. The world isn't always black and white. Sometimes there aren't clean lines. There's just bad and worse. I was beginning to suspect that part of growing up is learning you really can only do your best with the hand you're dealt.

But even though I was standing outside time, I felt a sense of urgency pulling at me. Lazarus and his cronies still had their supply of Neodeath, and I had to do something about it. Somehow I had managed to make myself indispensable to the one of the most pivotal plotlines in Reality. That weight was unsurprisingly heavy on my shoulders, like a sack of concrete powder.

I was one of the few living people who could understand what the victims of Lazarus's Neodeath were going through. My soul was stolen too. It wasn't exactly the same situation. My little orange orb wasn't headed for whatever new, dark prison these monsters had created—but I wasn't going anywhere nice either. There was no vacation paradise waiting for me when I died.

Just the tenth circle of a Hell.

It didn't matter how I had gotten here, though, or how hard the responsibility was to carry. I needed to do it. For Maria. For the other souls that had their agency taken from them. I knew firsthand how easy it was for those who were lost to be forgotten. A single soul among the trillions that have and would ever live was easy to lose track of. But I had them in my sights, and I wasn't going to look away.

The door to TERRA, good old Mother Earth, wasn't far. I walked to it with my hands in my pockets, checking to make sure that my precious cargo was still with me. I had no false impressions about what would happen to me if I lost them. Kane had explained the brutal punishment in exquisite detail.

I popped my key in the lock and eased the door open, powering up my phone as I did, letting it reconnect to the network now that I was back on earth's plane. Then I stepped out of what was normally my closet door into my bedroom, bracing myself for the work to come.

My phone erupted, vibrating furiously as a swarm of missed messages and calls came in at once. I stared at the device in my hand, looking at the notifications from everyone I knew: Alex, Robin, Dawn, and Ash. There were several numbers I didn't know on the list as well. I hadn't been gone long, but it seemed time had kept moving without me. That wasn't unusual when I dipped out of the world, but the deluge of messages told me that something had happened.

"Uh-oh," I muttered to myself as I tried to catch up.

CHAPTER THIRTY-SEVEN

MY HEART POUNDED in my chest as I stepped into the elevator at the MCIAW building. I wasn't entirely sure what I was walking into. The amount of information waiting for me was overwhelming was, but one thing was *crystal-clear.*

Ash was not pleased.

I have faced more than my share of monsters and men. Things that defy my understanding of Reality. Dragons that can fly. Squid monsters the size of a city block. But none of them scared me like my betrothed did.

An uncharitable person might attribute that to her lineage. As the daughter of the former Queen of All Fae and the Devil himself, she certainly inherited an impressive set of genes. But if I'm being honest, her parents weren't what made her scary. She accomplished that all on her own.

Ding, went the elevator as it opened on the thirteenth floor, causing my heart to skip a beat. Mentally I racked my brain, trying to figure out what I'd done wrong, but for the life of me, I couldn't see it. I knew it had to be something; Ash wasn't the type of person to be upset over nothing. I just didn't have the eyes to see.

Alex had been no help either. My friend had only gotten back about an hour before I did. The time dilution between the Veil and here meant that he was just as far out of the loop as I was. He could only give me an encouraging thumbs-up as we stepped out of the elevator together.

I glanced down the hallway to where the door with my cartoonish face was waiting, relieved to see it was closed. I half expected to find my betrothed standing with it open, ready to murder me with her bare hands.

I led the two of us to the office. If I didn't know better, I would say Alex was hiding behind me. In fact, I was pretty sure that was exactly what he was doing, but I couldn't blame him. Ash wasn't his betrothed. I had made that decision all on my own.

The caricature of my own face greeted me warmly as I opened the door. Somehow, I just knew Robin was behind that. He must have commissioned it, because it was technically "art." I stepped into the lobby where Leila, the young receptionist, sat behind the desk as always. Her face was tight with stress as she looked up from her screen at the sound of our entrance.

"Good afternoon, sir," she said formally. "I'll let the CEO know that you are here." She picked up the receiver of her office phone and punched a button.

"Please do," I replied, trying to sound more relaxed than I felt.

Alex and I exchanged nervous glances. That did not sound good at all. One thing about the Fae: They get more formal the angrier they are.

"Ma'am? *He's* here," Leila announced into her phone, her expression neutral. "Understood." She clicked it back into its cradle before looking back up at us.

"She's waiting for you in the Flame conference room." Leila's gaze tracked from me to Alex, who lurked in my shadow. "She is expecting this to be a one-on-one meeting, sir." I thought I heard my friend let out a relieved sigh behind me. I struggled not to roll my eyes.

"Sounds good," I replied as brightly as I could. "Do you mind keeping an eye on him while I'm gone?"

"Of course." Leila did not smile at my joke, which only further made me feel like I was marching to my execution. What had I done? I knew I was an idiot, but clearly, I was an even bigger one than I'd thought.

I made my way to the conference room section of the office, beyond the open-concept bullpen. The hairs on the back of my neck stood on end as the employees of my company watched me walk by. None of them stopped their work or greeted me, but I could feel their eyes as I passed.

Something had happened.

I had never been in the Flame before. Why any company needed so many different meeting rooms was beyond me. It was smaller than the one that we'd used with Robin the last time I was here. Like its namesake, the room was full of red accents. A copse of tiny trees grew scarlet leaves along the far wall. The small table was made of cherry. It was supposed to feel bright and warm, but to me it only felt threatening.

Ash was sitting at the far end of the room when I entered. She wore a subtle gray pantsuit that was entirely professional and not royal at all. Something Dawn would not be caught dead in. But she was striking and powerful. I briefly forgot that I was in trouble, just marveling at the sight of her. How in the world had I ended up here? I may be cursed, but sometimes I am luckier than I deserve.

What a strange life that had bound us together.

For a moment my betrothed and I stared at each other. I couldn't tell if we were experiencing relief to find both of us in one piece or if she was sizing me up like a fencing opponent.

"Hi," I offered softly after the silence grew oppressive. I extended it like an olive branch, still hoping for peace.

"Hi?" she replied dangerously. So much for that. I swallowed, resorting to waiting in silence for her to make the next move. I may be dumb enough to charge in where angels fear to tread, but even I was smart enough to sense the danger here.

"Do you wish to continue this betrothal, Matthew?" Ash asked in that same cold, dangerous tone. My jaw dropped open in shock.

"Of—of course," I sputtered, any pretense of self-defense gone. "What are you talking about?" I took two long steps toward her, but she held up a hand, stopping me in place.

"Dawn would switch places with me if you wished it."

Something very cold squeezed its hand around my heart, and I froze, doing my best to emulate the shocked immobility of an immortal. Her eyes were in their green, human form, and they held mine with a quiet, watery strength. Every instinct in my body screamed at me to run, but I ignored it.

"I am confused," I said slowly after the silence had amassed thick enough to be some sort of shield. "Why do you think that I would want that?"

"You took her, not me, into the lands beyond." I cocked my head in surprise. That was a significantly more *human* complaint than I had been expecting. Not that Ash is inhuman, but she isn't mortal. I guess sisters are sisters no matter what.

"We needed a way to convince the market that we were on the

level," I answered, still speaking slowly and carefully. "Dawn is a queen. We hoped that would make the security less likely to inspect her closely."

"If it is a queen you need—"

"But the most important part of the plan," I continued, flinching at the irritation that rose in her eyes when I cut her off, "was that she is bound to Sylph and able to make things invisible." Ash was silent, staring at me. I took that as an invitation to press forward, a sign that the danger had begun to fade, if only a little.

"You are a force, betrothed," I said, taking another step toward her. "But you shine far too bright to hide." The Lady of Autumn's gaze did not falter as she watched me, measuring something I could not define.

At last she sighed, and a little bit of the tension seemed to bleed out of her shoulders. "Your words may be true, but you did it without *telling* me," she hissed. "What is the point of our union if we act individually?"

"I'm sorry—" I began, but a thought cut me off, catching the rest of my apology in my throat. "I'm sorry, but what exactly do you call all this?" I gestured at the office around us in a sweeping motion. "Which conversation was this discussed in?"

Ash's eyes widened and for a second, they flickered the solid gold of the Fae before turning back to their vibrant green. "That's different."

"Is it?" I felt my own irritation grow in my question. After the trouble she had pulled me into without my knowledge, she dared to complain that I wasn't telling her everything? Ridiculous.

"This company is in *my* name. The IRS is coming after *me.* But for some reason, I had no idea that it existed. Tell me how that is different or better than me not telling you about my plan with Dawn?"

"It was supposed to be a surprise," the Lady of Autumn murmured, looking to the side for the first time. I felt my eyebrow start to arch, but with some effort I managed to catch it before it got too far. Winning a point against a Faerie is enough. Gloating is dangerous.

"Well, surprise!" I replied with a smile, forgetting my own wisdom. "I stopped the source of Neodeath." Ash's gaze snapped back to me, and I saw a flash of resentment flicker underneath her long eyelashes. I gritted my teeth, frustrated at myself for damaging the progress I had already made.

"Did you know that the IRS agents came looking for you while you were gone?" she asked, changing the subject. I grimaced, assuming I had some angry messages from them still to sort through on my phone. They had told me not to leave the state. "They threatened me with obstruction of justice for not revealing your location. They didn't believe for a second that your *fiancée* did not know where you were."

"It's not like you could have told them anything they would have believed," I pointed out. "Why didn't Robin just tell them lawyer things until they went away?"

"That's not the problem. The question is, What is the point?" she repeated softly. "If we are not united, then we are better off alone."

I took a moment to organize my thoughts. Fae are not humans. They look like us, but they are bound in ways that do not mesh with our culture. Ash couldn't lie, which meant she was telling me the truth. She really did feel…left out, useless, abandoned. In fact, given how poorly her "surprise" had gone, I wouldn't doubt that she was beating herself up about it. My harping on it wasn't helping fix the problem, only widening the fissure that was growing between the two of us.

Ostensibly, she was right. What was the point? I had made this deal with a queen who was nothing but dust now. Dawn had held up her mother's side of the bargain, but I didn't need the same protection I once did. If there was a way to get out of the deal, it might be worth considering.

That was only if I truly was being mercenary about it. It was a moot point; Dawn would never let me go. I wasn't sure Ash was right about the queen being willing to take her place, but I didn't care. As fun as the former Lady of Summer could be, there was a reason I didn't pick her when I had the chance.

But if I was being honest with myself—a thing that I hated doing—then the truth was, I wasn't still here just because of the arrangement. I might have been betrothed to Ash because of politics, but I had come to value and respect her. To want to be around her. No matter how the circumstances had changed, I wasn't ready to walk away from that just yet.

"You're right," I said with a sigh, crossing my arms and trying to look penitent rather than irritated. "It's something that we're going to need to fix." Ash's head came up in surprise at my words. For a moment we stared at each other, man and woman, having a conversation with only our eyes. I have no idea what I said, but it must have been enough to keep her interested.

"And you want to fix it?"

"I can fix half of it." I gave her another gentle glare. "The other bit isn't up to me." The Lady of Autumn studied me, as if looking for a trap. She must have seen some of the sincerity in me, because after a few heartbeats she nodded.

"Very well," she murmured, leaning back in her chair. "If you are willing to make a change, I will play my part too."

"Is this a deal?" I felt my lips quirk in the ghost of a smile. "Will I have to make a contract with my Faerie betrothed every time we have a domestic dispute?" Ash's eyes flashed golden once more, and she tilted her head at me, as if seeing me for the first time.

"Yes," she said flatly. A shiver ran down my spine at her words. We were so different. At least this would be binding. She would change. Which meant that I had to as well. I felt my throat tighten as I realized how dangerous this was going to be.

"Well, in the spirit of new cooperation—" I reached out at the table and pulled out the chair next to hers. "—I do have a project that I need your help on."

Ash leaned forward, a predator catching a whiff of blood.

"How would you like to help me kill Lazarus again?"

Ash's expression sharpened, and for a moment she was a perfect reflection of her cruel mother, thrilled by the prospect of a hunt worthy of her time. A smile grew on my own face to match hers, our earlier argument forgotten. In some ways, we were very alike.

"Let's try something new," I told her, still smiling. "Here's my plan."

"Hang on," she said, holding up a hand. "How much of this is already in motion, unable to be stopped or changed?"

"Uhh." I paused, trying to think how to explain what I was carrying in my pockets as anything other than a pretty concrete plan. "A lot of it?"

"You *so* do not get full credit for this," she warned before relenting with a wave. "Very well, proceed. Tell me your needlessly reckless scheme, then I will fix it as best I can."

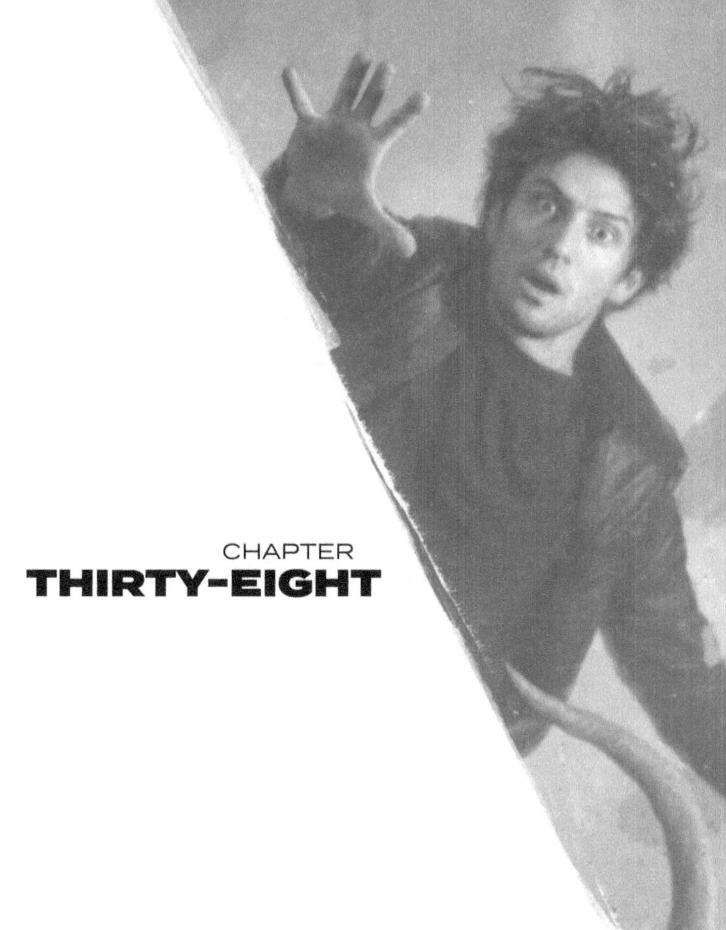

CHAPTER THIRTY-EIGHT

I KNEW I WAS on the right track when sleep found me instantly. I climbed into bed and lay back for only a moment before I was swallowed by the darkness. I'm not sure I have ever passed out that quickly in my entire life.

I hung in a pocket outside the normal passing of time, relishing the peaceful darkness. My mind soaked up the rest like it had just escaped the desert. Oh, how I'd missed *sleep*! Then the void exploded with the dark purple of Somnus's power, and I was ripped forward into his world.

A thousand impossible things flickered by me as I caught tastes of the dreams that played in other sleepers' minds like movies. I saw passion and fear, hope and desire, and a bunch of really weird stuff.

One guy's teeth kept falling out of his head in a flood that might as well have been a waterfall.

Then I was through the honeycomb and into the home of the sleep god. I crashed down into a plush, modern chair like I had just fallen from a great height. The rest of the modern building formed itself around me, coming together like the jaws of a trap.

I glanced down at myself, patting my front pockets to make sure I still carried my precious cargo. I was relieved to discover that I was dressed. I wore a pair of dark jeans and a matching jacket that were similar enough to my normal style that I was certain my subconscious was watching out for me.

A shadow coalesced, growing weight as it darkened until it formed the Romanic deity who ruled this expanse. He wore the same frayed toga as before. His dark beard was immaculately trimmed, and his purple eyes peered at me over his steepled fingers. I gave him a smile and waited.

"You are either very brave or very stupid," he mused after a moment.

"I'm pretty sure it's possible to be both at the same time."

"You taunt me, mortal?" Somnus's expression darkened in something like suspicion or anger. "You come into my world and dare to speak to me so? You may have bested my brother, but I assure you that I have not let my power rot and fester like he did. There are many more dreamers here than there were souls in Hades." I felt my eyebrows jump at that. Pluto's power had been directly tied to the number of prisoners he kept in his Underworld. As he sold them off, he had begun to wane. It made sense that the source of Somnus's own strength was similar but different.

"My good man, I have not yet begun to taunt," I insisted, puffing up my chest.

"I warned you not to trifle with me," Somnus snarled, a hint of rage growing on his face. "Now you will face the consequences of your choices." I got the feeling that he wasn't used to being sassed. I guess most things that called themselves deities probably weren't. Mortals generally had the good sense to shut up when bigger things cast their shadows. Not me. That's when I get louder.

I wonder what that says about me.

"Trifle?" I asked, leaning back in my chair, forcing my expression to be more disinterested than I felt. "I barely know what that means. Does it have anything to do with bringing you a soul?" As I spoke, I slid my hand into my jacket, or the approximation of it that I was wearing in this dream.

Somnus went preternaturally still as I pulled my hand out, holding the orange sphere that held a mortal soul in it. The Romanic god stared, naked hunger on his face. After a dozen heartbeats his purple gaze flickered from his prize to my face.

"What happened to your reluctance to deliver one of your kind over to me?" he asked. "Did a few missed slumbers truly break you so easily?"

I tilted my head, surprised that he had seen through me so fast. Maybe being a god gave him an extra sense of intuition about the mortal condition. Or maybe I'm just not that subtle. Either way, he had clearly read me like a book.

My exposure to Neodeath had forced me to consider what Death was—what it meant to a mortal like me. The true horror of the counterfeit was not necessarily *where* they were sending the souls they took. I had no idea what such an Underworld might even be like. It was that they were taking the agency, the choice away from their fellow humans.

I have been fortunate enough to see behind the curtain more than most. But even now, I do not have all the answers to the Big Mysteries. I don't know how we got here or what we're doing. I do know that we mortals get the short end of the stick in a lot of ways.

We are finite sparks of light burning in an infinite darkness. We are born. We live.

We die.

That's the deal. Nobody gets much of a choice about that part of it. But the one thing we do get is some modicum of control about what happens next. For the most part, we get to stamp our package with the delivery address to go and *find out.*

I'm not saying that it all ends up okay, or good, or right, or fair. I'm just saying that at least we get to choose our destiny. Free will is our gift and curse. While I was loath to steal someone's orb for my sake, who was I to gainsay another's choice? I didn't even have possession of my own soul; I don't think I'm qualified to be making decisions for other people.

"This is Cornelius Rufus, who died almost two thousand years ago," I said softly, staring into the orange depths of the sphere in my hands. "He was, according to all the paperwork that we have on him, a faithful pagan, intent on finding himself in Hades upon his passing."

"Two millennia?" Somnus hissed, true irritation passing across his face. "Why was he never delivered into our care? If this is the quality of service that one can expect from Death Delivery—"

"Yeah, if only he had been there in time for your brother to sell him off," I drawled, interrupting the god's rant. His teeth snapped shut in irritation, but he did not protest. How could he? We both knew what Pluto had gotten up to.

"Fortunately for you, his delivery was delayed." I held up the soul for his inspection. "Cornelius was abducted by a Dreadknight of the Lost. He was only recently recovered from the abyss."

"A Dreadknight?" Somnus sputtered. "They haven't been seen in an—"

"Eon, I know," I cut in smoothly, showing him a professional smile that was all teeth. "That's what I was told when I killed it and reclaimed the souls that it had stolen."

The silence between us was sharper this time. I felt my lips curl in a delighted little sneer as the god looked at me a little differently. Was that fear? Perhaps it should be. I still did not know what a Dreadknight is. I did not know what a god is either, if I was being honest. But I knew that people were scared of the big Lost that I had consumed.

"Unfortunately, by the time we finished verifying the soul and preparing it for delivery, Hades had already fallen into the Nothing." My eyes flicked back to the god, watching his reaction. This next part was going to be tricky. I needed to play it just right.

"This meant that poor Cornelius here was languishing in the Lost and Found, bound for an address that could not be delivered to. So to answer your question, the way I see it, this is as close as I can get him to where he always wanted to go in the first place." Somnus cocked his head, considering my words.

"Kane knows about this," I told him, trying to give him one last bit of reassurance. "He is prepared to restore delivery to Hades under your supervision once you have reestablished the Underworld, provided Reapers are allowed to inspect the souls in your inventory every century." Somnus leaned back in his chair, tension flooding out of his shoulders.

"Very well, mortal, I accept this offering. Give me the soul, and I shall release the bind upon your sleep. No longer will you be barred from the world of slumber. You may dream and rest once more."

"Well, that is very kind of you," I replied, letting what I hoped was a warm smile take over my face. "And under normal circumstances, I would be more than happy to be done with this."

"This sounds suspiciously like trifling," Somnus replied, arching an eyebrow. I noticed that he didn't seem as irritated as he had when I first got here. Maybe he knew what else I carried with me, or perhaps he was just confident that he was going to get what he wanted.

"I prefer to think of it as renegotiating." I grinned as I reached with my empty hand into my jacket pocket to pull out a second orange orb. "You see, we need to discuss what to do with his wife, Julia." Somnus stared at the new soul with rapt attention. Whatever he had been expecting, it clearly wasn't *that.*

"It seems to me that, if Death Delivery is recognizing me as the new director of Hades, the only logical course of action is for Julia to be delivered to our new facilities, *posthaste.*" The god's purple eyes flickered back toward me. "Don't you agree."

"I mean, eventually, yes." I shrugged, starting to slip the orb back toward my pocket. "But we're currently operating under *quite* the backlog. Who knows how long it would be before we are able to do a full audit of our Lost and Found section to make sure that every individual soul has made its way home?"

"You're threatening a god with bureaucracy?"

"It's the scariest thing I can think of."

"Enough of these games. Tell me what you want, mortal," Somnus spat. "Since it seems all your posturing about free will was for naught, spit out your price." I bit my lip, choosing to ignore the aptness of his criticism. Desperation makes liars of us all. Besides, I had no intention of keeping Julia hostage. I just needed him to think that I would.

"Oh, relax," I laughed, feeling a sense of relief flood into me as he took the bait. "I'm going to give her to you. I just have two tiny requests in exchange for expediting her paperwork to the top of the list."

"And what are they?" Somnus's expression was unamused, but the greed in his voice was impossible to miss.

"It's just a couple of little favors from the god of sleep. I promise you won't even notice."

CHAPTER THIRTY-NINE

AFTER SOMNUS AGREED to my extra conditions, he released me from his nightmare mansion and dropped me into the true darkness of slumber. When I finally opened my eyes, I was shocked to see morning's bright light streaming around the blackout curtains in my room.

My head felt lighter, and I rose from my bed more rested than I had felt in months. It was as if I had been carrying a great weight on my shoulders that sloughed off. A bright smile ripped across my face at solving one piece of my horrible puzzle.

For all I knew, I'd need twelve hours a day for the next five years to catch up on my lost slumber, but at least my sleep debt was paid for now. I would never miss the opportunity to snooze ever again. For a moment I stared at my bed, tempted to take a quick nap, just to prove how serious I was about my new commitment to my relationship with sleeping, but I decided that would be a bit extreme.

I had some other debts to collect on.

Whistling brightly, I burst from my room, making my way down the rectangular staircase from the third floor to the first. Was it my imagination, or did the sun seem brighter and the day warmer?

"Well, if it isn't Sleeping Beauty," a familiar royal voice drawled from the living room as I reached the ground, stopping me in my tracks. Sheepishly, I turned to face the audience that had gathered in my living room, apparently waiting for me to wake up. The five of them were gathered around the coffee table, enjoying what looked like a decadent brunch.

Dawn and Ash sat next to each other, their expressions perfectly serene, like two cats that were currently on good terms with each other. Robin reclined just beyond them; he raised a half-eaten pastry in greeting, a languid smile spreading across his face. Across from them, Alex and Megan shared a love seat, watching the rest of the Fae with something like mild suspicion. All of them were dressed for a fight. I glanced down at my sweats and suddenly felt like I wasn't properly attired for my own home.

I gave my sister a broad smile and a wink. Even after having her out of her coma-like state for a few months, I still felt a jolt of surprise every time I saw her. I had only just begun to accept her death before she came back. Now I struggled with this new reality—but it was definitely better.

Dawn shot me a half-lidded glare that was mostly for show over the lip of her mimosa in a champagne flute. I have no idea where she got one of those. Alex and I definitely did not own any. "I know some of us are immortal, darling, but a little respect for our time would be appreciated." The Queen of All Fae wore a pair of tight black tactical pants with a matching top. They were somehow still too fashionable, despite being on brand for the occasion. Unless I was an idiot, they looked like they were made of velvet instead of polyester like everyone else's.

"Save your breath. He's been like this his whole life," Megan agreed with disgust. I scoffed in mock outrage but didn't otherwise protest. There wasn't much of an argument to be made. I have never been what anyone would call a morning person.

"Save your breath, *Your Majesty*," Dawn corrected absently, as if by rote. Meg rolled her eyes when she thought the queen wasn't looking. I shook my head, amused at their antics but choosing not to pick a side.

Dawn was incredibly tolerant for royalty. But she had a pride that could be pricked. I knew my sister was already on thin ice for her attempts on Mav's life, and I saw no reason to add my weight to the cracks of their relationship.

"You came back from Goldhall for this?" I asked Meg instead, stepping forward to paw through the remaining pastries on the table. I settled on a chocolate croissant before taking a step back and hovering awkwardly.

Somehow I only had enough chairs for five guests. This had never been a problem before; I guess I was accumulating more people who were important to me. A momentary shadow of sadness passed over me, like a small cloud briefly blocking out the sun.

Seven. There should be enough seats for seven—just in case.

"Yes, little brother, I made the *impossible* journey to come to your aid." Meg rolled her green eyes at me with more gusto than she had used on Dawn. "Honestly, where do you even get off asking a question like that? You just don't ever ask for help."

"I couldn't agree more," Ash murmured, giving my sister a small smile. I was fortunate that my sister and my betrothed got along better than either did with my queen.

"I dunno," Alex offered, his mouth full of doughnut. "He asks me for favors all the time."

"Not helping," I told my best friend, shooting him a glare. Even with the whole room ganging up on me, I couldn't help but feel light and refreshed. I have seen more magic than most, but a good night's sleep might be the most powerful thing I have ever experienced. Nothing could shake me today.

"Something's different," Robin said shrewdly, studying me with narrow eyes.

"With me?" I pressed a hand against my chest, making a shocked face.

"Now that you mention it, dear Robin, there is a general lack of miasma roiling off our most difficult subject," Dawn mused, studying me with bright-golden eyes.

"You look like you slept," Ash said, her green eyes glinting. She alone of the Fae wore her human ones, standing apart from her kin's immortal gazes.

"I did," I replied with a broad smile. "It was delightful. I might do it again sometime."

"I take it Somnus was pleased by your terms?" My betrothed arched a single red eyebrow. She knew the answer, but she was playing a role for the room. While these five were some of my closest non-incarcerated friends, they weren't exactly the most trusting when it came to my plans.

"Oh, he complained," I replied airily, "but we both knew it was just a formality. He got what he wanted, and now Sleep can become Death."

"Look at how far you have come, Little Flame," Dawn murmured, watching me through her heavy-lidded gaze. "Matthew Carver, Underworld Real Estate Agent. What ever happened to the foolish boy who stormed up to my front door demanding to be invited to my pool party? I'm tempted to feel a hint of pride."

"Don't hurt yourself," I grumbled, taking a bite of my flaky pastry, but feeling pleased. The first part of my plan was audacious, but I had pulled it off. We were moving, like a gymnast flying off the pommel horse into the air. Now all I had to do was land the trick.

It turned out that the timing of my bite was off, because the five of them sat quietly, waiting for me to continue. I scrambled to swallow in the awkward silence before it could get too weird.

"Thank you, for coming," I said honestly, when my mouth was clear enough to speak in front of royalty. "I know that this isn't necessarily your fight, but—"

"Oh, do spare us the feel-good section of the speech," Dawn groused, earning her a glare from both my sister and Ash.

"He can't help himself," Robin agreed, shaking his head disappointedly, as if he was not the most melodramatic being I have ever met in my life.

Alex just mouthed *brothers-in-law* across the couch at me. I shook my head, refusing to rise to his bait. It was like trying to plan a raid with a roomful of failed stand-up comedians.

"No feelings," I promised, raising my hands to fend off the Queen of All Fae. "Just a quick expression of gratitude before I ask all of you to risk your lives." That caught all their attention.

"Lazarus has wronged this family," I reminded them, looking around the room. "We're a weird one, but that is what we are." I *refused* to look in Alex's direction.

It felt weird to prioritize the personal vendetta over the half-soul man's other crimes. To me, stealing souls and risking the balance of the universe was a little worse, but the Fae are a prickly sort. I wanted them to remember that the gangster owed them a pound of flesh.

"His other crimes are almost as heinous," I continued, earning a snort from Robin. My golden-eyed lawyer gave me a light round of applause. He knew what I was doing, of course. They were self-aware;

they just appreciated me having my priorities in order.

"Death himself is aware of this operation," I told them. "He sends his appreciation."

"Appreciation." Dawn stretched the word, as if studying it from all angles. "That sounds suspiciously like something that I cannot spend." Robin echoed his queen in a displeased growl. I laughed, delighted at how predictable the two of them were. I really have come a long way.

"I wouldn't say that," I said. "I'm pretty sure this is worth its weight in at least gold." As I spoke, I drew a third orange sphere from my pocket, chuckling as the queen's eyes widened in pure shock. It is not often that one gets to stun a Faerie. I was going to burn this memory into my mind. The three members of the Dandelion Court stared at the soul in my hands for a long time before, as one, they turned their gazes to spear me with physical force. Dimly I noticed Ash's eyes had flickered back to solid gold.

Annwn, the Fae Underworld, was closed and powered down. There was no new collection to be made to restart the Dandelion Court's intake process. The Faerie Lands were a grim little bunker, a world in permanent twilight until its last day.

But now I knew a little more about what was going on and how much a single soul mattered. Hades had been held up by only one. I had no doubt that even this orb could make a world of difference.

"A little birdie told me you were looking to get back into the Underworld business. This is Berywn," I told them, glancing at the orange ball in my hand. "She was lost to the darkness eons ago, but her soul was recently recovered by me." I tried not to let my smile grow wider than it already was. "Kane sent her with me to apologize for the tardiness."

Dawn reached out to accept the soul from me with shaking hands. I marveled at that, stunned by the depth of concern that she displayed. I have seen her turn down ten thousand stolen souls without blinking, but a single glowing light rendered her awestruck—and perhaps even more surprisingly—speechless.

The Queen of All Fae let out a slight gasp as she lifted it from my hand. Reverently she pulled it to her chest, cradling it like a newborn child. The room was silent as we watched her collect the first soul her fallen empire had seen in centuries.

I couldn't help but feel strange being a part of this transaction, but at this point, what about my life was normal? Berywn had made her choice, and that had been taken from her. I had no idea if it was a *good* one, but it was hers. If helping her get to where she wanted to go was all I accomplished, then that was better than most.

When Dawn finally looked up from the soul in her hands, her golden eyes were glinting with a wetness that could only be tears. My jaw tried to slam into the coffee table in front of me, but I managed to keep my mouth shut.

"Thank you, Matthew," she said softly, an expression that I could not place on her face.

"You're welcome." I gave her a crooked smile, suddenly feeling a little…not nervous, but like I was swimming in deeper waters than I'd thought. Ash's expression was decidedly neutral, and I decided to move on quickly.

"Don't get too excited," I warned them. "I'm counting on you bringing that fancy new spear of yours with us. Now that the payment is out of the way, here's how this is going to work."

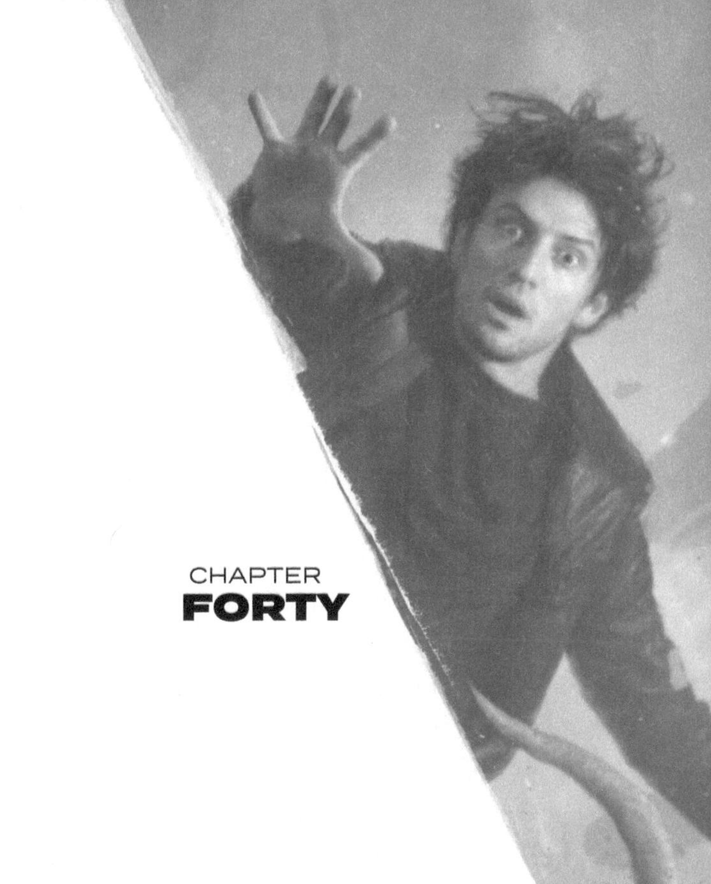

CHAPTER
FORTY

FINDING LAZARUS WAS easier than I thought it would be.

Well, that's not entirely true. I figured it would be either simple or impossible. If he was dumb enough to stay with his supply of Neodeath, then it would be a breeze for me to hunt him down. But if he abandoned the goods and went to ground, finding him was going to be trickier. The man had enough resources to compete with entire nations.

When my superpowered Death senses found that he had stashed the supply in the same building that he'd kept me in for three months before sending me to the Veil, I could only laugh. I knew we had him right where we wanted him.

"It almost feels like coming home," Alex grumbled from the driver's seat of his van as we eyed the squat office building from across the street. We were parked in a public lot, trying to blend in with the normal traffic.

"Matthew, if we're going to make a habit out of using your… vehicular accommodations, I am going to insist that you use some of your Hell-money to buy something nicer," Dawn complained from the seat behind me, where she and Ash sat in the captain's chairs in the middle row.

"Trust me, the experience does not improve as you get farther from the front," Robin called from where he was wedged into the back.

"Speak for yourself, giant," Meg complained. "This baby has plenty of room, you're just being greedy and invading *my* side."

"Yes, something much larger, and gold, I think," Dawn continued, ignoring the glare I threw over my shoulder at her. I guess bringing her a soul had only bought me a couple hours of peace. The meter must have run out already.

"How gaudy," Megan muttered just loud enough for all of us to hear.

"Speaking of annoyances," Dawn continued, something venomous curling in her tone, "I don't suppose you've managed to kidnap or murder my more earthy sister, have you?" The tension inside the car spiked as the two women turned to stare at each other.

"Tania? No, she's your problem." Megan replied coolly. "I'm after the ice one."

The queen was silent for a long moment before sniffing and turning away. "A pity," I thought I heard her murmur. With all the scheming, I hadn't had the time to wonder about Tania's mysterious disappearance. Dawn's disappointment could only mean that whatever she suspected was worse than my sister finally catching some of her prey.

"It's going to be fortified like a bunker in there," Alex warned, deliberately moving the conversation to safer topics.

"I remember."

"And he will know that you do, which means they're going to have made improvements." Alex gave me a long look. "You know how sometimes we walk into traps, and we're surprised and say something like, *Oh no, that was a trap*? And it's a whole thing, and then we get out the other side?"

"I'm not sure that's exactly how I would describe—"

"This is a trap. An omega trap. The trappiest trap that has ever trapped."

"Oh, okay, I guess we shouldn't go in then," I said, relaxing back in my seat. "Driver, take us home!"

"Wait, really?"

"No."

Alex stared at me like I was an alien. I rolled my eyes at being sucked into this game. "What else do you want me to say? We gotta go in."

"I know, I just wanted to feel like my complaints were being heard."

"I sympathize," Ash murmured from the second row.

I turned to give her a pained expression. "Not you too." Our conversation had helped, but clearly there was still some work to do on the old relationship. My betrothed gave me a sharp smile that was both playful and dangerous, like most of the best things in life. I took a deep breath and forced myself to find my center, to seize control of the situation before it became any more ridiculous.

"It is going to be a trap. We know this, which means we can be prepared. Lazarus and his cronies will be ready for us, but unfortunately for them, I've brought a few of my friends to even the odds."

"You don't have any other friends," scoffed Megan from the back of the van.

A knock sounded on my door, causing everyone to start in surprise.

I felt my grin grow wide as I rolled down my window. "Hi, Evangeline!" I said brightly, trying not to gloat at my sister being proven wrong so quickly. "We were just talking about you."

"I do not know why you called me here. I am still forbidden from meddling with the mortals in this operation," the angel replied tightly, not responding to my greeting.

"Ah," I replied with a smile. "It just so happens that the mastermind of this plot *is not mortal.*"

Evangeline's expression sharpened as she twitched in surprise. "What?"

"Hop in." I jerked my thumb over my shoulder at the back of the already overcrowded van. "I'll tell you all about Lazarus and his half soul."

We waited in the parking lot as afternoon set in, and the sun began to dip toward the western horizon. The immortals in the car squirmed uncomfortably, but no one in the third row dared to complain with an angel wedged in there with them. The mood was tense and silent, the way it always is when a stranger is added to a group of people who are far too comfortable with one another.

When most of the civilians had left for the day, I finally judged that it was time. "Let's go," I called, popping open my door and rising into a stretch. The sliding doors behind me groaned as they opened for the two Fae women. I dug into my pocket and pulled out a set of leather bracelets, each bound with a single golden feather.

"We have uniforms! Put these on," I commanded, passing one to each of my friends. Evangeline took it with a wry expression on her face, lifting it between two fingers like it was sticky. I had a feeling she could tell exactly who had given it to me. She accepted that my information was a good enough excuse to allow her to act, but that didn't mean I had completely won her over yet.

"Better safe than sorry," I told her.

"I agree," she replied, reluctantly slipping it onto her left wrist. "Which is why *she* cannot come with us." Her right hand snapped to point at Ash without looking. I felt my stomach drop in shock as I stared at the angel.

Of course.

"She's coming." I crossed my arms, matching Evangeline's white stare with ease. She was intimidating, but she had nothing on Orion, or Kane.

"Absolutely not. She is a demon."

"Technically she is a Faerie princess," I replied, holding up a finger as if I had made a perfect point. "You are being rude to the wrong team right now."

"She is Lucifer's daughter; I can smell his brimstone burning from her. No child of the Prince of Lies is welcome among us."

"She's also standing right here and can speak for herself," Ash growled, inserting herself into the conversation with her head tilted to the side. Her golden eyes were fixed on the angel with fiery intensity.

"Of course," I held up my hands in surrender, taking a step back. "I was just trying to stave off an interdimensional incident."

"Do you have a problem with me, angel?" Ash asked, ignoring me. Evangeline took a step toward her radiating danger. On instinct I glanced at Dawn, who was watching the interaction with a sharp expression. At my movement, her gaze tracked to me, and I felt a thrill run down my spine as I stared into her eyes. This was dangerous territory.

"I do, demonspawn. You are a cancer, born of rot and destined to become it."

"You speak of a father I do not know—that I have neither seen nor met. If I am an heir to his ways, then I am lost, for I have lived my whole life in the house of my mother. I am more Fae than Devil. Or does intention count for nothing in your halls?" Evangeline flinched as if Ash had struck her. For a moment, I was reminded of my first conversation with Father Bryant, more than two years ago, when he had scourged me for things that were beyond my control.

"That is something he would teach you to say," Evangeline hissed after a moment, but her expression was confused, as if she wasn't sure she believed her own words. It occurred to me that the Devil must be something of a bogeyman to his fellow angels. The story of their failure, the great betrayer.

"He would have to teach me something first."

"It doesn't matter anyway," I snapped, growing tired of having this squabble in the fading daylight. "This is a Death Corp operation, authorized by Kane and Azrael themselves." Evangeline turned toward me to protest, but I held up a hand, cutting her off.

"I know you report to Raguel and are under a different chain of command, which is why I *invited you out of courtesy.*" I took a step toward where the two women were still staring at each other. "It was my team of Reapers that sealed the Veil and prevented the murder of Azrael. This is my jurisdiction, angel, not yours."

Evangeline's eyes flashed a dangerous white, but after a moment she withdrew a step. She knew that the other reason I brought her was because she was the case agent assigned to my soul fraud. The sooner this Neodeath situation was cleaned up, the sooner I would move up to the top of her priority list.

Was it selfish? Sure.

Did I feel bad about it?

Not one bit.

"Now if we're done fighting like children on the playground, let's go and stop this crime against humanity." I nodded toward the brick office building across the street, where my senses told me the Neodeath supply waited—although it was bothering me how little there was. A meager tithe compared to what I had found in the Land of Darkness.

All of LA was clear, except for a trace amount here at this facility I knew so well. Yet another clue that this was a trap.

I turned on my heel, not waiting for Evangeline to reply, trusting my words to be enough of a stick to goad her into following me. I wasn't even sure if they were completely true. Kane and Azarael had told me to do this, but that didn't mean they'd told me I was in charge per se. It wasn't even really implied.

Alex was waiting for me at the back of the van, and he gave me a silent nod of respect before passing me the most precious thing in our possession. I hesitated for a moment, staring at the sheathed form of Azrael's blade. I am often hesitant to carry it, but given how much its original owner was invested in the outcome of this operation, it felt right. I slid the belt over my head, letting the sword's hilt dangle off my right shoulder like Orion had done so many times before me. Then I scooped up an assault rifle and slung it on my left. Might as well bring the big guns.

"Look at us, both carrying weapons of ancient and terrible power," Dawn mused brightly, pulling the Spear of Lugh from the back of the van. Her golden eyes sparkled with delight as she held the relic of her people.

"The check cleared, I see," I remarked dryly. "I'm surprised they still delivered it to you after Lazarus caught me running around his warehouse."

"Oh, they were furious," Dawn chuckled. "But the deal was between Esra and me. They had no choice but to fulfill their obligation, darling." I grinned at the Faerie's delight. At least that part of the plan had worked out. If Dawn had been deprived of her treasure at the end of my plan, I would've never heard the end of it.

"You should not take that," Evangeline murmured to me, interjecting herself once again. I knew she was some sort of angel cop, but I had not expected her to be such a *stickler.* It was really starting to get under my skin.

"What now?" I demanded, turning to look at her. "I'm well aware that I'm not worthy. The sword has made its opinion on me very clear in the past." I raised my right hand to show her the outline of the weapon's hilt seared into my palm. "But Azrael gave it to Orion, who gave it to me for safekeeping. So I'm the best foster option that it has right now."

"It's not that," Evangeline said softly, a strange cloud passing across her face. "When you carry one of those blades, its true bearer can see everything that it does." That caused me to pause, and I blinked at her in surprise for a moment. It occurred to me that her own sword was nowhere to be seen. So Azrael was watching, was he?

"Well, he was there when I was sent to accomplish this task," I told her after a moment of consideration. "He can watch if he wants." I breezed past her without another word, tired of her endless objections.

"Who are you and what have you done with Matthew Carver?" Meg asked as she slid into step next to me. My previously dead sister was dressed in a pair of black combat pants with a matching tank top. Her brown hair was pulled back in a tight ponytail, and I wondered if my own expression was as grim as hers.

"It's been a tough few years," I murmured back, looking both ways before jogging across the road toward the mostly empty parking lot outside Lazarus's building. I could have tried to be sneaky, but that felt like I would be doing a disservice to both teams. I knew enough about how the security worked here to assume that they would see us no matter what we tried. Even invisible people give off a thermal signature. There was no hiding from the amount of technology and magic that Lazarus had at his disposal.

"Really? I was having a peach of a time in Hell." Meg's voice had just a hint of bitterness, and it pierced my side like a sharp knife.

I gave her a frustrated look, but she waved away my apology.

"I'm not mad at you," she said with a sigh. "Just a little broken still." I swallowed heavily, trying to think of what to say. "My halves are still…melding back together. It feels like I'm trying to mix two different pieces of chocolate, but they have to melt a little first."

"That sounds unpleasant."

"It is. So it would be nice if my little brother managed to be more available when I'm falling apart."

"I thought you had Damien." I couldn't bring myself to even say the word *father*. Most of that was probably my own guilty reaction to my sister's words. But some of it was definitely his fault.

"Dad has been helpful," Megan agreed gently, well aware of the minefield she was stepping in. "He's taught me how to commune with Willow and how to navigate life as a member of the Dandelion Court." I snorted, unable to contain my disgust. What must that be like?

"But he's not my brother." She pressed forward, gentle but relentless. "He is not the one who came to pull me out of the Pit. I know you and he are not…close, but he's not a replacement for you." Something warm grew in my chest, a strangle blend of anger and shame.

I had been staying distant from Megan since she had fallen back in with our father. Part of that was because I had no interest in being in the same room as the man, but I would be lying if I didn't admit that some of it had to do with feeling like I was unnecessary.

"Okay," I said softly. "I'll work on that. I promise. But you gotta do something for me."

"What's that?" My sister shot me a wry glance, as if she already knew what I was going to say.

"Please stop trying to murder Mav? At least for now?"

"Nope."

I let out a little sigh of defeat. At least I could tell Dawn I tried.

I led my band of misfits straight to the front door, the same one I escaped from three months ago after killing Lazarus the first time.

Goose bumps crawled up and down my spine as I approached, telling me that I was being watched. My shoulders were tense, waiting for the fiery bite of a bullet. But no snipers opened fire on us as we crossed the open space. Our enemy must want to look into our eyes as he killed us.

That was fine with me.

The door was unlocked, and I pulled it open easily, leading the proverbial charge into the atrium. As before, the seal of the Lazarus corporation was set into the floor tiles: a hand grasping a sheaf of wheat. But instead of being a warm tan color, the entire relief had been painted black, making it seem much more sinister than before.

I gave Bellerophon and his waiting squadron of twenty armed guards a crooked smile. The scarred Nephilim glared at me, his black eyes promising payback for the last time we'd met. I felt my smile grow wider as he clocked the rest of my party, including the angel. I shoved my hands in my pockets and gave the room a casual scan.

"Hi there, Belly," I said softly, letting him see how unperturbed I was by all the guns pointed in my general direction. I was sure they were loaded with cold iron, but I doubted that was enough to really slow down a being like Evangeline.

"Where's the boss?"

"You made a mistake in coming here," Bellerophon snarled, taking a step toward me, curling his hands into fists. Boots pounded on the marble as another score of guards swept out behind us, closing the "trap" that had been laid for us.

"Did I?" I tried to keep some of my wry amusement to myself, but it was bubbling just beneath the surface. If the Hunter-runner-up noticed, he made no sign. Instead he pulled something from his belt and snapped it in half before throwing it on the ground.

All around us, the floor began to glow as a hidden circle, holding a five-pointed star, began to glow. Evangeline let out a gasp of surprise, and out of the corner of my eye I saw her stagger to the side ever so slightly. Begrudgingly I nodded in respect at my counterpart. It seemed they had accounted for everything.

"Hands up," Bellerophon ordered, his own fist wrapped around the hilt of his blade. "You have no power here."

"Eh," I said, shrugging. "I'm not sure that's true." Bellerophon's face tightened as if he was truly concerned about what trick I might have up my sleeve. Which, honestly, was the nicest compliment anyone had given me in a long time. The ancient and deadly Nephilim saw me as a threat. If I thought about it too much, I might shed a little tear.

Instead I pulled my hands free of my pockets, palming the little souvenir that my new best friend, Somnus, had given me in exchange for Julia's soul. It was a small leather bag, no bigger than my fist. Moving slowly, I managed to loosen the thong holding it shut and gave Orion's biggest hater a smile.

"Is all of this really for us?" I asked, moving my right hand in a wide, sweeping gesture. As I swung, time seemed to dilate for just a moment. A thousand sparkling grains of sand flew from my palm like dandelion seeds caught on the wind.

Bellerophon's eyes widened in surprise as the mortals surrounding him collapsed in waves. For a second, I thought his demonic blood would make him immune to the sleep god's working, but then his jaw went slack, and he collapsed.

A great wave of drowsiness hammered me. But the feathered bracelet around my wrist grew warm and the sensation retreated, banished by my protection. Smiling broadly, I slid the strap of my rifle off my shoulder and raised its sight to my eyes. With a quick burst of fire, I shattered the marble tiles at the end of the circle designed to trap Evangeline.

I looked up to find my friends staring at me in shock. Even the angel looked surprised. I gave them a cheeky grin right as a harsh alarm began to sound through the compound.

"Come on," I said with a toss of my head. "We have a rat to hunt."

CHAPTER
FORTY-ONE

WE LEFT BELLEROPHON snoring with the rest of his squad. Dawn wanted to cut his throat, but Alex had intervened. "He's Orion's," he reminded us. The Queen of All Fae had merely shrugged. Even she would not dare gainsay the Hunter his hunt.

Somnus's sleeping sand packed quite the punch. There seemed to be no one awake to respond to the alarm that flashed red lights above us as we made our way through the fortress-like structure.

Thick steel doors had been installed as checkpoints. Fortunately, Death's scythe was not repelled by the metal in the least, so it was easy work for me to cut a path through them.

"Where do you think he's holed up?" Ash asked me as we carved our way deeper.

"I have some ideas," I replied. "The first thing we should check is his office."

"Really?" Meg's skepticism was thick. "The big bad man cowers in his personal library?" I glanced at her hands, which were wrapped with Willow's light, and was struck once more by how odd it was to see her following in my footsteps.

"He's fond of his books." I shrugged, not convinced either. I just wanted to eliminate any other possibilities before we followed him to where I suspected the final showdown would take place.

"Matthew, if you made us all sit in your crowded car for hours for nothing because all Lazarus's guards are asleep, I shall be quite cross with you," Dawn commented from the back of the group.

"Don't worry, Your Majesty, I have a feeling your shiny new spear will come in quite handy," I called back, not bothering to turn in her direction. "Call it a bad feeling."

Dawn huffed but did not complain further. I knew she was itching for a chance to find out what the Spear of Lugh could really do.

As I suspected, Lazarus's office was empty. But I was truly surprised to find that it looked *abandoned.* A layer of dust hung over the room as if no one had been in it since the moment I killed the older version sitting behind the desk.

It gave me chills, being back in that place. As justified as it was, it still weighed heavily on me. I had struck down a monster, but he had been defenseless and unarmed. Did that make me a monster too?

Questions for a smarter Matthew on a less busy day.

"So much for that plan," Meg commented when we left the study.

"Come on, we have more holes to check," I commanded, leading my squad deeper into the facility. The room where I was briefly killed to send me to the Veil was similarly empty, although a telltale rusty stain on the floor near the circle told of darker rituals that had been performed here since the one on me. I let my anger grow as I led the group even deeper into the facility, swiping a keycard I'd taken off a sleeping guard to gain access to the secure elevators.

Ding! The doors slid open into a large, dusty floor deep in the earth. It was full of junk. A half-assembled old car rusted away on cinder blocks. A dozen antique pieces of furniture sat around in various states of disrepair. But in the far corner of the room, tucked away almost out of sight beneath a blue tarp, was a pair of marble pillars.

One of them was shorter than the other, sliced at an angle as if something sharper than a thought had cut it in half. I glanced at the black scythe in my hands, remembering how cleanly it had carved through the doors on our way here. Maybe I knew exactly what had done the cutting. As we approached, it became clear that the air between the two pillars was shimmering, as if the space between them was made of liquid instead of air.

"What is that?" Dawn demanded, catching sight of the portal as I began to walk toward it.

"I promised you I would take you on an adventure to another world. This is a gateway to one," I told her. "A fallen place that has been forgotten. Once it was called Elysium. But now it's just empty."

"Elysium," Robin breathed in awe. "A deathless land for heroes. What a lost treasure." The Faerie lawyer turned to look at me for a long moment. "Can you kill him in there?"

"Your guess is as good as mine," I chuckled. "But there are always ways." Lazarus had taken me to Elysium before he sent me to the Veil. According to him, it was a safe house where Death could not tread. At the time, I thought he had been talking about spies—that Kane could not snoop on him while he was there. But now I wondered if the world had another purpose. If Death wasn't present, was it possible to die there? Knowing how crafty the old man had been, I doubted it.

"Apostasy," Evangeline hissed, glaring daggers at the portal but showing no reluctance. I wondered if she realized how ridiculous she sounded. She hadn't been nearly this uptight the first time we worked together. Maybe having Lucifer's literal daughter next to her was putting her on edge.

"Well, what do you say, gang? Fancy a trip to a lost world?" I gave my companions a broad smile. "It will be quite the show, I promise."

"You do have something up your sleeve, don't you, Matthew?" Dawn asked, her eyes narrowing.

"I'm no magician," I said, turning to lead them into the shimmering air. "I just have great stage presence." I felt a light tickle as I slipped out of Terra and into Elysium, like a thousand feathers traced over my skin.

Like before, I stood in an almost endless wheat field under a perfect, cloudless sky. The only break in the rolling waves of grain was a breathtaking coastline where waves rolled in with elegant perfection.

On a hunch, I reached for the coiled power of Death in the back of my mind, but no matter how hard I tried, I could not grasp it. It slipped out of my hands like an oiled serpent.

Well, that was one part of the theory confirmed: I could not use my extra senses to hunt for the Neodeath. Still, I was certain that the majority of the stores were hidden here, away from Kane's prying eyes.

"Dark Abyss," Alex murmured from next to me as he emerged from the portal. "This is perfect." That truly was the best word for it. The weather was as close to room temperature as it could get. There was no trace of humidity, no so sense of discomfort.

"Well, we're here." Dawn glanced around the empty world with a skeptical eye. "Now what, O fearless leader?"

"They'll be waiting for us in the village," I said confidently, remembering my last trip here. I pointed at a small collection of huts a couple hundred yards away. Somehow I knew my words would prove true.

We trooped through the wheat, carving half a dozen paths, leaving bent grain stalks in our wake. As we walked, I studied the distant collection of huts, looking for any sign of our quarry.

"Are you sure you can kill him?" Alex asked, sliding into step behind me. My best friend could clearly read my thoughts, and I tossed him a small, tired smile.

"No," I said honestly. "I don't know what the rules of this place are, but I have some ideas."

"I love your ideas."

"You say that, but I didn't hear any complaints that time we put onions on our pizza."

"Even a broken clock is right once a day."

"Isn't it twice?"

"Yeah, I guess, but you're, like, *really* broken."

"Gee, thanks." I shot him a mock glare.

"You're welcome."

"No, I actually meant it." I felt far lighter than I should. Somehow I was leading a contingent of Fae, Nephilim, demonspawn, and an angel, and nothing had gone horribly wrong yet. I was getting far too comfortable with how weird my life was. "Thanks for being here."

"Wouldn't miss it for the world." Alex grinned. "Even if it will end up killing me at some point."

"There's a cheerful thought," I replied, laughing to avoid the sense of doom creeping over my flesh. So far this had all been too easy. But I knew Lazarus wouldn't make the mistake of underestimating me twice.

"Movement," Evangeline said sharply, her voice cutting through our conversation like a knife. My eyes snapped back to the clearing in the center of the ruins, and I saw the angel was right. A group of figures were waiting for us.

"Showtime," I told my friends with a grin. My heart began to race in my chest, and I felt my palms go slick with a hint of sweat. It was time to see how the cards fell. I had stacked the deck the best I could.

The Lesser Lazarus stood in the center of the group. He was

still dressed in his drab gray Overseer outfit, complete with a set of familiar horn-rimmed glasses. His cruel blue eyes held my gaze as I stared at him.

He did not seem surprised to see me, just confident that he had the upper hand. Doubt ran through me at the serene expression on his face. What did he know that I didn't? My gaze roved over his companions: a dozen guards in the gray uniform of the Abaddon Market, carrying rifles that they held pointed at the ground. There were two others beside him whom I recognized.

On his left was Beatrice, the technomancer I owed for the poor woman in Long Beach. The mousy woman looked at me with wide eyes. She at least was not used to this kind of confrontation.

At Lazarus's right hand stood the dragon Dracaena. I blinked in surprise at the sight of her. Her blue scales almost matched the perfect sky, and her cat pupils shone brightly as she sneered at me. The last time I'd seen her, she had been burning down Douglas's home around me.

That certainly explained a few things. I guess I shouldn't have been surprised to see her. The first time I'd ever encountered stolen souls, they had been in the hands of the Dragon Dons. It only made sense that they would be in bed with Lazarus over this. But this also told me that their embezzlement hadn't been merely for petty revenge. They had wanted to keep me, the only living Reaper, distracted while they manufactured their Neodeath.

"You are tenacious, Matthew Carver," Lazarus called from the center of the ruins as we walked up. "I wondered if you would remember this place. How did you know?"

"There wasn't enough of your Neodeath on the outside," I said with a shrug. "You had to be hiding it somewhere I couldn't see."

The gangster nodded once, as if that made sense. "Your Majesty. Messenger." He nodded politely to the most important members of my party as if he were welcoming them to a formal social event instead of facing them in a brewing shoot-out.

"How long have the two of you been hanging out?" I asked, nodding at the dragon. "I owe her." The woman smiled at me, a flash of pointed, inhuman fangs.

"Oh, you've met Dracaena?" Lazarus's voice dripped with honeyed sarcasm. "You really do get around."

"Says the guy with two bodies," I snorted. "Spare me the lecture. Let's get down to business, shall we? Give me the Neodeath and the abomination, and the rest of you can live." I glanced at Beatrice, feeling a surge of hatred. "Probably."

"Remarkable," Lazarus breathed, staring at me like I was an exotic animal he was thrilled to get to study. I supposed that his memories of me were not truly his. In some ways this was him getting to experience his own version of the dance with me. "You are as dumb as I remember."

"You do remember dying when I killed you, right?"

"This is Elysium, an undying land. Go ahead, *Reaper,* summon your deadly powers." He leaned forward, glaring at me with self-righteous madness. "Draw that angelic sword and cut me down. It will do *nothing,* for there is no Death here to claim me."

I arched an eyebrow and was silent, letting him think this was news to me. I could feel my companions shift uncomfortably behind me.

"We could start shooting at each other if you don't believe me." Lazarus jerked a thumb at the dozen guards standing behind him. "I brought some friends in case you need a more hands-on demonstration."

"Why do I get the feeling that there's an 'or' coming?" I asked.

"*Or* you can take my deal and spare both of us a giant waste of time."

"There it is." I gave Alex a knowing look. He played along, nodding sagely as if I predicted this from the beginning. "The bad guys always want to make a deal. It's really getting tired at this point. Go ahead, let's hear what you got."

"It's simple, really. I want you to fail in your mission, but not completely. Return to earth, and destroy all the Neodeath that was left behind. Show Kane you have purged all of it that he can see. Unfortunately, I escaped, but somehow you have blocked the path to making it, have you not? He will be unhappy but satisfied."

"I don't think you really know what it's like when Death is upset with your performance, but sure. What do I get if I play along with your little skit?"

"This." Lazarus reached into his pocket and pulled out a small object, holding it out for me to inspect. Despite myself, I leaned forward to get a better look. It was an apple, but of an unfamiliar color. It was neither red nor green, but instead bright, shining gold. It would match Ash's eyes if I held it up next to her face. The air around it seemed to shimmer. A thrill ran through me as I realized what it must be.

"Is that…?"

"An apple of Iðunn." Lazarus nodded sharply. "I seem to recall you putting that on your Abaddon Market application. Perhaps it would be useful for you to get your soul back. Or would you rather keep *wishing to be a Faerie*?" I could practically feel Dawn's and Ash's eyes burning into the back of my neck, but I didn't turn to look at them. I was too distracted by what was before me.

My first Impossible Task. I needed that apple.

All I had to do was agree to lie to Kane. I'd already done that once. Doing it a second time did not seem like a good idea. Even worse, I would have to consign more people to a fate like Maria's. To let Lazarus and his cabal take free will from more of my fellow mortals, just to save my own hide.

It might seem like it should have been a hard decision, but it really wasn't. I don't think that I am particularly selfless or heroic. It was just the same decision I had already made before. I was getting tired of having to make it over and over again.

"No dice."

Something dark and sinister flickered in the depths of Lazarus's blue eyes, like a monster in the deep. He did not hide his rage nearly as well as the older model of him used to.

"So where do we go from here?"

"It would seem that we are at something of an impasse," he replied with a sigh. "I had hoped you would be willing to see reason, but there is nothing you can do to us here, in this place."

"What about her?" I asked, pointing at Evangeline lurking off to my side. "I bet she could go under the hood and start breaking this place." The angel gave me a strained look that told me I was half right. There were probably going to be *rules* to it.

"Oh, she could." Lazarus's smile turned almost sinister as he considered Evangeline. "But there would be a price to pay."

"What kind of price?"

"It would be an overstep of her Authority," Lazarus continued, his eyes still locked on the angel. "We mortals tend to call that a Fall."

"Bureaucracy strikes again." I snapped my fingers in defeat. "I guess we're stuck here." Dracaena's eyes narrowed as she took in my sarcastic tone. I gave her a smile that was full of my teeth. They weren't as sharp as hers, but I hoped the threat was the same.

"Unless." I rubbed at my chin as if deep in thought. Inwardly, my heart was pounding as my body sensed a fight. "Robin, remind me: What culture is Elysium from?"

"It's Greek, I believe." My lawyer didn't need to pretend to be confused by my question. "Homer mentioned it in *The Odyssey,* as did Hesiod—"

I coughed pointedly to interrupt him. "That's close enough for our purposes," I said with a bright smile. "If it's Greek, it falls under the same purview as Roman. Which means Pluto would have been in charge of this place once upon a time, right?" Lazarus's expression clouded in sudden concern, but before he could react, I took a step back, drew my knife from my belt, and slashed my palm. A small burst of my red blood stained the ground. I paused for a moment, fascinated as the wound stitched itself back together: Elysium's magic healing me. When it was done, I looked up and cried out in a loud voice.

"Come, Hypnos, Father of Night!

"Attend to me, King of Dreams!

"Somnus, God of Sleep, I summon thee!"

There was a peal like thunder and an explosion of force beside me, rolling over the ocean of wheat like a tidal wave. I staggered a step to the side, but the fury of the god's entrance passed by me harmlessly.

Silence descended upon the glade as everyone took in the sight of the freestanding deity floating among us. Somnus wore a white toga, although it was no longer torn. A pair of white-feathered wings erupted from his back, and he hovered a few inches off the ground. His black hair was immaculately trimmed, and his purple gaze took in the scene with heavy displeasure.

"Are you mad?" Lazarus screamed, looking at me like I could somehow undo what I had just done. "You summoned a god here among us, free of a circle or any binding?"

"Well, I wouldn't say that," I replied, my smile growing.

"So it is true," Somnus breathed in angry awe, turning to take in the ruin of one of the worlds vaguely attached to his pantheon. "I had thought this place lost forever." Lazarus's face turned purple as he realized I had planned this.

"There is one problem, my lord," I told the god, jerking my head at the group gathered across from us. "You've got squatters. And they brought *rot* with them." Somnus's head tilted as he took in the sight of the dragon for the first time. I didn't warn him about that part.

"What is this corruption?" he thundered. I chuckled under my breath. If I didn't know better, I'd think he was enjoying this performance.

"Sire, I beg your pardon," Lazarus announced, stepping forward and dropping smoothly to one knee. "My people and I stumbled across these lands with no knowledge of what we'd found or who might own it. If I had known we were trespassing against you, I would never have allowed it."

"But you did allow it." Somnus's voice took on a dark, threatening tone.

"Surely there is a price to make this right," Lazarus insisted from the ground. "I will gladly pay to atone for my accidental insult." The newly minted Roman god of death looked at the man below him for a long moment before turning to check with me.

"What do you think?" he asked. Lazarus's head snapped up in shock, and he stared at me with mounting horror as he realized what I had done. I hadn't summoned an unbound god. True, Somnus wasn't inside a circle, but that was because he and I had already made a deal. It had been only too easy when I told him I'd help him find one of his lost worlds.

"I was kind of hoping you would put this place into maintenance mode for a little while and then go get a coffee or something. Whatever is you gods do when you take a break," I replied, glaring daggers at the dragon across from me. "That way we could finally have a proper conversation." Lazarus went pale as he realized what that would mean. *Gotcha.*

"And if I do this, our pact is complete?" The god cocked his head at me, waiting for my assent.

"You're free and clear of me. I told you it would be easy."

"Very well." Somnus grew still and closed his eyes for a moment. The tension in the world spiked as everyone stared at him. After a dozen heartbeats, he opened them, and he smiled at me before snapping his fingers once. The crack reverberated through the world like a gunshot.

Immediately the sky darkened and the wheat around us began to decay and rot as entropy and ruin poured back into this place that they had been denied for so very long. Lightning crackled as a massive storm began to form over the now tumultuous ocean. The pendulum had swung with a fury.

"I will be back in a while," Somnus announced, looking among us like we were a group of children he was leaving unattended in his home. "I expect this to be handled by the time I return." He flickered and was gone. For a moment our two parties stared at each other, neither side ready for such an immediate start. Even I was stunned by the abrupt change around us.

Then all hell broke loose.

CHAPTER FORTY-TWO

"KILL THEM ALL!" Lazarus screamed, pointing toward us. His firing squad of guards reacted immediately, lifting their assault rifles to their shoulders with the smooth efficiency of highly trained operators.

Unfortunately for them, I'd brought with me a pack of super friends who were even quicker. Harsh light erupted behind me, casting long shadows on the ground as Ash opened her connection to Willow.

The Lady of Autumn and I might technically have been bound to the same spirit, but she'd been practicing for centuries. The fire elemental's bright nimbus surrounded Ash's body like a glove. My betrothed floated into the air and let out a cry of rage as she cast her hand forward, sending a giant fireball toward the assembled gunmen.

Immediately the air around us whipped up, goaded into rage by Sylph, Dawn's companion. The furious wind grabbed the fireball and hurtled it toward its target at blinding speed. The guards scattered like bowling pins, but not all of them were fast enough. A pair screamed in horror as the living fire swept over them, devouring their flesh.

That was the last I saw of that exchange, because Dracaena launched herself at me like a blue missile. I pointed my left hand at the ground and summoned my own Willow, using their power to trigger a concussive blast that launched me out of the dragon's path.

The woman flashed by me, her claws raking at my chest. I dropped into a roll, coming to my feet as I spun to face her. Quick as a cat, Dracaena whirled, ready to pounce on me. She was still in her human form, and I felt a thrill of fear as the blue scales on her cheeks began to grow, covering more of her body like armor.

I really hoped she didn't have access to the same serum that Doyle did. I had no desire to face a fully unleashed dragon here in the wide-open ruins of Elysium with nowhere to hide. But as she rippled, she did not grow larger, which was a small mercy.

That was not to say that she wasn't terrifying. Sharp ridges grew out of her skull and at her elbows, tearing through her clothes like knives. Her claws sharpened into talons that could carve me to shreds. She looked like the human version of a dinosaur, missing only the bestial snout that many of the lesser members of her species could not seem to get rid of.

"I will enjoy breaking your bones and sucking the marrow from them, mortal," she hissed. "I will be honored beyond measure for killing you."

"Oh, get in line," I snapped, throwing a fireball at her face. She laughed, raising her arm to block the fireball with ease. Willow's flame bit hungrily into her shirt, burning the clothes, but the dragon showed no sign of discomfort, and the blue scales revealed by the burning remained undamaged.

That was fine—pretty much exactly what I'd expected. I'd tried to burn dragons before. They were immune to any fire I could produce except for their own, and something told me that Dracaena wasn't about to start spitting flames anytime soon.

But it was a great distraction. It gave Alex just enough time to get behind her. My friend tackled her from behind, which normally probably wouldn't do much. If the reptilian was anything like the rest of her kind that I had fought, she was insanely strong. But Alex's cheerful features were hidden behind the black veneer of a mummer's mask, a relic stolen from the massacre of my birthday party in the Faerie Lands. Fueled by some demon apparatus, it made him far stronger than he would ever be on his own. It also made him usually try to kill me. Fortunately, we had been practicing what to do in those situations.

Dracaena let out a surprised grunt and staggered under the force of his assault. Alex grappled her, dragging her to the ground with surprising ease. But the monster wasn't a quitter. She hissed in rage, twisting her body with her strange shapeshifting powers to produce a row of spikes along her back.

Alex cried in pain and released her as a pair of them pierced the flesh of his chest, leaving puncture wounds that began to leak bright blood on the ground. Before either of us could react, the dragon was on her feet and launching toward me, face twisted.

"Ack!" I shouted, ducking under her vicious lunge. My hair rustled with the wind of her passing as I narrowly avoided getting my face turned into mincemeat. Rising out of my crouch, I reached a hand over my shoulder to draw Orion's sword. The angelic blade burst into flames as I stood, casting its own light onto the battlefield.

To my surprise, the hilt was warm and welcoming in my hand. I got no sense of apprehension from it like I usually did. It seemed that it was a big fan of being used in this situation. I don't know if it had learned to hate dragons from its time with Orion or if angels hate the reptiles just as much.

"*Enough!*" thundered a voice fraught with power. I looked in time to see Evangeline blur forward, her own hand stretched out to grab the dragon. It was Dracaena's turn to dodge as the angel almost tackled her at blinding speed.

"Come, lizard," I taunted, circling to stand on the opposite side of the fight from where Evangeline recovered, so that Dracaena would be forced to look in both directions at once. "Let's see if you are as dangerous as Don Doyle."

My stomach churned as her face twisted, stretching and becoming squatter as she moved one of her eyes to the side of her head to better watch me, like some hideous mockery of a hammerhead shark on land.

"Yesss, let'sss," she hissed, her mouth warped by the shifting of her body. Beyond us, the rest of my party assaulted the guards. Dawn flew by, carrying the Spear of Lugh in one hand, summoning lightning from the darkening sky. I had no time to check on Alex or Megan, but there was enough fire being thrown around that I was confident my sister at least was still in the fight.

As one, the angel and I leapt forward, trying to overwhelm the dragon's defenses. Dracaena whirled, growing a long tail from her back as she did. The blue-scaled whip sailed at Evangeline, dotted with sharp spines.

Quick as light, Evangeline halted her charge and snatched the limb out of the air, catching it easily in her hands. Dracaena let out a surprised grunt as the angel braced herself and *pulled,* ripping the dragon from her feet in one smooth motion.

Heart racing, I leapt forward, eager to take advantage of the prone lizard. The burning blade in my hand seemed to sing with delight as I stabbed it toward her prone form. *I hope you're enjoying the show, Azrael,* I thought grimly.

But despite being down, Dracaena was very much not out. The reptilian let out a scream and twisted, rolling out of the way of my blow by literally breaking off her own tail like a lizard trying to escape a predator. Evangeline's white eyes blinked in surprise as she was suddenly holding a detached, scaled appendage no longer connected to Dracaena. It flopped mechanically in her hands as if still alive.

"Disgusting," Evangeline growled in disgust. But she did not drop the tail. Instead she pressed the attack, flipping the thing in her hands to use its barbed end like a scourge. "I will beat you with your own flesh, monster!"

Dracaena did not respond. She launched herself at me, but I forced her to dodge back with a swing of my burning blade. Her eyes were wild, the catlike pupils massive, as if she was trying to see in the dark. Panic was setting in.

A hail of gunfire ripped toward me, and it was my turn to duck to the side with a curse. A glance over my shoulder showed me that Lazarus had gotten his hands on one of his guard's assault rifles. He strode toward me with purpose.

"You won't kill me again!" he shouted. At least, I'm pretty sure that's what he said. I could only hear about three words, but I got the gist. A lightning bolt sizzled out of the sky, erupting at his feet, tossing him like a toy.

I screamed in pain, closing my eyes and covering my face with my free hand at the painful burst of light. A bright, jagged line carved its way across my vision, even in the dark. "Dammit, Dawn, watch where you're pointing that thing!" I yelled.

"Ware, mortal!" Evangeline shouted. I opened my hurting eyes, just in time to see Dracaena bear down on me, claws extended. She hit me like a scaled freight train, sending both of us flying to the ground. Pain lanced through my chest as she tore at my flesh. But even as we fell, my instincts took over. Orion's relentless training had burned a response in me, and my body flowed through the motions he had pounded into my brain.

I did not lose my grip on the angelic blade. Instead, I drew it close as we fell, getting it low and in line with the dragon that was hammering me. I had just enough time to see the too-wide pupils of her eyes flashing in rage before we slammed into the ground.

I let the force of our sudden stop be the impetus behind my thrust and jammed the blade's point upward with all my strength. Dracaena screamed, and we rolled through the dirt, locked together in combat.

After a couple of revolutions our momentum bled out, and we separated. I lost my grip on the hilt of the sword and slid free of her cutting claws. Gasping for air, I scrabbled to my feet, pressing a hand to my chest to probe the long wound she had left in my flesh. My hand came away bloody, but it felt like my ribs were still intact.

Dracaena, on the other hand, wasn't getting up. The dragon lay on her back, Orion's sword sticking out of her chest like a planted flag. Slowly, through a dazed lack of oxygen, I moved toward her.

Her eyes were open, and she was taking short, shallow breaths. She twitched at the sound of my coming but did not look at me. Instead, she stared at the open sky above us, as if she was dreaming of flying in it.

"You will not win," she hissed, voice tight with pain. "He is awake. The World Eater comes. And when he does, he will devour you and the light with you."

"It's always *somebody* with you guys," I complained breathlessly. "Why can't there ever just be, like, Steve, or maybe Eunice? Why does it always have to be so dramatic?"

"Leviathan is free. I am but a shadow of the dread to come." I was so shocked that for a moment I forgot to breathe. I knew that name: the target of my second task. In order to get my soul back, I had to slay Leviathan.

"You know him?" I demanded, stepping forward to grab the hilt of my blade. "Where is he?" I ripped the sword free of her chest and held it toward her face. The flames burned bright, as if excited to be so close to their enemy. "Tell me where I can find this monster," I shouted, no longer paying any attention to the battlefield around me.

"You don't need to worry." Dracaena sighed, a look of triumph passing across her face as her eyes lost focus. "He will find you." Then she was still, the tension flooded out of her body, and she turned from a dragon into an empty sack of scales.

"Tell me!" I screamed once more at her corpse, feeling a little bit of hope slip out of my fingers, leaving only emptiness and despair in its wake. "Tell me," I pleaded once more. But Dracaena had no more secrets to give.

Snarling in frustration, I rose from her corpse to survey the battle around us. Ash and Dawn hovered together above the battlefield, raining lightning and fire down on a ruined cottage where the last couple of guards had hunkered down. Megan was crouched behind a rock, throwing bursts of flame in the windows with mechanical precision. Evangeline stood next to me, studying me with a curious expression.

"Why do you care about Leviathan?" she asked.

"I have a date with—" I started to explain, but then I spotted Alex and Robin locked in a vicious struggle. My friend had my lawyer pinned to the ground and was choking the life out of him with his demon-enhanced strength.

"Dark Abyss," I cursed, sheathing Orion's sword behind my shoulder and breaking into a sprint. I wasn't sure Robin could be killed by strangulation; it seemed like too mundane a way to kill the old Faerie. But I had no desire to test that theory.

"Alex, no!" I shouted, flying toward my friend. The black mummer mask turned to face me as I drew close, and even though I could not see his eyes, I could practically feel the hate radiating off it. Me being one of the Devil's personal enemies had weird side effects on the power that fueled him.

"Get off!" I shouted, reaching out to flick the large tab we had installed on the forehead of the mask. With a *pop,* it snapped free of his head. My friend's face was twisted in a rictus snarl, but he blinked as his brain rebooted, and the rage that drove him vanished.

"Oh no," he said in horror as he realized he was choking Robin. With a jerk, he pulled his hands free and stared down at the blond Faerie. "I am going to hear about this for the rest of my life."

"You have no idea," Robin groused, rubbing at his neck with a grimace of pain. "Now get off me before I hire all the poets in the world to write devastating limericks about your back acne." Alex groaned as he stood up, holding a hand to his chest where Dracaena had sliced him. Without his demonic mask, he was clearly feeling his wound. He grimaced in pain as he bent to offer Robin a hand.

"Did we win?" Alex asked, looking around with wide eyes. His blue eyes focused on Dracaena's corpse on the ground with an expression of surprise. "That seems like a good sign."

"So far we're still in one piece," I confirmed. "Just got to take care of the last couple of line items." As I spoke, the building that Dawn and Ash were hammering let out a violent *crack* before collapsing in on itself, crushing whoever had been cowering in there.

"I *love* this spear," Dawn announced, drifting down from where she floated to stand beside me. "You may have many faults, Matthew Carver, but you are an excellent gift-giver. Which, as far as we Fae are concerned, is one of the best things you can be." She shot me a knowing look as she spoke. Clearly, she had understood Lazarus's comment about my wish.

I shook my head, refusing to fall for her bait. This wasn't over yet. "Are you all right?" I called to Meg as she walked over. My sister gave me a tight smile and thumbs-up. I could see the stress written on her face, but she waved me off when I tried to catch her eye.

"I'm fine too," Ash sniffed, coming to stand next to me. She softened her comment with a smile, and I laughed, finally allowing myself to relax. It had worked—I couldn't believe it. My plan had been *perfect.*

"I saw the fireballs you were throwing around. I was more worried for them."

"You're wounded."

"Just a scratch," I promised. I winced as I pressed another probing hand to my chest. Now that my adrenaline was wearing off, the gouges were starting to *sting.* "I don't think she broke anything important."

Ash's gaze tracked to the still corpse of Dracaena, studying it for a moment before flickering back to me.

"What?" I asked, my brow furrowing.

"Dragonslayer," she murmured. I blinked, turning to look back at my dead enemy with new eyes. I had forgotten about that whole part of it. After fighting Doyle, it just didn't seem quite as impressive.

"You're a regular chip off the old block," Alex told me, and I was surprised to hear there was no bitterness in his voice. I gave him a grateful smile before turning to look at the broken man who lay in the dirt.

"Where is the Neodeath?" Evangeline growled, cutting into our conversation. "It must be destroyed."

"Yeah." I nodded, letting her pull me out of the conversation. I reached out with the with sense that Death gave me to sweep the area. The oily rotten corruption of Lazarus's synthetic death leapt to me, burning darkly against my senses.

"There." I laughed, pointing at one of the still-standing huts. "All nice and stacked for us."

"All of it?" the angel asked me sharply. I made another sweep before nodding.

Evangeline raised her hand, and her brilliant halo blazed to life above her head once more. I looked away from its brightness. There was a crack of thunder, although it was so much deeper and more powerful that it made me feel like I had never heard real *thunder* before, just pretenders.

A beam of light speared down from the sky like a laser. It radiated power that rattled me to my bones. I screwed my eyes shut, trying to protect them, but it was still painfully bright behind my lids. When the roar faded, and the light ended, there was a white bar burned into my vision. I opened my eyes to discover the ruined hut was gone, replaced with a charred crater. My Reaper senses detected no hint of Neodeath.

It was done.

"Let's end this," I said, leading the party toward where Lazarus landed after Dawn struck him with lightning. His horn-rimmed glasses were shattered, and there was blood leaking from both of his ears. Being at the focal point of that *boom* seemed like it had been an unpleasant experience.

He blinked owlishly at me, looking lost and out of sorts and not like a dangerous man who'd stolen countless souls and almost destroyed the world.

I crouched down to pick up the object that lay next to him. The golden apple of Iðunn was cold and metallic to my touch. Curious, I squeezed it softly and found there was a bit of give to it. It felt like it was part fruit, part gold. Thankfully it seemed undamaged by its fall, and I buffed it against my ruined shirt for a moment, then lifted it to inspect it one last time before I took a bite.

My hand was shaking as I studied it. My first Impossible Task was about to be completed. I was one third of the way toward getting my soul back and being free. I couldn't believe it. Everything around me was muted, as if I was back in Somnus's dream world.

Finally, some good news.

"I would wait!" Dawn snapped, interrupting me before I could take a bite.

"Why?" I asked, cradling the precious fruit to my chest. "This isn't like a Snow White thing, is it?" I turned to give Lazarus a skeptical eye. "Do you think he poisoned it?"

"The apples of Iðunn are not just fruit, Matthew," Dawn explained with a sigh, her expression telling me that I was being an idiot. "They are what the Norse gods used to make themselves Immortal."

"Oh," I said stupidly, staring at the fruit with new eyes. I guess I should have known that. I remember what happened to the White Witch in Narnia. "What will it do to me?"

"Make you ageless and undying, for a little while," the Queen of All Fae told me. "But it does not last. The gods had to eat them regularly to maintain their power."

"If it doesn't last, why should I save it?"

"You never know when it might come in handy to be Immortal," she told me. Crap. I hate it when Dawn has a good point. It always feels foreboding and ominous. But the more I stared at that golden apple, the more certain I was that she was right. With a grumbled curse, I slipped it into my pocket, worried that I might be making a mistake, but unable to convince myself to eat it now.

"Do you want to do the honors?" I asked, turning to look at Evangeline. The angel was hanging back from the rest of us, watching our exchange with hooded eyes. Although she was our ally in this venture, she was not one of us.

"Honors?" Megan's voice came from behind me, full of confusion.

"Someone has to send this monster to the dark," I said, not looking away from Evangeline's face. A shadow of something passed over her expression, but she smothered it quickly, running her hands down her stained pants.

"It's better if it is you," she replied softly, giving me a sad smile. "Less paperwork if it is mortal-on-mostly-mortal." We stared at each other for a moment, each of us trying to see something about the other's mettle.

I had no choice, I knew. Kane would never accept me walking away from Lazarus. I wouldn't either. Forgiveness and second chances are important and necessary things. But as far as I was concerned, this had been his second chance, and he had somehow managed to be even more evil on his new go-round.

"Very well," I said at last, turning away from the angel's white eyes. Lazarus let out a whimper as I came to stand above him. There is no one more afraid to die than someone who has sacrificed so much of themselves to avoid it. Beatrice lay a dozen paces away, charred and still. I had no sympathy for her.

I wonder what he saw through his broken glasses. If he knew it was me or if he just saw a tall, black outline, the last long shadow cast over him before he was consigned to the dark. I held out my right hand and reached for Death's dark power.

It flowed to me easily, no longer barred from this place. The sword would not appreciate being used for such a task. Dragon killing might be its favorite hobby, so it would tolerate my presence to do that, but anything else was pushing it.

Death's scythe formed in my hands, made of cold, hard shadow. I stared down at the cowering man at my feet, who was shaking with fear, and tried to feel anything. But all I felt was numb. The crushing weight of justice had ground my emotions out of me. This must be, and so it would.

"By the power vested in me by Kane, CEO of Death Corp, guarantor of the Death Treaty, and protector of mortal souls, I sentence you to die," I told him coldly. I didn't think he could hear me, but it was important anyway. "May judgment find you wherever you go."

I raised my scythe and cut down a monster.

So naturally, that was when all hell broke loose.

CHAPTER
FORTY-THREE

ELYSIUM SHOOK AS something massive tore its way into the fallen world. Reality seemed to stretch to just short of its shattering point before it snapped back in place. I staggered to the side as the ground beneath my feet rumbled in response.

A shadow stood before us in the shape and size of a man but somehow also a dragon as large as a mountain. It flickered between those two forms for a dozen heartbeats, as if he was trying to decide which to become.

Then the dragon aspect shattered, and he stood before us as a man, clothed only in scales the color of midnight. Red eyes swept through the scene in a heartbeat before they fixed on me with hatred.

"Begone, creature of despair!" Evangeline shouted, stepping forward to put herself between us and the new being. I felt a ray of hope from her presence, grateful that she was here to protect us from his thing.

"Your suffering will be endless," he screamed with a voice that could destroy worlds. The shadow blurred as he lunged forward. Evangeline was the closest to him, and he snatched her in his clawlike hands so quickly that even she did not have time to react.

Before I could cry out, the monster ripped the angel in half with his raw strength. White blood erupted from her, catching fire as it baptized the ground. With a disdainful snort, he tossed both pieces to the side, turning to fix his anger on me once more.

The light of the world went out.

In the dark, the true thunder she had summoned to destroy the Neodeath rumbled once more, this time in anger. Underneath its fury I thought I heard the faint peal of a trumpet. Then with a flicker, the light came back, as if someone had turned the sun back on. But it seemed dimmer now—less than it had been.

I stared at the two halves of her torn body in stunned silence. Evangeline was dead. He had torn an angel apart with his *bare hands.* She was supposed to help me. If she didn't have the power to withstand this thing, what hope did we have?

"I know thee, Hunter's whelp," the monster seethed, his anger hot like lava. "I smell his stink upon you." I stammered, unable to come up with a reply, too horrified at what I had just witnessed.

But before he could move, Dawn stepped forward. The Queen of All Fae held her head high. Her blond hair was pulled back into a ponytail, and some distant part of my shell-shocked mind thought this might be the only time I had ever seen her not wearing a tiara or crown of some sort.

Her expression was taut, but the Spear of Lugh that she held before her did not shake. She was fearless and brave, and for a brief moment, hope soared in my chest.

"I know thee too, wench," the scaled thing snarled, its twisted voice tearing at my ears. "I can smell thy whore Faerie mother's blood. Step aside, and I shall repay a favor that she once granted to me." And suddenly it clicked. I knew who this was. Who it had to be. I remembered a story that Robin once told me, about how Gloriana had refused to give Orion the Spear of Ascalon when he had been at war with—

"Draco," I whispered in horror.

The horrifying progenitor of the dragon race, their Constellation, their god, was free from Tartarus, and he had come looking for me. True terror crashed down on me, and slowly, I reached my hand for Orion's blade, desperate to hold it and draw strength from its bright fire.

"He's mine, dragon," Dawn hissed, somehow taking a step toward the beast, spear still held high. I thought I heard Alex let out a little cheer from behind me.

"If thou shall not move, then thou shalt *be* moved," the draconic god promised, red eyes glinting with the promise of blood.

"I will not move," the Queen of All Fae promised, lifting her head, "and we both know I cannot lie."

Draco let out a low chuckle, amused and teeming with violence. "So be it," he thundered, unveiling a Presence that hammered into us. It was as if a mighty invisible hand reached down from the sky to squash us flat. I collapsed to my knees, gritting my teeth as I desperately tried to hold myself upright.

One by one, the rest of the party fell next to me, grimacing in pain from the suppressing power that Draco wielded like a club. Only Dawn remained standing. A bright-yellow aura began to glow around her, emanating from the spear but growing to encompass her whole body.

"So you have found some of your lost power," Draco mused, taking a step toward Dawn, his black-scaled face revealed a set of white fangs as he smiled. "You should have saved that for someone who could be killed." Dawn was shaking now, but still she stood tall. Terror plagued me, a heavier weight than even the dragon's power. I could not stand to watch her die. I had to do something. I had to save her. Then in a flash of insight, I knew how.

"Somnus! Somnus! Somnus!" I cried through gritted teeth. There was a *pop* as the newly minted god of death flickered into being behind Draco. His expression shifted from mild annoyance to horror at the sight of the dragon god.

"Leviathan? What are you doing in my realm?" Somnus demanded.

Oh no. Ohnonononono.

Draco *was* Leviathan? The god of the dragons was who I had to kill to get my soul back? This creature who had casually knocked us to the ground using only his mind? Who had torn an angel into pieces? I had a better chance of standing up to the Devil himself than this monstrosity.

"How do you get yourself in these situations?" Somnus asked, turning back to stare at me with an incredulous expression. "When I took my break, this all seemed like it was going rather well."

"Turn it back on!"

"Are you sure?" he asked, taking in the scene. "Once I do, our deal will be complete."

"Stay out of this, Sleeper," Draco hissed, not even turning to look at the new god. "This doesn't concern you."

"Do it!" I managed to wheeze through the pressure that was holding me in place.

"Very well." Somnus sounded like he disapproved, but he *snapped* his fingers, and the world righted itself. The storm clouds vanished, replaced by a perfect blue sky. The waves settled, and new wheat began to grow out of the fallow ground. Only the bodies remained as testimony to the Death that had visited here for a few short moments.

But the pressure upon us did not abate. I was still trapped on my knees.

"I told you not to *interfere,*" Draco snarled, whirling with violent speed to stare at Somnus.

"I was *bound.*" The two deities stared at each other for a long moment before the dragon hissed in annoyance but let it go. I guess they both understood the rules well enough. If he truly was bound, then there was nothing Somnus could do.

"But you are not any longer?" A note of crafty suspicion entered Draco's voice.

"I am not."

"Then go, and leave me to my work." A chill ran down my spine at the casual command.

"I will need the place back eventually," Somnus mused.

"Go!" Draco roared, causing the junior Death god to flinch back a step.

"Fine," he snapped, his purple eyes flashing with rage and insult. "I will leave you to your amusements." With a flicker, he vanished, leaving us alone with an irate dragon.

For a moment, Draco stared at us, like a chef evaluating produce. Then with a huff of disgust, he turned his back on us and strode to where Dracaena lay. The power that held us in place did not slacken, and we stood immobile, watching as the dragon god inspected his fallen comrade.

"You were ever fearless, my daughter," he said softly. "May you fly through the clouds of eternity in the darkness beyond." With a gentle motion he reached out and closed her sightless, staring eyes.

You gotta be kidding me.

The dragon stood over his daughter's corpse for several moments, head bowed as he said goodbye. I railed against the mental bonds that held me in place, but it was no use. I could barely wiggle my toes, let alone stand up.

When he was finished, Draco turned to stare at me with cruel red eyes. "This was cleverly done, pup," he commended me, drifting toward me with languid, predatory slowness. "The Hunter would never have thought of such a loophole. But I suppose that's why he rots in my old prison, isn't it?"

He extended a single claw to tilt my chin up so I could stare into his red eyes. "I cannot kill you. Not here. This is an undying land. There is no Death to finish the job." I felt a surge of relief at having my reckless theory confirmed. I wasn't sure if the god of dragons would somehow trump that rule.

"But just because you cannot die, does not mean you cannot *suffer.* You will feel every ounce of the agony you have caused me." Before I could blink, he lunged forward, burying his claws in my abdomen. I tried to scream, but there was no voice left in me.

I was trapped, held by his will as he ravaged me, slicing me with his claws. The world was on fire; it was only agony and despair. I could not think—I could not breathe. I was suffering incarnate. He tore me to shreds, destroying me until I was no more. Any part of Matthew Carver's physical form that could be broken was, and when it re-formed because there was no decay to claim it, he broke me again. I began to dream of the Tenth Circle of Hell like a man dying of thirst in the desert dreams of seeing an oasis.

I do not know how long the dragon god took his frustration out on me. In that place, it could have been an eternity. For a brief moment I was like the Death Board, always being tortured and never being tortured.

When his rage was finally vented, he withdrew a couple of paces to stare at me with disgust. I was lying on the ground. I had no memory of falling, but as my mind slowly began to process thoughts once more, I could feel my body slowly stitching itself back together to the state it was in when Somnus flicked the switch. I still bore the wounds from my fight with Dracaena, but all the damage Draco had done was slowly undone.

"You have taken something priceless from me, whelp," he said when I was almost whole again. His voice was no longer tinged with uncontrollable rage, but cold and calculating.

"I would kill you the moment you leave this place, but there would be consequences." His red eyes flickered to Dawn for a moment before falling back on me. "So I will give you this choice as a member of the Dandelion Court and therefore part of the Constellation Congregation: either you will face me in a duel under the supervision of the North Star, or I will declare war on the Fae and burn their world to the ground." The pressure that bound me abruptly vanished, and I climbed to my feet on shaking legs.

"Well, which will it be?" He smiled, his white fangs flashing. "I know which choice the Hunter would make." I blinked, looking at Ash and Dawn, trying to decide what I should say. Of course Orion would say yes. But I'm not him.

"Are you afraid, little mortal?" Draco taunted me, leaning toward me. I flinched, cowering back a step from his ominous presence. "I will give you a boon. You will be allowed to bring two allies to die with you when you face me." Dawn could not move her head, but her eyes were moving frantically from side to side. *No.* Ash was glaring at me, already angry at me for what I was going to say.

But what choice did I have? Fate had made certain that Draco and I would meet. I guess old Atty was having the last laugh now. Saying no would only get my friends hurt and delay the inevitable. I closed my eyes and swayed, trying to maintain my balance in my weak, recently re-formed body.

"I accept."

"Excellent." Draco stared at me hungrily for a moment before turning away, satisfied for now. It terrified me how quickly he flowed from irate to pleased; he seemed completely mad.

"You and I will see each other soon," he promised. Then he raised a single claw and carved a hole in the air. His outline flickered, shifting for a second into a massive dragon before condensing once more into his human form. The world twisted, and he was gone.

All my companions could move again.

"You idiot," Ash screamed, sliding to grab my face with both of her hands. I winced, still fragile from being tortured at Draco's claws. My betrothed tilted my head so that I stared into her eyes. They were furious, but she kissed me, which was the best thing that had happened to me in the last while, so I didn't care.

In the distance I could hear Dawn ranting, "If the bloody dragons want a war, I'll *show* them a war." But I ignored her, losing myself in the gentle, safe warmth of Ash's embrace. There wasn't any more Matthew Carver left to give right now.

"Is it always like this?" Meg asked Alex as they stood next to us.

"You know, usually I'd say that it's worse, but this might be it."

"Be what?"

"The bottom of the barrel."

It took me some time before I was able to walk confidently again. To their credit, no one rushed me. Even Dawn didn't have an acerbic comment to make, for which I was unreasonably grateful. Alex and Robin buried Evangeline while they waited for me. I don't know if you're supposed to do that for angels, but I also don't think they're supposed to die.

I wasn't looking forward to explaining that to her superiors. I doubted Raguel was going to take it super well. But I was going to need to get another case officer assigned to my soul fraud because there was a chance I was going to be crossing the Veil again real soon. I had signed my own death warrant, but I did it to protect my friends. That didn't mean I was giving up, but if I were a betting man, this felt like a hand that was going to bust.

When I could walk again, I used one of the doors of the still-standing ruins to slip us into the Between. None of us had any desire to return to Lazarus's fortress and find an army waking from their slumber.

The six of us emerged from the eternal hallway into my house. We were silent as we filed into the living room, lost in our own thoughts. Robin gave me a look full of tremendous pity, but I shook my head. I didn't need that. I already knew I was doomed.

I made my way up to my room to clean my wounds and change out of my shredded clothing. I hissed in pain as I peeled the blood-soaked cloth away from the cuts I earned while Elysium was not a paradise. But compared with the agony that a god had just inflicted on me, it was essentially nothing.

With a groan, I reached out and turned on the shower, letting it steam up the room as hot water shot out. I've said it before, but the only correct shower is one hot enough that it effectively gives you a fever, and I felt that way *before* I bound a Faerie fire spirit.

I waited a few moments for it to get warm enough, then slipped in, letting out a sigh of relief as the gore and grime sluiced off my body. The pressure stung, so I turned my back to the water, letting its warmth fill me to chase away the chill.

Finally feeling something close to relaxed, I closed my eyes and leaned forward, placing my forehead against the cool tile of the shower. I turned off my brain, trying to shove my despair into a corner so I could just exist in the life-giving heat.

But it didn't work.

Harbinger, a voice whispered in the back of my mind.

What was it Azrael called me? The canary in the coal mine? I am the warning light of death. Everywhere I go, bonds are broken, and violence rises. Death walks in my shadow, claiming everyone but me.

I wanted to deny it, to say they were wrong and that it was a curse I did not bear. But I couldn't. Its evidence was written in my life from the beginning. My mother and sisters could not escape the long shadow that it cast. Yuki didn't make it either. Not even an angel could survive being around me.

I was a lightning rod for killing, and if the Angel of Death was to be believed, it wasn't going to get any better. How soon until it was Alex? Or Megan again? What if it was…Ash?

I was nothing but a danger to those around me. A liability to their peace. Orion might be the safest one of my friends, locked up in Tartarus away from the danger that walks in my footsteps. *I am going to get them killed.* The thought sank its claws into me as easily as a tiger's slice its prey. My skin was not armored to protect me from this truth.

Distracted by my despair, I was caught completely off guard when a pair of hands slipped around my sides, hugging me gently, taking care to avoid my wound.

"Ack!" I shouted, starting to twist, but the hands held me tightly, locking me in place. I felt a body, colder than mine but much softer, press against my back, cutting off some of the water.

"It's just me," Ash murmured, her head pressed to the back of my neck. "I came to check on you. To see if you needed help."

"Oh, I definitely do," I breathed, a silent sob racking my body as something I had been trying to hold at bay suddenly slipped free. It was as if her calming presence gave me permission to acknowledge the horror I had just lived.

The agony that Draco had visited upon me felt endless. The rules of time are loose and inconsistent, so it was possible that it was still occurring. That, somehow, I was in two places at once while the Dragon god vented his rage upon me. I had spent months without sleeping only to be thrown into a nightmare from which I could not wake.

Something in my mind was cracked. I could feel the lines on my psyche. My sanity had already been weakened by Somnus's sleep debt, and Draco had hammered at that damaged foundation with all his might.

I wasn't okay.

I wasn't sure if I ever would be again.

"Shh," Ash whispered softly, holding me tighter. "I'm here."

Her presence was a balm, a fire holding back the darkness of the night that surrounded me. We stayed like that for a long time. When the hot water began to run out, Ash summoned her Willow to keep the enclosed space steaming even as the temperature dropped. My wounds were still open and oozing, but her presence was healing in a different way, stitching up a hole inside me.

"Hey, uh, not to interrupt or anything." Alex's voice sounded from my bedroom, pulling out of my almost peaceful trance. I could hear his awkward panic, which made me laugh softly. I smiled as I felt Ash echo it, still pressed against me.

"But there are, like, some IRS agents here, and they seem pretty upset."

"Tell them to get in line!" Ash called, not letting go of me.

"I'll be down in a moment," I groaned, reaching to pry her arms from my waist. I should have known there was one more piece of the puzzle left. But for the life of me, I did not know how I was going to get out of this one. Should have stolen some of the priceless art while I was in the Abaddon Market escrow.

Ash and I made our way down the stairs a few moments later. One perk of being bound to a fire spirit is that drying off is very easy. Neither of us looked like we had just spent the better part of an hour in the shower. I wore a crewneck and jeans over my fresh bandages. I had chosen dark gray in case my wounds started leaking. I didn't want to have to explain to the government why I was bleeding.

Agents Peters and Wong were in my living room, standing awkwardly in the corner as they stared down at my bedraggled comrades. Their sharp business suits were a stark contrast with my friends, who looked like they had been dragged through a…well, a war zone. Everyone was covered in mud and char. Dawn glared at the government officials with a sharp distaste that even a blind man couldn't fail to see.

"Mr. Carver," Agent Wong greeted me coolly. "I thought we made it clear that you were not to leave the city."

"I have not left town," I lied, somehow unable to make myself afraid of this woman after everything I had been through today. I knew the IRS had a lot of power, and she could probably drag me off to jail, but whatever. I'd just leave. The Key of Portunus meant no prison could hold me.

"Your phone was missing from the network for an extended period of—"

"Yeah, it keeps dying." I gave a casual flick of my wrist. "I'm not sure if you know this, but I am a little in debt right now, so I'm trying to save money and not buy a new one right away."

"We know you were gone," Peters snapped, falling into his bad-cop persona, taking a step toward me. I rolled my eyes and gestured at Robin to step in.

"Prove it," he called.

"What?" Peters asked, caught off guard.

"I'm his lawyer. Show me the flight logs, the toll charges. Surely you have some evidence of him being *somewhere* instead of just 'not being here.'" Robin made scare quotes with his fingers as he mocked them.

"You missed your deadline," Wong interjected, cutting Peters off before he could get into a verbal sparring match that it was obvious he would lose. "With no submitted payment plan, we will be forced—"

"But you see, darling, that is why we are here," Dawn called from her couch, a smile far too much like a shark's spreading across her face. I had a sudden flash of concern.

"What?" Wong said, completely caught off guard.

"I'm investing in Mr. Carver's firm," Dawn informed the woman, her smile growing larger as the pit in my stomach copied it. "We're just finalizing the paperwork, but that's the purpose of this meeting. If you are willing to wait until the end of business today, the influx of cash used for the purchase of my shares will more than meet the outstanding debt."

"Is this true?" Peters demanded, turning to glare at me with a distrustful expression. Over his shoulder Dawn smiled at me sweetly, but her eyes flashed with dangerous promise. Slowly, I glanced at Ash. My betrothed's expression was closed and smooth, as it often was when her sister was playing her games. She was the queen, after all. Who could tell her no?

"That's right," I managed through gritted teeth. Somehow it was almost harder to agree to this than to Draco's duel. I didn't know what exactly I was giving up by letting Dawn into my company, but I was sure we were going to find out. "We've been working around the clock to solve this crisis."

"We will also be filing an embezzlement claim," Robin announced, leaning forward. He looked unbothered by Dawn's move, but then again, he was more like her than anyone else here. "Our financial team has been deep in our books untangling the damage."

"Fine," Wong said after a moment of consideration. "You have until the end of the day to show me a payment plan that will significantly reduce your outstanding taxes. Otherwise…"

"I understand," I told her with a tight smile. "You'll have it."

"Cheer up, Matthew," Dawn said from her seat. She leaned back against the couch, eyes still swirling with wickedness. This was my punishment for agreeing to the duel. She would never admit it, but I would suffer for the choice I made. "Now that you're debt-free, you can start getting ready to pay for a wedding!"

"What!?" Ash and I asked at the same time.

REVIEWS

I hoped you enjoyed reading *Sleep Debt* as much as I did writing it. If you did, the best way to help me spread the word is by leaving a review! Millions of books are published on Amazon every year. So if you enjoyed it, please let people know!

If, for some reason, you're not able to leave reviews, word of mouth is powerful! Tell your friends you think will like it. The better these books do, the more time I can spend working on them, and the more fish I can buy for my aquarium collection. (It's getting bigger. I have a problem.)

But no matter what, thanks for taking the time to read my story. I hope to find you again at the end of the next one!

- Andrew

PATREON

If you're unfamiliar, Patreon is a place where you can support your favorite authors and get access to books while they are still being worked on. You can get everything from my sincere thanks to a chance to give me feedback on the direction of the story. You can subscribe for a day, a month, or a year. It is not required by any means, but it does help me to continue this adventure!

To read the next book of the Debt Collection, *Present Day,* early, as well as my other writing projects, check out the link to the Patreon below or scan the QR code with your phone.

www.patreon.com/AndrewGivler

www.ingramcontent.com/pod-product-compliance
Lightning Source LLC
Chambersburg PA
CBHW020354310726
48979CB00015B/2591/J